The Eternal Kiss

13 VAMPIRE TALES OF
BLOOD AND DESIRE

Edited by Trisha Telep

RP|TEENS
PHILADELPHIA • LONDON

Library of Congress Cataloging-in-Publication Number 2009926683
ISBN 978-0-7624-3717-7

Cover photo: iStock
Cover and interior design: Frances J. Soo Ping Chow
Project editor: T.L. Bonaddio
Typography: Berthold Baskerville and Schneidler Initials

Published by Running Press Kids, an imprint of
Running Press Book Publishers
2300 Chestnut Street
Philadelphia, PA 19103-4371

Visit us on the web!
www.runningpress.com

Contents

Introduction

Thank heavens you've picked up this book.

Would you trade your life for just one kiss?

With the amount of readers itching for vampire stories these days, you can be sure there are more and more that would. Vampires are bigger and tastier than they've ever been. They are gorgeous and seductive and dangerous—what more could you ask for? It's easy to see why everybody is scrambling to get into a pair of fangs. You get to be young and beautiful forever and make-out eternally with an incredibly hot member of the Undead.

It seems to me that vampires are the gatekeepers of youth. If you reject their eternal kiss, you say yes to getting older (as well as yes to the sun, yes to eating food on a regular basis, no to blood drinking, etc.). As the editor of this book, I find that fascinating. Do I grow up, or do I refuse to? It's like Peter Pan all over again, only with pulsing veins and teeth, constant night and scary red eyes. Vampires are all Lost Boys (or Girls). Every one of them. Wandering the earth aimlessly, looking for love and blood.

These crimson-sweet tales, by some of the best living writers in the business of the dead, will satisfy your cravings. Whether your (blood) type is tall, dark and handsome or lonely and gorgeously Goth, you'll find a choice selection of vampires to quench your thirst.

A kiss may be just a kiss, but a kiss from a vampire is an eternal kiss. It's a kiss that can mean forever. Death or immortality. Which would you choose?

That is, if you're even given a choice.

—TRISHA TELEP

Falling to Ash

BY KAREN MAHONEY

THEO WAS LATE. It had been almost a year since she'd seen him, and he couldn't even be on time.

Moth growled, shifting her gaze to the moon so she could enjoy the cool rays as they bathed her pale skin. Moonlight was her favorite thing in the world—apart from brown eyes on a good-looking guy. She pulled her sunglasses down onto the tip of her nose and surveyed the alley, wondering what the hell had happened to Theo. She tapped her foot impatiently, enjoying the clicking sound the steel toe-caps of her boots made on the sidewalk.

Anything to avoid thinking about Mom's memorial service tomorrow. Well, not so much the service itself—she was far more afraid of facing her father. Her lips tightened as she remembered the last time she'd seen him; fatherly love had been the last thing on his mind. Her mother had been gone for a year, and yet her dad couldn't care less whether or not his middle daughter turned up to remember her.

Moth swallowed and pushed those thoughts away, instead admiring the pure white skin of her slender arms as she stretched them above her head. It wasn't like she'd ever been much for tanning, even before she became a vampire. She could still walk in daylight, but not in full-summer and never without some cloud cover or buildings to shade her. As each year passed, she noticed how the sun bothered her a little more; even SPF fifty wasn't always enough.

Pushing the cheap plastic sunglasses back into position, she leaned against the back door of *Subterranean* and wondered why they couldn't have met *inside* the club. It was ten-thirty on Saturday night—the place would be crawling with vampires, and she might even see some familiar faces. Despite her desperation to get away from this place, she'd been lonely the past few months.

And then Theo was there, sliding out of the shadows and gliding toward her with the cat-like grace she was so familiar with. His beauty never failed to take her breath away, even though she hated the knowing gleam in his eye as he touched her cheek in greeting.

Moth glared from behind her shades. "You're late."

"And your manners haven't improved."

"I was in Boston, Theo. Not a finishing school for naughty girls."

Theo raised his dark eyebrows and grinned his wicked pirate-smile. "Now there's an idea . . ."

Moth pushed the sunglasses up onto her head, balancing them among the thick black waves of her long hair. She knew that her silver eyes would be glowing brightly in recognition of her sire, but she couldn't bring herself to show him how happy she really was to see him. He hadn't earned that right—not since the day, ten years ago, when he'd stolen her innocence and made her a monster.

He reached out for the shades and snatched them before she could stop him. "Why are you wearing these ridiculous things?"

"My eyes keep glowing and the contacts hurt." She nodded up at the moon. "It's almost full."

"You haven't been feeding." Theo's tone was filled with reproach. "If you had, you wouldn't have this problem." His own eyes were currently light gray, his vampire nature hidden behind centuries of rigid control.

Moth glared. "I've fed more than enough."

He sniffed. "From blood banks. It's hardly the same thing."

"You said you wouldn't push me on this."

"I haven't pushed you on your eating habits for almost a decade. Perhaps I should start."

She scuffed her boot on the ground, deciding that a change of subject might be a good idea. "Why are we standing out here, anyway?"

Theo leaned against the wall and pushed his hands into the pockets of his custom-made jacket. His black hair was shorter than she remembered it, the curls resting neatly around his ears and stopping short of his collar. People often took them for family, which amused Theo. He liked to pretend she was his little sister—it gave him a sick charge.

Just as Moth began to wonder if he was going to answer, he met her eyes. "I don't want anyone to know you're back. Not yet."

She frowned. What the hell was he cooking up now? Wasn't it enough that he'd dragged her into the city for a meeting, just because he knew she'd be back for her mother's service? "You promised me a year of freedom, Theo. My time's not even up, yet. This isn't fair."

"*Life* isn't fair, my lovely." His eyes were like stone, his mouth unsmiling.

"But you *promised*," she said, hating herself for showing weakness. She wrapped her arms around her body, as though she could hold back the pain that began to gnaw at her belly. Being around Theo always made her feel hungry—that was one of the reasons she'd wanted to get away from Ironbridge in the first place.

"I have a job for you," Theo said, breaking into her thoughts. "It's something very special. Only my little Moth would do for this one."

Ten months into her ... vacation, and he wanted her for *this*? To steal something? That's all he ever wanted her for. "This is such crap. You don't need me—it's just an excuse."

His eyes grew wide and mock-innocent. "An *excuse*? For what?"

"To get me back. You're not happy unless you're controlling everyone around you."

Theo's face hardened and Moth felt the familiar tug of power in her chest. He owned her, body and soul—if she still even *had* a soul—and she hated him almost as much as she loved him. Right now, maybe she hated him more.

"Be grateful that you had as long as you did, child. It's hardly my fault you came back to cry over your mother's grave. Now, listen to me. Here's what I want you to do ..."

• • •

All this trouble for a stupid funeral urn? And why was death such a feature on this trip? Moth shook her head as she stomped through Ironbridge Common and avoided a group of kids who were taking turns swigging out of a bottle. She pushed down the sharp stab of envy somewhere in the region of her heart; she would never do those human things again. She sighed, and tried to remember what it had been like to be a "normal" teenager. If she was being honest with herself, it wasn't like she'd been all that happy back then, anyway.

It was a mild night and the sky was clear. Summer wasn't far away—she could already smell it in the air and dreaded the longer days to come. Moth flopped onto a bench under one of the old-fashioned iron lamps that lined the pathways. She tried not to remember the distressed expression on Caitlín's face when she'd left the city, ten months ago. They'd sat in this very spot and said their goodbyes. Moth had promised to call her younger sister as soon as she returned to Ironbridge, but instead here she was skulking around the Common and wondering if there was any way she could get out of doing this job for Theo.

"Hey, what freak show did *you* escape from?"

Two guys were standing in front of her, one of them posing with a cigarette dangling from the corner of his mouth. She'd been so busy thinking about Theo, and the crazy scheme he'd dragged her into, that she hadn't even smelled them coming.

Moth tried for the friendly approach. *Hey, it was worth a try.* "Nice to see you, too, boys." She grinned, while still managing to keep her fangs hidden. It was tricky, but possible, although it had taken her several years to master the art.

The boys were probably sixteen or seventeen; only a little younger than Moth had been when she was turned almost a decade ago. They wore blue jeans and long-sleeved T-shirts. One of them carried a jacket that caught her eye—it was soft black leather, covered in zips and pointed metal studs. *Nice.* She wondered how a kid like that could afford such a beautiful jacket.

"Don't know what you're grinning at, but you're sitting on our bench." This was said around the cigarette, so some of the force behind the words was lost. The guy had short brown hair, narrow eyes, and a *screw-you* attitude. His slightly hawkish nose reminded her of Theo's.

Leather Jacket Boy nodded agreement as he stood shoulder-to-shoulder with his buddy. He clearly thought he was doing a good job at playing the silent, menacing role, but his scruffy halo of soft-looking blonde hair ruined the effect.

Moth sighed and slowly shook her head. "Now, that's no way to talk to a lady, is it boys?" She leaned back and spread her arms out along the back of the bench. The studded bracelets on her right wrist caught the light.

The smoker leaned over her. "I don't see a 'lady' here. And I said, get off our bench."

"Can't you find another bench to make out on?" Moth kept her expression neutral, but she could smell the boy's anger and it was making her even hungrier.

"What are you saying?" Leather Jacket Boy demanded, his face flushing.

Moth stood in a single, fluid movement. She tugged down her short black skirt and cursed as she caught her fishnets on one of her rings. "Crap. Now look what you made me do." She glared at them both, remembering too late that the expression would be lost behind her sunglasses. She was tempted to give them a good look at her eyes, but Theo would be pissed and she'd only just gotten back. Probably not a wise move.

She reached out to the dark-haired kid, swiping the cigarette from his mouth. Before he could protest, she pressed the burning tip against her other palm and watched their faces as her white flesh sizzled. It hurt like hell, but there was no way she would show *them* that—and the burn would heal in a matter of minutes, anyway. Not that these assholes needed to know that.

Both guys backed up a step. "Shit," the one who'd been smoking said. "She must be high."

Moth grinned, not caring if she flashed fang this time. "Get lost." She threw the butt at them, laughing as they shot fearful glances at her.

"Crazy bitch," Leather Jacket Boy muttered. He grabbed his friend's arm and pulled him away from the bench. "C'mon, Todd."

Moth watched them through narrowed eyes, clamping down

hard on her hunger and keeping the desire to teach these punks a *real* lesson in check.

"Todd" turned back and gave her the finger.

Ah, what the hell. "Hey," she called.

She sauntered over to them, swinging her hips and twirling her hair between her fingers. She stood up close to Leather Jacket Boy and ruffled his blonde hair. "Nice jacket you got there. Your boyfriend buy it for you?"

"Shut up!" This was from Todd.

Moth ignored him. "Or maybe it was a gift from Mom and Dad. Do your folks know you're out here, smoking and causing trouble for vulnerable girls like me?"

She grabbed the jacket with ease and made a big show of admiring it. "Lovely piece of work. I bet it was a Christmas gift. Am I right?" She looked at the blonde kid and smiled.

"Give it back, or you'll be sorry."

"Yeah. Like I was sorry about sitting on your stupid bench," she replied. "I think I'll take this with me. Maybe it'll teach you boys some manners."

Todd took a step forward. "Give it back, freak." He lit another cigarette and watched her through those cunning eyes. Moth couldn't help admiring his bravado—his hands didn't shake at all. "Maybe we'll find out how you did that little trick before, see if it works when someone else tries it." He brandished the freshly glowing cigarette and blew a cloud of smoke at her.

Moth acted without thinking—something she did way too much, according to Theo. Okay, and according to her father and her "loving" older sister. She closed her mind to dark thoughts of Sinéad and her dad, determined not to see their disappointed faces.

Instead, she grabbed Todd by the throat and pulled him toward her so fast he lost his footing. She was so much shorter than him, it must've looked comical. At the same time, she wrestled the cigarette from his fingers and held the glowing tip close to his sweating face.

"Next time, you get this in your eye." She took a drag on it and blew a mouthful of smoke directly into his face. "From now on, that's *my* bench."

Moth shoved him away from her hard enough to dump him on his ass. She dropped the cigarette on him then picked up the leather jacket. Dusting it off while she watched the blonde boy, who was gazing at her with terrified saucer-eyes, she felt a surge of adrenalin. Part of her hated doing this, but there was a growing part that enjoyed the sense of power no matter how hard she tried to deny it. It helped that she pictured her father's face sneering at her whenever she played the tough-girl role.

She shrugged into the jacket, testing the fit and enjoying the feel of the smooth satin lining. It was too big, but that didn't matter.

"Very nice," she said. "Thanks."

Leaving them with their mouths hanging open, Moth walked back to the pathway. Heading back into the city, she tried to ignore the gnawing hunger that made her whole body buzz. She'd have to make an extra stop for blood now, dammit.

Theo wanted Moth to steal an urn filled with the ashes of a recently "deceased" vampire. It wasn't anyone she knew, which was something of a relief, but it was still a crazy assignment. Mainly because this particular vampire was a "master" who had been destroyed by a rogue vampire hunter. And not just any hunter, but one that had become a nasty thorn in Theo's side during the months that Moth had been gone. Apparently he was a middle-aged man who didn't look like he could slay a mosquito, much less a vampire, and yet the guy was still at-large after destroying six vampires. The most recent victim, Maxim, was an old business associate of Theo's. Moth didn't know what her sire wanted with the ashes, but knowing him it couldn't be for anything good.

Oh, and the urn was currently stored somewhere in the hunter's apartment.

How the hell she was going to find a way into a super-paranoid vampire hunter's private home—which was no doubt protected by all kinds of technology and magic—was something that Theo had left for Moth to figure out for herself.

Perfect.

She prowled the perimeter of the apartment block on the eastern edge of Ironbridge, wondering why a killer would choose somewhere like this to hole up. It was too high profile— way too up-market for a person who should, by rights, want to keep his head down and his business private. On the other hand, he probably made a ton of money doing what he did, so why not live in style? It wasn't like a vampire hunter had a high life-expectancy.

Moth ran her fingers over the cool metal of the intercom, wondering where Thomas Murdoch was hunting tonight.

"You need to get in?" The voice came from directly behind her, and Moth couldn't believe she hadn't sensed anybody approach. She was losing her touch.

She swung around to face a young guy, probably similar in age to her—before she was turned—with blonde spiky hair and intense dark eyes. She couldn't tell what color they were, even under the apartment-block security lights, but that didn't matter right now. What mattered was that he was freaking gorgeous. And tall—much taller than her.

The guy activated the electronic entry pad with a black fob hanging from his keyring. He gave her a strange look as he opened the door, probably because she was just staring at him. Moth wondered if she had drool running from the corner of her mouth.

"After you," he said.

"Thanks." This wasn't exactly how Moth had planned on entering the building, but what could she do? She couldn't be rude, not when he was so goddamn cute, and maybe this would turn out to be easier than climbing the outside wall.

She unzipped the leather jacket and noisily cracked her knuckles, immediately regretting the habitual action. It wasn't her most feminine trait. She ventured further into the lobby ... and slammed on the brakes as she walked past a huge copper-framed mirror. *Damn.* Way to advertise your undead status. She backed up and waited for the guy to walk by.

He gave her that look again, but headed for the far end of the foyer and hit the elevator call button. As soon as he disappeared inside, Moth scampered up the stairs and headed to the top floor. It figured that a kick-ass vampire hunter would live at the top of a ten-storey building. Luckily for her, endurance wasn't an issue since turning vamp.

Tenth floor, and the plush-carpeted hallway was quiet. No mirrors here—just ornate wood paneling lining the walls and low-key lighting humming quietly above her head. Moth tried not to think about the stranger who had let her in; his dark eyes seemed to burn in her mind, and it disturbed her that someone who was clearly only human could affect her that much. She'd spent so many years being drawn to Theo that she'd forgotten what it was like to feel a genuine spark of attraction for anyone else. She wondered who the young guy was and which apartment he lived in.

Moth shook her head, reminding herself how furious Theo would be if she screwed up. If she wanted to get out of Iron-bridge and enjoy her last couple months of freedom, she needed to succeed. She shivered as she walked underneath an air-conditioning unit that had been left running, glad that she'd changed into black jeans when she'd stopped at one of Theo's dens for a snack. Thankfully, despite his aversion to "bottled blood" (his name for the hospital supplies some vampires preferred to drink), he didn't stop his people from indulging their morals.

The door to apartment 1016 was at the far end of the corridor, set back in its own alcove. The bright copper handle stood out against dark wood, and Moth's heart began to pound when she noticed that the door stood open. Just a crack, but she still caught a glimpse of burgundy carpet and a small entry hall through the narrow gap. She pushed her sunglasses on top of her head and contemplated this whole situation being a setup.

No, that was crazy.

Licking her lips and wishing that being a vampire meant she didn't have to feel that human rush of adrenalin, Moth edged closer, trying to ignore the fear and excitement pulsing in her stomach. She pushed *out* with her senses to see if she could smell or hear what waited on the other side of the door. Too late, she caught the sliver of a human scent behind her—it was mixed with something oily and mechanical and utterly unfamiliar.

A sharp pain pierced the back of her neck, and suddenly she was falling...falling to the floor and beyond into darkness.

• • •

Moth opened her eyes but immediately regretted it, hissing in pain at the bright light shining in her face. She tried to move, but realized her arms were secured behind her with something hard and cool. Something that, although cold, still burned the bare flesh of her arms.

"Don't struggle, you'll hurt yourself."

Moth squinted in the direction of the male voice, but it was difficult to make out her surroundings with the spotlight aimed at her. The heat was making her skin itch, and her lips were dry and cracked. Someone had removed the leather jacket, leaving her in the tight black T-shirt that displayed a blood-red picture of Dr. Frank N. Furter from *The Rocky Horror Picture Show*.

She almost cried with relief when the solar lamp—or whatever it was—switched off, leaving the room illuminated by flickering candlelight. *Very atmospheric.* Moth was propped up against a wall beneath the only window in the room. To her left was a large bed covered in a gray velvet throw and, on the other side of that, floor-to-ceiling built-in wardrobes lined the wall. Two small glass-topped tables each held several candles of varying height. A man sat in an armchair to her right.

Moth tried to stand, but realized her legs were bound by heavy silver chains. At least her jeans offered some protection. She frowned, wondering why the silver that she assumed bound her wrists was so painful. Vampires were sensitive to silver, but it wasn't usually this bad. More like an irritating allergy—and even then, only with really good-quality silver.

She gazed at the suspiciously familiar-looking young man who was watching her. The first thing she noticed about him was that he held some kind of crossbow trained on her, and it was aimed straight at her heart.

He said, "The silver chains and handcuffs are blessed, that's why it hurts."

Moth scowled. "That's just mythology."

"So, that's why your wrists are burning?" His mouth twitched. "You must be a girl of faith for it to be so painful. Ironic, huh?"

"Who are you?" Moth resisted the temptation to bare her fangs, just in case he was simply a nutjob who didn't really know what he was talking about. Considering the blessed silver chains and the crossbow, she doubted that was true, but it offered some comfort while her mind raced to figure a way out of here.

The young guy with spiky blonde hair and dark eyes leaned forward as he smiled at her, but it wasn't a friendly smile. His face was flooded with candlelight.

"You," whispered Moth.

"Jason Murdoch, at your service. Sorry that Dad couldn't be here to say 'hi.'"

"You're Thomas Murdoch's *son?*"

He nodded, looking pleased that she'd figured it out. "Jace. I'd shake your hand, but you're a little tied up over there."

Moth was fighting a nauseating combination of fury and panic. *This* little (*Okay, not so little*) bastard was Jace Murdoch, son of the vampire hunter that had plagued Theo over the last few months? Theo had assured her it was safe to break into Thomas Murdoch's apartment at this time of night—he hunted during the witching hour—but there had been no mention of a hunter-in-training sharing space with Daddy. She mentally kicked herself. Hard. Why had she listened to Theo? She should've cased the job herself.

Jace shifted position again, leaning back and resting the crossbow on the arm of the chair. A silver ring flashed in his left eyebrow, something she hadn't noticed downstairs in the foyer.

He'd also taken off his jacket and was dressed simply in a white T-shirt and blue jeans, his powerful forearms covered in ink that led her to believe he might be older than she'd first thought. Moth squinted, managing to make out some kind of Celtic band around his right arm—the one that guided the crossbow and was as steady as a rock—and something that might have been a dragon or a phoenix on his left.

"What are you doing here?" Moth was glad to hear that her voice was strong.

He raised an eyebrow, the one with the piercing. "I live here." Jace must have seen the surprise on her face, because he shrugged. "Well, some of the time. I'm away at school mostly, but I spend whatever breaks I get back here in Ironbridge."

Moth tested the handcuffs that bit into her wrists. The pain was intense, but she tugged at them again and had to swallow a cry of triumph as she felt something give. Not enough—not yet—but maybe soon. "I don't know what you're bothering with school for if you're going into the family business with Daddy." She kept her tone light, mocking, hoping to distract her captor.

He grinned, and this time it seemed more genuine. "You don't know anything about me, but I know plenty about *you*." He stood and grabbed something that had been lying on the floor by his feet. Before she could see what it was, he approached—still keeping his weapon trained on her—and held the mirror up in front of her.

He glanced down, tilting his head slightly, and gazed back

at her. "Well, would you look at that? No reflection. Just like downstairs."

Moth wanted to kick out at him so desperately she could taste it, but he stayed just out of reach. He threw the mirror down and grasped the crossbow in both hands, pointing it higher, this time at her forehead.

Taking a deep breath, Moth tried to catch his eye in just the right way. If she could snare him in her gaze, she might be able to weaken his will enough to get him to free her.

Jace shook his head. "Uh, uh, no you don't little vampire." He produced her sunglasses from the pocket of his jeans and slowly approached her from the side. "Stay right there like a good girl. I think you'll look a lot better in these, when you can't use those pretty eyes on me."

Infuriating as it was, Moth could do nothing as he placed the shades awkwardly over her eyes. One side wasn't sitting properly over her ear, but that was because she struggled despite the crossbow pointing at her head. Surely if he *really* wanted her dead, she'd already be a pile of ash. Moth tried to tell herself that. It helped.

And, bizarre as it sounded—even to herself—Jace Murdoch didn't seem like such a bad guy. Well, if you didn't count the fact that he'd shot her with a tranquilizer dart (or something like it) and then tied her up in the toughest silver she'd ever heard of. And if you ignored the fact that he was holding a crossbow with the razor-sharp bolt locked and loaded.

Right.

Moth bared her fangs and hissed as he backed away, always keeping her in his line of sight. *What the hell*; might as well go for the whole vampire-show, see if she could shake his confidence.

He assumed his position back in the chair, seeming unaffected by her fangs. She couldn't help thinking that she probably looked sort of comical, tied up and helpless and wearing a pair of tacky oversized shades.

Confirming her suspicions, Jace grinned. "You look cute, you know that?"

"Screw yourself."

"That's no language for a lady."

Moth shifted position on the hard floor, using the movement to disguise the fact that she'd pulled the chain linking the handcuffs apart a little further. She couldn't see what she was doing, but she could feel it; every tug shot burning pain into her wrists. Even though she didn't like taking human blood from a live donor (and she liked the taste even less) she was seriously tempted to bite this guy when she got free. Just to scar him as surely as she would have to bear the scars of silver burns for the rest of her very long life.

Jace said, "You're not going to get out of those, you know."

Moth smirked at him in what she hoped was an irritating way. "Why the hell would I want to escape when you're such fascinating company?"

She watched him as he shifted the crossbow to his other hand while he checked his cell phone. "You waiting for Daddy to call?"

"Cute." Jace narrowed his eyes. "What's your name, little vampire?"

What would it hurt, to give him that? "Moth."

He shook his head. "Your real name. Not your stupid vampire name."

"That *is* my real name." Now, anyway. Now and forever.

He smiled that nasty smile again; not the flash of genuine humor she'd seen earlier. "Whatever you say, *Moth.*"

"What do you care what I'm called? You're going to kill me, anyway."

"You're already dead, as far as I'm concerned. You were the very moment you were bitten."

Moth felt something like grief stir in her chest. "You don't know that. Is that what your dad told you about us?" She swallowed. "Maybe you shouldn't just take his word for everything, and go find out some of this stuff for yourself."

"As soon as I've got my degree, I'll be traveling with him. That's the deal."

"*Hunting* with him, don't you mean?"

He shrugged. "So what? You're a hunter—you're all predators. Vamps, werewolves . . . All monsters kill whatever and whoever they can to survive." He gave her a hard look. "Don't tell me you've never killed a human."

She was suddenly relieved he couldn't see her eyes. Her mouth pulled into a tight line and she wished she were a better liar. "I don't have to answer to you. You're holding a freaking crossbow aimed at my heart."

"Yeah, that's what I thought." His lip curled. "You can't even answer the question."

"I don't owe you anything. You attacked me and tied me up, and then threatened to turn me into dust. How do you even know how long ago I was turned? Have you thought about that?"

He frowned. "What do you mean?"

"Hasn't Daddy told you? New vampires won't just disintegrate into a convenient pile of ash. You're going to end up with a lot of bodies that need to be disposed of. Have you got the stomach for that? How old *are* you, anyway? You're just a kid ..."

Jace stood, his face twisted with anger. The crossbow trembled in his hand. "Shut your mouth, bloodsucker."

Moth felt sick, her arms hurt and her legs were heavy against the floor, but she was getting to him. Finally. She tested the cuffs one last time and then *pulled*, thankful that her silver-induced weakness didn't stop her from breaking the bonds. The chain snapped, though that still left her wrists encased in the blessed metal. But so what? She could use her hands again, which was all that mattered.

Jace was much closer now. He seemed younger and less sure of himself. Moth licked her lips and shook her hair out of her eyes, dislodging the precariously perched sunglasses. They hit the ground just as Jace aimed the crossbow at her head. Moth was sure she could hear his heart beating, could almost taste his fear. The hunter's son probably had a lot to prove to Daddy. The irony wasn't lost on her.

She smiled at him, despite the fear that fluttered in her chest like a trapped bird. "You're aiming at the wrong place. My heart's a lot lower than that."

She watched, with a curious mixture of anger and compassion, as he swallowed. She could see his throat work as he licked his lips. He was almost in reach of her legs. Almost...

"Nice setup you've got here." Moth braced her palms against the floor. "Your dad must earn a lot of money dusting vamps, huh?"

A single bead of sweat trickled down Jace's temple. She wondered what it would taste like, whether she would get the chance to taste him.

His foot moved forward—one more step—and it was enough.

Moth moved. She pushed her hands down and flipped her legs up, slamming her bound feet into his knee and hearing the satisfying crunch of bone.

Jace collapsed, howling with pain. The crossbow fell beside him and released its deadly bolt, whizzing past Moth's ear and landing with a *thunk* just below the window as it buried itself in the aged plaster. Moth's momentum had carried her on top of her would-be captor. Her legs were hopelessly bound with those thick chains, but she still managed to roll onto her knees and pin Jace to the ground.

His face was the color of raw putty as he struggled beneath her, surprising her with his human strength despite the injury, but she held him with ease.

"Quit moving around." Moth smiled sweetly. "You don't want to hurt yourself now, do you?" She'd just broken the guy's kneecap, and she knew she was being a cow but . . . *what the hell.* He deserved it.

Even without the use of her legs—even with the broken silver cuffs still circling her wrists—Moth was stronger than him. Despite the difference in their sizes, she pushed down on his arms and lay on top of him with her knees resting between his legs. If she pressed her knees in just the right way, Jace was going to be in a lot more pain than he already was.

"So," she said, with a wicked smile. "Does your father know you do this kind of thing?"

He took shallow breaths. "Of course he does. He trained me."

"And how old are you?"

"How old are *you*?"

She cocked her head to one side. "Eighteen."

"That's when you were turned. How old are you? *Really*."

Moth pursed her lips and thought about playing with him some more. But what did she have to lose? "I'm twenty-eight."

Jace looked surprised. "You've been a vamp for ten years? No way."

"You're saying I look younger? Aw, thanks." She fluttered her eyelashes.

Grimacing as he shifted position beneath her, he sucked in a breath. "No, I mean you *seem* younger. You act it."

Moth gave him the benefit of her silver stare. "Sometimes. So, c'mon. Your turn."

"I'm nineteen."

She wiggled her eyebrows. "Ooh, I love a younger man ..."

"Get off me, freak."

"Flattery will get you everywhere." Moth dug her knees in. Hard.

Jace's eyes rolled with pain and, if it was possible, his face became even paler. "Bitch," he gasped.

"Says the guy who drugged me—and I don't know how the hell you managed *that*—tied me up in chains and handcuffs made of blessed silver, and then threatened to dust me with Daddy's crossbow."

"So ... what? You're going to bite me now, is that it?"

"Would you like me to?" Moth could smell his fear. It was intoxicating, and she was already trying to fight the bloodlust rising in her gut. She could feel the panicked drumbeat of his heart as their bodies pressed together. Just because she had an aversion to the taste of blood—especially the fresh stuff—didn't mean she wouldn't do what she had to do. Not when it came to survival.

She studied Jace's pain-wracked face. This wasn't survival, it was revenge, but didn't she deserve a little of that? She wouldn't drain him, of course. She would only take a little. Just a taste ...

Moth slid her hands down his solid arms and grabbed his wrists, forcing them above his head. He was powerless. He could wriggle beneath her, but with the busted kneecap he only had one leg that was working, and he was probably in too much pain to do too much damage with it.

His blonde spikes had wilted, and sweat ran freely down his neck and onto the carpet. She stared into his dark eyes—his *brown* eyes—and did something she hadn't done for a very long time. Oh, the days she'd spent dreaming of Theo and those full lips. But there was something about Jace's thinner mouth that drew her to him. Even though he was beaten and in pain, the grim determination that pulled it into a tight line spoke of the sort of man he was going to become.

Moth licked her lips and leaned in close.

Jace's eyes widened as she captured him in her gaze, willing him to hold still, just for a moment, while she pressed her lips to his and delivered the softest of kisses. He tasted of fear and rage, desire and pain, and it was truly delicious. Filled with regret and growing bloodlust, Moth pulled away—she had to get out of there. But first she had to find that damn funeral urn.

Before she could move away, Jace's uninjured leg suddenly swung around, clamping down on her chained legs and holding her in place as he pushed his lips back against hers.

Moth's brain registered a fleeting moment of, *WTF?* as he deepened the kiss. Wasn't he supposed to be transfixed by her silver eyes? She still hadn't fully mastered the art of compulsion, but she had *some* ability. And then she purposely switched off that part of her mind—the part that was afraid—as she enjoyed the moment; it had been too long since she'd been kissed like this. Too long since she had been held and touched.

Moth finally opened her eyes and pulled away. She looked down into his face and he stared back, a dark challenge hidden in the depths of his eyes. His lips quirked in a half-smile, and the movement sent a drop of blood running down his chin.

Before she could control the impulse, Moth darted forward and caught the shining crimson bead on the tip of her tongue. It tasted harsh and tangy, and she shuddered with a mixture of desire and disgust as she swallowed it. She licked her lips and tried to push down the wave of guilt that washed over her. *Crazy to feel that way, just for nicking him with her teeth.* It had been an accident—heat of the moment.

"If you'd let go of my hands, I could wipe the rest of the blood away." Jace's tone was neutral, all signs of pain and panic appeared to have gone. He'd regained his control, just as she had lost hers.

Moth gazed at the new blood welling from the cut on his bottom lip. She released his arms and pushed away from him, rolling to one side and dragging herself across the room and against the wall nearest the door. Her newly acquired leather jacket was hanging from a hook against the dark wood. She grabbed it and tugged it down, ripping the bronze coat hook from its moorings. Wrapping the material around her hands, she gripped the thick silver chains encasing her legs and *pulled.*

The metal was heavy and tough—even without the so-called "blessing" (which Moth was beginning to suspect was actually some kind of magical warding)—but she was fast regaining her strength.

The chains snapped, the miniature padlocks shattering into pieces and scattering around her on the carpet.

Jace lay exactly where she'd left him. His injured leg was bent at a strange angle and Moth began to wonder if she should leave him there like that. She shook her head. *What the hell was she thinking?* She was going soft, forgetting what he'd done to her in the first place. One kiss and she'd completely lost her head.

Flipping onto her feet, she shrugged into the jacket and tried to ignore the faint burning sensation around each wrist. Moth approached the would-be vampire hunter and nudged him with the toe of her boot.

"Okay, Van Helsing. Where does your father keep his trophies?"

He coughed and propped himself up on his elbows. He tried to hide a wince as he attempted to lift himself into a sitting position. "What do you mean?"

"Come on, I don't have time for this. You cost me . . ." She glanced at the clock on the bedside table and almost gasped. "*Two freaking hours?!* What the hell did you plug me with?" She narrowed her eyes. "Forget that. What time will Daddy be home?"

Jace glared at her. "He's never home before dawn."

Moth felt the tension in her gut ease. "So . . . The trophy room?"

"He doesn't take scalps, if that's what you mean."

She rolled her eyes. "Ashes, Jace. Where does he keep the ashes?"

"He doesn't."

"Yeah, right. Tell me, or I'll rip the place apart *after* I take out your other knee." She gave him an evil grin. "How do you fancy a wheelchair for the next three months?"

Moth was amazed to see his fingers twitch in the direction of the unloaded crossbow. She brought her heavy boot down on it with a satisfying *crunch*.

"Tick-tock, Jace."

"Fine. There's no trophy room." He raised his hand as he saw Moth about to reply. "There really isn't. Dad keeps some funeral urns in the kitchen."

She frowned. "Um . . . The *kitchen*?"

"Cupboard under the sink." He lay back against the floor and closed his eyes.

"Your old man's a freak, you know that?"

"Screw you."

Moth couldn't stop the grin that spread across her face. She blew him a kiss and pocketed his cell phone and her shades on her way past the armchair. She left the room and quickly checked all the other doors before finding the kitchen at the far end of the labyrinthine apartment.

The kitchen was surprisingly large, square and filled with chrome and modern appliances that didn't look like they saw much use. The small sink and disposal unit shone under the bright lights, and beneath those nestled the sort of cupboard where you'd expect to find cleaning products.

Except inside *this* cupboard were at least a dozen funeral urns. Why would a vampire hunter store trophies of his kills under the kitchen sink, of all places? Maybe it was simply because nobody would ever think to look there for his prize stash.

Or maybe Thomas Murdoch was a crazy bastard. What the hell did it matter, anyway? As long as she grabbed the right one, she was out of here.

Moth shuddered as she touched the urns at the front. *Ugh, creepy.* How was she supposed to know which one Theo wanted? She nibbled her lower lip, her mind straying to the kiss with Jace. He may be the son of a killer, with a serious attitude problem to boot, but he was still pretty damn hot. She should really give his phone back when she left—that knee was going to need a lot of medical attention.

She pushed away thoughts of teen-vampire hunters, and instead tried to remember what Theo had told her about the master vampire that'd been dusted. She carefully removed each urn, searching for clues, and breathed a sigh of relief when she thought to look underneath. Each one was inscribed with a date—presumably the date of death. Moth knew when Maxim had been killed, so it was only a matter of minutes before she found the right container. At least, she *hoped* it was the right container.

Tucking the ceramic urn under her arm, she prayed she wasn't going to have one of her clumsy nights. She would have to take the stairs, much as she was tempted to climb out of the window and just shimmy down the wall, but carrying ashes that were over five-hundred years old while sticking to the wall Spider-Man style, probably wasn't a good plan. Especially as the contents of this funeral urn—no matter how gross—were her ticket back out of Ironbridge for the next two months.

As she finally left the apartment, wondering how many invisible alarms she'd tripped in the kitchen, Moth dropped Jace's cell phone outside the bedroom door. Maybe he'd find it before his dad got home. She didn't have time to do more for him. Theo would be waiting for the urn, and was no doubt wondering where the hell she was.

Moth rolled her eyes. *Let him wait*—like he'd even care that she had almost been killed tonight.

Except Theo *had* cared. He had seemed to care a great deal, which left Moth confused and vulnerable when she faced her father the next day.

• • •

"I don't know what kind of deal you made with the Devil, Marie O'Neal, but do you honestly believe I haven't noticed you've not aged a day since your eighteenth birthday?"

Moth—still known as Marie to her family—stared at her father in shock. She wanted to say something sensible; something that would convince him that he was talking crap. Anything that might make him believe she wasn't the monster he suspected her of being. But the O'Neals were a superstitious bunch, and her father was the worst of them.

"Dad—"

"Get out of my house. Your mother's been in her grave this past year, so you've no business here anymore."

"You can't stop me from seeing Caitlín!" Her younger sister would be devastated when she heard what was happening. How could Moth explain this to her without revealing the truth?

Coming home had probably been a mistake, but Moth refused to miss her mother's memorial service. Apart from the fact that she *wanted* to be here for that, not putting in an appearance would've caused even more questions. She hadn't been home since Mom died last year, and even back then her father had been insistent that his middle daughter was now living a life of drugs and "*God-knows what else.*" However, the look of distaste on his lined face—the shadow of fear that lingered in his pale blue eyes—said that he now believed something else entirely.

Rory O'Neal had always been a God-fearing man, thanks to his strict Catholic upbringing by elderly immigrant parents, but he was looking at Moth as though she were the devil incarnate.

He scowled at her. "Caitlín's old enough to see you on her own time, away from here, and Sinéad feels the same way as I do."

She couldn't resist sneering at that. "Of course she does." Moth and her older sister had never been close.

"Don't speak about your sister in that tone. At least she didn't run away after your mother passed."

Moth ignored him and watched the family's arthritic dog shuffle around the untidy backyard. She tried not to think about her older sister's smug expression as she had watched their father lead Moth out onto the porch after the last guest had left. At least Dad had waited until people had properly paid their respects, before disowning her and telling her she was something other than human.

Much as she wanted to hate him, how could she truly blame her father?

Swallowing unshed tears, she shivered in the rapidly cooling shade. She couldn't help wondering what it would feel like to have the sun warming her face. As usual, she sat under cover of the wooden porch as the bright spring day came to a close.

"Do you even hear what I'm saying to you, Marie?" Her father's voice broke into her scattered thoughts. "You're not welcome here. Leave us in peace."

Tears burned in her eyes—the eyes her father had insisted she uncover after the service commemorating Mom's life and death—and the blue contacts caused her eyes to ache more than ever. Moth clutched her sunglasses between stiff fingers, and resisted the temptation to crush them into dust. She suddenly wished she'd left them back in that room with the wannabe vampire hunter.

A picture of Jace suddenly flashed in her mind, as bright and clear as a newly developed photograph. She gritted her teeth and pushed the image away. He was human, and not only that, he was her enemy.

Moth's voice was husky. "I understand *what* you're saying, Dad. I just don't know how you can say it to me. I'm your *daughter.*"

His eyes were blank. "No, you're not. Not anymore."

Marie "Moth" O'Neal gazed at her father for a long moment. His face was set in cold, hard lines that she knew would never again melt into a smile—not for her.

Caitlín was the only human being that she could rely on now. She had to learn to accept her new "family;" a family that worshipped the moon rather than the sun, and who didn't look at her as though she were a monster.

When she had returned to Theo with barely-healed scars on her arms—and the silver handcuffs causing fresh burns every moment—her sire had been furious. Not with her, as she'd feared, but with the young human who had dared to attack his "little Moth." He had ripped the blessed metal from her wrists without flinching, the mysterious urn seemingly forgotten as he held her in his arms and stroked her hair.

Turning away from the home she had grown up in, Moth tasted bitter ashes on her tongue. Her old life was crumbling around her, but she pinned a fierce smile on her lips as she headed out of the city. She tucked her sunglasses in place, hoisted her backpack higher on her shoulder, and wondered how long it would take her to hitchhike back to Boston.

She had earned her last two months of freedom, and she damn well intended to make the most of them.

Shelter Island

BY MELISSA DE LA CRUZ

IT WAS THE light that started it. Hannah woke up at three o'clock in the morning one cold February day and noticed that one of the old copper sconces along the wall was turned on, emitting a dim, barely perceptible halo. It flickered at first, then died, then abruptly came back to life again. At first she chalked it up to a faulty wire, or carelessness on her part—had she turned off the lights before bed? But when it happened again the next evening, and again two days later, she began to pay attention.

The fourth time, she was already awake when it happened. She felt around the nightstand for her glasses, put them on, then stared at the glowing bulb and frowned. She definitely remembered turning off the switch before going to bed. She watched as it slowly burned out, leaving the room dark once more. Then she went back to sleep.

Another girl would have been scared, maybe a bit frightened, but this was Hannah's third winter on Shelter Island and she was used to its "house noises" and assorted eccentricities. In the summer, the back screen door would never stay closed, it would bang over and over with the wind, or when someone walked in and out of the house—her mother's boyfriend, a neighbor, Hannah's friends whose parents had houses on the island and spent their summers there. No one ever locked their doors on Shelter Island. There was no crime (unless bike-stealing was considered a crime, and if your bike was gone, most likely someone just borrowed it to pedal down to the local market and you would find it on your front doorstep the next day) and the last murder was recorded sometime in the 1700s.

Hannah was fifteen years old, and her mother was a bartender at The Good Shop, a crunchy, all-organic café, restaurant and bar that was only open three months out of the year, during the high season, when the island was *infested* (her mother's word) with cityfolk on vacation. The *summer people* (also her mother's words) and their money made living on the island possible for year-rounders like them. During the off-season, in the winter, there were so few people on the island it was akin to living in a ghost town.

But Hannah liked the winters, liked watching the ferry cross the icy river, how the quiet snow covered everything like a fairy blanket. She would walk alone on the windswept beach where the slushy sound of her boots scuffing the damp sand was the only sound for miles. People always threatened to quit the island during the winter. They had enough of the brutal snowstorms that raged in the night, the wind howling like a crazed banshee against the windows. They complained of the loneliness, the isolation. Some people didn't like the sound of quiet, but Hannah reveled in it. Only then could she hear herself think.

Hannah and her mother had started out as summer people. Once upon a time, when her parents were still together, the family would vacation in one of the big, colonial mansions by the beach, near where the yachts docked by the Sunset Beach hotel. But things were different after the divorce. Hannah understood that their lives had been lessened by the split, that she and her mother were lesser people now in some way. Objects of pity ever since her dad ran off with his art dealer.

Not that Hannah cared very much what other people thought. She liked the house they lived in, a comfortable, ramshackle Cape Cod with a wrap-around porch and six bedrooms tucked away in its corners—one up on the attic, three on the ground floor, and two in the basement. There were antique nautical prints of the island and its surrounding waters framed in the wood-paneled living room. The house belonged to a family who never used it, and the caretaker didn't mind renting it to a single mother.

At first, they moved around the vast spaces like two marbles lost in a pinball table. But over time they adjusted and the house felt cozy and warm. Hannah never felt lonely or scared in the house. She always felt safe.

• • •

Still, the next night, at three o'clock in the morning, when the lights blinked on, and the door whooshed open with a bang, it startled Hannah and she sat up immediately, looking around. Where had the wind come from? The windows were all storm-proofed and she hadn't felt a draft. With a start, she noticed a shadow lingering by the doorway.

"Who's there?" She called out in a firm and no-nonsense voice. It was the kind of voice she used when she worked as a cashier at the marked-up grocery during the summers when the cityfolk would complain about the price of arugula.

She wasn't scared. Just curious. What would cause the lights to blink on and off and the door to bang open like that?

"Nobody," someone answered.

Hannah turned around.

There was a boy sitting in the chair in the corner.

Hannah almost screamed. That she was not prepared for. A cat. Maybe a lost squirrel of some sort, she had been expecting. But a boy...Hannah was shy around boys. She was fast approaching her sweet-sixteen-and-never-been-kissed milestone. It was awful how some girls made such a big deal out of it, but even more awful that Hannah agreed with them.

"Who are you? What are you doing here?" Hannah said, trying to feel braver than she felt.

"This is my home," the boy said calmly. He was her age, she could tell, maybe a bit older. He had dark shaggy hair that fell in his eyes, and he was wearing torn jeans and a dirty T-shirt. He was very handsome, but he looked pensive and pained. There was an ugly cut on his neck.

Hannah pulled up the covers to her chin, if only to hide her pajamas, which were flannel and printed with pictures of sushi. He must be a neighbor, one of the O'Malley boys who lived next door. How did he get into her room without her noticing? What did he want with her? Should she cry out? Let her mother know? Call for help? That wound on his neck—it looked ravaged. Something awful had happened to him, and Hannah felt her skin prickle with goose bumps.

"Who are you?" the boy asked, suddenly turning the tables.

"I'm Hannah," she said in a small voice. Why did she tell him her real name? Did it matter?

"Do you live here?"

"Yes."

"How strange," the boy said thoughtfully. "Well." He said. "Nice meeting you Hannah." Then he walked out of her room and closed the door. Soon after, the light blinked off.

• • •

Hannah lay in her bed, wide-awake for a very long time, her heart galloping in her chest. The next morning, she didn't tell her mom about the boy in her room. She convinced herself it was just a dream. That was it. She had just made him up. Especially the part about him looking like a younger Johnny Depp. She'd been wanting a boyfriend so much she'd made one appear. Not that he would be her boyfriend. But if she was ever going to have a boyfriend, she would like him to look like that. Not that boys who looked like that ever looked at girls like her. Hannah knew what she looked like. Small. Average. Quiet. Her nicest feature were her eyes, sea-glass green, framed with lush dark lashes. But they were hidden behind her eyeglasses most of the time.

Her mother always accused her of having an overactive imagination, and maybe that was all it was. She had finally let the winter crazies get to her. It was all in her mind.

But then he returned the next evening, wandering into her room as if he belonged there. She gaped at him, too frightened to say a word, and he gave her a courtly bow before disappearing. The next night, she didn't fall asleep. Instead, she waited.

• • •

Three in the morning.

Lights blazed on. Was it just Hannah's imagination or was the light actually growing stronger? The door banged. This time, Hannah was awake and had expected it. She saw the boy appear in front of her closet, materializing out of nowhere. She blinked her eyes, her blood roaring in her ears, trying to fight the panic welling up inside. Whatever he was . . . he wasn't *human*.

"You again," she called, trying to feel brave.

He turned around. He was wearing the same clothes as the two nights prior. He gave her a sad, wistful smile. "Yes."

"Who are you? What are you?" she demanded.

"Me?" He looked puzzled for a moment, and then stretched his neck. She could see the wound just underneath his chin more clearly this time. Two punctures. Scabby and . . . blue. They were a deep indigo color, not the brownish-red she had been expecting. "I think I'm what you call a vampire."

"A vampire?" Hannah recoiled. If he were a ghost, it would be a different story. Hannah's aunt had told her all about ghosts—

her aunt had gone through a Wiccan phase, as well as a spirit-guide phase. Hannah wasn't afraid of ghosts. Ghosts couldn't harm you, unless it was a poltergeist. Ghosts were vapors, spectral images, maybe even just a trick of the light.

But vampires ... There was a Shelter Island legend about a family of vampires who had terrorized the island a long time ago. Blood-sucking monsters, pale and undead, cold and clammy to the touch, creatures of the night that could turn into bats, or rats or worse. She shivered, and looked around the room, wondering how fast she could fly out of bed and out the door. If there was even time to escape. Could you outrun a vampire?

"Don't worry, I'm not that kind of vampire," he said soothingly, as if he'd read her mind.

"What kind would that be?"

"Oh you know, chomping on people without warning. All that Dracula nonsense. Growing horns out of my head," he shrugged. "For one thing, we're not ugly."

Hannah wanted to laugh but felt it would be rude. Her fright was slowly abating.

"Why are you here?"

"We live here," he said simply.

"No one's lived here in years," Hannah said. "John Carter—the caretaker, he said it's been empty forever."

"Huh," the boy shrugged. He took the corner seat, across from her bed.

Hannah glanced at him warily, wondering if she should let him get that close. If he was a vampire, he didn't look cold and clammy. He looked tired. Exhausted. There were dark circles underneath his eyes. He didn't look like a cold-blooded killer. But what did she know? Could she trust him? But he had visited her twice already, after all. If he'd wanted her dead then, he could have killed her at any time. There was something about him—he was almost too cute to be scared of.

"Why do you keep doing that?" she asked, when she found her voice.

"Oh, you mean the thing with the lights?"

She nodded.

"Dunno. For a long time, I couldn't do anything. I was sleeping in your closet, but you didn't see me. Then I realized I could turn the lights on and off, on and off. But it was only when you started noticing that I began to feel more like myself."

"Why are you here?"

The boy closed his eyes. "I'm hiding from someone."

"Who?"

He closed his eyes harder, so that his face was a painful grimace. "Somebody bad. Somebody who wants me dead—no, worse than dead." He shuddered.

"If you're a vampire aren't you already dead?" she asked in a practical tone. She felt herself relaxing. Why should she be scared of him when it was so obvious it was he who was frightened?

"No, not really. It's more like I've lived a long time. A long time," he murmured. "This is our house. I remember the fireplace downstairs. I put the plaque up myself." He must be talking about that dusty old plaque next to the fireplace, Hannah thought, but it was so old and dirty she had never thought to notice it before.

"Who's chasing you?" Hannah asked.

"It's compli..." but before the boy could finish his sentence, there was a rattle at the window. A thump, thump, thump, as if someone—or something—was throwing itself against it with all its might.

The boy jumped and vanished for a moment. He reappeared by the doorway, breathing fast and hard.

"What is that?" Hannah asked, her voice trembling.

"It's here. It's found me." He said sharply, edgy and wired as if he were about to flee. And yet he remained where he was, his eyes fixed on the vibrating glass.

"Who?"

"The bad...thing..."

Hannah stood up and peered out the window. Outside was dark and peaceful. The trees, skeletal and bare of branches, stood still in the snowy field and against the frozen water. Moonlight cast the view in a cold, blue glow.

"I don't see any—Oh!" She stepped back, as if stabbed. She had seen something. A presence. Crimson eyes and silver pupils. Staring at her from the dark. Outside the window, it was hovering. A dark mass. She could feel its rage, its violent desire. It wanted in, to consume, to feed.

Hannah...Hannah...

It knew her name.

Let me in...Let me in...

The words had a hypnotic effect, she walked back toward the window, and began to lift the latch.

"STOP!"

She turned. The boy stood at the doorway, a tense, frantic look on his face.

"Don't," he said. "That's what it wants you to do. Invite it inside. As long as you keep that window closed, it can't come in. And I'm safe."

"What *is* it?" Hannah asked, her heart pounding hard in her chest. She took her hand away from the window but kept her eyes on the view outside. There was nothing there anymore, but she could sense its presence. It was near.

"A vampire too. Like me, but different. It's . . . insane," he said. "It feeds on its own kind."

"A vampire that hunts vampires?"

The boy nodded. "I know it sounds ridiculous . . ."

"Did it . . . do that to you?" she said, brushing her fingers against the scabs on his neck. They felt rough to touch. She felt sorry for him.

"Yes."

"But you're all right?"

"I think so." He hung his head. "I hope so."

"How were you able to come inside? No one invited you," she asked.

"You're right. But I didn't need an invitation. The door was open when I came. But so many doors were open on all the houses, but I couldn't enter any of them but this one. Which made me think that I'd found it. My family's house."

Hannah nodded. That made sense. Of course he would be welcome in his own home.

The rattling stopped. The boy sighed. "It's gone for now. But it will be back."

He looked so relieved that her heart went out to him.

"What do you need me to do?" she asked. She wasn't scared anymore. Her mother always said Hannah had a head for emergencies. She was a stoic, dependable girl. More likely to plant a stake in the heart of a monster than scream for rescue from the railroad tracks. "How can I help?"

He raised his eyebrow and looked at her with respect. "I need to get away. I can't stay here forever. I need to go. I need to warn the others. Tell them what happened to me. That the danger is growing." He sagged against the wall. "What I ask you to do might hurt a bit, and I don't want to ask unless it's freely given."

"Blood, isn't it? You need blood. You're weak," Hannah said. "You need my blood."

"Yes." The shadows cast his face in sharp angles, and she could see the deep hollows in his cheeks. His sallow complexion. So perhaps some of the vampire legends were true.

"But won't I turn into . . . ?"

"No." He shook his head. "It doesn't work that way. No one can make a vampire. We were born like this. Cursed. You will be fine—tired and a little sleepy, maybe, but fine."

Hannah gulped. "Is it the only way?" She didn't much like

how that sounded. He would have to bite her. Suck her blood. She felt nauseous just thinking about it, but strangely excited as well.

The boy nodded slowly. "I understand if you don't want to. It's not something that most people would like to do."

"Can I think about it?" she asked.

"Of course," he said.

Then he disappeared.

. . .

The next night, he told her a little more about the thing that was after him. It had almost gotten him once before, but he had been able to get away. But now it was back to finish the job. It had tracked him down. Hannah listened to the boy's story. The more he talked, the closer she felt to him. He was running out of time, he said. He was growing weaker and weaker and one day he wouldn't be able to resist its call. He would walk out to meet his doom, helpless against the creature's will.

Something thumped on the window hard, breaking the spell of his speech. They both jumped. The glass vibrated, but held and didn't shatter. Hannah could sense the thing was back. It was out there. It was close. It wanted to feed.

She turned to him, reached out for his hand. Her eyes were wide and frightened. "I'm sorry, but I...I can't."

"It's all right," he said mournfully. "I didn't expect you to. It's a lot to ask."

The light blinked off, and he was gone.

. . .

Hannah thought about him all the next day, remembering his words, his desperation to get away from the creature in the night that was hunting him. How alone he had looked. How scared. He looked like how she had felt when her father had told her he was leaving them, and her mother had had no one to turn to. That evening, before going to bed, she put on her cutest night-gown—a black one her aunt had brought back from Paris. It was black and silk and trimmed with lace. Her aunt was her father's sister and something of a "bad influence" (again her mom's words). She had made a decision.

When he appeared at three in the morning, she told him she had changed her mind.

"Are you sure?" he asked.

"Yes. But do it quickly before I chicken out," she ordered.

"You don't have to help me," he said.

"I know." She swallowed. "But I want to."

"I won't hurt you," he said.

She put a hand to her neck as if to protect it. "Promise?" How could she trust this strange boy? How could she risk her life to save him? But there was something about him—his sleepy dark eyes, his haunted expression—that drew her to him. Hannah was the type of girl who took in stray dogs and fixed broken bird's wings. Plus, there was that thing out there in the dark. She had to help him get away from it.

"Do it." She decided.

"Are you sure?"

She nodded briskly, as if she were at the doctor's office and asked to give consent to a particularly troublesome, but much-needed operation. She took off her glasses, pulled the right strap of her nightgown to the side and arched her neck. She closed her eyes and prepared herself for the worst.

He walked over to her. He was so tall, and when he rested his hands on her bare skin, they were surprisingly warm to the touch. He pulled her closer to him and bent down.

"Wait," he said. "Open your eyes. Look at me."

She did. She stared into his dark eyes, wondering what he was doing.

"They're beautiful—your eyes, I mean. You're beautiful," he said. "I thought you should know."

She sighed and closed her eyes as his hand stroked her cheek.

"Thank you," he whispered.

She could feel his hot breath on her cheek, and then his lips brushed hers for a moment. He kissed her, pressing his lips firmly upon hers. She closed her eyes and kissed him back. His lips were hot and wet.

Her first kiss, and from a vampire.

She felt his lips start to kiss the side of her mouth, and then the bottom of her chin, and then the base of her neck. This was it. She steeled herself for pain.

But he was right, there was very little. Just two tiny pinpricks, then a deep feeling of sleep. She could hear him sucking and swallowing, feel herself begin to get dizzy, woozy. Just like giving blood at the donor drive. Except she probably wouldn't get a doughnut after this.

She slumped in his arms and he caught her. She could feel him walk her to the bed, and lay her down on top of the sheets, then cover her with the duvet.

"Will I ever see you again?" she asked. It was hard to keep her eyes open. She was so tired. But she could see him very vividly now. He seemed to glow. He looked more substantial.

"Maybe," he whispered. "But you'd be safer if you didn't."

She nodded dreamily, sinking into the pillows.

• • •

In the morning, she felt spent and logy, and told her mother she felt like she was coming down with the flu and didn't feel like going to school. When she looked in the mirror, she saw nothing on her neck—there was no wound, no scar. Did nothing happen last night? Was she indeed going crazy? She felt around her skin with her fingertips, and finally found it—a hardening of the skin, just two little bumps. Almost imperceptible, but there.

She'd made him tell her his name, before she had agreed to help him.

Dylan, he'd said. My name is Dylan Ward.

• • •

Later that day, she dusted the plaque near the fireplace and looked at it closely. It was inscribed with a family crest and underneath it read "Ward House." Wards were foster children. This was a home for the lost. A safe house on Shelter Island.

She thought of the beast out there in the night, rattling the windows, and hoped Dylan had made it to wherever he was going.

Sword Point

BY MARIA V. SNYDER

AVA GLANCED AT the grimy alley. *This can't be right,* she thought. Crushed newspapers, bags of garbage, and pools of muck lined the narrow street. But a faded sign with *Accadamia della Spada* hung above the door.

Odd. A famous establishment located in the armpit of Iron City.

She hitched her equipment bag higher on her aching shoulder and headed toward the building. Since she lived in the suburbs across town, it had taken her over an hour to reach this place by bus. Ava pulled her coat's hood over her head as cold raindrops dripped from the night sky.

An unsettled feeling rolled in her stomach. She should be ecstatic and thrilled. This was a dream come true. Perhaps the combination of the location and the rainy Monday had doused her excitement.

A prickle of unease raised the hairs on her arms. She paused, certain someone was watching her, but the teenager lounging on a stoop across the street had his hoodie pulled down over his face as if asleep.

When she spotted two large blue eyes staring at her, she

smiled in relief. A young boy peered at her through the dirty window of the building next to the Academy. He hid behind his mother when Ava drew closer.

Through the window, Ava recognized a karate dojo. Parents sat in folding chairs as their children, clad in oversized uniforms with bright colored belts, kicked in unison. A young man with a black belt wove between them, correcting postures or giving praise. His shoulder-length hair had been pulled back into a ponytail, revealing a tattoo on his neck. The two black marks resembled Chinese calligraphy.

Ava lingered by the window, observing the lesson. I'm not procrastinating. I'm learning. That shuffle-kick is very similar to fencing footwork.

The teacher paired the children, and they practiced kicking into a pad. Ava caught the teacher's attention, and he scowled at her. She jerked away as if she'd been slapped and continued on to the Academy.

The Academy's elaborate stone entrance was marred with graffiti. She wrinkled her nose at the smell of urine and pressed the buzzer.

"Name?" The intercom squawked.

"Ava Vaughn."

The ornate door clicked open. The depressed inner-city exterior hid a modern fencing studio. Amazed, Ava stared. In the wide open space, students in white fencing gear sparred on long thin red strips. Others practiced lunges and attacks in front of mirrors. The ring of metal, the hum of voices, and the mechanical chug of fitness equipment filled the air.

An instructor carrying a clipboard approached. "Ms. Vaughn?"

She nodded.

He eyed her, clearly not impressed. "Change and warm up. Then we'll evaluate you."

Before he could shoo her away, she said, "But Bossemi—"

"Invited you, I know. Doesn't mean you'll train with him. You have to impress us first." He poked his pencil toward the locker rooms in the back.

As Ava changed clothes, she thought about the Three Rivers Regional Competition. She had fought well and won all her bouts, gaining the notice of Sandro Bossemi, a three-time Olympic Champion from Italy.

Fencers from around the world re-located just to train at the Accademia della Spada, which translated to the Academy of the Sword. Admittance to the school was by invitation only. Ava dreamed about being asked to train here.

However, reality proved to be another matter. Even though she had out-fenced all her opponents at the competition, the students at the Academy countered her efforts to spar them with ease. She couldn't even claim her youth as an excuse. A few fourteen- and fifteen-year-olds trained here, making her feel old at seventeen. After her first night of practice, Ava doubted she would be asked back.

A moment of panic engulfed her. *What will I do?* She steadied her hyperactive heart. *I'll train even harder and Bossemi will invite me again.*

When she lost her last bout, Mr. Clipboard joined her. He had been evaluating her all evening. She braced for the dismissal.

"Tomorrow you'll work with Signore Salvatori," he said. He flipped a paper. "We'll arrange a practice time with your tutor. I'll need contact information."

It took her a moment to recover from her surprise. "I go to James Edward High."

"Oh." Scanning the page, he marked it. "Then you can have Salvatori's seven to ten p.m. slot. Do you speak Italian?"

"No, but I'm fluent in French." Since fencing bouts were officiated in French, she had been determined to learn it.

"Salvatori only teaches in Italian so you may want to learn a few words for your lessons each evening."

"Each?" Ava tried to keep up with the information.

"If we are to teach you anything, you're to be here every night, and from two to five on Saturday. You have Sunday off; Sandro Bossemi is a devout Catholic."

Dazed, Ava walked to the locker room. Conflicting emotions warred in her. She was thrilled to not be dismissed, but daunted by the training schedule.

By the time she changed, the room was empty. She would have loved to leave her heavy gear bag here, but she had school practice tomorrow afternoon. Guess I'll be doing my homework on the bus. When she calculated her travel time, she realized she would also be eating her dinner on the bus. Peanut butter and jelly sandwiches with a side order of diesel fumes. Wonderful.

Pulling out her cell phone, she called her mother.

"Donny's 24-Hour Diner, can I help you?"

"I'd like an extra large banana split to go please," Ava said.

Mom laughed. "Ava, sweetie! How was practice?"

"Like a *Pirates of the Caribbean* movie, Mom. I pillaged and burned."

"Showing off on the first night isn't a good way to make friends." Her mother kept her tone light, but Ava knew the little dig was aimed directly at her.

For Ava, fencing had always come first. She didn't have time for friends she didn't need. Her mother disagreed.

Ava drew in a calming breath. "How soon can you pick me up?"

Silence. Her mother worked full-time and attended college classes at night, but to pay for Ava's training at the Academy, she scaled back her course load to one class so she could take another job as the night manager of Donny's.

You don't reach the Olympics without sacrifice.

"You can come during your dinner break," Ava prompted.

"Ava, I can't. I only get thirty minutes to eat. Can you get a ride? It could be a good ice breaker for making a friend."

Her fingers tightened on the phone. Her mother just wouldn't quit. Perhaps if she had an imaginary friend her mother would get off her back.

"I already made a friend," Ava said.

"Already?" Doubt laced her mom's voice.

"Yeah. Her name's Tammy, she lives in Copperstown. Her parents own the Copper Tea Kettle."

"Oh! The place with all those fancy teas?"

"Yeah. They're big tea drinkers. Look, Mom, I've gotta go. I'll get a ride with her. Bye." Ava closed her phone, and checked the time. Ten minutes until the next bus.

She left the locker room and almost ran into a group of fencing coaches, including Mr. Clipboard talking with the karate instructor. They all jumped back when they spotted her, and conversation ceased.

"Sorry. Didn't mean to surprise you," she said into the silence. No response. As she passed them, her back burned with their stares.

That was creepy. If the Karate Dude doesn't want people to watch through his window, he should buy curtains.

When she reached the bus stop, she dropped her heavy bag on the sidewalk in relief.

"You lied to your mother," a man said behind her.

She spun. The Karate Dude stood five feet away, peering at her with loathing. "Tammy isn't one of the Academy students."

Anger flared. "You perv. You shouldn't be hanging around the girls' locker room."

"And you shouldn't have come here alone." His intent gaze pierced her body like the point of a sword. "Your kind is always overconfident," he said.

"My kind? Fencers?" Fear brushed her stomach. Perhaps this was one of those situations her mother warned her about.

"You can quit with the charade. I know what you are."

And he was a dangerous wacko. Should she scream or call the

police? He put his hand in the pocket of his black leather jacket. Ava grabbed her phone, searching the street for help. No one.

The Karate Dude yanked out a bottle. In one fluid motion, he flipped the lid off and flung the contents into her face.

She yelped and swiped at her cheeks. Acid? Wiping her eyes in panic, she steeled herself for the pain. Nothing. A few drops of the liquid dripped into her mouth. Water?

Karate Dude's satisfied smirk faded.

"What the hell was that for?" she demanded. Ava dried her face on the sleeve of her coat, and smoothed her—now wet—blonde hair from her eyes.

"You're not...I thought..." He sputtered and seemed shocked. "But you're so pale..."

Ava spotted the bus. "Stay away from me, you sicko freak, or the next time I'll call the police."

The bus squealed to a stop and the door hissed open. She grabbed her bag, sprinted up the steps, and dropped into the seat behind the driver. Glaring at the freak, she didn't relax until the doors shut and the bus drove away.

...

Ava dreaded returning to the Academy. All because of that Karate Freak. But it wouldn't stop her from going. Oh no. She loved fencing, and hoped to join gold medalist Mariel Zagunis in the record books. Mariel was a goddess! She was the first American woman in a century to win fencing gold with a saber. *A century!* Ava dreamed of doing the same with the foil.

She had competed with all three weapons, but a foil's bout with its feints, ducks and sudden attacks appealed to Ava more than the épée or saber. The sport fed her competitive streak, while the rhythm and cadence of the moves made her feel elegant and graceful. She even enjoyed researching the long history of the sport, which surprised her mother since anything not involving a foil in her hand tended to be done under protest and as quickly as possible.

Holding her cell phone—with 911 already dialed—in one hand, and her bag in the other, Ava stepped from the bus. With her thumb ready to push the send button, she scanned the street. A few parents hustled their kids to karate class, and two Academy students walked toward school.

Ava sprinted to catch up with the fencers. She trailed behind them despite their annoyed looks. When she spotted the Karate Freak teaching his class, she remembered to breathe. Once inside the Academy, she should be safe.

Mr. Clipboard seemed surprised to see her. Ava debated. Should she ask him about last night or not? He had been in the group talking to Karate Freak. He tapped his watch when she approached. She didn't have time. *I'll ask him later.*

By the time the session ended, Ava no longer cared about the Karate Freak. All she wanted to do was crawl inside a locker and hide. Salvatori hadn't spoken any of the Italian words she learned. Eventually, he stopped talking and used gestures for most of the session, adjusting her stance by touch.

He corrected everything she had learned from Coach

Phillips. When she thought she had mastered a move, he proved her wrong. Frustrated and humiliated, Ava felt like a beginner again. Coach Phillips treated her like a professional, while Salvatori acted like he worked with an amateur. Perhaps she should ask for another coach.

At the end of the lesson, Salvatori dismissed her with a curt wave. Exhausted, she aimed for the locker room and stopped.

Karate Freak leaned against a side wall, watching her. No one seemed bothered by his presence, and Ava didn't have the energy to care. She changed in a hurry, wanting to leave before the Academy emptied.

Once again she armed herself with her pre-dialed phone. She was halfway to the door before Karate Freak caught up to her. At least this time a few people milled nearby.

"Go away," she said, brandishing the phone.

"Look, Ava, I'm sorry about last night," he said.

He knew her name. She stepped back. *Wait a minute. Did he just apologize?* According to her mother, the male species was incapable of apologizing.

"I thought you were someone else." He pulled his hair away from his face, attempting to look sincere.

If he wasn't a freak, he'd be hot—grayish blue eyes, hawk nose and a slight Asian cut to his features. But he overdid the whole karate warrior look with his tight black T-shirt and black jeans. Maybe she should call him the Ninja Freak. Either way, his explanation was lame. She remained unconvinced.

"I know it sounds weird. We've been having trouble with . . .

another school. And I thought you were one of them, spying on us."

"So you threw water on me? That's weak. Get lost." She walked around him. But he trailed her.

"It's a long story, and you wouldn't believe it if I told you."

"Fine. Whatever. Apology accepted, now go away." She pushed through the door, hoping to leave him behind.

He kept pace with her. "At least let me make it up to you. How about a free lesson?"

"On how to be a jerk? No, thanks."

Unfazed, he gestured toward the school. "No. Isshinryu karate. You know, martial arts? All fencers should cross-train. Karate is great for improving your reflexes and footwork."

"No." She didn't trust him.

"If this is about last—"

"Look, I don't even know you, and frankly, I don't have any interest." She continued to the bus stop.

He walked with her. "I can rectify one of those." He held out his hand. "I'm Jarett White, owner of the White Hawks Isshin-ryu Club."

Owner? He didn't look old enough, but she shook his warm hand. He held hers a moment past awkward.

"Your hand is ice cold." He studied her face as if that was a bad thing.

She pulled away. "It's November."

"How about a free session on self defense? It could help you around here."

"I really don't have time." Except Sunday, but that was her day to get everything else done. And her "to do" list spanned pages.

He considered. "Yeah. I guess Salvatori has you on the novice training schedule. That's brutal."

Despite her irritation, she was intrigued. "How do you know?"

"I trained with Sal for two years before Sandro took me on." His gaze grew distant. "Sandro helped me qualify for the Junior Olympic Fencing Championships."

Impressive. He must have been recruited by the best universities. "Where did you go to college?"

"I'm taking business classes at the community college."

She gaped at him in pure astonishment. With a fencing scholarship, he could have gone anywhere.

Jarett noticed. "I earned my black belt at age twelve, and I enjoy teaching karate. Plus I'm my own boss. How many twenty-year-olds can say that?"

Weak excuses. Ava felt sorry for him. Teaching a bunch of snot-nosed kids instead of competing at the Cadet level. He must have burnt out. Before she could remark, the familiar roar of the bus signaled its approach.

"You really shouldn't be taking the bus this late," Jarett said. "Besides lying to your mother about getting a ride home, there's dangerous people downtown."

She hefted her bag. "I didn't lie to my mother." The bus's door opened, revealing the smiling red-haired driver. "Jarett, meet my friend Tammy." Ava gestured to the bus driver.

He gave her a wry grin. "Let me guess, her parents own the Copper Tea Kettle."

"Yep. And the most dangerous person I met so far...is you." She stepped onto the bus.

Jarett saluted her with an imaginary sword. "Touché."

• • •

Much to Ava's annoyance, Jarett insisted on walking her to the bus stop every night. He'd talk about karate and fencing, but he always kept watch, scanning the area as if expecting an ambush.

After a few nights she actually looked forward to his company. And he agreed with her about Mariel being a goddess.

"She was added to the 2004 Olympic team as a replacement, then goes on to win the gold. How sweet is that?" He stabbed a hand in the air.

"Pretty sweet. To be at the Olympics has to be ..." Ava searched for the word, but couldn't find the perfect one.

"Awesome."

She thought about Jarett's many talents. "Does your community college have a fencing program?"

"No. But I went to Penn State University for a year. Their coaches are excellent."

"Why didn't you stay?" The question just popped from her mouth. She wished she could erase it as his smile faded.

"I needed to be home. Some things are more important than fencing."

Ava found that hard to believe. *Nothing* was more important than fencing. *Nothing.*

. . .

Jarett was extra jumpy. He spooked at any noise, and stared at everyone who walked by them as they waited for the bus. There were more people out tonight than Ava had seen before. *Friday night.*

When he glanced around for the fourth time in a minute, she asked, "Why do you do that?"

"Habit. You should always know who is around you so you're not surprised."

"Sounds paranoid."

"Consider the first night I met you. You were completely oblivious to the fact I was right behind you all the way to the bus stop. I could have grabbed your bag and been gone before you even reacted."

"I have fast reflexes," she said.

"Consider how much faster you'd be if you knew a few seconds sooner?"

She conceded the point. All too soon, the bus arrived. Ava mounted the steps with reluctance. She almost laughed out loud. Five days ago, she ran up these steps to get away from Jarett. Now she didn't want to leave. The door hissed shut behind her. Tammy gave her a distracted hello as Ava sat in her usual seat.

"Full bus tonight," she said to Tammy.

"Yeah. All the college kids from the burbs are headed down-town." She tilted her head to look into the big mirror above her and checked out the passengers.

Ava looked back. Groups of friends hung together, laughing and talking loudly. A few high school kids tried to look cool in front of the college kids. One kid sat alone, staring out the window. He wore a black hoodie with a grinning skull on it. When the bus pulled away from the curb, he waved to someone outside.

Settling in for a long ride, she pulled out her history book to study. It remained unopened in her lap. She was distracted by thoughts of Jarett and by Tammy glancing in her mirror every few seconds. Ava finally asked her why.

"There's a punk in a black hoodie. I think he's on drugs so I'm keeping an eye on him," Tammy said.

As Tammy slowed for the next stop, Ava turned around. The punk stared at her. Pale skin clung to his skeletal face. He grinned, displaying crooked teeth and black gums. Yikes.

"Got a runner," Tammy said with delight. Her hand hovered over the door switch. As soon as a runner reached the point that they might actually catch the bus, Tammy would shut the door and pull away.

"You're evil," Ava said.

"Everyone needs a hobby. He's getting closer . . . Wait for it . . . Wait for it . . . Ah, hell." She slumped back in her seat. "It's your friend."

Jarett bounded up the steps and dropped a token into

the fare collector. "Thanks," he said, not even out of breath. He didn't acknowledge Ava, but she recognized his hard expression—the sword point. The same cold fury had burned in his eyes when he had thrown the water on her. But this time, he focused it on the grinning skull punk.

As the bus accelerated, Jarett knelt on the seat next to her, facing backward. "I thought I should make sure the bus was safe," he said. He kept his right hand inside his jacket pocket and his gaze never left Grinning Skull.

Ava suspected he knew the kid. When the bus reached the trendy downtown area, it emptied of students, leaving her, Jarett and the punk. They rode for a while in silence. Tension radiated, filling the air. Ava startled when the kid dinged the signal for the next stop. Jarett jumped to his feet. Grinning Skull stood in the aisle, facing him.

Tammy opened the exit door in the middle of the bus.

"Next time," Grinning Skull said, waggling boney fingers at Jarett. In a blink, he was gone.

"I told you that guy was on drugs," Tammy said. "Did you see how fast he moved?"

Jarett relaxed into his seat as the bus drove away.

"A friend of yours?" Ava asked.

"No. He's a troublemaker in my neighborhood. When I saw him on your bus, I just wanted to make sure he didn't bother you."

Conflicting emotions fought in her chest. She was pleased at his concern but annoyed he thought she couldn't defend herself.

"Don't you have other things to do? It's Friday night. Won't your girlfriend be mad?" *So lame!*

By his sly smile, Ava knew he saw right through her.

"No worries, my harem will wait for me," he teased. Then he sobered. "I wish. Between training, classes and work, there's no time for fun. I'm guessing it's the same with you. Although I'm sure the guys at your school must be lined up three-deep trying to get your attention."

"Of course." She flicked her long ponytail dramatically. "There's a daily fight over me in the hallways."

He laughed. The rich sound buzzed through her. She decided it didn't matter why he was here, she would just enjoy his company. For Ava, the ride home flew by.

...

Ava used the access code Mr. Clipboard had given her to enter the now-empty Academy. Her mother followed, exclaiming over the equipment. Ava had two hours until her lesson with Salvatori, but a ride downtown from her mother was worth the wait. Plus her mother wanted a tour of the school.

"I'll pick you up after my economics class." Her mom left.

The silent studio gave Ava the creeps. She should warm up and practice before the others arrived, but she hesitated outside the dark locker rooms. Instead of changing, she explored the Academy. A few of the coaches' offices lined the far left wall. Bulletin boards with flyers decorated the space between them.

Ava discovered a hallway in the far left corner of the building. Here the modern renovations ended and the original wood floor and arched windows remained. Half-moon-shaped stained glass transoms sat atop thick ornate doors. Curious to see what lurked behind this double wide entrance, Ava found Sandro Bossemi's private studio and office.

She entered. The office held the typical furniture and clutter. Foils, épées and sabers rested in the corners. A large, almost life-sized crucifix hung on the far wall with a realistic Jesus nailed to it. The poor guy was frozen with his face creased in agony and wounds bleeding. Yikes.

None of Bossemi's gold medals were on display. Disappointed, she returned to the corridor. Two other doors remained. One connected to Jarrett's office, which explained how he'd magically appeared in the studio. The room led to his dojo.

Through the open office door, she watched him teach a few adults. They failed to look as impressive in their white uniforms as Jarett did. His flexibility and speed was striking compared to their awkward attempts. How could she have thought he was a perverted jerk?

She returned to the Academy. The last door had *Vietato L'ingresso* written on it. *More Italian words I don't know. Probably an equipment room.* Ava turned the knob. Despite the strong smell of garlic, her guess seemed right, but the row of swords didn't glint in the weak light. She picked one up. The heavy weapon was made of wood and the tip had been sharpened to a nasty point. *I could stab someone with this.*

Bottles of water lined the shelves, matching the one Jarett

had used when he threw water on her. Crossbows with wooden bolts hung on the wall. Even the points of the arrows were made of wood. Her queasiness turned into apprehension when she found crosses and wooden stakes. *This is beyond weird. It's bordering on serious mental illness. Did Bossemi believe in—*

"What are you doing in here?" Jarrett demanded.

Ava jumped. Her heart lunged in her chest.

Before she could reply, he gestured to the door, "Can't you read?"

"Not Italian."

He tapped the words with his index finger. "*Vietato L'ingresso.* No admittance."

Ignoring her heart's antics, she shrugged. "If you really wanted to keep people out, you should lock the door."

He motioned her from the room, then shut the door when she joined him in the hallway. "We need to be able to get in there quickly."

"Why? What're all those weapons for?"

He shook his head. "Not yet. Sandro decides who is ready or not."

She wanted to protest, but he changed the subject.

"I'm done with my class and you still have time before training. How about that self-defense lesson?"

Ava considered the incident last night. Perhaps he wouldn't be so protective if she agreed. Odd. The thought of walking to the bus alone didn't produce the relief she expected.

"Okay, but you have to answer one question."

Wariness touched his eyes. "What's the question?"

She had a million to ask, but knew he'd probably dodge most of them. Ava pointed to the left side of his neck. "What do your tattoos mean?"

He relaxed. "It's Okinawan for hawk. Isshinryu is an Okinawan marital art." Jarett guided her through the door and into his office. Framed pictures decorated the walls. He pointed to a photo of a red-tailed hawk. "Hawks are a symbol of victory. My sensei tattooed the characters onto his neck when he earned his black belt, starting a tradition."

"Your sensei?"

"Okinawan for teacher." He huffed in amusement. "Hang around here long enough and you'll learn Okinawan and Italian." He stopped before the mats and gestured to her feet. "No shoes."

She kicked off her street shoes and stepped onto the thin black foam. The mats interlocked like a jigsaw puzzle. Next to the main entrance, the window spanned the whole front of the dojo.

Jarett faced Ava and grabbed her wrist. His thumb overlapped his fingers. "Holy chicken wings, Batman. Don't you eat?"

She tried to jerk her arm free, but he held on.

"When we work on self-defense techniques, I'm not going to let you go unless you force me. Now, to break my grip, pull through my thumb. It's the weakest part of the hold." Jarett demonstrated.

Ava tried again and managed to free herself. They practiced a variety of wrist and arm holds for a while.

"You're stronger than you look," he said. "And quick to learn. Some of my students just don't get it."

He taught her how to break a bear hold and other body locks. Ava liked being held by him. He smelled of Polo Sport. When she managed to roll him off of her, she paused as a brief surge of pride followed an "ah ha" moment.

Jarett met her gaze and beamed. "If you know what to do, you can escape from anyone, no matter how big."

"What if they have a knife or a gun?"

"That's a whole other lesson. I'll show you next week."

The prospect thrilled her. When it was time for her fencing lesson, she cut through Jarett's office and noticed a framed photo propped on his desk. In the picture, Jarett stood next to an older Asian man. Both wore karate uniforms with black belts. Both had matching tattoos and the same shaped face.

"Is that your sensei or your father?" she asked.

Jarett plopped into his chair. "He was both." Sadness tainted his voice.

She frowned and tried to think of something appropriate to say.

"Looking for the perfect Hallmark words of comfort?" He gave her a wry grin. "They don't exist in this case. My father was murdered."

She thought she felt bad before. "That's horrible. Did the police arrest anyone?"

Jarett's expression hardened. "The killer was taken care of. We made sure of that."

A thousand questions lodged in her throat. Afraid of the answers, she swallowed them and retreated to the Academy.

The Saturday afternoon practice included a welcome change in routine. During the last hour, the coaches staged a mock tournament. Ava endured being embarrassed, but not because of her fencing skills. With just a week of training, her attacks and parries had vastly improved, surprising her. Signore Salvatori even gave her a "buono." High praise indeed.

No. The embarrassment came from her mother. She arrived in time to watch the bouts. Bad enough to have her mother there, but then the woman compounds Ava's mortification by cheering and hooting for her. Good thing the fencing mask hid her red face.

When Ava finally slinked from the locker room, she stopped in horror. Jarett was talking to her mother. *Just kill me now.*

She rushed over, intent on hustling her mother out the door.

"...Did you see her feint-disengage attack? It was perfect," her mother exclaimed.

Ava jumped into the conversation. "It wasn't perfect, Mom. I didn't win any bouts."

Her mother swept her hand as if waving away a fly. "It's just a matter of persistence, practice and experience."

Ava rolled her eyes. *Mom's such a dork.*

"I like that. Can I tell it to my students?" Jarett asked. He even managed to appear sincere.

Bonus points.

Her mother blinked at him for a few seconds. "Ah ... sure." She cleared her throat. "I'm sorry, I thought you trained here."

"I do, but I teach karate, too."

"Oh."

"Did you have trouble parking?" Ava asked her mother, hoping the change in topic would get her moving away from him.

"Not at all, but, Ava . . . Do you think you can get a ride home with Tammy?"

"Why?"

"A few of my classmates invited me to dinner nearby." Her mother practically bounced on the balls of her feet in excitement.

Ava was tired, hungry and had been looking forward to a quick ride home. She opened her mouth to complain, but stopped. Her mother had already read Ava's disappointed expression. She no longer bounced.

If Ava said she couldn't get a ride, her mother would skip dinner to take her home. She couldn't even recall the last time her mother did something for herself. She had given up her social life for Ava, and her daughter had been too focused on fencing to notice.

So why did I realize this now? Jarett. Perhaps the water thrown in her face had woken her up. A good thing. Now the only other things she had to worry about were punks on the bus, and strange wooden stakes in Bossemi's closet.

"Sure, Mom. I'll get a ride."

Delight flashed in her eyes. "Thanks, sweetie. See you at home!" She kissed Ava's forehead and swept out the door.

"Sweetie?" Jarett smirked.

"Don't start."

"That was pretty clever. You told her you'd get a ride home, but didn't say how, so technically you didn't lie to her. Does Tammy work Saturdays?"

"No." She dug in her bag for the bus schedule. She'd missed the five fifteen bus by ten minutes, and the next one wasn't due until six thirty. Her stomach grumbled. She hunted for money, finding only a few bucks. "Is there a hot dog cart around here?"

He winced. "Hot dogs? No wonder you're so thin. You should be eating healthy foods."

She clamped down on a laugh. He'd probably have a fit over her daily diet of junk food.

Despite his protest over her food choices, he led her to a local food stand. The shoppers had gone home, and it was too early for the theater crowd, so the area was empty. Jarett set a quick pace, and Ava hustled to keep up.

On the way back to the bus stop, Jarett entertained her with stories about his karate students.

"...Little guy was so proud of his new move, he ran over to his father and kicked him right in the...Damn." Jarett grabbed her upper arm. "Listen," he said in a tight voice. "If I tell you to run, you run to the Academy. Understand?" He talked to her, but he watched three figures walking toward them.

"Yes, but—"

"Not now." He squeezed once and let go. Reaching inside his jacket, he pulled out a mini crossbow, loaded a small bolt and aimed it at them. "Don't come any closer," he said.

They stopped. A street light illuminated their pale and gaunt faces. Resembling half-starved street punks, they wore ripped baggy jeans that sagged around thin waists, exposing colorful boxers. A ton of bling hung from their necks on thick gold chains. Hoods had been pulled up.

Ava recognized Grinning Skull from the bus. His friend's shirt had skeletons playing in a band on it, and a cobra design wrapped around the punk on the right's sleeve.

"You can only shoot one of us before we move," Grinning Skull said. "That leaves two and I doubt your girlfriend is armed."

Ava's stomach twisted as the small bit of confidence she had gained by learning a few self-defense moves fled.

"She knows nothing about this," Jarett said. "Her bus will be here soon. Once she goes, we can . . . talk."

Skeleton Band cackled. The sound scraped like glass against stone. "You didn't tell her about us? What a naughty boy you've been Jarett White Hawk. Tisk, tisk."

"Irresponsible," Cobra agreed. "Jarett will pay with his life. Like father like son."

"And the girl?" Skeleton Band asked.

"Ours." Grinning Skull looked at Ava with hunger.

Ice pumped through her veins yet she felt hot and sweaty.

The three advanced.

"Run," Jarett ordered. He shot the crossbow, hitting Cobra in the stomach.

Before she even moved, the punks flickered. One second they stood fifteen feet away, the next they surrounded Jarett and Ava. *Like a cartoon. Except this is like a badly-drawn horror cartoon.*

Jarett dropped the crossbow, pulled a bottle from his pocket, and tossed water into Skeleton Band's face. The punk shrieked as his skin melted and steamed.

Another flicker and Grinning Skull grabbed Ava in a steel grip. She couldn't move. Panicked, she yelled for Jarett, but he was caught tight by Cobra. Grinning Skull opened his mouth. The putrid stench of decay gagged her. He bent close to her face. She cringed as his ice-cold cheek brushed hers.

When he bit her neck, she screamed. She never thought she'd be the kind of girl to scream, but terror and pure revulsion had built inside her to such a degree that screaming was the only way to release it.

Grinning Skull pushed against her as if slammed from behind. He grunted and went slack, knocking Ava to the ground. He landed on top of her. A dead weight. She stared at his face and nausea boiled up in her throat. The skin disintegrated before her eyes, peeling off the bone, which crumbled into powder.

Ava kicked the dusty clothes off of her. She wanted to puke, to scream and to faint, but she held it together and focused on Jarett and Bossemi. The master fencer held a wood sword. Two piles of clothes lay at his feet—the remains of Cobra and Skeleton Band.

Bossemi gestured to the clothes and shoes. Jarett swept them up.

"All'interno. Rapidamente!" He barked before running to the Academy.

Ava scrambled upright and followed him with Jarett fast on her heels. When the door shut behind them, they sagged with relief.

"Sandro, I'm—" Jarett started.

"Idiota." Bossemi turned to Ava. "Prossimo . . . Come. We must clean your wound."

In all the excitement, she had forgotten about the bite. Pain throbbed when she touched her neck. Blood coated her fingers. Her vision blurred, but a sharp order from Bossemi snapped her out of it. She didn't even realize Jarett supported her until they reached his office.

She met Jarett's gaze. He looked miserable. But she didn't have time to question him. Bossemi instructed her to lie down flat on his couch. He put a towel under her neck.

"This will hurt," he said.

When he brandished a spray bottle and metal hook-shaped tool, she closed her eyes. He might not have much of a couch-side manner, but he was honest. It hurt. By the time he had cleaned the bite and bandaged it, tears had puddled in her ears.

Jarett sat on the edge of the couch, holding her hand. Bossemi dumped the blood-soaked towel into a hamper.

"Tell her what she needs to know," Bossemi said. "I'll organize a watch." He handed Jarett his wooden sword, then left.

Jarett stared at the weapon with resignation.

Ava pulled her hand away from his and struggled to a sitting position. She wanted answers. "Talk. Now."

He sighed. "At least I don't have to convince you they're real."

"The punks?"

His gaze focused on the life-sized crucifix. "Not punks. Vampiros."

Vampiros. Italian for "vampire." Instinctively, she wanted to protest—vampires populated horror novels, not real life. But she couldn't explain how the punks disintegrated into powder. "Go on," she said.

"They've been around since biblical times." Jarett said.

Ava thought back to the attack. "They flickered and were so strong." She shuddered.

"That's why we use swords and crossbows. If they grab you, you're almost as good as dead."

"What about the stakes I saw in the closet?"

"We use those during the day. We hunt them while they sleep. Safer that way."

"We?"

"The Hawks. Sandro taught us how to find and fight the vampiros. He recruits candidates from the fencers he invites to his school. Some join us. Others leave. And some won't get recruited at all."

"Would I have been recruited?"

He considered. "If I hadn't messed it up, probably not."

"How did you ... Oh."

"'Oh' is right. I thought you were a vampiro. You're pale

and thin. I wasn't the only one." He sounded defensive. "The other coaches suspected you, too. Plus we had just attacked one of their nests, and thought you were trying to get revenge."

"A nest of them? How many vampiros are there?" she asked.

"There are nests in most of the major cities of the world. The Hawks are there too. It's an on-going battle. Sometimes we manage to wipe out an entire cluster, and sometimes they get to us first."

Ava remembered his sad story. "Did they kill your father?"

Jarett's body tensed and his grip tightened on the sword. "Yes. They drained his blood, starving his brain of oxygen. Once the brain dies, a demon takes possession of the body. It's not like in the movies. Police don't find a bloodless corpse. There is no burial and no dramatic rising from the dead. The victim just changes. They lose weight, becoming pale, nocturnal creatures."

She followed the logic. "Then your father is a ..." She couldn't say the word.

"Not anymore." Anguish strained his voice. He closed his eyes. "He came to visit me at school. They go after their relatives and friends first. I knew as soon as I saw him."

Ava waited. Despite the obvious outcome, Jarett needed to tell the story.

"My father had been a Hawk all my life. We moved from city to city, hunting vampiros. But I didn't want to join the Hawks. I wanted to fence. I was selfish, and my father died."

"You can't blame—"

"Yes I can. I'm the one who flung the holy water on him. He dissolved before my eyes."

She searched for the appropriate words. What did Jarett call them? Hallmark words. She didn't think she would find a sorry-your-father-was-a-vampire sympathy card. Instead she asked him why the vampiros disintegrated.

"The demon keeps the body alive. Once the demon is killed, the body is destroyed. The older they are, the faster they go. If they're very new, we use holy water to help them along."

They sat for a while in silence. Ava's wound burned and pulsed. She touched the bandage.

"You better call your mom and tell you won't be home tonight," Jarett said.

"Why?"

He braced as if about to deliver bad news. "You need to stay here until the venom runs its course. Sandro cleaned your wound, but the vampiro's saliva mixed with your blood."

Her insides twisted. "Will I—"

"No. You're not going to turn into a vampire. But they know you've been bitten, and they'll come for you."

That was truly horrifying. "Aren't we protected?" Ava gestured toward the crucifix.

"No. The wood has to touch them."

Bossemi burst into the room, panting and brandishing another wood sword. "The Accadamia . . . surrounded."

Jarett shot to his feet. "The Hawks?"

"On the way." He inclined his head toward Ava.

"She believes."

"Buono." Bossemi tossed Ava his sword. She caught it in mid-air. He thumped a finger on his chest. "Aim for...il Cuore."

Her own heart increased its tempo, signaling its desire to retreat.

"She doesn't know how—" Jarett began.

"Vampiros will break-in before Hawks arrive. Prossimo!" Bossemi raced across the hall, stopping at the equipment room. Leaving the door unlocked now made horrifying sense. Jarett armed himself with holy water and Bossemi grabbed another sword.

The loud crackle of breaking glass cut through Ava. She clutched her weapon to her stomach which threatened to expel her dinner.

Bossemi and Jarett exchanged a surprised glance. They positioned themselves by the door to the dojo. Ava stayed behind them to protect their backs.

"They're bold. What did you do?" Bossemi asked Jarett.

"Killed Vincent."

"Idiota! I told you to wait. You can't kill the leader without taking out the entire nest."

"He murdered my father. I—" His argument was cut short by the arrival of the vampires.

Ava marveled at Bossemi's lethal speed. Between him and Jarett, the doorway filled with dusty clothes. A splitting noise sounded behind Ava, she turned in time to see the boarded up windows of the Academy open and dark figures climb inside.

She yelled, "Vampiros!"

Jarett joined her at the end of the hallway as the two vampiros flickered. Bossemi remained by the dojo's door. Ava held her weapon with the point down, backing up as a vampire stalked her.

"En garde, Ava. Attack!"

Jarett's order broke through her fear. She raised the tip and lunged, stabbing the point into the vampire's heart. But there was no time to reflect on her action, as another vampire sprinted toward her.

Time blurred. Her arms ached from wielding the heavy sword and her breath puffed. But she kept the sword's point moving. If a vampiro grabbed her weapon, she would be done.

The three of them had found a good defensive position. The studio filled with other vampires. The Hawks had arrived, but even more vampiros poured into the room. The sheer number of vampires soon overpowered and disarmed the Hawks. The ones attacking Jarett and Ava stepped out of range. Bossemi stood behind her.

"We have seven of your members, Sandro. All we want is Jarett White Hawk and Ava. Two for seven. You can't beat that."

Ava glanced at the captured Hawks. She recognized Signore Salvatori and Mr. Clipboard. They both shook their heads "no" when she met their gaze. They were willing to give up their lives for her. *Why?*

"Leave Ava alone and I'll come," Jarett said. He dropped his sword.

"No." The word burst from Ava's mouth. She didn't want to lose him. He was right, some things were more important than fencing. His life and the lives of all the Hawks.

"Tirer le signal d'incendie," Bossemi whispered in a language Ava understood—French.

She tossed her weapon to the floor.

"Ava, you are *not* going with them," Jarett said.

"Shut up! I'm tired of taking orders from you." She pushed him, giving him a pointed look. "First you assume I'm one of them." *Push.*

He caught on, and backed up.

"Then you nag me about taking the bus." *Push.*

The vampiros watched them with amusement.

"And you don't even warn me about these things!" She shoved him hard. He fell to the floor with a solid thump, and she had reached the fire alarm. She yanked the handle down.

Ear splitting bells pierced the air. Everyone hunched against the noise, but the vampires remained unharmed. Ava appealed to Bossemi. He held up a finger as if to say wait.

The sprinkler system switched on. Water sprayed and the vampires began to melt.

"I never thought they'd dare attack me in my Accadamia," Bossemi said. "But having a priest bless the water in my fire system, just in case, seemed like a good idea."

Jarett whooped and hugged Ava.

"You will now train with me," Bossemi said to Ava.

"To be a Hawk?"

"Do you want to be one?"

Ava didn't hesitate. "Yes."

"Maybe. Maybe Olympics first, then a Hawk. We'll see." He moved away, shouting orders in Italian.

Surprised by his comment, Ava pulled away from Jarett so she could see his face. "But you—"

"Would never have qualified for the Olympic team. Once I realized the truth, I decided to stay here and be a Hawk."

"Does that mean Bossemi believes I might qualify?"

He smirked. "It's just a matter of persistence, practice and experience, Sweetie."

She groaned and punched him in the gut.

The Coldest Girl in Coldtown
BY HOLLY BLACK

MATILDA WAS DRUNK, but then she was always drunk. Dizzy drunk. Stumbling drunk. Stupid drunk. Whatever kind of drunk she could get.

The man she stood with snaked his hand around her back, warm fingers digging into her side as he pulled her closer. He and his friend with the open-necked shirt grinned down at her like underage equaled dumb, and dumb equaled gullible enough to sleep with them.

She thought they might just be right.

"You want to have a party back at my place?" the man asked. He'd told her his name was Mark, but his friend kept slipping up and calling him by a name that started with a D. Maybe Dan or Dave. They had been smuggling her drinks from the bar whenever they went outside to smoke—drinks mixed sickly sweet, that dripped down her throat like candy.

"Sure," she said, grinding her cigarette against the brick wall. She missed the hot ash in her hand, but concentrated on the alcoholic numbness turning her limbs to lead. Smiled. "Can we pick up more beer?"

They exchanged an obnoxious glance she pretended not to

notice. The friend—he called himself Ben—looked at her glassy eyes and her cold-flushed cheeks. Her sloppy hair. He probably made guesses about a troubled home life. She hoped so.

"You're not going to get sick on us?" he asked. Just out of the hot bar, beads of sweat had collected in the hollow of his throat. The skin shimmered with each swallow.

She shook her head to stop staring. "I'm barely tipsy," she lied.

"I've got plenty of stuff back at my place," said MarkDan-Dave. *Mardave*, Matilda thought and giggled.

"Buy me a 40," she said. She knew it was stupid to go with them, but it was even stupider if she sobered up. "One of those wine coolers. They have them at the bodega on the corner. Otherwise, no party."

Both of the guys laughed. She tried to laugh with them even though she knew she wasn't included in the joke. She was the joke. The trashy little slut. The girl who can be bought for a big fat wine cooler and three cranberry-and-vodkas.

"Okay, okay," said Mardave.

They walked down the street, and she found herself leaning easily into the heat of their bodies, inhaling the sweat and iron scent. It would be easy for her to close her eyes and pretend Mardave was someone else, someone she wanted to be touched by, but she wouldn't let herself soil her memories of Julian.

They passed by a store with flat-screens in the window, each one showing different channels. One streamed video from Coldtown—a girl who went by the name Demonia made some kind of deal with one of the stations to show what it was really like behind the gates. She filmed the Eternal Ball, a party that started in 1998 and had gone on ceaselessly ever since. In the background, girls and boys in rubber harnesses swung through the air. They stopped occasionally, opening what looked like a molded hospital tube stuck on the inside of their arms just below the crook of the elbow. They twisted a knob and spilled blood into little paper cups for the partygoers. A boy who looked to be about nine, wearing a string of glowing beads around his neck, gulped down the contents of one of the cups and then licked the paper with a tongue as red as his eyes. The camera angle changed suddenly, veering up, and the viewers saw the domed top of the hall, full of cracked windows through which you could glimpse the stars.

"I know where they are," Mardave said. "I can see that building from my apartment."

"Aren't you scared of living so close to the vampires?" she asked, a small smile pulling at the corner of her mouth.

"We'll protect you," said Ben, smiling back at her.

"We should do what other countries do and blow those corpses sky high," Mardave said.

Matilda bit her tongue not to point out that Europe's vampire hunting led to the highest levels of infection in the world. So many of Belgium's citizens were vampires that shops barely opened their doors until nightfall. The truce with Coldtown worked. Mostly.

She didn't care if Mardave hated vampires. She hated them too.

When they got to the store, she waited outside to avoid getting carded and lit another cigarette with Julian's silver lighter—the one she was going to give back to him in thirty-one days. Sitting down on the curb, she let the chill of the pavement deaden the backs of her thighs. Let it freeze her belly and frost her throat with ice that even liquor couldn't melt.

Hunger turned her stomach. She couldn't remember the last time she'd eaten anything solid without throwing it back up. Her mouth hungered for dark, rich feasts; her skin felt tight, like a seed thirsting to bloom. All she could trust herself to eat was smoke.

When she was a little girl, vampires had been costumes for Halloween. They were the bad guys in movies, plastic fangs and polyester capes. They were Muppets on television, endlessly counting.

Now she was the one that was counting. Fifty-seven days. Eighty-eight days. Eighty-eight nights.

"Matilda?"

She looked up and saw Dante saunter up to her, earbuds dangling out of his ears like he needed a soundtrack for everything he did. He wore a pair of skin-tight jeans and smoked a cigarette out of one of those long, movie-star holders. He looked pretentious as hell. "I'd almost given up on finding you."

"You should have started with the gutter," she said, gesturing to the wet, clogged tide beneath her feet. "I take my gutter-dwelling very seriously."

"Seriously." He pointed at her with the cigarette holder. "Even your mother thinks you're dead. Julian's crying over you."

Matilda looked down and picked at the thread of her jeans. It hurt to think about Julian, while waiting for Mardave and Ben. She was disgusted with herself and she could only guess how disgusted he'd be. "I got Cold," she said. "One of them bit me."

Dante nodded his head.

That's what they'd started calling it when the infection kicked in—Cold—because of how cold people's skin became after they were bitten. And because of the way the poison in their veins caused them to crave heat and blood. One taste of human blood and the infection mutated. It killed the host and then raised them back up again, colder than before. Cold through and through, forever and ever.

"I didn't think you'd be alive," he said.

She hadn't thought she'd make it this long either without giving in. But going it alone on the street was better than forcing her mother to choose between chaining her up in the basement or shipping her off to Coldtown. It was better, too, than taking the chance that Matilda might get loose from the chains and attack people she loved. Stories like that were in the news all the time; almost as frequent as the ones about people who let vampires into their homes because they seemed so nice and clean-cut.

"Then what are you doing looking for me?" she asked. Dante had lived down the street from her family for years, but they didn't hang out. She'd wave to him as she mowed the lawn while he loaded his panel van with DJ equipment. He shouldn't have been here.

She looked back at the store window. Mardave and Ben

were at the counter with a case of beer and her wine cooler. They were getting change from a clerk.

"I was hoping you, er, *wouldn't* be alive," Dante said. "You'd be more help if you were dead."

She stood up, stumbling slightly. "Well screw you too."

It took eighty-eight days for the venom to sweat out a person's pores. She only had thirty-seven to go. Thirty-seven days to stay so drunk that she could ignore the buzz in her head that made her want to bite, rend, devour.

"That came out wrong," he said, taking a step toward her. Close enough that she felt the warmth of him radiating off him like licking tongues of flame. She shivered. Her veins sang with need.

"I can't help you," said Matilda. "Look, I can barely help myself. Whatever it is, I'm sorry. I can't. You have to get out of here."

"My sister Lydia and your boyfriend, Julian, are gone," Dante said. "Together. She's looking to get bitten. I don't know what he's looking for . . . but he's going to get hurt."

Matilda gaped at him as Mardave and Ben walked out of the store. Ben carried a box on his shoulder and a bag on his arm. "That guy bothering you?" he asked her.

"No," she said, then turned to Dante. "You better go."

"Wait," said Dante.

Matilda's stomach hurt. She was sobering up. The smell of blood seemed to float up from underneath their skin.

She reached into Ben's bag and grabbed a beer. She popped

the top, licked off the foam. If she didn't get a lot drunker, she was going to attack someone.

"Jesus," Mardave said. "Slow down. What if someone sees you?"

She drank it in huge gulps, right there on the street. Ben laughed, but it wasn't a good laugh. He was laughing at the drunk.

"She's infected," Dante says.

Matilda whirled toward him, chucking the mostly empty can in his direction automatically. "Shut up, asshole."

"Feel her skin," Dante said. "Cold. She ran away from home when it happened and no one's seen her since."

"I'm cold because it's cold out," she said.

She saw Ben's evaluation of her change from *damaged enough to sleep with strangers* to *dangerous enough to attack strangers.*

Mardave touched his hand gently to her arm. "Hey," he said.

She almost hissed with delight at the press of his hot fingers. She smiled up at him and hoped her eyes weren't as hungry as her skin. "I really like you."

He flinched. "Look, it's late. Maybe we could meet up another time." Then he backed away, which made her so angry that she bit the inside of her own cheek.

Her mouth flooded with the taste of copper, and a red haze floated in front of her eyes.

· · ·

Fifty-seven days ago, Matilda had been sober. She'd had a boyfriend named Julian, and they would dress up together in her bedroom. He liked to wear skinny ties and glittery eye shadow. She liked to wear vintage rock T-shirts and boots that laced up so high that they would constantly be late because they were busy tying them.

Matilda and Julian would dress up and prowl the streets and party at lockdown clubs that barred the doors from dusk to dawn. Matilda wasn't particularly careless; she was just careless enough.

She'd been at a friend's party. It had been stiflingly hot, and she was mad because Julian and Lydia were doing some dance thing from the musical they were in at school. Matilda just wanted to get some air. She opened a window and climbed out under the bobbing garland of garlic.

Another girl was already on the lawn. Matilda should have noticed that the girl's breath didn't crystallize in the air, but she didn't.

"Do you have a light?" the girl had asked.

Matilda did. She reached for Julian's lighter when the girl caught her arm and bent her backward. Matilda's scream turned into a shocked cry when she felt the girl's cold mouth against her neck, the girl's cold fingers holding her off balance.

Then it was as though someone slid two shards of ice into her skin.

• • •

The spread of vampirism could be traced to one person— Caspar Morales. Films and books and television had started romanticizing vampires, and maybe it was only a matter of time before a vampire started romanticizing *himself.*

Crazy, romantic Caspar decided that he wouldn't kill his victims. He'd just drink a little blood and then move on, city to city. By the time other vampires caught up with him and ripped him to pieces, he'd infected hundreds of people. And those new vampires, with no idea how to prevent the spread, infected thousands.

When the first outbreak happened in Tokyo, it seemed like a journalist's prank. Then there was another outbreak in Hong Kong and another in San Francisco.

The military put up barricades around the area where the infection broke out. That was the way the first Coldtown was founded.

· · ·

Matilda's body twitched involuntarily. She could feel the spasm start in the muscles of her back and move to her face. She wrapped her arms around herself to try and stop it, but her hands were shaking pretty hard. "You want my help, you better get me some booze."

"You're killing yourself," Dante said, shaking his head.

"I just need another drink," she said. "Then I'll be fine."

He shook his head. "You can't keep going like this. You can't just stay drunk to avoid your problems. I know, people do. It's a classic move even, but I didn't figure you for fetishizing your own doom."

She started laughing. "You don't understand. When I'm wasted I don't crave blood. It's the only thing keeping me human."

"What?" He looked at Matilda like he couldn't quite make sense of her words.

"Let me spell it out: if you don't get me some alcohol, I am going to bite you."

"Oh." He fumbled for his wallet. "Oh. Okay."

Matilda had spent all the cash she'd brought with her in the first few weeks, so it'd been a long time since she could simply overpay some homeless guy to go into a liquor store and get her a fifth of vodka. She gulped gratefully from the bottle Dante gave her in a nearby alley.

A few moments later, warmth started to creep up from her belly and her mouth felt like it was full of needles and Novocain.

"You okay?" he asked her.

"Better now," she said, her words slurring slightly. "But I still don't understand. Why do you need me to help you find Lydia and Julian?

"Lydia got obsessed with becoming a vampire," Dante said, irritably brushing back the stray hair that fell across his face.

"Why?"

He shrugged. "She used to be really scared of vampires. When we were kids, she begged Mom to let her camp in the hallway because she wanted to sleep where there were no windows. But then I guess she started to be fascinated instead. She thinks that human annihilation is coming. She says that we all have to choose sides, and she's already chosen."

"I'm not a vampire," Matilda says.

Dante gestured irritably with his cigarette holder. The

cigarette had long burned out. He didn't look like his usual contemptuous self; he looked lost. "I know. I thought you would be. And—I don't know—you're on the street. Maybe you know more than the video feeds do about where someone might go to get themselves bitten."

Matilda thought about lying on the floor of Julian's parents' living room. They were sweaty from dancing and kissed languidly. On the television, a list of missing people flashed. She had closed her eyes and kissed him again.

She nodded slowly. "I know a couple of places. Have you heard from her at all?"

He shook his head. "She won't take any of my calls, but she's been updating her blog. I'll show you."

He loaded it on his phone. The latest entry was titled: *I Need A Vampire*. Matilda scrolled down and read. Basically, it was Lydia's plea to be bitten. She wanted any vampires looking for victims to contact her. In the comments, someone suggested Coldtown and then another person commented in ALL CAPS to say that everyone knew that the vampires in Coldtown were careful to keep their food source alive.

It was impossible to know which comments Lydia had read and which ones she believed.

. . .

Runaways went to Coldtown all the time, along with the sick, the sad, and the maudlin. There was supposed to be a constant party, theirs for the price of blood. But once they went inside, humans—

even human children, even babies born in Coldtown—wouldn't be allowed to leave. The National Guard patrolled the barbed-wire-wrapped and garlic-covered walls to make sure that Coldtown stayed contained.

People said that vampires found ways through the walls to the outside world. Maybe that was just a rumor, although Matilda remembered reading something online about a documentary that proved the truth. She hadn't seen it.

But everyone knew there was only one way to get out of Coldtown if you were still human. Your family had to be rich enough to afford hiring a vampire hunter. Vampire hunters got money from the government for each vampire they put in Coldtown, but they could give up the cash reward in favor of a voucher for a single human's release. One vampire in, one human out.

There was a popular reality television series about one of the hunters, called *Hemlok*. Girls hung posters of him on the insides of their lockers, often right next to pictures of the vampires he hunted.

Most people didn't have the money to outbid the government for a hunter's services. Matilda didn't think that Dante's family did and knew Julian's didn't. Her only chance was to catch Lydia and Julian before they crossed over.

. . .

"What's with Julian?" Matilda asked. She'd been avoiding the question for hours as they walked through the alleys that grew progressively more empty the closer they got to the gates.

"What do you mean?" Dante was hunched over against the wind, his long skinny frame offering little protection against the chill. Still, she knew he was warm underneath. Inside.

"Why did Julian go with her?" She tried to keep the hurt out of her voice. She didn't think Dante would understand. He DJed at a club in town and was rumored to see a different boy or girl every day of the week. The only person he actually seemed to care about was his sister.

Dante shrugged slim shoulders. "Maybe he was looking for you."

That was the answer she wanted to hear. She smiled and let herself imagine saving Julian right before he could enter Coldtown. He would tell her that he'd been coming to save her, and then they'd laugh and she wouldn't bite him, no matter how warm his skin felt.

Dante snapped his fingers in front of Matilda, and she stumbled.

"Hey," she said. "Drunk girl here. No messing with me."

He chuckled.

Melinda and Dante checked all the places she knew, all the places she'd slept on cardboard near runaways and begged for change. Dante had a picture of Lydia in his wallet, but no one who looked at it remembered her.

Finally, outside a bar, they bumped into a girl who said she had seen Lydia and Julian. Dante traded her the rest of his pack of cigarettes for her story.

"They were headed for Coldtown," she said, lighting up. In

the flickering flame of her lighter, Melinda noticed the shallow cuts along her wrists. "Said she was tired of waiting."

"What about the guy?" Matilda asked. She stared at the girl's dried garnet scabs. They looked like crusts of sugar, like the lines of salt left on the beach when the tide goes out. She wanted to lick them.

"He said his girlfriend was a vampire," said the girl, inhaling deeply. She blew out smoke and then started to cough.

"When was that?" Dante asked.

The girl shrugged her shoulders. "Just a couple of hours ago."

Dante took out his phone and pressed some buttons. "Load," he muttered. "Come on, *load.*"

"What happened to your arms?" Matilda asked.

The girl shrugged again. "They bought some blood off me. Said that they might need it inside. They had a real professional setup too. Sharp razor and a one of those glass bowls with the plastic lids."

Matilda's stomach clenched with hunger. She turned against the wall and breathed slowly. She needed a drink.

"Is something wrong with her?" the girl asked.

"Matilda," Dante said, and Matilda half-turned. He was holding out his phone. There was a new entry up on Lydia's blog, entitled: *One-Way Ticket to Coldtown.*

• • •

"You should post about it," Dante said. "On the message boards."

Matilda was sitting on the ground, picking at the brick wall to give her fingers something to do. Dante had massively over-paid for another bottle of vodka and was cradling it in a crinkled paper bag.

She frowned. "Post about what?"

"About the alcohol. About it helping you keep from turning."

"Where would I post about that?"

Dante twisted off the cap. The heat seemed to radiate off his skin as he swigged from the bottle. "There are forums for people who have to restrain someone for eighty-eight days. They hang out and exchange tips on straps and dealing with the begging for blood. Haven't you seen them?"

She shook her head. "I bet sedation's already a hot topic of discussion. I doubt I'd be telling them anything they don't already know."

He laughed, but it was a bitter laugh. "Then there's all the people that want to be vampires. The websites reminding all the corpsebait out there that being bitten by an infected person isn't enough; it has to be a vampire. The ones listing gimmicks to get vampires to notice you."

"Like what?"

"I dated a girl who cut thin lines on her thighs before she went out dancing so if there was a vampire in the club, it'd be drawn to her scent." Dante didn't look extravagant or affected anymore. He looked defeated.

Matilda smiled at him. "She was probably a better bet than me for getting you into Coldtown."

He returned the smile wanly. "The worst part is that Lydia's not going to get what she wants. She's going to become the human servant of some vampire who's going to make her a whole bunch of promises and never turn her. The last thing they need in Coldtown is new vampires."

Matilda imagined Lydia and Julian dancing at the endless Eternal Ball. She pictured them on the streets she'd seen in pictures uploaded to Facebook and Flickr, trying to trade a bowl full of blood for their own deaths.

When Dante passed the bottle to her, she pretended to swig. On the eve of her fifty-eighth day of being infected, Matilda started sobering up.

Crawling over, she straddled Dante's waist before he had a chance to shift positions. His mouth tasted like tobacco. When she pulled back from him, his eyes were wide with surprise, his pupils blown and black even in the dim streetlight.

"Matilda," he said and there was nothing in his voice but longing.

"If you really want your sister, I am going to need one more thing from you," she said.

His blood tasted like tears.

• • •

Matilda's skin felt like it had caught fire. She'd turned into lit paper, burning up. Curling into black ash.

She licked his neck over and over and over.

• • •

The gates of Coldtown were large and made of consecrated wood, barbed wire covering them like heavy, thorny vines. The guards slouched at their posts, guns over their shoulders, sharing a cigarette. The smell of percolating coffee wafted out of the guardhouse.

"Um, hello," Matilda said. Blood was still sticky where it half-dried around her mouth and on her neck. It had dribbled down her shirt, stiffening it nearly to cracking when she moved. Her body felt strange now that she was dying. Hot. More alive than it had in weeks.

Dante would be all right; she wasn't contagious and she didn't think she'd hurt him too badly. She hoped she hadn't hurt him too badly. She touched the phone in her pocket, his phone, the one she'd used to call 911 after she'd left him.

"Hello," she called to the guards again.

One turned. "Oh my god," he said and reached for his rifle.

"I'm here to turn in a vampire. For a voucher. I want to turn in a vampire in exchange for letting a human out of Coldtown."

"What vampire?" asked the other guard. He'd dropped the cigarette, but hadn't stepped on the filter so that it just smoked on the asphalt.

"Me," said Matilda. "I want to turn in me."

• • •

They made her wait as her pulse thrummed slower and slower. She wasn't a vampire yet, and after a few phone calls, they discovered that technically she could only have the voucher after undeath. They did let her wash her face in the bathroom of the guardhouse and wring the thin cloth of her shirt until the water ran down the drain clear, instead of murky with blood.

When she looked into the mirror, her skin had unfamiliar purple shadows, like bruises. She was still staring at them when she stopped being able to catch her breath. The hollow feeling in her chest expanded and she found herself panicked, falling to her knees on the filthy tile floor. She died there, a moment later.

It didn't hurt as much as she'd worried it would. Like most things, the surprise was the worst part.

•••

The guards released Matilda into Coldtown just a little before dawn. The world looked strange—everything had taken on a smudgy, silvery cast, like she was watching an old movie. Sometimes people's heads seemed to blur into black smears. Only one color was distinct—a pulsing, oozing color that seemed to glow from beneath skin.

Red.

Her teeth ached to look at it.

There was a silence inside of her. No longer did she move to the rhythmic drumming of her heart. Her body felt strange, hard as marble, free of pain. She's never realized how many small agonies were alive in the creak of her bones, the pull of muscle. Now, free of them, she felt like she was floating.

Matilda looked around with her strange new eyes. Everything was beautiful. And the light at the edge of the sky was the most beautiful thing of all.

"What are you doing?" a girl called from a doorway. She had long black hair but her roots were growing in blonde. "Get in here! Are you crazy?"

In a daze, Matilda did as she was told. Everything smeared as she moved, like the world was painted in watercolors. The girl's pinkish-red face swirled along with it.

It was obvious the house had once been grand, but looked like it'd been abandoned for a long time. Graffiti covered the peeling wallpaper and couches had been pushed up against the walls. A boy wearing jeans but no shirt was painting makeup onto a girl with stiff pink pigtails while another girl in a retro polka-dotted dress pulled on mesh stockings.

In a corner, another boy—this one with glossy brown hair that fell to his waist—stacked jars of creamed corn into a precarious pyramid.

"What is this place?" Matilda asked.

The boy stacking the jars turned. "Look at her eyes. She's a vampire!" He didn't seem afraid, though; he seemed delighted.

"Get her into the cellar," one of the other girls said.

"Come on," said the black-haired girl and pulled Matilda toward a doorway. "You're fresh-made, right?"

"Yeah," Matilda said. Her tongue swept over her own sharp teeth. "I guess that's pretty obvious."

"Don't you know that vampires can't go outside in the daylight?" the girl asked, shaking her head. "The guards try that trick with every new vampire, but I never saw one almost fall for it."

"Oh, right," Matilda said. They went down the rickety steps to a filthy basement with a mattress on the floor underneath a single bulb. Crates of foodstuffs were shoved against the walls and the high, small windows had been painted over with a tarry substance that let no light through.

The black-haired girl who'd waved her inside smiled. "We trade with the border guards. Black-market food, clothes, little luxuries like chocolate and cigarettes for some action. Vampires don't own everything."

"And you're going to owe us for letting you stay the night," the boy said from the top of the stairs.

"I don't have anything," Matilda says. "I didn't bring any cans of food or whatever."

"You have to bite us."

"What?" Matilda asked.

"One of us," the girl said. "How about one of us? You can even pick which one."

"Why would you want me to do that?"

The girl's expression clearly said that Matilda was stupid. "Who doesn't want to live forever?"

I don't, Matilda wanted to say, but she swallowed the words. She could tell they already thought she didn't deserve to be a vampire. Besides, she wanted to taste blood. She wanted to taste the red throbbing pulsing insides of the girl in front of her. It wasn't the pain she'd felt when she was infected, the hunger that made her stomach clench, the craving for warmth. It was heady, greedy desire.

"Tomorrow," Matilda said. "When it's night again."

"Okay," the girl said, "but you promise, right? You'll turn one of us?"

"Yeah," said Matilda, numbly. It was hard to even wait that long.

She was relieved when they went upstairs, but less relieved when she heard something heavy slide in front of the basement door. She told herself that didn't matter. The only thing that mattered was getting through the day so that she could find Julian and Lydia.

She shook her head to clear it of thoughts of blood and turned on Dante's phone. Although she didn't expect it, a text message was waiting: *I cant tell if I luv u or if I want to kill u.*

Relief washed over her. Her mouth twisted into a smile and her newly sharp canines cut her lip. She winced. Dante was okay.

She opened up Lydia's blog and posted an anonymous message: *Tell Julian his girlfriend wants to see him . . . and you.*

Matilda made herself comfortable on the dirty mattress. She looked up at the rotted boards of the ceiling and thought of Julian. She had a single ticket out of Coldtown and two humans to rescue with it, but it was easy to picture herself saving Lydia as Julian valiantly offered to stay with her, even promised her his eternal devotion.

She licked her lips at the image. When she closed her eyes, all her imaginings drowned in a sea of red.

Waking at dusk, Matilda checked Lydia's blog. Lydia had posted a reply: *Meet us at the Festival of Sinners.*

Five kids sat at the top of the stairs, watching her with liquid eyes.

"Are you awake?" the black-haired girl asked. She seemed to pulse with color. Her moving mouth was hypnotic.

"Come here," Matilda said to her in a voice that seemed so distant that she was surprised to find it was her own. She hadn't meant to speak, hadn't meant to beckon the girl over to her.

"That's not fair," one of the boys called. "I was the one that said she owed us something. It should be me. You should pick me."

Matilda ignored him as the girl knelt down on the dirty mattress and swept aside her hair, baring a long, unmarked neck. She seemed dazzling, this creature of blood and breath, a fragile mannequin as brittle as sticks.

Tiny golden hairs tickled Matilda's nose as she bit down.

And gulped.

Blood was heat and heart and running-thrumming-beating through the fat roots of veins to drip syrup slowly, spurting molten hot across tongue, mouth, teeth, chin.

Dimly, Matilda felt someone shoving her and someone else screaming, but it seemed distant and unimportant. Eventually the words became clearer.

"Stop," someone was screaming. "Stop!"

Hands dragged Matilda off the girl. Her neck was a glistening red mess. Gore stained the mattress and covered Matilda's hands and hair. The girl coughed, blood bubbles frothing on her lip, and then went abruptly silent.

"What did you do?" the boy wailed, cradling the girl's body. "She's dead. She's dead. You killed her."

Matilda backed away from the body. Her hand went automatically to her mouth, covering it. "I didn't mean to," she said.

"Maybe she'll be okay," said the other boy, his voice cracking. "We have to get bandages."

"She's *dead*," the boy holding the girl's body moaned.

A thin wail came from deep inside of Matilda as she backed toward the stairs. Her belly felt full, distended. She wanted to be sick.

Another girl grabbed Matilda's arm. "Wait," the girl said, eyes wide and imploring. "You have to bite me next. You're full now so you won't have to hurt me—"

With a cry, Matilda tore herself free and ran up the stairs— if she went fast enough maybe she could escape from herself.

...

By the time Matilda got to the Festival of Sinners, her mouth tasted metallic and she was numb with fear. She wasn't human, wasn't good, and wasn't sure what she might do next. She kept pawing at her shirt, as if that much blood could ever be wiped off, as if it hadn't already soaked down into her skin and her soiled insides.

The Festival was easy to find, even as confused as she was. People were happy to give her directions, apparently not bothered that she was drenched in blood. Their casual demeanor was horrifying, but not as horrifying as how much she already wanted to feed again.

On the way, she passed the Eternal Ball. Strobe lights lit up the remains of the windows along the dome and a girl with blue hair in a dozen braids held up a video camera to interview three men dressed all in white with gleaming red eyes.

Vampires.

A ripple of fear passed through her. She reminded herself that there was nothing they could do to her. She was already like them. Already dead.

The Festival of Sinners was being held at a church with stained-glass windows painted black on the inside. The door, papered with pink-stenciled posters, was painted the same thick tarry black. Music thrummed from within and a few people sat on the steps, smoking and talking.

Matilda went inside.

A doorman pulled aside a velvet rope for her, letting her past a small line of people waiting to pay the cover charge. The rules were different for vampires, perhaps especially for vampires accessorizing their grungy attire with so much blood.

Matilda scanned the room. She didn't see Julian or Lydia, just a throng of dancers and a bar that served alcohol from vast copper distilling vats. It spilled into mismatched mugs. Then one of the people near the bar moved and Matilda saw Lydia and Julian. He was bending over her, shouting into her ear.

Matilda pushed her way through the crowd, until she was close enough to touch Julian's arm. She reached out, but couldn't quite bring herself to brush his skin with her foulness.

Julian looked up, startled. "Tilda?"

She snatched back her hand like she'd been about to touch fire.

"Tilda," he said. "What happened to you? Are you hurt?"

Matilda flinched, looking down at herself. "I . . ."

Lydia laughed. "She ate someone, moron."

"Tilda?" Julian asked.

"I'm sorry," Matilda said. There was so much she had to be sorry for, but at least he was here now. Julian would tell her what to do and how to turn herself back into something decent again. She would save Lydia, and Julian would save her.

He touched her shoulder, let his hand rest gingerly on her blood-stiffened shirt. "We were looking for you everywhere." His gentle expression was tinged with terror; fear pulled his smile into something closer to a grimace.

"I wasn't in Coldtown," Matilda said. "I came here so that Lydia could leave. I have a pass."

"But I don't want to leave," said Lydia. "You understand that, right? I want what you have—eternal life."

"You're not infected," Matilda said. "You have to go. You can still be okay. Please, I need you to go."

"One pass?" Julian said, his eyes going to Lydia. Matilda saw the truth in the weight of that gaze—Julian had not come to Coldtown for Matilda. Even though she knew she didn't deserve him to think of her as anything but a monster, it hurt savagely.

"I'm not leaving," Lydia said, turning to Julian, pouting.

"You said she wouldn't be like this."

"*I killed a girl*," Matilda said. "I killed her. Do you understand that?"

"Who cares about some mortal girl?" Lydia tossed back her hair. In that moment, she reminded Matilda of Lydia's brother, pretentious Dante who'd turned out to be an actual nice guy. Just like sweet Lydia had turned out cruel.

"You're a girl," Matilda said. "You're mortal."

"I know that!" Lydia rolled her eyes. "I just mean that we don't care who you killed. Turn us and then we can kill lots of people."

"No," Matilda said, swallowing. She looked down, not wanting to hear what she was about to say. There was still a chance. "Look, I have the pass. If you don't want it, then Julian should take it and go. But I'm not turning you. I'm never turning you, understand."

"Julian doesn't want to leave," Lydia said. Her eyes looked bright and two feverish spots appeared on her cheeks. "Who are you to judge me anyway? You're the murderer."

Matilda took a step back. She desperately wanted Julian to say something in her defense or even to look at her, but his gaze remained steadfastly on Lydia.

"So neither one of you want the pass," Matilda said.

"Go to hell," spat Lydia.

Matilda turned away.

"Wait," Julian said. His voice sounded weak.

Matilda spun, unable to keep the hope off her face, and saw

why Julian had called to her. Lydia stood behind him, a long knife to his throat.

"Turn me," Lydia said. "Turn me or I'm going to kill him."

Julian's eyes were wide. He started to protest or beg or something, and Lydia pressed the knife harder, silencing him.

People had stopped dancing nearby, backing away. One girl with red-glazed eyes stared hungrily at the knife.

"Turn me!" Lydia shouted. "I'm tired of waiting! I want my life to begin!"

"You won't be alive—" Matilda started.

"I'll be alive—more alive than ever. Just like you are."

"Okay," Matilda said softly. "Give me your wrist."

The crowd seemed to close in tighter, watching as Lydia held out her arm. Matilda crouched low bending down over it.

"Take the knife away from his throat," Matilda said.

Lydia, all her attention on Matilda, let Julian go. He stumbled a little and pressed his fingers to his neck.

"I loved you," Julian shouted.

Matilda looked up to see that he wasn't speaking to her. She gave him a glittering smile and bit down on Lydia's wrist.

The girl screamed, but the scream was lost in Matilda's ears. Lost in the pulse of blood, the tide of gluttonous pleasure and the music throbbing around them like Lydia's slowing heartbeat.

• • •

Matilda sat on the blood-soaked mattress and turned on the video camera to check that the live feed was working.

Julian was gone. She'd given him the pass after stripping him of all his cash and credit cards; there was no point in trying to force Lydia to leave since she'd just come right back in. He'd made stammering apologies that Matilda ignored then he fled for the gate. She didn't miss him. Her fantasy of Julian felt as ephemeral as her old life.

"It's working," one of the boys—Michael—said from the stairs, a computer cradled on his lap. Even though she'd killed one of them, they welcomed her back, eager enough for eternal life to risk more deaths. "You're streaming live video."

Matilda set the camera on the stack of crates, pointed toward her and the wall where she'd tied a gagged Lydia. The girl thrashed and kicked, but Matilda ignored her. She stepped in front of the camera and smiled.

• • •

My name is Matilda Green. I was born on April 10, 1997. I died on September 3rd, 2013. Please tell my mother I'm okay. And Dante, if you're watching this, I'm sorry.

You've probably seen lots of video feeds from inside Coldtown. I saw them too. Pictures of girls and boys grinding together in clubs or bleeding elegantly for their celebrity vampire masters. Here's what you never see. What I'm going to show you.

For eighty-eight days you are going to watch someone sweat out the infection. You are going to watch her beg and scream and cry. You're going to watch her throw up food and piss her pants and pass out. You're going to watch me feed her can after can of creamed corn. It's not going to pretty.

You're going to watch me too. I'm the kind of vampire that you'd be, one that's new at this and basically out of control. I've already killed someone and I can't guarantee I'm not going to do it again. I'm the one that infected this girl.

This is the real Coldtown.

I'm the real Coldtown.

You still want in?

Undead Is Very Hot
Right Now

BY SARAH REES BRENNAN

"SO DID YOU come all the way from Transylvania to join this totally awesome band, Chris?"

"Er," said Christian. "I'm from Birmingham."

The lights in the studio hurt Christian's eyes, and their interviewer was blowing a pink, bobbing balloon of bubblegum while she interviewed them. Every time she blew up the bubble a vein in her neck jumped under her makeup.

She'd introduced herself as Tracy. Christian didn't like to think such filthy things about a girl he'd just met, but he couldn't help suspecting she spelled it with an "i."

"So tell me, boys," said Traci, swallowing the bubble, which collapsed and folded neatly into her mouth. "Any of you found that special girl yet?"

Bradley, who Christian might well have hated the most of all, gave her his best smile.

"Still searching, Traci," he said, and looked bashful. "It's hard to find someone really real in the music biz, you know? I just want a normal girl. Someone who gets me."

Christian knew for a fact Bradley had been sneaking off with

Faye, which was a bad idea both because she was their manager and because she was possibly Satan's emissary on this earth.

"How about you, Chris?" Traci chirped, turning her eyes on Christian like two blue helicopter beams. "Do you have a girlfriend?"

"Christian," said Christian. "And, um, of course I don't."

"*Of course* you don't?" Traci asked with sudden, terrifying intentness. In the shadows Christian could see Faye uncoil like a viper about to strike. Traci leaned toward him, her smile inviting honesty and her breath smelling of Bubblicious watermelon. "And why is that, Chris?"

"Uh," said Christian. "Because I'm *undead*?"

"Do the girls not get the real you, Chris?" Traci drawled, leaning back and looking a little disappointed.

"I think they probably do, to be honest," Christian said. "I think that's sort of the problem. I mean, they're aware of the fact that I drink blood, so I can't take them out for dinner, plus understandably they worry about getting all the blood drained from their bodies. And if they asked me on a date to a barbecue, I might wind up on the end of a chargrilled stake. The prospect isn't exactly appealing."

Faye was pacing like a caged leopard, which alarmed Christian extremely. She'd said "just be yourself," before the interview, and this was the only self Christian knew how to be, even though Faye seemed intent on redesigning him.

Bradley laughed far too loudly in Christian's ear. Christian jumped.

"Good thing you're cute, am I right, Traci?"

Traci winked back at Bradley. "How right you are, Bradders. So, Josh and Pez," she said, turning to the rest of the band.
"Do you two have girlfriends?"

Josh looked terrified. Pez looked distracted by Traci's shiny
earrings.

Christian wondered what having girlfriends had to do with
music. They'd just come in from recording the last song for their
first album—why hadn't Traci opened the interview by asking
about that?

It wasn't like Christian had enjoyed much success with girls
when he'd been alive anyhow. He'd been shy, and he'd had all
that acne. Whenever he liked a girl she'd claim she valued their
friendship too much, and in the name of said friendship she'd be
forced to make out with rugby players while Christian held her
purse. His mum had always said that there was plenty of time,
that soon he'd be in college and there would be a thousand different paths for him to choose.

There had only been one path, though—the alley Christian
had used as a shortcut home from school. It had been dark and
cold, Christian stumbling along with his hands in the pockets of
his thin school-uniform trousers and being glum that he'd forgotten his gloves. There was the huddled form of someone he had
thought was homeless, who he'd stopped to help, and then there
was the bloody attack that Christian didn't remember clearly. It
had been so fast, the brutal snarling creature leaping on top of
him. He'd managed to open the blade on his Swiss Army knife

and score a long line up the vampire's face. The wound had opened, dark and dripping blood into Christian's mouth.

And then there were no more choices.

Christian was roused from the memory of that dark alley by Bradley's loud laugh and the terribly bright television lights.

Why they had made the vampire with the super-hearing sit next to the man with the laugh of a hyena on speed, Christian didn't know.

"I'm sweet seventeen," said Bradley, who was a liar and a fiend and at least twenty. "And never been—"

He waggled his eyebrows without finishing his sentence and Traci laughed uproariously.

"Oh Bradders, you are so bad! How about you, Chris?"

Christian blinked. "Me?"

"How old are you?" Traci asked. "Two hundred? Three hundred?"

"Er," said Christian. "I'm nineteen."

At that point Traci leaned in again, covering his hand with hers and not drawing back at the chill. She looked deep into his eyes and said, in a warm, understanding voice:

"Would that be nineteen in . . . *vampire* years?"

• • •

"You didn't have to get so narky with her, Chris," Faye said as she shepherded them back to the limo which was meant to take them to their concert.

"Vampire years!" Christian repeated.

"Like dog years, but in reverse," Bradley explained helpfully.

Christian did not hit him because the pamphlet they had given him at the re-education clinic after his attack—*The Responsible Citizen's Guide to Vampirism*—was very clear about the fact that he had the strength to knock Bradley's head clean off his shoulders and into the bucket of champagne set in front of them. Bradley was the stupidest person Christian had ever met, but he didn't deserve that.

Besides, Faye would have given him hell.

"Yes, I understood her horribly speciesist and insensitive point, actually. Thanks," he said instead, and rubbed at his temples. When he was annoyed his fangs tingled, and it always ended up giving him a migraine.

"I can't believe we're going to do our first concert right now," Josh said, avoiding Christian's eyes as usual and bouncing nervously in his seat. The roof of the limo was making his fuzzy brown curls a little static.

"Nor can I, since we don't even have fans yet. What with only finishing up recording our first album today and everything."

Josh carefully pretended he hadn't heard Christian. *Vampire in the limo?* his body language screamed. *What vampire in the limo? I have no idea what you mean!*

"We released the single and the photo-shoot pictures to all the best mags a month ago," Faye pointed out cheerfully. "You guys already have five message boards dedicated to you. And the fan mail's been pouring in, mostly for Bradley and Chris."

"Oh ha ha ha," said Christian, staring out of the darkened limo windows.

People were peering in as the car passed, curious and a little excited. Christian would have done it himself a year ago, presuming that the limo meant that those inside it had glamorous and interesting lives.

"Chris, Chris," said Bradley, hitting him over the head to attract his attention as if Christian was deaf rather than, for example, a *vampire* with *super hearing*. "Are you really only nineteen? I thought vampires lived to be hundreds and hundreds of years old."

"We do," Christian said shortly. "And we get to be hundreds and hundreds of years old by living one year at a time. I've only been a vampire for a year."

"That's deep," Pez told him.

They all stared at Pez who beamed benignly back at them. At last Faye cleared her throat.

"Right," she said. "Let's go through your program again, boys."

They'd had it drilled into them for weeks. Christian looked out of the darkened windows again, and thought about how it had been at the first audition to become part of 4 The One, him desperately hoping to be chosen and hopeless about it, watching Faye's eyes light up at Bradley's careless, golden good looks.

"You'll be the hot one," she'd said calmly, then turned her eyes to Josh, who stared back beseechingly. "You can be the nerd. Geek chic is very in."

"Lady, I think I got confused. I thought this was an interview for a job at a fast-food place," said a guy with dreadlocks and crazy eyes who Christian would later learn claimed to be called Pez.

"You'll be the drummer, obviously," Faye told him.

Then she turned to Christian, who barely dared to hope in case she snatched it away from him and ground it to pieces under her scarily high heels. He'd had to leave home. Mum had told him that his little brother couldn't sleep with a vampire in the house. He had no place else to go.

Faye smiled at him, almost as beautiful as she was terrifying.

"You'll be the gimmick."

It had seemed like a good idea at the time.

• • •

There was a screaming crowd outside the auditorium.

"Um," said Christian. "Did we go to a Stephen King signing by mistake?"

"You read, Chris?" Faye asked. "That's good. Make them think you have layers, that you're deep and interesting. The kind of guy who will write them poetry—better yet, *songs*. Be sure to mention that in the next interview."

"Come on, guys," said Bradley, flinging open the door of the limo. "Our public awaits!"

He launched himself out of the limo and onto the red carpet, where he actually did a backflip. The crowd made a sound a little bit like applause and a little bit more like baying wolves, and Christian covered his eyes from the sheer shame of being associated with such a ridiculous person.

Faye jabbed Christian in the stomach with her pen.

"Get out there! And if you could possibly do that thing where you shield your face with your caped arm and hiss—"

"Faye," said Chris earnestly. "I will never do that thing."

Faye snorted and crossed her admittedly excellent legs with a rasp of silk. "At least get out there and flash them some fang."

Pez and Josh had already climbed out of the limo, knocking shoulders as the crowds screamed. They huddled together. Christian drew his cape around himself.

"I miss my hoodie," he informed Faye as a parting shot. "I know you stole it."

"You're talking crazy, you never had a hoodie," Faye said. "Don't let me hear you speak of it again."

Christian climbed out onto the red carpet. He'd thought that the studio lights at the interview were bad, but the dozen clicking, flashing cameras were so much worse. He lifted his hand to cover his eyes, then realized Faye had glued his cape to his sleeve somehow and now he was doing *that thing*. That *vampire* thing.

When he lowered his hand he saw Bradley was blowing kisses to the yelling girls, pretending to move forward on the carpet and then doing a little backward walk to blow more kisses.

Christian gave up and shielded his eyes, even though it meant he was doing *that thing* again. He felt so cheap.

Pez and Josh, at this point shamelessly clinging to each

other, were making a rush for the door of the auditorium. Chris started to flee after them, picking up speed even though Faye had made it very clear that specific and terrible things would happen to anyone who ran, hid behind someone else or—and this was directed specifically at him—used supernatural powers to evade a camera.

Even Christian's hearing could barely make out all the sounds as he passed the crowd. There was so much screaming it was making his migraine worse, his fangs stabbing into his lower lip as his head pounded, random shrieks interspersed with shouts of their names coming from the mob.

"Bradley, Bradley, look at me!"

"Bradley, I want your babies!" yelled a guy who looked about forty years old and was wearing a purple feather boa. Bradley winked and blew him a kiss.

"Chris!"

"Pez!"

"Josh!" Josh looked around, his face puzzled and a little pleased by the sound of his name, and Christian almost walked into his back. Josh looked terrified and backed sharply away.

"Chris, bite me!"

"I love you, Bradley!"

"Chris, I wanna be your queen of the night!"

That was the feather boa guy again, Christian couldn't help but notice.

"Christian! Christian, help!"

That turned Christian's head. It wasn't only that the girl

had used his real name, which nobody had done since he'd left home, but there was a pitch and urgency to her voice that said she was in real trouble.

He could see a particularly dense part of the crowd, a nexus where there were too many bodies crammed and things had become frenzied, people shoving too hard. In the midst of the crushed bodies Christian saw a hand waving, going down, as if there was a girl drowning in that human sea.

Christian grabbed hold of the rail on top of the barricades and vaulted over it in one easy vampiric movement. He spread out an arm to clear the space before him and watched people scattering in panic.

That was when he realized that when he'd spread his arm his stupid cape had flared out, a swathe of billowing darkness, and he'd exposed his face, lips curling back from his teeth.

How embarrassing. Faye was going to be thrilled.

He knelt down and lifted the girl up gently by her elbows. She was pink and breathless, with red pigtail braids that had gone wispy and eyes that had gone big. Christian could hear her heart racing with the speed and strength of a charging rhinoceros. He was worried she was going to faint.

"Are you all right?"

"I—um—yes?" said the girl.

Christian smiled. "Are you not sure?"

"Um," said the girl.

"Come on, you should get..." Christian paused and tried to think of something that might persuade a girl not to faint. All he could think of were smelling salts, which just went to show he should never have started reading mum's Mills & Boon novels. "A glass of water? There are probably chairs backstage. Or boxes to sit on. I mean, I hope you can have a chair, but I want to prepare you for boxes."

The crowd was no longer screaming, but they were drawing in. Christian wrapped an arm protectively around the girl's fragile shoulders, his cape settling around her like a blanket.

"Thank you," she said, low into his ear, her heart still pounding. "My name's Laura. Thank you."

Christian led her back to the barricades and then boosted her over them. She was light and he could throw her like a tennis ball. She had to grab the rail as she passed over it to slow her trajectory, and she landed kind of hard.

"You're welcome," said Christian, leaping after her and steadying her as she wobbled from the impact. "Sorry about that. I'm a bit—" *terrible at being a vampire* "—strong."

"That's okay," Laura whispered, warm against him. She was underneath his cape again somehow.

He walked her toward the door of the auditorium, slipping out of the night full of mysteriously screaming people and into a cool concrete refuge.

At his side, Laura spoke. "I'm really sorry for bothering you on your big night," she told him. "I was just scared and I panicked. I knew you'd come to save me."

Christian looked down at her, startled. She wasn't red and breathless anymore, but pale with golden freckles. Her eyes were summer-sky blue and still wide, and she was looking at him like he was a hero.

"Er," said Christian. "You need water! I know this because humans... need to drink water. For living."

He stopped himself from adding, "this is just one of the many things that I know" and shaming himself further.

He led her up a steel flight of stairs into the labyrinth of corridors and curtains that counted as backstage, and then they went on a quest for a water cooler. Christian was beginning to get panicky over not finding one, so when Faye appeared and zeroed in on him like a manicured torpedo he actually felt a moment of relief.

But the usual paralyzing terror kicked in when she smiled at him, her white teeth like a row of tombstones. Christian suspected his name was written on every one.

"Chris, you have to go to your dressing room. Bradley and the others are already in makeup!"

"I want to get Laura some water," Christian said decisively so that Laura would not think Faye bossed him around, and so that she might forget the mention of him putting on makeup.

"And of course Laura should have water, shouldn't you, sweetheart?"

Laura looked at Faye with fear, which showed she was smart as well as pretty.

Faye clicked her fingers and her evil-twin assistants appeared, possibly out of the walls. Whenever Faye clicked her fingers it was as if she'd rubbed a magic lamp—her wishes were instantly granted. Christian had a theory that reality was scared of her too and so bent to her will.

"Water her," said Faye. "Give her a place to watch the show. I love her. She's news."

Laura was led very firmly away. Christian cleared his throat and said: "I'll see you after the show!" in a voice that cracked. She just stared at him with beseeching eyes, unable to escape from the custody of the dreaded Marcel and Marcy.

"Thanks very much, Faye."

"Thank *you* very much, Chris," said Faye, who was immune to all sarcasm but her own. She took his arm and started dragging him toward the dressing room. "You saved a girl's life and you did the cape thing and you and she are going to be on the front of every magazine in this country. You even *wrapped* her in your cape. I love you today, Chris. I could kiss you on your stupid, fangy mouth."

"Faye, please don't. I'm scared of you," Chris pleaded, terror making him blunt.

She stopped at the door of their dressing room, reached up and pinched his cheek between two pointy fingernails.

"I know you are, my little vampire cupcake. Now get in there."

Christian's dressing room was alarmingly large and had lights that reminded him of the lights in the TV studio, dazzling and oppressive.

He felt a lot more oppressed when he was tackled into a large leather chair by several women who looked at him with cold, dead eyes and wielded powder puffs with no mercy.

His first concert seemed like it was going to be as much of a nightmare as his first television interview by the time he was released by the powder-puff torturers and staggered with the others out toward the stage. His skin felt caked, and it shimmered under the neon lights.

"Lookin' good," Bradley drawled.

"Bite me," Christian snapped, then shut his eyes and recited from the pamphlet. *"Except do no such thing, because joking about biting from either side of the species divide is in poor taste, and also the blood would have long-term effects which might well prove detrimental to your health."*

"Okay," said Bradley. "4 The One, are we ready to *reach new heights of awesome* tonight?"

"Er, yeah!" said Josh.

"Sorry, what was that?" asked Pez.

"I cannot believe you just said that," Christian squinted at Bradley. "I am judging you so hard right now."

"Okay, never mind," said Bradley. "Josh, remember to pop your hips, we don't want a repeat of what happened last week. Let's go!"

They walked out onto the stage, which was bathed in purple and pink spotlights, the noise of screams rising to greet them from the pit and the sound of a loudspeaker blaring behind them. Christian winced.

"The moment you've all been waiting for, ladies and gentlemen. This is . . . 4 The One!"

Bradley strode over to the microphone as Christian was swinging his guitar strap over his head, settling the instrument against his hip, fingers touching the strings and getting familiar.

"I wrote this song myself," said Bradley—a barefaced lie. He sounded just like he did when he was waggling his eyebrows. "It's called 'Lock Up Your Daughters'. And to all the mothers out there, I suggest you do!"

There was a scream of approval. "All the mothers out there" seemed to be intending to lock up their daughters, so they could have Bradley for themselves.

Pez started in on the drums, and they swung into the song. It was a good song, catchy. Christian liked these songs best, when everyone was playing instruments and Bradley was actually singing, his voice improbably good for someone with such an annoying laugh. These songs made up for the ones where Bradley, Pez, and Josh did a weird synchronized dance with enough hip-popping to cause injury, or at least induce high blood pressure in the crowd.

Christian was deeply thankful that Faye had told him he didn't have to dance, though his role of standing in front of the wind machine with his cape blowing and his hair falling into his eyes as he leaned in and murmured into the microphone was not significantly better.

He was even more thankful for an opening song like the one they were playing now, the crowd singing along, Bradley's voice convincing them that they all knew the words. Christian could be a little quiet at times like these, sink into the background, once again be the shy boy who loved his guitar and dreamed of being a superstar.

He liked it when that boy stirred briefly back to life.

Between the curtains to the left of the stage he saw Laura dragging a box as close to the stage as she could get without being revealed. She dusted off her hands and perched herself on top of it as he watched her. She noticed him watching and shot him a smile, blushing, giving him a sidelong glance as if they had an in-joke.

He looked at the box she was sitting on and realized they did. He smiled back at her and then turned his smile to the audience, loving them all, loving the band, loving the girl watching him from the side of the stage. His heart beat as theirs did for a minute, all of them swept away.

Euphoria carried him through the concert and the dash back onstage to play that first song again as an encore. Safely backstage, the band members were all laughing and breathless, the humans' skin warm and sweaty. Bradley put his arm around Christian and Christian let him, even leaned against him. Bradley's other arm was around Pez, and Josh was not keeping his distance from Christian like he usually was. They were a team for an instant, victorious.

Then Pez said: "That was an awesome rehearsal. When are we having the concert?" and Bradley let out a crack of laughter. Christian pulled away and turned to Laura.

She was still sitting on her box, face turned up to him like some pale flower turned up toward the sun.

He reached out a hand to her and she took it.

He said: "Do you want to go for a walk with me?"

• • •

"I love walking in the night time," Laura told him shyly. "Do you?"

"It beats walking in the day time. I barely get any exercise done before I burst into flames."

Christian regretted that as soon as he'd said it. Here he was with a beautiful girl on a nighttime stroll and he'd said something that roughly translated to, "Yes, the scenery is very nice, which reminds me that I am the blood-drinking undead. Check out the teeth!"

He tried to look at the night as she was seeing it, deliberately crossing his eyes so his vision blurred a little, so that what was clear and rather dull became mysterious shadows. A tree heaped with dead leaves at the end of the road became a towering oak wearing a bright crown. The moonlit road became a silver path of infinite possibilities.

"It's a beautiful night, though," he said softly, and almost believed it.

He was rewarded by Laura slipping her hand in his. Her hand was warm, and he curled his fingers around it, hoping at least to shield it from the night air and keep her warm, even if he could not share any real warmth with her.

"I write poetry," said Laura.

"I'd like to read some."

"I write poems about . . . the night. And death."

"Um," said Christian. His own death hadn't been particularly poetic, but deaths probably varied. "Okay."

"I never let anybody read them," Laura continued. "But I would. I think I could let you."

She gave him that look again, as if he was a shining hero. It warmed Christian through and through.

"Yeah?" he asked. "Thanks."

She swung his hand a bit, companionably, and he wasn't a shining hero—they just seemed like an ordinary boy and girl alone together. That was better.

When they reached the tree at the end of the road, she stopped and looked up at him.

"I saw your picture in *Bubbly*," she said. "It was an interview with the band. You were wearing a dark-green cloak with a sort of metal clasp at the throat."

Christian remembered that Faye had stabbed it into his throat when she was putting the cloak on. He still wasn't convinced that had been an accident: she'd been very annoyed with him for rebelling against the public-relations orders she'd given and showing up in jeans and a football shirt.

That was the last day he'd ever seen his hoodie, too.

"I was wondering," Laura said. "How were you feeling that day?"

He'd felt like a total idiot. He was living in a house with strangers, he hadn't understood at the time that Bradley was a moron (he'd seemed golden and perfect, able to answer every question the interviewer fired), or that Pez wasn't constantly mocking him. He had understood that Josh—shy, nerdy Josh—

the boy who was most like him, and who he would have chosen for a friend out of them all, was so scared of him that he felt sick every time they were in a room together.

"Lonely," said Christian.

"That's what I thought," Laura told him, hushed. "I could just tell."

"Really?"

"I came to the concert to see you," Laura continued, looking up into his eyes.

A cold breeze cut through the dead leaves over their heads. Laura shivered and Christian drew off his cape, using his vampire strength as sneakily as he could to break the thread that Faye had used to sew the ends of the cape to his sleeves. He wrapped Laura in his cape, tilting up her face to tie the ribbons under her soft chin.

"Well," said Christian. "You're seeing me."

Her heart was beating too fast again. Christian could hear it, warm and pounding fast, over all the distant noises of the night.

"This is going to sound silly," Laura whispered. "But I think I knew then, when I saw the picture. That we'd meet. That we'd be . . . together."

"Here we are," said Christian.

She was standing very close. He didn't *think* she was scared.

He leaned in a little, and Laura reached up to sweep his stupid black bangs (that Faye had insisted on) out of his eyes with a small, gentle hand.

That was a good sign, he thought, and he leaned in closer to catch her soft lips with his, her breath in his mouth strange and sweet. He drew his arm around her and held her more carefully than he had ever held anything. She shut her eyes and kissed him back. For a while, it felt like he was breathing too.

When her breath stuttered against his lips, he stopped. He didn't want to hurt her.

She didn't live far away. He walked her to her door, one of many similar doors in a trim little suburban street. There were begonias in her front garden. His mother had grown roses along a crazy-paving path just like the one he walked Laura down. They said good night, and she went inside.

Christian knew it was wrong and intrusive and incredibly creepy, but being a vampire meant you kind of lost touch with boundaries. Super senses meant he knew whenever Bradley and Faye were kissing in the kitchen even if he was clear across the house. He knew when Josh was about to have an asthma attack before Josh did, though the last time he'd handed him his inhaler, Josh had screamed and dived under the table. So, although looking up at a lit window was a perfectly normal thing to do, with vampire vision it meant he could see right through the gauzy curtains to Laura's pink-decorated bedroom which had a poster of . . .

Christian cut his eyes away from the horrifying vision of himself on the poster, wearing the terrible green cloak, and instead looked to Laura's full bookshelves and then to Laura herself, spinning in the center of the room.

She looked happy and beautiful, skirt flaring around her like a flower. She must have spun until she was dizzy, because just then she collapsed backward onto her bed with hands clasped over her heart.

Outside in the darkness, Christian smiled.

· · ·

He woke up the next evening to the sound of Bradley singing off-key in the kitchen, an annoying sound that brought his head up so sharply that he thumped it on his coffin lid.

He threw the now-dented lid off, said a word his mum would not have liked, and stormed up the basement stairs to the kitchen.

"I know you can sing in tune because that's your job!" Christian called as he came toward the kitchen.

Bradley was filling mugs of tea.

"Not my whole job," he said calmly. "There's also my fantastic dance moves, and being dead sexy."

"I think you take my point."

"Well, I like variety, it appeals to my artistic soul," Bradley said. "Sometimes I dance badly too. Can't seem to do anything about the sexy. Nothing puts a dent in that."

Christian was tempted to bash his own head against the cupboard, but he already had a headache and besides that his pamphlet said that wanton destruction of property was socially irresponsible.

"Augh," he said instead.

"You're cranky when you get up," Bradley observed and

winked. "How was the groupie?"

"Her name is Laura," Christian said coldly. "And she's not a groupie."

Bradley waved a kitchen mitt at him in what seemed to be an entirely random gesture. Christian stared, and then Bradley grinned.

"She came to your concert and threw herself at you because you're famous. Kind of the working definition of a groupie, dude. Your first one. Nice."

"She did not throw herself at me!"

She understands me, Christian wanted to say. *She knew from seeing a stupid picture that I was lonely.* But he wasn't going to tell Bradley that.

"Okay, Chris," Bradley said, rolling his eyes. "You'll learn to be at peace with your new undead-stud identity in time. There'll be more groupies at the party later."

"I invited Laura to the party," Christian informed him stiffly.

"Aw," Bradley said. "Aw, *man*."

Christian raised a sardonic eyebrow.

"I'm not really cut out to be a mentor," Bradley said. "Charismatic leader, yes. Idol of millions and object of crazed lust, sure. But Josh is a baby, and Pez is a registered citizen of la-la land, so that leaves me, and I thought you were older and we had an understanding."

"An understanding?" Christian echoed. "Bradley, I hate you."

"Yeah," Bradley said. "That's our thing."

"No, Bradley, I *actually* hate you."

"Mmm, sure," said Bradley dismissively. "The thing is, you're kind of a baby, too, aren't you? New to the business. These girls, right, they all *want* to have a special connection with you, but that doesn't mean they do, you get me? This girl doesn't know you. You don't know her. There's no way to get to know each other either. There's this great big technicolor picture of your, like, image in between you. You're better off sticking with your band-mates. We've got each others' backs, know what I mean?"

He punched Christian and his fist rebounded off Christian's arm. Bradley stared at his hand for a moment and then shrugged philosophically.

"You think I'm better off sticking with Josh?" Christian asked. "He won't even talk to me."

Bradley shrugged, leaning against the shiny, black marble countertop and taking a sip of chai tea. He looked rumpled and perfectly at home in his white cashmere sweater, in this overly-expensive house, among glass-fronted cupboards with crystal glasses and matching plates inside them.

"I know things are a bit rough for you, man."

He took another sip of tea, then spat it out and dropped the cup when Christian pinned him up against the wall, one arm against his throat. He certainly knew his own strength: the pamphlets had informed him of it painstakingly and at length. He knew his arm must feel like an iron bar to Bradley, unyielding, cutting off his supply of air.

"What do you know," he hissed through bared teeth, "about how rough things are for me?"

Bradley made a strangled sound and clawed at Christian's arm.

Christian tilted his head the way Faye had taught him so that his fangs glittered, long and sharp, hovering far too close for comfort.

"You have no idea! You people are not my friends. I don't have friends, and I don't have a family anymore, because I am no longer human. But I do have the ability to rip out your throat and drink you down like a milkshake, so I suggest you shut your mouth and stay out of my business!"

He let Bradley go, shoving him backward so he hit the wall, but not as hard as Christian would've liked. Bradley staggered but stayed upright.

Christian let his lips skin back over his fangs.

"She said that we were going to be together," Christian said tightly. "And I—I want to believe her. So just leave out the groupie talk."

Bradley nodded, slowly, and they stared at each other until Faye came in, stilettos tapping. Christian couldn't help but notice she'd bought a lot of shoes with pointed wooden heels since they'd first met.

He was *pretty* sure it was just a scare tactic.

"What is going on here?" Faye inquired sharply. "If you boys feel the urge to wrestle, you will do it under my supervision, in a fountain, with key members of the press present!"

The microwave pinged. Bradley popped it open and took out a mug. He pushed it along the counter in Christian's direction.

It was a mug full of heated blood, a smiley face with tiny fangs on the front. Written underneath it were the words: WE'RE FANG-TASTIC!

Christian picked up the mug, curling his cold fingers around its warmth and feeling simultaneously guilty and overcome by how ridiculous Bradley was.

Eventually he muttered, "Thanks," into the cup. Bradley just nodded.

• • •

He had arranged to meet Laura under the tree from last night. He had it all planned. He had left his stupid cape at home, though if Faye found out she'd probably stake him and put his ashes onstage in an urn. And the cape.

He'd thought Laura might be standing under the tree, her back to him, and her hair might be loose and rippling red. The leaves would frame her, moonlight gilding them and her alike, and she'd turn around and smile.

It all happened exactly like that, aside from the two other girls. They were a rather big difference, and sort of spoiled the vision. One of them had wild bright-blonde hair and the other had wild pitch-black eyelashes, and they reminded Christian of the girls at school who'd either sneered at him or seemed honestly unaware he existed.

He disliked them both on sight. The fact that their presence interfered with his plans to kiss Laura "hello" might have had something to do with it.

"Oh my God," said the wild blonde. "It *is* Chris. Oh my God!"

"He's not wearing the cape," said the wild eyelashes. She sounded extremely disappointed. "And he's not—" She gestured to her face.

"That was makeup," said Christian. "I don't wear it every day."

"You should," Eyelashes told him seriously. "It makes you look much better."

"I can't believe you were telling the truth!" Blondie exclaimed.

"I was," Laura said.

Laura looked small and uneasy. Christian felt the impulse to rescue her, put his arm around her and fold her tight against him, but she was lingering close by the other girls as if drawn in by the pull of their gravity. They towered over her, shimmering and confident.

"Of course she was telling the truth," Christian said.

Laura threw him a smile, grateful and sweet. "These are my friends, Haley and Rochelle. Um, I said that they could— maybe—I mean, can they come to the party too?"

Christian's mum had raised him to be polite. "Um," he said. "That sounds like—fun."

Eyelashes and Blondie (he thought Eyelashes was Haley and Blondie was Rochelle) each grabbed hold of one of Christian's arms.

"Sooooo," said Haley, "will the rest of the *band* be at the party?"

Christian found himself disliking the fawning way she said

band, like it was an entity apart from, and more important than, them as individuals.

"Yes."

"Will *Bradley* be there?" Haley pursued, a sudden glassy look in her eyes.

"Yes, the whole band will be there," Christian said patiently.

The entire walk back was like an interview, in which Haley-Eyelashes indicated she was deeply disappointed in him for not knowing basic and vital facts like Bradley's favorite color.

Christian was massively relieved when they reached the house. Every window was shining, and the house itself appeared to be swaying gently from side to side, as if someone had got it intoxicated.

Haley squealed and dragged Christian by brute force toward the door, where Faye's usual doorman Terence was standing outside, looking burly. He did that well.

"Hey, Chris."

"Um," said Christian. "They're all with me."

"Respect," said Terence, and gave him two thumbs up.

Christian took a moment to be deeply thankful that vampires could not blush, and walked into the hall. The carpet was squishing oddly under his feet. A man wearing a papier-mâché elephant head dashed across the hall and up the spiral staircase. Somewhere upstairs people were applauding.

"Ah, I see Pez's friends are here," said Christian, as he and his strange and awful harem climbed the spiral stairs after the elephant-headed man.

"This is so cool," said Rochelle. "Hey, do you drink the blood of the other members of the band?"

"What? No, I certainly do not!" Christian exclaimed, scandalized.

"Really?" Rochelle asked. "Not any of them? Not even Bradley's?"

"Especially not Bradley's!"

"You two are so funny," Rochelle told him, laughing, and pressed his arm. "Like that one interview in *Just Pretend We're Twenty-One*, when you were all asked to name your favorite person in the band. Bradley said you, and Josh said Bradley, and Pez said Bradley, and you said you just hated Bradley. That was so funny!"

"No, you see, I actually *do* hate Bradley," Christian explained.

"So funny," Rochelle repeated, shaking her head.

They were at the top of the stairs now, and witness to the conga line forming down the gallery. Someone had constructed Bradley a throne out of gilt-painted cardboard and he was drinking something out of a pineapple.

"Hey, Chris!" he called out, waving his pineapple.

"Bradley!" screeched Haley, in a voice that vibrated in weird and terrifying ways. She let go of Christian's arm and barreled her way through the conga line.

Christian hoped Rochelle would follow her, but Rochelle stayed hanging onto his arm. Laura just stood on Rochelle's other side, nervously hovering. Christian's attempts to establish eye contact were foiled by Rochelle's hair.

"Can I get you girls a drink?" he offered desperately at last.

"Such a gentleman," said Rochelle, and Christian took that as a "yes." He went downstairs and retrieved the cans of Coke that he always had hidden over the fridge because Josh had low blood sugar and sometimes required one right away.

He came back up holding the cans and met Bradley at the top of the stairs cradling his pineapple.

"Good call bringing that girl with the eyelashes," he said. "She dived, but I ducked. Now I think she's planning to make Josh a man. It'll be good for him."

"Er, that's nice," said Christian.

Christian's pamphlet had advised that the correct way to deal with a vampire on the verge of going feral was to report him to the authorities and, in extreme cases, push him into some sunlight and watch carefully as he became a small pile of ashes.

At no point had the pamphlet suggested that smiling and waving a pineapple was an appropriate technique to subdue such a vampire.

"I'm sorry about before. I lost my temper," Christian said. Apparently, pineapples were more powerful than he had supposed.

Bradley gestured with his pineapple in what seemed to be a peaceful manner.

"That's all right," he said. "I'm very zen about that sort of thing. You are young, my little fanged grasshopper, but you will learn."

"Hi, Christian," said a voice behind Bradley. Christian knew who it was at once because nobody else used his real name.

Bradley shifted aside to reveal Laura, who looked at him with wide startled eyes.

"Oh, I'm sorry."

"Quite all right, Laura," said Bradley, waving his pineapple benevolently. "I have to go see if Pez has added something unfortunate to the punch again. It's not his fault, he actually seems to like the taste of bubble bath . . ."

Before wandering off, Bradley gave Christian a significant look. Christian chose to completely ignore him.

Laura was haloed by the chandeliers, hair vivid and her dress snow-pale. She drew in close, without Christian pulling her to him, curls tickling the side of his face, and whispered: "You don't have to dress that way for me."

Christian looked down at his rugby shirt and jeans.

"You can be your real self," Laura told him, her eyes intent.

"I am my real self," Christian said. "I don't understand."

He was starting to feel very uneasy, but before he could ask her exactly what she meant, or what she thought of him, Laura leaned in again, warm lips against his ear, and said: "Will you take me to your room?"

Explanations could wait.

"Yes," Christian said. "Absolutely. I'm sure you will enjoy it. Uh, my room, that is. It's decorated. Faye hired a decorator to do that."

Laura laughed at him as if she understood, and he led her back down the stairs, cradled in the corner of his arm. Her heart was beating very fast. His thoughts seemed set to the nervous rhythm of her pulse, leaping around erratically.

"Your bedroom is in the basement?" Laura asked, and then laughed nervously. "No, of course, that makes sense. Obviously."

Christian opened the door to his room and thanked Faye silently for her good taste in interior design. "Subtle," Faye had said at the time. "We're going for subtle." When Bradley then chimed in, "We don't want to let it all fang out," she had beaten him with her Blackberry.

Christian's room was done all in cream colors, a reproduction of Monet's *Water Lilies* above the fireplace. The only touch of brightness were the crimson curtains curling at the edges of a door that led to nowhere, which has been installed to cover the only window in the room.

It would all have looked really classy, except for the fact Christian had left his coffin out in the center of the room with the lid on the floor, instead of tucking the whole thing away under the extra bed.

"Er, sorry," Christian said, and dived toward it.

"No," Laura said. "It's fine. Leave it."

He'd heard that girls liked to set the mood, but he didn't even like to think about what kind of mood a coffin set.

"We do kind of need to get it out of the way," Christian pointed out, "so we can get to the—"

Laura looked at him, her face a blank.

"Unless you've changed your mind," Christian said hastily, "which is absolutely, completely fine. I would understand. We could go back to the party—"

He was interrupted by Laura walking into his open arms. He closed them around her almost by reflex, drawing her close because she was warm, because she felt soft and smelled sweet and he wanted her there, wanted her to want to be there so badly.

She turned up her face to his, and he kissed her, light and exploring, letting her breathe, letting her set the pace. Her pulse thundered beneath her skin, singing a song of life and pleasure to him every time he touched her. He kissed her mouth lightly, the corner of her lips, her chin, and then her mouth again. She started, as if she had not expected him to be so tender, and the tip of his fang cut her. Christian tasted blood.

"Oh, I'm sorry," he murmured, drawing back.

"It's fine," Laura whispered, her voice trembling a little, but it must have been with excitement because she threaded her fingers through his hair and brought his face down to hers again.

He kissed her again, delicately, mouth lingering against hers with all the gentleness he possessed. He didn't want to taste her blood. This wasn't about feeding.

Her mouth opened, yielding and lovely. Her fingers in his hair tugged. He kissed her a little harder, kissed her cheek, her chin, brushing butterfly kisses along her jaw. She pulled his head down again so his mouth slid from her jaw to her throat.

Even then, he didn't get it. He kissed her there, where her pulse was beating fast but safe beneath her fragile skin.

"Do it," she said, breathing hard and determined.

He lost the rhythm of her warm heart and breath then, slid back into a cold place.

"Do what?" he asked, but he was already drawing back. He already knew.

Christian stepped away and walked alone to the crimson curtains, stood on the threshold of the door that went nowhere.

"Don't you want to?" Laura asked, her voice breaking. "My friend Rochelle said that if you liked me, you'd want to."

"Did she?"

"I thought human blood was best—"

"I don't care if it is. I do not want to be something who thinks about human beings as food," Christian said, keeping his voice low.

"That's really noble," Laura began.

"No," Christian told her. "*No, it isn't.* I do not think about you as food. I do not want the blood, so I am not noble for not taking it. Can't you give me credit for a little human decency?"

Laura's silence made her still. It was the silence of anyone hurt and embarrassed and being shouted at by a stranger.

Christian took a deep breath he didn't need at all. "No. Of course you can't. That's the problem, isn't it?"

He shouldn't be shouting at her. She wasn't wrong, after all. He'd threatened to drink Bradley's blood this very evening. He and Laura were just strangers who didn't understand each other. It was now they were learning that.

He'd wanted her to be human for him. That was just as insulting.

"I'm sorry that I upset you," Laura said in a small voice, her eyes combing the corners of the room as if searching for places she could hide. "I don't quite...I don't know what I did wrong."

Christian's mother had taught him at a very early age that it was wrong to make girls cry.

"You did nothing wrong," he said as gently as he could. "I guess I'm just not vampire enough for you."

Not yet.

He offered her his arm and led her gently back to Rochelle, who would be her friend for the night because she had got them invited to this great party. They both seemed willing to engage in a little human deception.

"I'll see you around?" Laura asked. She sounded both uncertain about whether she would and about whether she wanted to.

Christian lied to her, intentionally, for the first time, and said, "You will."

• • •

When Christian tried to go back down to his room, he almost tripped over Haley and Josh on the basement stairs.

"I'm terribly sorry," he said, and backpedaled hastily before Josh could become asthmatic with combined terror and passion.

He crashed into a man wearing a papier-mâché lion head who turned out to be Pez.

"Oh, hey, man," said Pez. "Where's your lady friend?"

Christian was mildly surprised that Pez had noticed Laura

existed at all. Many things happening on Planet Earth passed Pez right by. "I think she only liked me because I'm a vampire."

Pez looked stunned. "Hang on," he said. "You're *actually* a vampire?"

"Ah, yes?"

"I thought that was a gimmick Faye came up with!"

"Yes, Pez," Christian said wearily. "I'm a gimmick. I'm also a vampire."

Pez nodded his fluffy, dreadlocked head which bounced with all the product that Faye ordered into it every day.

"Huh."

Christian waited while Pez processed the idea, feeling slight dread at the thought of how terrified Josh was of him.

"Dude," said Pez. "If you're actually a vampire, it is really nice of you to go grocery shopping so much."

"Oh, well," Christian mumbled, feeling unexpectedly flustered. "There's a late-night grocery shop down the road. I don't mind. I know Josh needs sugar, and Bradley drinks all that milk, and you kind of use up all the bubble bath."

"It's tangy," Pez assured him. "Very refreshing."

"Okay."

Pez punched him in the chest and then swayed back, laughing. "Appreciate it, man," he said, and then rejoined the conga line.

Christian was feeling a bit too fragile to cope with a conga line full of unlikely and intoxicated papier-mâché animals, so he went down to the projection room where he thought he could hear the video recording of their first concert being played.

He did not at all mean to see Bradley and Faye kissing in the darkened room, but that was exactly what he saw, and his vampire vision left nothing to the imagination.

Christian blinked hard three times to dispel the terrible sight.

"Chris, you are in so much trouble," said Faye, disentangling herself from Bradley's embrace, her lipstick blurred.

"I am so sorry, I had no idea. The music was up very loud. Please don't kill me."

"You keep sidling away from the wind machine," Faye said, ignoring him superbly, as she did when she had decided people were being stupid. "Don't try to lie to me. It's extremely clear."

Christian looked at his blown-up image on the farthest wall, bathed in violet light and definitely shying away from the wind machine.

"Hey, where's Laura?" Bradley asked. He was wearing Faye's lipstick, too. It made him look monumentally ridiculous.

"Not with me," Christian said. "You were right."

Bradley looked sympathetic, which Christian appreciated. The look on Faye's face gave him chills.

"Chris, do you mean that you just gave me a dramatic rescue and a tragic love affair, all in only two days?" she asked slowly. "Because if you've done that, I have to say, I think I love you."

Bradley made a distressed face. "Faye, give the guy a break. He has feelings."

"I know—torment, isolation, longing for love," Faye said, as if checking boxes in the terrible list that lived inside her brain. "Adore it. Totally classic."

"I'm not . . ." Christian burst out, and stopped.

He wasn't that vampire *thing* Laura had longed for. That was what he wanted to say. But to Faye and Bradley, of all people, he just couldn't do it.

Faye's face softened a little. She walked over to him, hair mussed and lipstick smeared. For a moment, Christian thought that she might actually be experiencing a wave of womanly sympathy.

"But you are," she said, stabbing her perfectly manicured nail in his direction, and his wild dream died. "You're the vampire wishing for his lost humanity, yearning for love as a way to recapture it, always thinking that someday, someone will understand."

"You don't understand," Christian said reflexively, and then bit his tongue (that was extremely painful for a vampire).

"Oh, I know," Faye said. "Nobody does. But you'll keep thinking maybe someone will. You'll keep searching for the one, and they'll keep hoping they could be the one, and the album will go to the top of the charts!"

"I feel somewhat exploited," Christian said. "I think that's due to the fact that *you're exploiting me.*"

He looked over Faye's shoulder at the images onscreen. Bradley was shaking what his mother and his plastic surgeon had given him, Josh and Pez shuffling behind him. Christian was all alone, his black hair lifted like wings by the wind machine.

"Sure," Faye agreed. "But what else are you going to do? What else are you going to *be*? You're a vampire, Chris. And I'm going to make you a star."

The haircut on that lit-up musician on the big screen didn't look as stupid as it always did in the mirror. Even the cloak didn't look stupid.

"It's not so bad, Chris," Bradley said encouragingly. "Stop moping."

Faye whirled on him. "Never tell him that again!"

"Sorry, Faye."

"Keep moping, Chris," said Faye sternly. "Mope your little heart out. Now, I'm tired of this party. Nobody is doing anything scandalous or newsworthy at all. We're going to my house, Bradley. Feel free to mope here alone, Chris. Or if you like, you can join us."

Chris took a moment to ponder the possible implications of Faye's offer, and feel his head go all swimmy with horror. He looked at Bradley to check that Bradley was also horrified, and Bradley gave him a thumbs-up.

Christian's horror reached almost cosmic proportions.

"I think," he said coldly, "I will fetch my cape and go for a walk."

"It's raining, man," Bradley informed him.

"I think that I will fetch my cape and go for a long, miserable walk in the rain."

Faye smiled brilliantly. "And that's why we all love you, honey."

Christian paused on his way out to cast one more reproachful and traumatized look at the pair of them.

Over their heads he saw his own image: the rock star vampire, eyes shut, lost in the music and the moment of love. Christian saw himself looking wistful and oddly beautiful, pale in neon lights and makeup, yet somehow divorced from both, shining like an icon. He looked happy and almost human.

Almost, but not quite. He was smiling a little.

In the spotlights, his fangs gleamed.

Kat

BY KELLEY ARMSTRONG

THE VAMPIRE HUNTERS came just before dawn. I was sound asleep—a total knock-out sleep, deep and dreamless, after a night spent sparring with Marguerite. I woke to her cool fingers gripping my bare shoulder.

"Kat?" she whispered. "Katiana?"

I pushed her away, muttering that I'd skip the bus and jog to school, but her fingers bit into my shoulder as she shook me.

"It's not school, *mon chaton*," she said in her soft French accent. "It's the hunters. They've found me."

My eyes snapped open. Marguerite was leaning over me, blue eyes wide, her heart-shaped face ringed with blonde curls. When I was little, I used to think she was an angel. I knew better now, but it didn't change anything. She was still *my* guardian angel.

I rolled out of bed and peered around the dark room. If I blinked hard enough, I could see. Cat's-eye vision, Marguerite called it. I was a supernatural, too, though not a vampire. We had no idea *what* I was. At sixteen, I still didn't have any powers other than this bit of night vision.

Marguerite pushed clothing into my hand. For two years,

we'd slept with an outfit and packed backpack under our beds, ready to grab if the hunters came. Two years of running. Two years of staying one step ahead of them. Until now.

"Where are they?" I whispered as I tugged on my jeans.

"Outside. Watching the house."

"Waiting for daylight, I bet." I snorted. "Idiots. Probably think once the sun comes up, you'll be trapped in here."

"If so, they will be in for a surprise. But I would like to be gone by then, to be sure they are not waiting for reinforcements."

"Going up, then?" I asked.

She nodded, and we set out.

• • •

We snuck through the top-floor apartment we rented in the old house. In the living room, I hopped onto the couch, and Marguerite handed me a screwdriver. I popped off the ventilation shaft cover, handed it down to her, grabbed the edge and swung up and through.

Ever seen a TV show where the hero sneaks into the villain's lair through a ventilation shaft? Ever thought it looked easy? It's not. First, your average ventilation shaft is not action hero-sized. Second, they're lined with metal, meaning it's like crawling through a tin can, every thump of your knee echoing.

Fortunately, neither Marguerite nor I are action hero-sized either. And we know how to move without making a sound. For Marguerite, it comes naturally. Vampires are predators, and she's never sugar-coated that for me. My skill comes from training. I'm a competition-level gymnast, a brown belt in karate and a second-degree black belt in aikido.

I'd been taking lessons since I came to live with Marguerite eleven years ago. All supernaturals need to be able to defend themselves, she says. I might eventually get powers that help me, but if I turn out to be something like a necromancer, I'm shit outta luck. Not that she'd use those exact words. Marguerite doesn't swear and doesn't like me to either. She has no problem with me kicking someone's ass—she just doesn't want me saying the word.

When my elbow bumped the metal side, I managed to swallow my curse, turning it into a soft growl.

"You're doing fine," her whisper floated to me. "Keep going."

We finally reached the attic, where we'd removed the screws from the vent right after moving in. As I pushed it up and out of the way, I mentally cursed again, this time cussing out the landlady for nailing shut the attic hatch, which would have made for a much easier escape route. That was why we'd rented the place—Marguerite had seen the hatch in our apartment and slapped down the cash...only to realize it was nailed closed, the wood too rotted to pry open.

Once in the attic, Marguerite took over. She can see better in the dark than I can. In the vent, she'd let me go first to cover my back, but here she led to make sure I didn't trip or step on anything nasty. That's the way it's always been. She trains me to defend myself, but when she's there, she's always the one taking the risks. When I was five, it made me feel safe and loved. Now

. . . well, there's part of me that wants to say it pisses me off, but the truth is, I still like it.

Marguerite walked to the dormer window. Oak branches scraped against it like fingernails on a chalkboard, setting my already stretched nerves twanging. She wrenched off the rotted window frame. Those branches, creepy as they were, made excellent cover, hiding us as we swung up and onto the roof. Following her lead, I slid across the old shingles, feeling them scrape a layer or two off my palms. We crept along to the shadow of the chimney, then huddled against it and peered out into the night.

Marguerite started to close her eyes, then opened them wide, her nostrils flaring.

"Yes, I'm bleeding," I whispered. "Scraped palms. I'll live."

She handed me a tissue anyway. Then she closed her eyes, trying to pinpoint the vampire hunters with her special senses. A vampire can sense living beings. Marguerite doesn't know how it works, but years ago I saw this show on sharks and how they have this sixth sense that detects electrical impulses, making them perfectly evolved predators. So I've decided that's what vampires have—a shark's electrosensory system. Perfect predators.

Tonight her shark-sense wasn't up to snuff, and Marguerite kept shaking her head sharply, like she was trying to tune it in. She looked tired, too, her eyes dim, face drawn. I remembered how cool her skin had been when she woke me up.

"When's the last time you ate?" I whispered.

"I had a storage pouch—"

"Not that stale blood crap. A real meal, I mean."

Her silence answered. While she can get by on packaged stuff, it's like humans eating at McDonald's every day. Not very healthy. She needs real food, hot and fresh. Though she doesn't need to kill people to feed—she just drinks some blood, like a mosquito—it's always dangerous, and since we've been on the run she doesn't do it nearly enough.

"You can't do that. You need to feed more to keep up your energy."

"*Oui, maman.*"

I made a face at her and hunkered down, letting her concentrate. After a moment, she pointed to the east.

"Two of them, over there. Watching and waiting. We must go."

I nodded, and followed her back to the rear of the house and down the tree, hidden by its branches. We hop-scotched through yards as the darkness lifted, giving way to predawn gray, pink touching the sky to the east. The rising sun wasn't a problem. Bram Stoker got one thing right with Dracula—vampires can walk around in daylight just fine.

We headed for the bus station three blocks away. These days, when we looked for a place to live, Marguerite didn't ask how many bedrooms and baths it had or even how much it cost. She picked apartments based on how easily we could escape them—and get far away, fast.

"I'm sorry, *mon chaton*," she said for the umpteenth time as we ran. "I know you liked it here, and I know you were looking forward to your date Saturday."

"I'll live."

"You liked him."

I shrugged. "Just a guy. Probably turn out to be another jock-jerk anyway."

Being on the run meant home-schooling. Home-schooling meant limited opportunities to meet guys. So I did most of my socializing at the gym, which had lots of really hot guys. Unfortunately, most of them knew how hot they were. Luke had seemed different, but I told myself it was just a front. That always made leaving easier.

We dashed behind a convenience store. I leapt onto the wooden fence and ran along the top of it.

"Slow down, Kat," Marguerite called behind me. "You will fall."

I shot a grin back. "Never. I'm a werecat, remember?"

She rolled her eyes. "There is no such thing."

"Because I'm the first."

It was an old routine, and we knew our lines by heart. I've loved cats for as long as I can remember, and I'm convinced it has something to do with my supernatural type. Marguerite says no—there are no werecats. She says the reason I like felines so much is just because, when I was little, people always told me I looked like one, with my sleek, golden brown hair and tilted green eyes. Even from the day we met, Marguerite had called me *chaton*—kitten.

Back when I lived with my parents and was named Kathy, I'd always wanted to be called Kat, but my mother said that was silly and Kathy was a perfectly good name. When I went away with Marguerite, I had to change my name, and I'd done so happily, wanting something fancier, more exotic, like her name. So I became Katiana, but everyone called me Kat.

I darted along the top of the wooden fence, then hopped down behind the bus station. When I headed for it, Marguerite caught my arm.

"You will stay close to me when we are inside," she said. "No running off."

"I'm not five, Mags," I said.

I could also point out that she was the one the hunters were after, but she'd only say that still put me in danger. Given a chance, they'd grab me as bait for her. I'd say if they did grab me expecting a hysterical sixteen-year-old girl, they'd be in for a shock, but I wasn't dumb enough to put myself in harm's way. Rule one of martial arts: never underestimate your opponent, and I didn't know a thing about these opponents. Marguerite said they'd be supernaturals—all vampire hunters are, because humans don't know about our world—so we could be facing anything from spellcasters to half-demons to werewolves.

As we entered the trash-strewn alley, I noticed a foot poking out from a cardboard box.

"Dinner," I said, pointing.

"We do not have time—"

"We'll make time," I said, lowering my voice as I strode to the box. "You need your energy."

I bent and peered into the box. The guy inside was sound

asleep. I motioned Marguerite over. She took a look and hesitated, glancing over at me. She'd rather not do this with me watching, but I was right—she needed the energy boost. So, she daintily wedged her shoulders into the box, moving soundlessly. Another pause. I couldn't see her face, but I knew what she was doing—extending her fangs.

When she struck, it was with the speed and precision of a hawk. Her fangs sank in. The homeless guy jerked awake, but before he could make a sound, he slumped back into the box, out cold again. A vampire's saliva contains a sedative to knock their prey out while they feed. Like I said, perfectly evolved predators.

I didn't look away as Marguerite fed. Why would I? She didn't turn her head when I downed a burger. Humans kill animals for food. Vampires knock out humans and borrow some blood. People would donate that pint at a clinic to keep a human alive, so what's wrong with taking it fresh from the source to keep a vampire alive? Marguerite says I'm oversimplifying things. I say she overcomplicates them.

When Marguerite finished feeding, she took a moment to seal the wound and make sure the man was comfortable. Then she tucked five twenty-dollar bills into his pocket, and motioned for me to fall in behind her as she continued to the end of the alley.

Of the five people inside the bus depot, two were sprawled out asleep on the seats. They clutched tickets in their hands, as if to prove they had a reason to be there, but I bet if I checked the tickets they'd be months old. Homeless, like the guy in the alley.

Marguerite caught my elbow and whispered, "We will go home, Katiana. I promise."

"I wasn't thinking about that."

But, of course, I was. I missed home. Not the house or even the neighborhood, just the feeling of having a house and a neighborhood. Even as I walked past the posted bus schedule, I couldn't help looking down the list of names, finding my city. Montreal. Not the city where I was born, but my real home with Marguerite, the one we'd been forced to leave when the hunters tracked her down two years ago.

We walked to the counter.

"Kathy," a woman called.

I didn't turn. Marguerite had drilled that instinct out of me years ago. But I still tensed and looked up. Reflected in the glass of the ticket booth, I saw a woman approaching me, smiling.

"Kathy."

Marguerite caught my hand, squeezing tight. I glanced over, slowly, saw the woman and my gut went cold—a sudden, mindless reaction, something deep in me that said I knew her, and I should run, run as fast as I could.

Still gripping my hand, Marguerite started for the door. The woman only watched us as we hurried outside.

"She knew my name," I said.

"Yes, they know about you. That is why—"

"She knew my *real* name."

Marguerite looked away. I stopped walking. When she tugged my hand, I locked my knees.

"What's going—?"

"Not now. We must leave."

I didn't move.

She met my gaze. "Do you trust me, Kat?"

I answered by letting her lead me to the sidewalk.

"We will call a taxi," she said, fumbling with her cell phone.

Two figures stepped from behind the bus depot and started bearing down on us.

"Marguerite?"

She looked up. *"Merde!"* She grabbed my hand again. "Run, Kat."

"But we're in a public place. Shouldn't we just go back inside—?"

"They will not care. Run!"

I raced back down the alley, past the homeless guy in his cardboard box, and vaulted the fence, Marguerite at my heels. As I tore down the next alley, two more figures stepped across the end of it. I wheeled. The other two men were coming over the fence.

Trapped.

The men in front of us didn't say a word, just started walking slowly our way. I squared my shoulders and flexed my hands, then broke into a sprint, running straight for them, hoping that would catch them off-guard. If not, I'd rather start the fight before the other two joined in.

One of the men reached into his pocket. He pulled out something. It was still barely dawn, the alley dark with shadows, and

I saw only a silver object. A cell phone maybe. Or a radio. Or—

He lifted a gun. Pointed at me.

"Kat!" Marguerite shrieked.

She grabbed my shirt and wrenched me back. I flew off my feet. She dashed in front of me. The gun fired—a quiet *pfft*. The bullet hit her in the chest. She toppled beside me, hands clutching her heart, gasping. Her face, though, was perfectly calm. No blood flowed between her fingers.

"On my count," she whispered. "Three, two, one..."

We leapt up. Marguerite went for the guy with the gun. He fell back in surprise. She grabbed the gun as I caught the second guy by the wrist and threw him down. Behind us, the other two were running, feet pounding the pavement, getting louder by the second.

Marguerite kicked her opponent to the ground, and we ran. As we did, I glanced over. The hole in her chest was closing fast, leaving only a rip in her shirt.

"—vampire?" one of the men behind us was saying. "Why the hell didn't someone know she was a vampire?"

I looked at Marguerite. She met my gaze, then tore hers away, and we kept going.

· · ·

On the next street, we saw a city bus and flagged it down. The driver was nice enough to stop. We climbed on. I looked out the window as we pulled away from the curb, but there was no sign of our pursuers.

"They aren't vampire hunters, are they?" I murmured.

"No."

I looked over at her. "Were there ever vampire hunters?"

She shook her head, gaze down. "No. Only them."

"Coming for me, not you. They're from that place, aren't they? Part of that group that experimented on me."

"The Edison Group. Yes. At first, I thought they might be vampire hunters. There is such a thing, though rare, so I should have known..." She shook her head. "I wanted them to be vampire hunters. When I realized otherwise...I should have told you."

"Yeah." I met her gaze. "You should have."

"I'm sorry."

I nodded. She put her arm around my shoulders, and I rested my head on hers and closed my eyes.

• • •

I don't remember much about my mother and father. They'd always seemed more like paid guardians than parents. They'd treated me well and given me everything I needed. *Almost* everything. There was no cuddling at my house. No curling up on Daddy's lap with a book. No bedtime tuck-in with hugs, kisses, and tickles from Mommy. I hadn't known I was missing anything, only that I wasn't a happy child.

The hospital visits didn't help. Once a month, late at night, my father would wake me up and we'd drive to this place that he said was a hospital, but looking back, I know it was a laboratory.

We always had to go in through the back door, where we'd be met by a tall man named Dr. Davidoff. He'd whisk us into a room and run all kinds of tests on me. Painful tests that left me weak and sore for days. My parents said I was sick and needed these visits. I'd say I felt fine, and they'd say, "Yes, that's why you need to keep going."

When I was in kindergarten, a new library assistant came to our school. Her name was Marguerite and she was the prettiest lady I'd ever seen. The nicest, too. All the kids wanted to help her put away books and listen to her talk with that exotic accent. But I was her special pet. Her kitten. Whenever I was alone at recess, she'd come over and talk to me. And she'd keep me company after school, while I waited for my father to pick me up.

One day, Marguerite said she had to leave and asked me to come with her. I said yes. Simple as that. I was five and I loved Marguerite, and I didn't particularly love my parents, so it seemed like a good trade-up. I went to live with her in Montreal, where I was Katiana and she was my Aunt Marguerite, and the story of how I came to live with her was a delicious secret between us.

When I'd been with her a few years, Marguerite told me the truth. I was a supernatural, and a subject in a genetic modification experiment, supposedly to reduce the negative side-effects of supernatural powers. Marguerite had been part of a network of supernaturals concerned about the experiments. She'd been assigned to monitor me, so she'd taken the job at my school.

When she saw how miserable I was, she told the group, but they wouldn't let her do anything—her job was to only watch and report. Marguerite couldn't do that. So she'd asked me to come away with her, and no matter what has happened since, I've never regretted saying yes.

· · ·

The bus went downtown, so that's where we got off.

"There is a car rental place on the other side of the river," Marguerite said. "We will go there."

I nodded and said nothing. It was barely seven, and the downtown streets were almost empty. A vehicle rolled by now and then, most of them cube vans making early deliveries. A few police cars crawled along the streets, looking for trouble left over from the night before.

Sleepy-eyed businessman dragged themselves into office buildings, coffee clutched in their hands, the smell making my stomach perk up. If we'd been back at the apartment, I'd be just rolling out of bed, a steaming mug of hazelnut coffee on my nightstand, Marguerite knowing that woke me better than any alarm clock.

As we reached the end of the block, the smell of coffee was overwhelmed by a far less enticing odor: the river. I could hear it, too, the crash of the dam not yet swallowed by the roar of downtown traffic. As we turned the corner, a blast of wind hit, and I swore I could feel the spray of water.

I shivered. Marguerite reached for my backpack. "Let me get your sweater."

"I'm okay."

"A coffee then." She gave a wan smile. "I know you like your morning coffee. It will not be your fancy flavored sort, but—"

"I'm okay."

She turned another corner, getting us out of the wind. "You're not okay, Kat. I know that. I . . ."

"You thought it was for the best. I get that." I cleared my throat, anxious to change the subject. "I recognized the woman in the bus station. I think she was one of the nurses from the lab. I guess they finally tracked me down, and now they want to kill me."

"No. They would not do that. You are too valuable."

I snorted. "Yeah, as a trophy. If you didn't think he meant to shoot me, you wouldn't have jumped in the way."

She walked a few more steps before answering. "I am certain they would not kill you. But certain enough to risk your life on it? No." She looked over at me. "You *are* valuable, Kat. Even in their experiment, you were special. That is why you had to go to the laboratory at night, away from the other children, hidden from most of those who worked there."

"So I was a top-secret part of a top-secret experiment?"

A tiny smile. "Something like that."

"A werecat. Gotta be."

I expected her to roll her eyes, shoot back her usual line, but she only hunched her shoulders against the cold morning air, and stared off down the empty street.

"The bullet," I said. "Is it still . . . in you?"

She nodded. When I tried to press her on that, worried that it might be dangerous, she brushed off my concern with uncharacteristic impatience, her gaze fixed on the next corner. Then she caught my arm.

"Someone is there. He stopped at the corner."

I could come up with a dozen logical explanations for someone to pause at a corner, but Marguerite held me still as she strained to look, listen and sense.

"Someone else is approaching," she whispered. "He stops beside the first..."

Vampires don't have super-sonic hearing, but it was so quiet that even I could pick up the murmur of conversation. Marguerite pushed me into an alcove as footsteps sounded. Then a man cursed. Marguerite pushed me farther into the alcove, and we huddled there, listening.

"Are you sure your spell picked them up?" the man asked.

"It detected the girl," a woman said. "It only works on the living. And only intermittently with her."

The man said something I didn't catch.

"I suppose so," his companion replied. "Let me cast again."

She murmured words in a foreign language. A spell. I shivered. Marguerite rubbed my arm, but it wasn't the cold that made me tremble now. I might be a supernatural, and I might live with one, but their world was still foreign to me, mysterious. I don't like mysteries. I like what I can see, feel, touch and understand. I like what I can fight. Spells? I had no idea how to defend myself against those.

We pressed deeper into the shadows as the voices approached.

"Nothing," the woman said.

"We—"

"Shhh," she said. "I heard something."

We'd barely breathed, so it wasn't us. A door creaked open. Footsteps again, but it was another pair, coming from the opposite direction, like someone had stepped out of a shop down the road. The footsteps headed our way.

Marguerite's slender hands flew in familiar code, outlining a plan. I barely needed to watch—I knew what she'd be thinking. With a bystander approaching, our pursuers would be focused on getting past him, any weapons hidden. So when they reached the alcove—

Marguerite sprang first, grabbing the man as he stepped into view, then yanking him into the darkened alcove. I leapt out behind her. The woman backpedaled, hands sailing up, lips parting. An invisible blow hit me in the chest. I tottered backward. That was it—just thrown off balance. I smiled. Now *that* I could handle.

I charged. Her hands flew up again. I chopped them down, disrupting her spell. She started to cast again, this time not using her hands. A witch spell. A roundhouse kick knocked her off her feet and cut that one short.

Marguerite leapt between us. She grabbed the woman and dragged her into the alcove. Inside, the man lay on his back, out cold from her bite.

As Marguerite took the woman into the shadows for the

same treatment, I looked down the street. A chubby guy in a business suit stood twenty feet away. Just stood there, travel mug raised halfway to his lips, like he'd been frozen there the whole time, watching the fight.

"Morning," I said.

He skittered across the road and took off the other way.

"Looks like he didn't want to play Good Samaritan today," I said as Marguerite joined me on the sidewalk. "But he probably has a cell, so he might call . . ." I stopped, seeing her holding what looked like a phone. "Did *they* manage to call someone?"

"A radio with a GPS." She lifted the box. "They sent our coordinates."

She dropped it over the side of a trash bin, and we took off. As we turned the corner, we saw the woman from the bus station rounding the next one down the block. I wheeled. Two unfamiliar men were approaching from the rear. I hesitated, telling myself they were just humans, bystanders, heading off to work. Then one reached into his coat and pulled out a gun.

Marguerite grabbed my shoulder, steering me to the nearest exit: a service lane just ahead. At the mouth, she caught my arm and peered down the lane, making sure it wasn't a dead end. There was a wall thirty feet down, but the lane continued, turning left.

We raced to the end, veered around the corner . . . and found a single parking space, enclosed on all other sides by soaring walls.

"No, no, no," Marguerite whispered.

I pointed. "A door."

As we ran to it, Marguerite pulled out her lock picks. I tried the handle, just in case, but of course it was locked. She pushed a pick into the keyhole.

Footfalls pounded down the service lane. She stopped and turned.

"Just open—" I began.

"No time."

She looked around, then her chin shot up. I followed her gaze to a fire escape. I ran for it. She boosted me, and I grabbed the bottom rung. I scrambled up, hand over hand, as fast as I could. At a shout, I looked down to see the woman skidding to a halt at the end of the alley... and Marguerite, still on the ground.

"Marguerite!"

"Go!" When I didn't budge, she glowered up at me, fangs extended as she snarled, "Go!"

She ran at the woman. I climbed, slower now, fingers trembling, forcing myself to take each step, my gut screaming for me to stop, to go back for her. But I knew she was right. I had no defenses against a gun. She did. I had to get away and trust she'd follow.

When I reached the top, I turned. The first thing I saw was the woman, unconscious on the ground. Then the two men, one holding Marguerite in a head-lock, the other with his gun trained on me. I hesitated. He fired.

The bullet hit the brick below my foot. He lifted the barrel higher. I lunged onto the rooftop, heart thudding. The metal fire escape groaned as someone began to climb it. I scrambled to my feet and took off across the roof.

. . .

I got away. As soon as I did, I realized I had to go back.

They'd already tried to kill Marguerite. She was just an obstacle to getting me and, now, a way to get to me, to lure me in. She'd survived being shot, but now that they knew what she was, they'd know how to kill her. I shivered just thinking about what they might do to try to convince her to give me up. And when they couldn't, they'd kill her. No question.

I shivered, gulping icy air as I stood pressed against a wall, catching my breath. Then I closed my eyes and listened. No one was coming. I kept listening, trying to hear the roar of the dam to orient myself. It was close by, just to my right. I turned the other way and started walking.

. . .

I found them in the same service lane we'd run into. They'd backed a van in and had the rear doors open as one of the men dragged Marguerite, hands behind her back, gagged and struggling, toward it.

As I strode into the alley, the driver leapt out, raising his gun.

"I come in peace," I said, lifting my fingers in a V.

He paused, half out of the van, his broad face screwing up in confusion.

I raised my hands. "See? No pistol. No switchblade. Not even a ray gun."

The witch I'd taken out earlier came around the other side of the van, approaching slowly. I watched her lips, ready for the first sign of a spellcast.

"I want to make a deal," I said.

She didn't answer, just stopped, her gaze traveling over me like she was looking for a hidden weapon. The driver eased back into the van, door still open, radio going to his lips.

"You can stop looking for her," he said. "She's right here." Pause. "Yeah, it's the O'Sullivan kid. Says she wants to make a deal." His voice dropped. "Better hurry."

The other man resumed dragging Marguerite to the van.

"Uh-uh," I said. "Put her in there and I'm gone. This deal is a trade. You take me and you let her go."

Marguerite shook her head wildly, her eyes blazing. I looked away and focused on the witch.

"You do want me, right?" I said.

"We do."

"And you aren't interested in her."

Her lips twisted with undisguised distaste. Marguerite told me that's how other supernaturals see vampires—unnatural and inhuman, worthy only of fear and disgust. They would kill her as soon as they could. I was sure of it now.

I continued, "So you take the prodigal science experiment home to the lab, and the vampire goes free. Fair enough?"

The witch hesitated, then nodded. "Come along then, Kathy."

"It's Kat."

A flicker of annoyance, quickly hidden. "All right then. Kat. Come—"

"I'm not coming anywhere until you release her. She'll walk this way. I'll walk that way. Crisscross. Everyone's happy." *Except me, going back to that horrible place, those awful experiments.* I pushed the thought away. I was valuable, so I'd survive, which was more than I could say for Marguerite if I didn't do this. She'd given up her freedom to look after me. Now it was time for me to do the same for her.

When the witch didn't move, I said, "I'm not going anywhere. You guys have guns, spells, demonic powers, whatever. I have zip. Just let her go, so I'm sure you're holding up your end of the bargain."

Another brief pause, then the witch signaled to the man holding Marguerite. He released her. As she walked toward me, I headed for the witch, my gaze still fixed on her. Out of the corner of my eye, I could see Marguerite pull down the gag, mouthing to me, trying to get my attention, trying to tell me to wait for her signal, then run. I ignored her. I had to go through with this.

I was about five feet from Marguerite when a truck backfired behind me, the sound cracking like gunfire. I jumped and spun. That's *all* I did. I didn't lunge. I didn't run. I didn't even back up. It didn't matter. I'd moved, and when I did, I heard the *pfft* of a silenced shot.

Marguerite screamed. I felt her hit me in the back, the blow so hard it knocked me off my feet, and as I fell, I twisted, and saw her running toward me, still three feet away, too far to have hit me. A spell, it had to be a—

I hit the pavement, flat on my back, blood spraying up from my chest.

Blood. Spraying up. From me. From my chest.

I lifted my head, looking down at myself, and saw—and saw—and saw—

"You shot her!" the witch screeched.

"She was trying to—"

"You were *waiting* for an excuse. You ..."

She kept shouting as Marguerite dropped beside me, tears plopping onto my face as I lay on the pavement and all I could think was, *I didn't know vampires could cry.*

"...like Davidoff's going to complain," the man was saying. "I gave him the excuse to test his secret experiment..."

The voices drifted away again. Or maybe I drifted. I wasn't sure. The next thing I knew, I was sitting up with Marguerite's arm around me, her face buried in my hair, tears wet against my scalp as she whispered, "I'm sorry, *mon chaton*. I'm so sorry."

"...just get the body in the van..." the woman was saying.

Body? I jerked up at that, looking around wildly, reassuring myself I was alive. I could still see them, could still hear Marguerite telling me it would be okay, everything would be okay.

Marguerite had me on my feet now, her arm still around me as she whispered, "We're going to run, Kat. We *must* run. Do you understand?"

Run? Was she crazy? I'd been shot. I couldn't—

Everything went black. Then, suddenly, I was on the sidewalk, running as she supported me. The pain in my chest was indescribable. Every breath felt like a knife stabbing through me. Marguerite had one hand pressed to the hole in my chest, trying to keep it closed, but it didn't matter. The blood ran over her fingers, over my shirt, dripping onto the pavement. Yet somehow we ran.

As we stumbled onto the road, a truck horn blasted. We kept going. The truck tried to stop, brakes and tires squealing. We raced past it, cutting so close that the draft as it passed nearly toppled us. The truck screeched to a halt. The driver shouted. Our pursuers shouted back, but they were stuck on the other side of the vehicle, out of sight.

We ducked into the first alley and kept going.

As we ran, the ground tilted under my feet. I tried to focus, but could see only a haze of dull shapes. Then I heard something. Water. The thunder of the dam, growing closer with each step. I heard Marguerite too, on her cell phone. Emergency. Shooting. The dam. Ambulance. Police. Please hurry.

What was she doing? I couldn't go to a regular doctor. I'd been told that all my life, even before I went away with Marguerite. *In an emergency, call home. Don't let them take you to a hospital.* My parents said it was because they wouldn't understand my condition. True. They just hadn't mentioned that the condition was being a genetically-modified supernatural whose blood tests would make the doctors call the guys in the Hazmat suits.

I guess that didn't matter now. I needed immediate medical attention. We'd deal with the fallout later.

The roar of rushing water grew steadily louder. Then another sound cut through it. The wail of sirens. I remembered seeing the police cars downtown. That's why Marguerite had asked for the police—they'd get here quickly, and that would scare off our pursuers. In an emergency, she always said, cause a scene and get the humans involved. No supernatural would risk doing anything with them around.

Marguerite lowered me to the ground, my back brushing against a metal railing. A cold mist of water sprayed my neck. When I blinked, I could focus enough to see we were at the dam. Police lights strobed against the buildings, the sirens deafening now.

There was no sign of our pursuers. This trapped them worse than the truck. They couldn't approach. We were safe.

"Mags," I whispered. I tried to say more, but could only cough, pain ripping through me, bloody spit splattering my clothes.

"Shhh, shhh." She kissed the top of my head, tears raining down her cheeks. "I'm sorry, *mon chaton*. So sorry. I should have told you, should have warned you. You are so young. So young."

Told me what? Young? Too young for what? To die? No. She couldn't mean that. I was fine. The ambulance was coming. I could hear the siren.

Doors slammed, and a police officer shouted for Marguerite to step back. Her trembling fingers fumbled around my neck, finding my necklace. A Star of David. I wasn't Jewish, but we always said I was. Just part of the cover.

When she found it, she breathed a sigh of relief, murmuring, *"Bien, bien."*

Why good?

"Step away from the girl," another officer shouted.

"I love you, Kat. You know that, don't you?" She kissed my forehead again. "I love you and I'll never leave you."

She stood then. I tried to call out to her but couldn't. The fog was descending again and it took everything I had just to focus, just to see her, a faint shape in the grayness as the mist from the dam and the fog from my brain swirled together.

"I'll see you on the other side," she whispered. Her fingers grazed my chin as she stepped back.

I twisted my head to watch her as she climbed onto the railing. The police shouted. I shouted, too, but only in my head, shouting her name over and over, telling her to stop, to come back, not to leave me . . .

She blew me a kiss and mouthed, "I'll see you soon," then back-flipped off the railing. The last thing I saw was Marguerite plummeting down, out of sight, into the river a hundred feet below.

And then . . .

Nothing.

• • •

I woke up cold, a chilled-to-the-bone kind of cold, with only a thin sheet pulled up to my chin. Under me, my bed was rock hard. I stretched and my muscles screamed in protest.

Damn, I really needed a workout.

I laughed at the thought. I'd been shot in the chest. Something told me it'd be a while before I was training again.

I inhaled, and resisted the urge to gag as my nostrils filled with the stink of antiseptic and chemicals. The smell of a hospital, bringing back old memories. I shivered. At least I wouldn't be going back to *that* hospital again. Almost worth being shot.

I wiggled my fingers and toes. God, everything ached and I was freezing. Did they have the air-conditioning on? My bed was so cold it was like lying on a marble slab.

I rubbed the bed . . . and my fingertips squeaked across the surface. I stopped. Mattresses didn't squeak. Was it covered in plastic? Did it need to be? Had I pissed myself?

I lifted my head. It took some effort—my head was flat on the bed. No pillow? I looked down and caught the flash of my reflection. I was lying on a metal table.

I jumped up so fast I nearly tumbled to the floor. I looked around. Metal. All I saw was metal. Metal table. Metal equipment. Metal trays covered with metal surgical instruments.

Had I woken up in surgery? Oh, God. Had they *finished*? My fingers flew to my chest, finding the spot under my left breast where the bullet had—

There was no bullet hole. No stitches. No bandages.

And no heartbeat.

I shook my head sharply, and pressed my fingers to the spot and closed my eyes, trying to feel . . .

There was nothing to feel. My chest didn't move at all. No

heartbeat and no breathing.

As I turned, I caught a glimpse of my reflection in the bank of metal berths behind me. I saw me—just me, same as always, tanned skin, brown hair, green eyes, gold pendant gleaming on my chest.

I caught the pendant and ran my fingers over the points of the star. The Star of David. Now I knew why Marguerite had been so happy to see me wearing my pendant. So they wouldn't embalm me.

I heard the words of the man who'd shot me. *Like Davidoff's going to complain. I gave him the excuse to test his secret experiment.*

An excuse to test whether their genetic modification had any effect on my supernatural blood-right, my destiny. To die . . . and rise again.

"Katiana."

I glanced over to see Marguerite in the doorway. She stepped inside and pulled the doors closed.

I couldn't have been asleep long, but she looked like she hadn't fed in weeks. She was pale and unsteady, her eyes sunken and red.

"Guess you were right," I said. "I'm not a werecat."

Her face crumpled. I didn't ask if she'd known I was a vampire. Of course she had. That's why she'd been assigned to me. Why she'd taken me away. I'd always felt like Marguerite was more my family than my parents had ever been. Now I knew why.

I didn't ask why she hadn't told me the truth. I knew. Of

every supernatural creature I could have been, this one would be the biggest blow, and she'd wanted to spare me the truth until I was older. I suppose she figured she had plenty of time before I needed to know. Time to let me grow up. Time to let me be normal.

A thought struck. "So, I'm going to be sixteen forever?"

"No, no," she said quickly. "That was one of the modifications, with the experiment. You are supposed to live a normal life, with only the other powers of a vampire."

Supposed to. That was only a theory, of course. No one could know for sure. I'd age or I wouldn't.

"Someone's coming." The words slipped out before I realized I was saying them. I turned toward the closed hall doors, but didn't hear anything. Still, I knew someone was out there. I could feel him.

A shark's sixth sense.

The perfect predator.

I shivered. Marguerite started to hug me, then lifted her head, catching the same weird sense, and quickly handed me new clothing. I took it and we hurried to the corner. Whoever was coming down the hall passed the room without stopping.

"So what happens now?" I whispered as I dressed. "The Edison Group must know I'm here. They'll be waiting for me to...rise."

"They are."

"And when I disappear? They'll know. They'll come—"

"I have made arrangements. Money can buy many things.

The records will show you were cremated by accident. You cannot be reborn from that. They will think they have lost you. We are safe." She helped me into my shirt and caught my gaze. "I know you have questions, Katiana. There is so much you must be wondering."

There was. So much. So many questions. So many worries and fears. *Too* many. I pushed them aside and focused on the easiest question, the only one I could deal with.

"Can we go home?"

She nodded. "Yes."

"Then, right now, that's all I want."

She nodded, put her arm around me, and led me from the room.

The Thirteenth Step

BY LIBBA BRAY

One

BY THE TIME the train pulled into the station, and Lauren wound her way down the stairs and out onto the desolate stretch of York Street, the sun was only a pale yellow sliver of warning slipping fast below the darkening horizon. She didn't like being out after dark—no one did these days—but she needed the job, and so here she was hurrying past empty storefronts, abandoned cars, and long-gone ironworks factories untouched by Brooklyn's gentrification boom. It was July in the city, the heat bullying in its humidity. In the distance, the half-lit towers of the Farragut Houses rose like an ugly Lego attempt. She glanced at the tiny ad in her hand: Part-time assistant needed for Angelus House. Good pay and flexible hours. There was an address scribbled on the side, an address she'd been given over the phone when she foolishly booked the appointment for eight-thirty, an address she was now trying desperately to find even as her gut told her it was madness to be walking unprotected at this hour. A torn page from a newspaper scuttled along the sidewalk and got caught on her foot. BLOODLUST SICKO KILLS AGAIN read the headline. Lauren shook it from her shoe and hurried along.

Angelus House occupied a corner on one of Vinegar Hill's cobblestone streets next to a litter-strewn, weed-choked lot surrounded by a rickety fence. It had been a small Victorian hospital that overlooked the Brooklyn Navy Yards at one point, but now tinted-glass privacy windows, thick iron gates, layers of graffiti, and heavy vines obscured its former limestone glory. Lauren buzzed, and when no one opened the heavy security door, she walked around the side looking for a usable entrance.

"You one of them, huh? You one of those freaks?" A dark-haired guy in a Knicks tank stepped out and dropped into a karate stance, brandishing a spray-paint can.

She screamed loud and high, which sent the guy running. A second later, a door banged open, and there was a guy offering her his hand.

"Are you okay?"

Golden. That was the word that popped into her mind. With the glow of lower Manhattan shining behind him, he appeared like a golden god, his long pale hair falling in thick waves to his shoulders. "Do you need help? What are you on?"

"What? N-nothing!" she said in a shaking voice. "There was a guy. He was spray painting something on the fence over there. He took off when you came out."

The golden one scanned the empty lot, scowling. "What are you doing out here? It's not safe after dark, and this is private property."

"I came about the assistant's job," she said, showing him the ad still clutched tightly in her hand. "I have an appointment for eight-thirty. But nobody answered the buzzer at the front door, so I came back here. I'm Lauren."

"Oh. Jeez. Sorry. Sometimes nobody gets to the buzzer. That's why we need an assistant. Come on in. I'm Johannes."

Lauren sat across from Johannes the Golden Boy in a drab chair in a cheerless square of an office with only one dim banker's lamp for light. He turned a pen end on end while asking her a series of questions: Was she proficient on a Mac? Did she mind answering phones and filing? Would she be willing to run errands during her shift—go for food or supplies that they might need? Did she understand that this was a place for troubled teens and that she might see and hear things that were kind of rough? Was she discreet? Did she spook easily?

She answered yes, no, yes, yes, yes, no.

He stared at her. He had deep brown eyes flecked with gold, which seemed to burn in the lamplight. "So tell me what you know about Angelus House?"

"I know you're the last hope for the toughest addiction cases. You take in homeless teens, runaways, kids from the projects, the ones everybody else has given up on."

He stopped playing with the pen. "Why do you want this job?"

Lauren stared at the ceiling and wondered how much she should tell him about herself. About the last three years. Her sister Carla.

"I just graduated from high school. I need a job, and I'd like to give back somehow."

He glanced at her flimsy resume that mostly consisted of part-time retail jobs. "No college plans? No rushing off to Gimme Gimme You or something?" She thought she saw a hint of a smirk on his face.

"No."

"Where do you see yourself in five years?"

Somewhere else. It was uncomfortably cold in the room. The air chilled the sweat on her neck and made her want to go outside into the heat again. "I have no idea."

"You're really honest." Golden Boy stared at her, and she couldn't begin to know what he was thinking. Had she blown it? She must have blown it. "Congratulations, Lauren," he said, giving her a beautiful smile. "You've got yourself a job."

Johannes insisted on walking her to the subway in the dark. It had begun to rain a little, which only made the humidity worse. "Great. Just what we needed. Our own hater." Johannes pointed at the wall where the tagger had come back to finish his work. Over the Angelus House insignia of a lone winged knight, the words *Los Vampiros* had been sprayed in red paint, and the letters dripped like blood.

Two

LAUREN WAS STANDING on the mostly empty subway platform when she saw the tagger in the Knicks shirt coming her way. She scanned the few people around her—a homeless guy, an old couple having a fight in Chinese, some oblivious hipsters across the tracks on the Manhattan side.

"I have 911 on speed dial," she said, holding out her phone.

"Yeah? You get reception down here? Who's your carrier— the *Matrix*? Look, I'm just trying to warn you, a'ight?" He wasn't so scary up close. About five-eight with short-cropped dark hair, a face from a Renaissance painting, and a large cross medallion hanging around his slender neck.

"Warn me about what?" Lauren forced herself to make eye contact.

"You need to stay away from those Angelus House assholes. They are seriously bad news."

"Says the guy who vandalizes buildings and stalks teenage girls," Lauren said, trying to put some snark into her voice. She hoped he couldn't tell how uneasy she was. That was the first rule of survival in New York: a shrug and a *that-all-you-got* attitude.

"I'm serious, yo. They go into the projects, and they take people."

"Yeah. It's called helping."

"They're not helping. They're *recruiting*."

"For what?"

"Something very bad. This guy I know, Isaiah Jones, he told me all about it. He used to roll with them, but he got out. Said they were up to some freaky shit. Now he's in hiding. Won't even tell his mom where he's staying."

Light filled the tunnel. Lauren could hear the train scuttling closer.

"Don't take that job, yo. You be sorry."

"Yeah? Says who?"

"Just a friend."

The train blasted into the station, sending the trash on the platform swirling around Lauren's feet. The doors opened and she leapt inside, willing them to close again. The guy stood on the platform, shoulders hunched, hands in his pockets.

"I got a name for you to remember: Sabrina Rodriquez. She used to be one of theirs. When the cops found her body, there wasn't a single drop of blood left in it."

The doors closed with a loud ding-dong that made Lauren jump, and then the train hurtled into the darkness.

Three

ON MONDAY AT two o'clock, Lauren showed up for her first day at Angelus House. The buzzer let her in, and inside, a girl with a purple-blue Mohawk and heavy eyeliner greeted her. She smelled strongly of patchouli and looked to be about Lauren's age or a little older. She wore a sleeveless sundress, which showed off her many tattoos, including one on her neck of the Angelus House insignia.

The Mohawk girl beamed. "Hey, you must be Lauren. Awesome! Welcome to Angelus House. I'm Alex. God! Isn't it miserably hot out? We've got the AC cranked."

Alex wore an ankle bracelet heavy with charms that tinkled like bells with every step. "We're, like, soooo crazy happy you're here. Seriously? I cannot keep up with the filing and phones and stuff. Don't get me wrong—it's all because Angelus House is a successful program, and that is totally cool. But still. There's only so much we can do without help. Hey Rakim! Come meet Lauren!"

A tall, skinny guy with an old-school fade and oversized black-frame glasses bounded up, his hand out for a shake. "Nice to meet you, Lauren." He made up a silly song about her name on the spot, rhyming Lauren with Darwin, Sauron, and Kilimanjaro-n, and Lauren found herself hoping that this was the start of something new and good.

They showed her around, introducing her to more smiling teens working on posters or playing ping-pong in the rec room. The first floor had been turned into "sharing" rooms and common areas. The second and third floors housed a dormitory that could take as many as thirty teens at a time. The staff lived on the top floor. On the surface, Angelus House was like every other drug rehab center she'd visited in the past three years. There were the ratty, secondhand couches and chairs grouped around a wall-mounted TV. Here were the requisite inspirational posters sharing space with cheaply framed photos of rehabbed teens doing inspirational activities—a dance-off, arts & crafts day, basketball, quilt-making. Captions had been supplied: "Brian shows us his moves!" "Grace for two, nothing but net!" "Amber and Gabby love DDR night!" "Sing it, Rakim!"

"You know I make that picture look good," Rakim said with mock seriousness.

Alex punched him in the arm. "Modest much?"

"Looks fun," Lauren offered. She was never very good at small talk.

They showed her the kitchen area with its chipped cupboards and an old refrigerator marked by a laminated "Newbies" sign. "You'll need to keep this stocked with healthy foods for the new teens who come in. Juice is great because a lot of the addicts crave sweets. The rest of us can take care of ourselves, so it's just this one fridge you have to worry about," Rakim said, showing off the inside of the fridge with its three juice cartons.

"Sorry. I know it's kinda disgusting in here," Alex said, making a face. "But once we take over the Navy Yards to do some new building, we're gonna have, like, crazy amazing new facilities—almost a mini-city."

"And then we can kiss this shit goodbye," Rakim said.

"Is Johannes here?" Lauren asked as they made their way down another long corridor turned faintly green by the bad florescent lighting. She'd looked for the golden one on every stop of the tour but hadn't seen him.

"Usually he does a lot of field work," Rakim answered. "Going into the projects and out on the streets. He helped save my ass for real."

"And he is such the hotness," Alex said, giggling as if she and Lauren were sharing their first girl secret. "Oops, not that way." She steered Lauren away from a set of stairs leading down into complete darkness.

"What's down there?"

"Detox," Alex said, grimacing. "Not pretty. Don't worry, though. You don't have to deal with that."

"Don't get freaked out if you hear weird noises and shit coming from there. Just turn up the radio and learn to block it out," Rakim said. "You get used to it after a while."

Lauren stared down into the darkness. She heard nothing but the asthmatic hum of the overburdened air-conditioning. "What happened to the last girl who worked here—Sabrina?"

Alex looked confused. "We've had a Lisa and now we've got a Lauren. No Sabrina. Besides, you're the first assistant we've ever had."

"And not a minute too soon, 'cause I cannot file another thing," Rakim said, palms up in surrender. "I just remembered: We've got kick-ass brownies in one of the sharing rooms. You like brownies?"

Alex offered her arm and Lauren took hold.

"Who doesn't?" she said.

. . .

Lauren worked at Angelus House Monday through Friday from three o'clock until eight. The job was fairly easy, she discovered. As none of the teens were allowed off the grounds and the staff was needed to look after the place, Lauren was often sent outside to do the grocery shopping or pick up medical supplies. There was plenty of time to read. And everybody made her feel like she was wanted, like she was contributing to something important. No one was really around to miss her at home, anyway. Since her sister Carla had been court-ordered to the Eagle Feather Center for Hope and Healing, her parents made the drive upstate every weekend for visiting hours. Sunday nights, they'd come back looking gray, their words of parental encouragement scooped out of them. The TV was on a lot.

Lauren was glad to have somewhere to be with people who might possibly become friends—or more. And there was Johannes. Whenever he swept through, the air in the room felt different to Lauren, charged with possibility. She watched him—leaning one arm against the door frame, lean and long in a worn-thin Vampire Weekend T-shirt that showed the outline of muscle across his broad back, his deep-set eyes taking everything in, that lazy smile showing up along with a pair of dimples and a low growl of a laugh that did things to her stomach. She'd seen the way he was with the teens who came through the doors, how he calmed them, took in their stories, nodding. It was hard to believe he was only twenty-two. Sometimes he'd drop by her desk or pop into the long, musty filing room where she sat sorting through manila folders with badly-typed patient names on the tabs, putting them in alphabetical order.

"How's it going in here?"

"Fine," Lauren would answer, wishing she could think of something clever to say to keep him there.

"Got those supplies for me?"

She would hand over whatever she'd been asked to procure that day—boxes of gauze, economy-sized bottles of hydrogen peroxide, pine floor cleaner, rubber tubing, new sheets and towels.

Once, she'd had to make a run to the home improvement center for long, flat pieces of lumber, nails, and ten-pound bags of mulch. "Might want to do some retaining walls and some plantings in the parks. Good project for the newbies," Johannes had explained when she and the delivery guy had dropped it all in the freight elevator for Johannes and Rakim to take down to the basement.

Sometimes, Johannes would pop his head into the filing room and ask, "Need anything?"

Yes. I would like you to ravage me here on the floor and swear your undying love to me. "No. Thanks. I'm good."

"Keep up the good work," he'd say, and Lauren would creep to the door to watch him walk away, his beautiful ass perfectly showcased by his Levi's, as he took the stairs down to detox.

Four

FRIDAYS WERE RECYCLING day at home, and since no one else bothered to do it anymore, Lauren hauled the newspapers down to the recycling area behind their new rental with its view of traffic on Fourth Avenue. Their old apartment had windows that looked out onto Prospect Park, but that was before Carla's medical bills poured in, and they were forced to move down Park Slope into a fourth-floor walk-up in a building with a super who liked to chatter whenever he saw Lauren. She dropped the tightly-bundled papers, the blue bags of spent plastic and metal in the bins and wiped the sweat from her brow with her forearm. The super nodded to the day's paper with its two-inch headline:

Blood Gangs of New York.

"Another body," he said in his heavily French-inflected English. "That make ten so far. They find this one with her throat ripped out."

Lauren didn't want to get drawn in or she'd be late for work. "The police think it's some gang thing."

"In Haiti, the Tonton Macoute would come in the night like ghosts. If you spoke out, they would come. If you didn't, sometimes they still come. Everyone lived in fear then. They would come and come until our spirits were silenced and we all felt dead."

A loud blast came from Fourth Avenue, and two cabbies cursed each other until a full-scale fight broke out.

"Crazy people," the super said, dropping the lid on the recycling bin.

When she slipped back into the apartment, the TV was on with the sound muted. Lauren saw garish images of kneeling prisoners in orange jumpsuits, black hoods covering their faces. Lauren's mom sat in her chair by the window unit wearing her reading glasses as she sorted through a stack of mail that Lauren knew were bills. Her dad was at work. He would stay in the safe bubble of his office, with its office jokes, water cooler, kitchen coffee pot, and shared stories about the "putz" boss, until he was forced to come home.

"I'm off to work, Mom," Lauren said.

A minute later, as she was closing the door, her mother answered. "Okay. Be careful."

The day passed slowly. By six o'clock, Lauren had accomplished her to-do list and finished the last forty pages of her book, so she loitered in the hallway outside the sharing room where people did their 12-step work. The voices inside were hushed murmurs. A big guy named Brian stepped out. He had a shaved head that had been tattooed with intricate designs and smack in the middle was the Angelus House insignia. He headed to the men's room without noticing Lauren. A snippet of confession drifted through the cracked door.

"...it was just the most incredible feeling, and I like feeling powerful now, not like before..."

"...I'm gettin' my mark at the end of the week..."

"...that's awesome, bro. Stick with the program. You won't be sorry..."

"...let's say the Angelus prayer. 'We are the fallen angels. We are the shadows in the night. We are the Alpha and the Omega...'"

Lauren pressed closer, trying to hear more. A hand pushed the door closed.

"Sorry. You're not supposed to listen in. Privacy and all that." Brian was back. He towered over her, smiling.

"Oh, I-I'm sorry. I was just...sorry."

"No problem." He gave her a dazzling smile before slipping inside and shutting the door tightly behind him.

Lauren wandered the halls staring at the photos of those smiling teens, wondering what made them succeed. "Everybody likes a winner," she whispered to the wall.

A long, chest-rattling moan of pain drifted up from the detox floor, and Lauren found herself taking the stairs down into the shadows, drawn to the sound. It was cooler as she descended and so dark she had to hold fast to the banister to be sure of her steps. She'd reached some sort of wide door, but it was locked. She put her ear to it, hearing nothing but the AC hum. And then came a piercing scream that prickled the hair on her neck and sent her stumbling back up the stairs toward the light. She sat at her desk with her headphones on, blasting her music until it was time to go.

Five

IT WAS THURSDAY night, just before the end of her shift, when the guy got inside.

Somebody had accidentally left the back door open, and now he was standing in the common area screaming obscenities, with a wild-eyed look and a knife in one hand.

"What did you do to me!" he shouted. His teeth were a mottled brown; angry sores dotted his face.

"Okay, take it easy, bro." Six-foot-two Brian tried to take him, but the guy smacked him hard, sending him reeling. The drugs made him fearless, and no one could get close.

"What did you do to me?" he screamed until the tendons of his neck bulged. "I can't sleep. I see things the way they really are. I know. I know!"

"Calm down. It's all right," another staffer said, extending her hand.

He jumped back and jabbed at the air with his knife. "You're out to get me!"

"They're out to get me, too," Lauren said suddenly. He noticed her for the first time.

"You know? You know what I'm talking about?"

She nodded and lowered her voice to a loud whisper. "We've got to get away. I've got a safe room. I'll take you there."

"Okay. Okay," he said.

Heart thumping, she led him to the filing room.

"The thirteenth step," he muttered. "I didn't finish it. Now I hurt so bad—worse than ever, and they're going to kill me." He showed her his arm where he'd scratched it to ribbons. Under the blood, she could just make out the ink of a tattoo.

"It's okay." Lauren opened the door to the filing room. She could hear the wail of sirens in the distance. "In here we'll be safe."

She let him go in ahead of her. Quickly, she locked the door behind him, the keys shaking in her hands. He screamed and flung himself against the door. Lauren jumped back.

"I'm not doing the thirteenth step! You hear me!" He bashed his head into the frosted-glass panel of the door once, twice. The sound of sirens grew closer. Lauren slid down the wall and placed her hands over her ears. The third time he bashed against the panel, a crack appeared in the glass like a flower stem dotted by petals of blood. Someone had gone for Johannes, and he was running down the hall toward her, beautiful and fast.

"You okay?" he asked, touching her shoulder.

"Sure," she said. Then the guy broke through the glass with his head and Lauren blacked out.

Six

AFTER THE PARAMEDICS left and Lauren had given a statement, Johannes insisted on taking her for something to eat. They settled on a hole-in-the-wall noodle shop called Lisa's Pieces where Lauren ordered a bowl of hot broth with noodles that felt slippery and good going down.

"You sure you're okay?" he asked for about the tenth time.

"Yeah. I'm okay. Who was that guy?"

"I heard he was in the program a long time ago, before I came in. Sometimes people go back out there—it's rare, but it happens." He reached over and rubbed her arm. "I heard you were amazing. How'd you think to do that?"

"You really want to know?"

"I asked, didn't I?"

She stared at her spoon. "My sister Carla used to get like that when she was tweaked out of her head. If she wasn't giddy and planning to become a famous movie star, she was paranoid and ready to take your head off."

"I'm sorry," he said so sincerely that Lauren blushed a bit. "This job must be hell for you."

"Sometimes. Sometimes it's cathartic, you know?"

He nodded slowly. "Yeah. I know. I killed my best friend, driving drunk when I was sixteen. There's not a day that goes by that I don't think about that. Not a day that goes by that I don't pray for forgiveness. But with each person we save, I get a little closer to it." He looked so sad and helpless then, and Lauren wanted to throw her arms around him, save him with a kiss. "I guess my penance became my calling."

Lauren felt a sudden twinge of envy that he seemed to know his place in the world. "I guess I haven't found my calling yet."

"Maybe your calling will find *you*." He smiled. "Maybe it's here at Angelus. Maybe you'll even run some missions with us. I know I'd love it if you stayed on."

He reached past the bowl of untouched fried noodles and took her hand in his. His fingers were long and swallowed hers easily.

"They found another one," the waiter said, and somebody turned up the TV mounted over the bar.

"The decapitated body of sixteen-year-old Shawna Lenore of the Farragut Houses was found down by the Navy Piers," the lacquered TV reporter said. "Police had no comment about whether this murder is related to a string of brutal killings that have terrified New York for the past several months, and which some are speculating could be part of an escalating gang war."

On the flickering TV screen, a crowd of angry residents shouted at police from the sidewalks in front of the Farragut Houses. "How come they don't do nothing to help us?" a lady holding a baby said to the camera, "They blaming us and we didn't have nothing to do with it. They just gonna let us die."

The report switched to one of the fancy restaurants a few

blocks away and a couple enjoying a meal at a table outside. "It's so scary. Makes us wonder whether we should move to the suburbs."

"Hey," Johannes whispered, stroking his thumb against Lauren's palm in a way that made her heart beat faster. "You want to get out of here?"

They walked along the water. Across the river, Manhattan had restructured itself for night as a fractured geometry of light. A homeless couple argued in the street: *"You made me do it!" "I didn't make you do nothing!" "You coulda stopped it." "It don't never stop."*

The woman fell on the pavement and started crying like a child.

"Should we do something?" Lauren asked.

"Nothing to be done," he answered and drew her into the velvet darkness of an alley. He backed her against the brick wall with a mural of two towers under the words "Never Forget," and then his mouth was on hers, sweet and warm and obliterating.

"Don't you touch me! Leave me alone—I never did nothing to you!" the homeless woman half-yelled, half-cried, but they were moving away now, out of sight and caring. Johannes leaned into her and pressed his body against hers. He tilted her head with one hand and sucked down the length of her taut neck until it was almost painful, but Lauren refused to cry out. She never wanted him to stop. Nothing else mattered but this. The sounds of the city—the shouts, the taunts, the threats, the distant cries—faded away, and when the police cars screamed past, red lights flashing a warning on their way to some new horror, Lauren didn't even flinch.

Seven

LAUREN'S FIRST MISSION with Angelus was on a Friday night, second week in August. She, Johannes, Rakim, Alex, and a few others headed down to Admiral's Row, a length of street marked by dilapidated row houses protected by an iron fence that did nothing to keep them from becoming shooting galleries. The houses were so decayed Lauren could smell the rot. Inside, it reeked of shit and piss and they had to step over the bodies of people half-dressed and barely conscious.

While the others fanned out trying to see if they could get anybody to come with them, Johannes leaned over a petite blonde girl in an NYU shirt. She looked like she'd been there for days. "Hey, what's your name?" he asked.

"Dana," the girl slurred, her eyelids fluttering.

"Listen, Dana. We're with Angelus House, and we can get you a bed for the night. Would you like that?"

She tried to grab for Johannes's crotch. "You got any glass? I'll do whatever you want for it."

Lauren imagined Carla like this, offering her body to anybody who could get her high for another hour or two. She wanted to kick the girl, not save her.

"Come on, Dana. We're taking you some place where you can get cleaned up," Johannes said evenly. "You guys get her in the van. I'm gonna see if I can save anyone else."

Alex and Rakim draped the girl's arms across their shoulders and stepped carefully over the shattered bottles and rusted syringes to where they had a van waiting.

"What was that?" Lauren asked, suddenly startled.

"What was what?" Alex asked.

"I heard screaming."

Alex craned her neck skyward. "Must've been the birds."

Lauren saw the birds outlined against the perpetual hazy glow of the New York night. They were enormous with what looked to be six-foot wing spans. That couldn't be right, she thought, as she watched them dive down and disappear into the dark behind the shadowed, broken houses.

"Holy shit. Did you see that?"

"Sorry. Kinda occupied with Dana here," Alex grunted as she and Rakim eased the girl into the back of the van.

"Those birds. They were huge!"

Rakim wiggled his eyebrows. "Must've been real New York pigeons then. Okay, we are good to go."

"Jesus Christ!" someone screamed in alarm, but Lauren couldn't be sure where it had come from and Rakim was gunning the motor.

"Kilimanjaro-n. It's time to move. You in or out?"

"In," she said. She slid the door closed and refused to look back.

"We'll take it from here," Rakim told her, once they'd returned to Angelus. He and Alex half-carried Dana down the stairs into the dark of detox and Lauren started a new file, putting it into Johannes's inbox for him to fill out later. Then she sat in the common area watching a vampire flick with the newbies and fell asleep. She woke two hours later to find herself alone on the couch feeling worried and more than a little annoyed that Johannes hadn't come for her.

"Forget this," she said, and took the stairs down to detox, pushing through the heavy door.

The hallway was mostly dark, but up ahead, where it curved left and right, she could see dim florescent lights flickering like strobes. There were no inspirational posters with pictures of smiling teens on these walls. It was grim as a Soviet-era apartment building. From behind the doors, she heard odd sounds—growls and gurgles, like animals eating. And something else—a constant buzzing machine whine that didn't match the sporadic popping of the overhead lights. It made her skin crawl. And then there was a loud, piercing shriek of agony that died into desperate cries. Lauren heard a rumbling noise coming closer. She stood trembling under the flickering lights too terrified to move. A shadow reached across the back wall, growing larger, then smaller, and then a pigtailed girl appeared, dancing to the music blaring from her headphones while pushing a mop and a big yellow bucket on wheels. The water was oddly dark, and the girl's gloved hands and apron were spattered with splotches.

"What are you doing here?" the girl asked in a thick New York accent that competed with the music blurting from her headphones. "You can't be here now. I gotta clean."

"Sorry," Lauren said, turning away from the shadows, the sounds, the girl, and the murky water in the bucket, running as fast as she could for the door. She ran smack into Johannes.

"Lauren? What are you doing? You're not supposed to go into detox." His face was grim, even a little angry.

"I... I was just looking for you."

"And I was up there looking for you." His smile relaxed her.

"I heard weird noises. And somebody screamed."

"That's why we tell you not to go there. Sometimes during withdrawal it can get really nasty. But I don't have to tell you that."

Lauren remembered going with Carla to the hospital that first time, how her sister fought and cursed, growled like an angry dog, spat and, yes, screamed. "I guess you're right."

Johannes kissed the top of her head and held her close. "Just looking out for you, babe. Besides," he licked her neck. "I require your assistance in other matters."

It had been a long time since Lauren had felt like someone was looking out for her, and she found herself grateful and hungry for the way Johannes took her hand in his long fingers and led her away from the shadows at the bottom of the stairs.

Eight

THE DRIVE TO Eagle Feather was pretty if you were on vacation, which Lauren wasn't, and so it was just trees and cows and more trees and three hours in the car with her parents saying nothing that mattered.

Carla had put on some weight since the last time they'd seen her, but she'd also taken up smoking, lighting one cigarette after the other during their visit. "Sometimes the patients exchange one addiction for another. We try to get them hooked on something healthier, like exercise or a hobby," the director, a small man with a wire-thin voice and very little hair told them. "But if there is a stop-gap addiction that is not as immediately detrimental, such as smoking or doughnuts, we allow it." Her parents ignored the smoking and made overly cheerful conversation about how good Carla looked and how much cooler it was upstate than it was in the city where everyone was just sweltering this summer. Lauren thought about the people at Angelus, about those kids who had nothing, who lived on the street or the projects, who'd overcome the worst possible scenarios to get clean and make something of themselves. And here was Carla—spoiled, entitled Carla, whose selfishness had driven them into a shitty rental and aged her parents by ten years. Carla, who couldn't get it together despite having everything. Lauren hated her for it.

"Can you bring me some new clothes next time?" Carla said when they were leaving. "All the candy around here is making my jeans tight."

"Of course," her mother said. "I'll get Lauren to help me pick something out."

"Great. Homeless Chic. Don't make me look like too much of a dork, okay Squirt?" Carla laughed. Lauren didn't.

Lauren slammed the car door hard. "Well, *that* was fun. What a fucking waste of time."

"Lauren! Watch your language," her mother said, catching

her eyes in the rearview mirror.

"Yeah, 'cause it's my language that's the problem here." She knew she should give it up—there was no point in having an argument—but she couldn't stop herself. "When are you going to get it? She's ruined everything. She's a loser, and she gets everything."

Lauren's mom blanched. "She's sick, honey."

"She's not sick. She's useless! This wouldn't happen at Angelus House."

"That's enough, Lauren," her father snapped.

Yeah, enough, Lauren thought. They didn't speak for the entire ride back to Brooklyn. The next day, she packed her clothes, her iPod, and some pictures, and moved into Angelus House.

Nine

THERE HAD BEEN a few brownouts due to the heat's demands on the city's ancient grid, and the mayor was telling everyone to cut back on their electricity. But inside Angelus House, the AC was working fine, keeping everything freezing cold. Now that Lauren was living there full time, she had to adjust to the chilliness of the place. No one else seemed to mind it, but Lauren found herself wearing a sweatshirt during the day and sleeping in flannels at night. There were other oddities. No one ever used the vending machine in the rec room. In fact, a fine layer of dust lay on the keys, and she realized that in her six weeks on the job, she'd never seen anyone come to refill it. Once, she hit the button for a package of M&Ms, and when she opened it, the candy was so old, the chocolates crumbled in her hand like pastel dirt. Only the fridge marked "Newbies" ever needed restocking. And sometimes, in the early hours of the morning, distant cries, shrieks, and moans cut through the stillness. The desperation of those sounds filled her with a dread she couldn't name, and so she pulled the pillow over her head, listening to her heartbeat until she managed to sleep and forget. And by noon, with everyone up and laughing, going about their work, offering hugs or back rubs or jokes, Lauren felt safe again. People looked out for each other here. Her family had imploded, but now she'd found a new family to take her in, and that was enough.

On a Friday, one week after Lauren had come to live at Angelus House, she found all the residents huddled together in one of the sharing rooms, speaking in hushed tones.

"...What was he doing out at that hour?"

"...He knew better than that..."

"...burned to a crisp..."

"What's going on?" Lauren asked.

Alex looked up, her face registering surprise. Her eyes were red and rimmed with tears. "It's Brian."

"Those bastards in the projects, they torched Brian," Rakim said, his nostrils flaring in anger. "He went in to help them, and they paid him back by setting him on fire."

Just then Johannes walked in. "If we get caught up in anger, we lose. Come on. Let's remember Brian as he'd want us to."

They formed a sharing circle, hands clasped. Lauren stood on the outside, watching. "We are the fallen angels," they intoned. "We are the shadows in the night. We are the Alpha and the Omega. Unto us is given this charge. Unto us will be the glory."

They hugged and comforted one another, especially the newbies who had come to see Brian as their protector.

"We remember and go on," Johannes said.

"Amen," the others answered.

Brian's death was front-page news. FALLEN ANGEL, the headline in the *Daily News* trumpeted, and there was a picture of Brian smiling out from under that shaved head full of tattoos. Everyone at the Farragut swore they'd had nothing to do with it, that nobody had even seen him around there and that it was all a setup by the cops or the real-estate developers or Angelus House itself. One anonymous source claimed that he'd seen Brian simply walk out into the daylight muttering "For the greater good," before bursting into flame.

They held a candlelight vigil for Brian that evening, marching from Angelus House through Vinegar Hill to the Navy Yards, where the mayor spoke and promised that those who were guilty would be brought to justice. The cops hit the city hard, taking people in for any and everything they could. After Brian's death, the tide of public opinion turned in favor of Angelus House taking over the empty warehouses along the waterfront.

"He sacrificed himself for us," Lauren overheard Rakim saying a few days later. He said it to Dana, who had cleaned up nicely and was attending meetings every day. "That's the

Angelus commitment. That's the extra step." He broke off when he saw Lauren. "Hey Lauren Sauron. You mind going for some groceries? I think the newbies need more juice."

"Sure."

He smiled, but something in his eyes made her uneasy, and she found herself wanting to escape the too-cold recycled air. "Hey, who's better than Kiliamanjaran?"

"Nobody," she said and went outside.

In the grocery cart, Lauren found an envelope with her name on it shoved under the bags she kept there. Inside was the day's paper with the headline: ANOTHER ONE BITES THE DUST. Lauren scanned the story. The body, drained of blood, had been discovered in a dumpster behind a Burger King in downtown Brooklyn, the head missing. Another victim in an escalating gang war. The victim's name was Isaiah Jones of the Farragut Houses.

Isaiah Jones.

A note had been scrawled at the bottom of the page: *I need to talk to you. You can find me today on the boardwalk at Coney, in front of Deno's. Tell nobody. A friend.*

That afternoon, Lauren pretended she had a dentist's appointment and biked down to Coney Island where she found the tagger on the boardwalk painting caricatures of tourists for extra cash. He looked up, shielding his eyes from the relentless sun. "Hey. What do you want—a drawing of you as Princess Leia or Barbarella? Personally, I think you would look hot as Wonder Woman."

"Sorry about your friend."

"Yeah," he said, gazing out at some point on the horizon. "Come on. Let's get outta this heat."

The tagger, whose name, she learned, was Antonio, sweet-talked an aquarium volunteer into letting them inside for free. They took refuge in the cool damp, wandering through the maze of watery exhibits full of exotic creatures, stopping in a secluded spot near the moray eel. Antonio leaned against the glass. The blue-gray light turned him ghostly pale.

"Remember I told you about my cousin, Sabrina? Right before she died, she called me up scared out of her mind and said she'd seen some weird shit going down at Angelus. Bad shit."

"Like what?"

He shook his head. "She wouldn't tell me over the phone. But she mailed me this postcard right before she disappeared." He pulled a card out of his back pocket. It was the Angelus House insignia. Across the front in a shaky script were the words *los vampiros*. "Two days later, she was dead. They killed her." Lauren started to object, and he held up a finger. "Wait. Just let me tell you about Isaiah now. Isaiah ran with a crew out of the Farragut. He liked to smoke, deal a little weed, nothing major, only he gets caught for a second time—he's eighteen now—and they give him a choice: Angelus House or time. So he joins up, does the program, but he doesn't take it serious. He's just going along till he can get out."

Lauren felt hate rising. "Nice."

"One night, he comes rolling back into the houses, smokes a blunt with his boys, and when he's all loose, he starts telling them how he got tapped for something big, something secret, like the damn Mafia. He told 'em that Angelus wasn't just a twelve-step program. They got a secret thirteenth step."

Lauren remembered the tweaker who'd broken in that night. He mentioned a thirteenth step, but he was out of his mind. "What do you mean?"

"Isaiah said once you were tapped, you got the mark to prove your commitment to Angelus House—the tattoo they all wear. Then you had twenty-four hours to prove yourself on a mission, and once you did that, you were untouchable. A bona fide immortal." He paused. "A vampire."

The eel bumped against the glass, startling Lauren. "This is, like, crazier than crazy," she said.

"Yeah? How do you explain what happened to that guy Brian?"

"The cops say somebody at the Farragut killed him."

"That crazy bastard burned up in the sun."

"You know this."

He shrugged. "I heard it."

"And that makes it automatically true."

"You want to hear this shit or not?"

She crossed her arms. "Whatever. You asked me down here."

"And you came," he offered. "Think about it: If you wanted to work up a crew of vampires without being noticed, where would you do it? You'd get the people no one wants to be bothered with, the lost causes who already got a craving they can't stop on their own so they're, like, ripe for whatever you throwing at 'em. And then you'd make up some bullshit turf war and blame it on a whole bunch of other people nobody wants to be bothered with, let them take the fall."

Lauren rolled her eyes. "Okay. Backing up. You said they had twenty-four hours after they got the mark to do a mission. What happens if they don't?"

He lowered his voice to a strained whisper. "It's like the worst withdrawal symptoms ever, and they never stop. You lose your mind."

And again Lauren thought of the man who'd bashed his head into the glass of the filing room door.

"So either you do what they want you to do, or they kill you one way or another," Antonio continued. "Isaiah said he saw it happen to this other cat, and that's why he was out of there the next morning without getting inked. That's why he went into hiding. But they got to him anyway. Just like Sabrina. And the worst part is, nobody knows. People are so blind they'll believe whatever they're told. Gang war." He spat. "My Puerto Rican ass."

The eel slithered along the bottom of the dark floor of the tank, back and forth. Lauren watched it searching for prey, and something hard and angry twisted in her guts. This guy and his bullshit theories was taking away the only good thing she'd had in three years.

"So let me get this straight. Some former drug dealer gets high and starts making up stories about vampires and you take it as gospel? You're such an idiot. He played you. He probably owed money to somebody. Listen, my sister used to tell me all kinds of crazy lies, and I believed her because I didn't want to know the truth. She's still pulling shit on my parents all the time. So excuse me if I'm all out of gullibility. Go play your games with somebody else."

She turned and threaded her way through a sea of yellow-shirted camp kids. Antonio ran after her. "Hold up. Just answer me this, okay? They hired you to run errands, right? *Because they needed somebody who could go out during the daylight hours for them.* Tell me—you ever go out during the day with your boyfriend?"

Lauren realized they had only gone out after dark. "He doesn't get off shift until nighttime."

Antonio nodded, a cruel smirk pulling at his lips. "Yeah. I'm sure that's it." He handed her his phone. "Here. Call him up. Tell him to come meet us out here at Coney in the nice warm sun. Hey, if he shows up, I will personally go to Nathan's and buy the hot dogs. Oh wait—he probably doesn't eat, either."

A sense of unease pricked at Lauren. She'd never once seen Johannes eat. Not Alex either. Not Rakim. Only the newbies. But that didn't mean anything, did it?

She shoved his phone at him. "I've got a better idea. Why don't you leave me alone?"

Lauren walked the long way to the train letting the sun bake into her skin. She watched the people bobbing in the gentle surf, the bright afternoon turning the sand into little prisms, and thought about what Antonio said. Vampires. That was completely insane. On the way to the train, Lauren texted Johannes. CN U MEET ME FOR PIZZA @ 4:00? She waited for his response. It never came.

Ten

THEY WERE CROSSING Atlantic Avenue on the way to the movie theater when Johannes nudged her with his elbow. "What's up? You're pretty quiet."

"It's nothing."

He stopped walking and turned her to face him. "Doesn't sound like nothing."

"It's just . . . you never texted me back."

"God. I'm so sorry, Lauren. We had this crazy long meeting with some suits today about the go-head with the building plans for the Navy Yards, and I couldn't get away. It was so boring I wanted to hang myself."

"Oh. Sure. Okay."

"That is not an okay face," he said, tilting her chin up so that she could look into those dark eyes.

Lauren forced herself to look away. "Okay. Um." She laughed uneasily. "This is so incredibly crazy that I sort of hate myself. But you remember that first night—the guy tagging the building? Well, he left me a note today."

Johannes's eyes widened. "What? Are you okay?"

"Yes. Totally fine, but I met up with him, which I know was stupid, but he's got this insane idea that you and everybody at

Angelus House are . . . vampires."

Johannes cocked one eyebrow in an amused fashion.

"Okay. Forget I said anything. Totally stupid."

"Um, you think? Maybe just a little bit?" He lost his grin. "What's creeping me out more is that he's been watching you. Especially with all the murders going on. I wish I knew who this guy was."

Lauren hesitated for a second, but Johannes's hand was rubbing her back, and she found she wanted his protection after all. "His name is Antonio Rodriguez. His cousin Sabrina was in your program for a while. He said she died."

Johannes's face darkened. "Antonio. I should have known."

"You know him?"

"Yeah. I do. He's always blamed us for the loss of Sabrina. She was a tough case, kind of like your sister. Hard to save."

Lauren flinched at the mention of Carla. "What happened?"

"Antonio happened. Sabrina was ninety days clean—she'd been through almost all her steps—and against our advice, Antonio signed her out. Two days later, they found her at the Farragut Houses. Heroin overdose."

"He told me she was drained of blood, like those others."

Johannes shook his head. "Heroin. If he'd let her complete the program, she might have made it." Johannes looked right into Lauren's eyes and she felt foolish, like a kid who'd been pranked. "Did you know he's obsessed with vampires? I mean obsessed. He visits all these sites on the Internet, chat rooms. Sick stuff. Sabrina said he was part of a crew that used to call themselves Los Vampiros, and they would freak people out by pretending to be the undead. It was a gang thing. To prove your loyalty, you had to do something pretty hardcore."

"How hardcore?"

"Like maybe kill somebody. I don't like this." He pulled her close and kissed her head. Lauren's felt shaky. She'd spent the afternoon talking to the guy without once realizing how dangerous he might be. "Lauren, please be careful. I don't know what Antonio's mixed up in these days, or how far his crazy obsession has gone. If you see him again, you should call the police. Or if you don't want to do that, you can call me. I promise to keep you safe." He kissed her long and slow. "You really want to go see that movie?" That easy grin was back, making Lauren sweat.

She shook her head.

"Me either," he said.

He took her back to Angelus House, leading her up to the top floors where the staff lived. She'd been up here very rarely as there wasn't much to see except dorm rooms, and all the action happened down in the common areas. Johannes stopped before one of the doors and pushed it open. "Come on in."

"This is your room?" Lauren wasn't sure why she asked except that it seemed so nondescript. There were no photos, no mementos, nothing except the Angelus House insignia poster, a chest of drawers, and a twin bed beside a small table with a banker's lamp.

"Do you trust me?" He took her face in his palms and looked into her eyes. "Because I need for you to trust me, and sometimes I feel like you don't."

"I do," Lauren whispered. "It's just—I've learned a lot about not trusting."

Lauren could feel tears welling up and suddenly, Johannes was kissing her, and she didn't care about anything else. He lay her down on the too-soft mattress, and she welcomed the weight of him as he nudged her thighs open with his own. She couldn't escape if she wanted to, and there was a sick little thrill in that kind of surrender.

"Is this okay?" Johannes whispered, planting small kisses down her neck.

"Yes," she moaned.

She kissed him hard, and he matched her intensity, gripping handfuls of her hair. He moved against her slowly but deliberately, and she arched to meet him.

"God. Lauren," he moaned. "You feel so good."

In one quick move, he yanked off his shirt exposing the Angelus tattoo in the center of his beautiful chest. Lauren reached out to touch it, and he sucked her fingers, making her shiver. He lay down beside Lauren and slid his fingers under the waistband of her cargo pants, moving down, touching her in a place that made her gasp.

"Yeah? You like that?" he purred, and Lauren could only gasp again. "I like making you feel good." His thumb made circles, and his mouth was on her neck, kissing, sucking hard. He nicked her with his teeth and she flinched. "Sorry," he said, his voice hoarse. "Sorry."

He buried his face in her hair, his thumb became more insistent, the pleasure building till Lauren's body shook and shuddered from the force of it.

"I love you," he whispered, and Lauren had never been happier.

Eleven

LAUREN WOKE TO an empty bed. It was late for her, around two in the afternoon. She showered and dressed and headed down to the common room where the TV weatherman promised a record high of one hundred and two with an absurd amount of humidity. Lauren groaned even though inside the Angelus House, it was dark and cool as the earth.

She plopped down next to Alex on the ratty old couch. "You want to go out for a walk or an ice cream?"

Alex grimaced. "Ugh. Too hot for me."

They ever go out in the daylight? She heard Antonio's voice in her head. But he was a thug and what he said was crazy; she would prove it. "Come on. I don't want to go by myself," Lauren said, tugging on Alex's limp arm. "Just five minutes."

"I can't leave," Alex insisted, sliding out of her grip. "I'm on duty."

"What could happen in five minutes?" Lauren taunted.

Alex's gaze was steely. "A lot."

Lauren got that same prickly feeling, but then Alex was smiling and nuzzling against her in that affectionate, hippie girl way. "I'm sorry, Lauren-a-manjaro. I wish I could go with you. Look, here's ten bucks. I'll take a cherry ice and get yourself whatever you want."

"Sure," Lauren said, staring at the tattoo on the back of Alex's neck.

On the way out, she found Dana sitting alone on the front steps, her face turned toward the sun. Rivulets of sweat ran down her neck. The heat was beastly.

"God. Aren't you dying out here?"

The girl shook her head. "I just wanted to soak it up while I can, you know?"

"I guess," Lauren said. She couldn't wait for the first cold snap to blow through.

"Tomorrow it will all be different," Dana said sadly.

"What's happening tomorrow?"

Dana lifted up her hair, showing off a brand-new tattoo on her left shoulder blade. It was still caked in dried blood. "Got the mark today. I'm fully committed to the program now. I'm ready."

"Right," Lauren said, her heartbeat quickening. "So you're ready for the thirteenth step."

"Exactly," she said smiling. "The first one's the hardest, but after that, it gets easier and easier. Anyway, I guess it's like they say—you have to be willing to commit."

"Dana—" Lauren started, but there was a scratching and then a pounding at the tinted window behind them.

"I think they're looking for me," the girl said. With a backward glance at the blazing sun, she went in.

...

Lauren didn't return with the ices. She spent the night in her old room at home. Her parents had gone to Eagle Feather, but the super let her in with his key, and she went to work right away researching vampire lore on the Internet, locking all the doors and windows, hanging garlic from them, hoping she was wrong. Johannes sent her a text at ten and another well after midnight—WHERE R U? and EVERYTHING OK?

CARLA TROUBLE, she texted back. SEE U MONDAY. She added x's and o's and willed herself not to cry.

When the first pink claw marks of dawn faded into a pale blue morning, Lauren headed out. She looked down to see the day's papers bundled in string. The front page showed a picture of Antonio. JUSTICE SERVED: ANGELUS HOUSE KILLER KILLED BY HIS OWN. Lauren ripped off the string and turned inside to the story. Antonio Rodriguez of the Farragut Houses had been found down by the Navy Yards with his chest torn open, his head ripped off, and every drop of his blood drained. An anonymous source claimed he was a member of the notorious Los Vampiros gang, rumored to be responsible for the city's spate of murders.

She ran for the subway.

Twelve

AT YORK, SHE got off and walked through the sleepy neighborhood up the cobblestone street to the top of the hill overlooking the Navy Yards. She let herself into Angelus House. It was eerily quiet, cool and dark as always with that slightly earthen smell she'd always attributed to the AC. Carefully and quickly, she made her way to the back, to the small hallway that housed the freight elevator. Rakim had said it was the only way down to the basement. It had a metal gate that had to be closed first. Lauren pushed the round B. It lit up, and then she was moving down into the bowels of the old hospital.

The doors opened onto utter darkness, and for a moment, Lauren thought about going upstairs to her desk and pretending there was no basement, no mysterious detox floor, nothing going on at all. She could file papers, read her book, buy juice for the newbies, and go on loving Johannes. But she had to know. She stepped out, letting the elevator doors close behind her, and then she was tiptoeing through the dark. Her knee banged against something hard, and she stifled a scream with her fist. Carefully, she reached down and felt. It was wood—a table? Too low. A bed frame? She wished she'd brought a flashlight. The damp earth odor was stronger here; it filled her nostrils and made her want to sneeze, but she didn't dare. Instead, she stood perfectly still, allowing her eyes to adjust. Soon, she could make out long, rectangular shapes in the dark that were oddly familiar. Coffins. Her breathing quickened as she remembered the lumber and mulch she'd hauled back from the home improvement center earlier in the summer. As gently as possible, she nudged aside the top to one of the coffins and squatted low, putting her face even with the opening. Her eyes started at the bottom, where she could make out the glint of Alex's ankle charm bracelet; her gaze traveled up to a moonlight-pale hand with impossibly long fingers topped by razor-sharp curved nails. She bit off the cry in her throat and half-stumbled back toward the freight elevator, which wouldn't come though she pressed the button furiously. She turned a corner, looking for a way out and found herself in another room of coffins, their new pine tops shining in the darkness, but at the far end, she could just make out a pair of double doors. Slowly, she inched her way through the room, her shaking breath the only sound among the sleeping undead. She didn't see the coffin until it was too late, and she flew over it, knocking into two others and sending their covers to the floor with a loud thunk. Gurgling animal noises filled the dark. And then one of the things burst up from the coffin. It was gray-white as the moon, long and barrel-chested with enormous, leathery wings, a mouthful of pointed teeth and yellow eyes that stared down at her in contempt. Then it threw back its head and shrieked in alarm, and Lauren was up and running. She burst through the doors into the flickering light of the detox floor. Behind her she could hear the thing screeching, awakening the others. She tried door after door trying to find one that would open. Down at the far end of the hall, she found a knob that turned, and she threw herself inside, locking the door.

"You're not supposed to be on this floor."

Lauren turned around slowly. Dana stood in the corner. Her mouth was a smear of bright red blood. Two long, serrated teeth poked down over her bottom lip. Pale, thin skeletons of wings had sprouted from her back, and her skin was the color of old bones. The bloodshot yellow of her eyes was interrupted by enormous pupils that were utterly without light, and Lauren could not stop staring at her, or at the mess of a body the thing that used to be Dana had left convulsing on the floor behind her, the jugular still spurting in a thinning stream.

"You can't be here," Dana said again, her voice more of a snarl now.

The door opened. She heard shouting. Human sounds. Something hit her hard, and then she fell into a merciful blackness.

Thirteen

SHE WOKE TO a high, whining, machine-like buzz and the sensation of pain. She was strapped to a table, and Rakim was bent over her left arm, the tattoo needle doing its work. Blood oozed from the miniscule holes he raised.

"Sorry, I didn't get a chance to ask you where you'd like it, so I went with the forearm. It's a classic." He wiped away her blood with gauze from the boxes she'd brought them every week.

From across the room, Johannes approached, so perfect and golden that it made her ache. He stroked her hair gently as she'd seen him do with the addicts, kissed her softly. "Lauren, it's okay. Just relax."

She squirmed anyway. "You killed Antonio."

"He brought it on himself. He should have left it alone."

"He wasn't very tasty, either," Rakim tutted. "I will be so glad when we run this town, and we don't have to dine out on its leftovers. Maybe I'll have me some nice Park Avenue socialite then. Hey, you should hold still if you don't want your mark to look all busted."

The pain was back in her arm. "I'll go with you for your first kill," Johannes promised sweetly. "It's not so bad. You'll see."

"You get used to it. And you feel totally amazing after." Alex stood framed in the doorway, smiling. "Before long, you don't care about what you're doing."

Rakim finished his work, wiping away the last of Lauren's blood with gauze. Her arm was sore and the Angelus insignia was black against the red of her skin. Johannes freed her from the table's restraints.

"You're free to go. You have twenty-four hours. If you don't make a kill, you'll get very, very sick. If you do choose to be one of us, you have to be back before sunrise. It's your choice."

Johannes's lips were on hers and she couldn't keep from kissing him back.

...

The night was hot; the sky was the oily black of old coffee. Lauren wandered the streets of Brooklyn in a haze, the humidity pressing down on her. She rode the F train all the way to Coney Island and back into the city. The bright white inside the train made her eyes burn and her head pound and she got off at Fourth Avenue. Above her, the vampires swarmed the skies shrieking. They were not birds; she knew that now. She was beginning to see and hear everything. Her ears picked up the smallest noises: rats scuttling in alleys, the sighs of discontented lovers, new life coming into the world on a tide of pain and blood, always blood. She passed by her apartment and listened to her parents breathing, could sense their worry. Outside the super's apartment, she felt his restlessness as he dreamed of his time with the Tonton Macoutes, his machete doing its grisly, silencing work. Everyone had something to hide.

She moved on, fighting the jittery need making itself known in her anxious heartbeat. The skin of her arm was puffy and tight beneath the new tattoo, and every part of her had begun to hurt, as if she could no longer be contained by the limits of her flesh. Bile churned in her gut; her blood, which pumped with a new ferocity, begged for satisfaction. She licked her lips and ran her tongue over the tiny nubs of fangs pushing through her upper gums, making her mouth tender and swollen. How long had it been since the tattoo? Twelve hours? Fifteen?

Here and there she saw the vampires, squatting on the burned-out shells of cars, climbing the fire escapes of the tenements, circling the bridges and the piers, crouched under the overpasses, yellow eyes flashing, tattered wings spread out, lips peeled back to show their bloody maws, bodies breaking in the grip of their unnaturally strong hands. One glanced at her and laughed.

. . .

It was an hour later than she had ever remembered knowing before. Sharp pain twisted round her muscles like squeezing vines. In the alley near the water where Johannes had kissed her so perfectly, Lauren fell onto the broken pavement in a cold sweat. She blinked. Her eyelids scratched. The homeless woman staggered up the street without her boyfriend this time. She sang a Stevie Wonder song off-key. As the woman moved closer, Lauren felt her body quickening, tensing, the nubs of her fangs descending. She shut her eyes tight and tried to hold very still.

"Hey."

Lauren opened her eyes to see the woman very near, so near that the scent of her blood beneath her skin was nearly unbearable. "Hey. You got some change you can spare? I'm hungry."

"Go away," Lauren rasped.

"You stupid little bitch."

"Go. Away," Lauren growled through gritted teeth.

"You think I like doing this? You think this is my idea of a good time?" The older woman spat on her and cursed until Lauren was forced to take refuge elsewhere. Lauren walked till she was numb, making her way through Red Hook, toward the water, to wait for the sun. At Lorraine Street, the blue of the pool tantalized her. She thought about going in for a last swim, about letting her lungs fill with water and ending it, but when she came around the corner, there was the girl sitting alone on the wall outside the recreation center in her day-camp shirt. It was close to dawn, maybe five-thirty. The sun would be up soon.

"What are you doing out here?" Lauren asked.

"Waiting for my aunt. She went to get me donuts."

"Donuts are good."

"I like the ones with the powdered sugar."

The girl smelled like powdered sugar to Lauren. Like something sweet and perfect. Lauren doubled over and wrapped her arms around herself.

The girl looked at her strangely. "You sick?"

"Yeah, sweetie," Lauren choked out. "You should stay back. I'm real sick."

The child was scared now. Lauren could smell the fear mixing in her blood, and Lauren wanted to tell her to get ready because the whole world was sick, as diseased as she felt inside. But this girl with the large eyes didn't know that yet. It was waiting for her, like a spoiled donut gone to maggots. And then, as Lauren's body shook with new agony, she realized the girl didn't have to know.

Lauren would save her.

Fourteen

LAUREN STOOD ON the old cobblestone street taking in the view of the yawning mouth of the city, its steel and stone teeth ready to devour the morning sky. Already, signs of dawn showed. At the top of the hill, Angelus House loomed. Someone had left the front light burning, and Lauren she made her way toward it now with slow, sure steps, adjusting to the tangy iron taste in her throat. She'd only vomited once at the beginning, but the girl was small and too weak to get away, and Lauren had held her with surprising strength. The girl's blood had tasted sweet and sugary and slightly creamy, as if she might have had a quick cup of milk that morning before leaving the house. It had been fairly quick, all in all. Her only mistake was looking into the girl's eyes and seeing her face mirrored there. She would not make that mistake next time.

She passed by her old desk. They'd have to find a new assistant, of course. A note had been left on her chair—*We're in the sharing room*. She found them standing in a circle, hands joined, waiting for her.

"We are the fallen angels," they intoned. "We are the shadows in the night."

Johannes held out his arm to welcome her into the circle, and she took her place, mouthing along with them, her whispers growing stronger, her words gaining power and conviction until her voice could not be distinguished from anyone else's.

All Hallows

BY RACHEL CAINE

DATING THE UNDEAD is a bad idea. Everybody in Morganville knows that—everybody breathing, that is.

Everybody but me, apparently. Eve Rosser, dater of the undead, dumb-ass breaker of rules. Yeah, I'm a rebel. But rebel or not, I froze, because that was what you did when a vampire looked at you with those scary red eyes, even if the vampire was your hunky best guy, Michael Glass.

None of them were fluffy bunnies at the best of times, but you really did *not* want to cross them when they were angry. It was like the Incredible Hulk, times infinity. And even though my sweet Michael had only been a vampire for a few months, that just made it worse; he hadn't had time to get used to his impulses, and I wasn't sure, right at this second, that he could control himself. Controlling *my*self seemed like the least I could do.

"Hey," I breathed, and slowly stepped back from him. I spread my hands out in obvious surrender. "Michael, stop."

He closed those awful, scary eyes and went very, very still. Eyes closed, he looked much closer to the Michael I'd grown up around...tall, dreamy, with curling blonde hair in a surfer's careless mop around a face that made girls swoon, and not just when he was on stage playing guitar.

He still looked human. That made it worse, somehow.

I tried to decide whether or not I ought to totally back off, or stand my ground. I stayed, mainly because, well, I've been in love with him since I was fourteen. Too late to run now, just because of a little thing like him being technically, you know, *dead*.

I wasn't in any real danger, or at least, that was what I told myself. After all, I was standing in the warm, cozy living room of the Glass House, and my housemates were around, and Michael wasn't a monster.

Technically, maybe yes, but actually, no.

When Michael's eyes opened again, they were back to clear, quiet blue, just the way I loved them. He took another breath and scrubbed his face with both hands, like he was trying to wash something off. "I scared you," he said. "Sorry. Caught me by surprise."

I nodded, not really ready to talk again quite yet. When he held out his hand, though, I put mine in it. I was the one in the black nail polish, rice-powder makeup, and dyed-black hair; what with my fondness for goth style, you'd think that I'd have been the one to end up with the fangs. Michael was way too gorgeous, too *human* to end up with immortality on his hands.

It hurt, sometimes. Both ways.

"You need to eat something," I said, in that careful tone I found myself using when speaking about sucking blood. "There's some O neg in the fridge. I could warm it up."

He looked mortally embarrassed. "I don't want you to do that. I'll go to the clinic," he said. "Eve? I'm really sorry. Really. I didn't think I'd need anything for another day or so."

I could tell that he was sorry. The light in his eyes was pure, hot love, and if there was any hunger complicating all that, he kept it well hidden deep inside.

"Hey, it's like being diabetic, right? Something goes wrong with your blood, you gotta take care of that," I said. "It's not a problem. We can all wait until you get back."

He was already shaking his head. "No," he said. "I want you guys to go on to the party, I'll meet you there."

I touched his face gently, then kissed him. His lips were cool, cooler than most people's, but they warmed up under mine. Ectothermic, according to Claire, the resident, scholarly nerd girl in our screwed-up little frat house of four. One vampire, one goth, one nerd, and one wannabe vampire slayer. Yeah. Screwed up, ain't it? Especially living in Morganville, where the relationship between humans and vampires is sometimes like that between deer and deer hunters. Even when vampires weren't hunting us, they had that look, like they were wondering when open season might start.

Not Michael, though.

Not usually, anyway.

He kissed the back of my hand. "Save the first dance for me?" he asked.

"Like I could say no, when you give me that oh-baby look, you dog."

He smiled, and that was a pure Michael smile, the kind that laid girls out in the aisles when he played. "I can't look at you any other way," he said. "It's my Eve look."

I batted at his arm, which had zero effect. "Get moving, before you see my mean look."

"Scary."

"You bet it is. Go on."

He kissed me again, gently, and whispered, "I'm sorry," one more time before he was suddenly gone.

He left me standing in the middle of the living room of the Glass House, aka Screwed-Up Frat Central, wearing a skin-tight, shiny pleather catsuit, cat ears, and a whip. Not to mention some killer stiletto heels. Add the mask, and I made a super-hot Catwoman.

The costume might have been the reason for Michael's shiny eyes and out-of-control hunger, actually. I'd intended to push his buttons for Halloween...I just hadn't intended to push them quite that *hard*.

I heard footsteps on the stairs, and Shane's voice drifted down ahead of him. "Hey, have you seen my meat cleaver— *holy shit!*"

I turned. Shane was standing frozen on the stairs, wearing a lab coat smeared with fake blood and some gruesome-looking Leatherface mask, which he quickly stripped off in order to stare at me without any latex barriers. What I was wearing suddenly felt like way too little.

"Eve—jeez. Warn a guy, would you?" He shook his head,

jammed the mask back on, and came down the rest of the stairs. "That was *not* my fault."

"The leering? I think yes," I said. And secretly, that was pretty cool, although hey, it was Shane. Not like he was exactly the guy I was hoping to impress. "Totally your fault."

"It's a guy thing. We have reactions to women in tight leather with whips. It's sort of involuntary." He looked around. "Where's Michael?"

"He had to go," I said. "He'll meet us at the party." No reason to tell Shane, who still couldn't quite get over his anti-vamp upbringing, that Michael had gone to snag himself a bag of fresh plasma so he wouldn't be snacking on mine. "Seriously—do I look okay?"

"No," Shane said, and flopped down on the sofa. He put his heavy boots up on the coffee table, sending a paper plate with the dried remains of a chili dog close to the edge. I rescued it, gave him a dirty look, and dumped the plate in his lap. "Hey!"

"It's your chili dog. Clean it up."

"It's *your* turn to clean."

"The *house*. Not your *trash*, which you can walk your Leatherfaced-ass into the kitchen to throw away."

He batted his long, silky eyelashes at me. "Didn't I tell you that you look great?" Shane said. "You do."

"Oh, *please*. Chilidog. Trash. Now."

"Seriously. Michael's going to have to watch himself around you. And watch out for every other guy in the room, too."

"That's the idea," I said. "Hey, it was this or the Naughty

Nurse costume."

Shane sent me a miserable look. "Do you *have* to say things like that?"

"Guy reaction?"

"You think?" He held out his plate to me, looking so pitiful that I couldn't help but take it. "You just destroyed my ability to get off this couch."

I had to laugh. Shane teased, but he wasn't serious; the two of us never were, and never would be. He was thinking of someone else, and so was I.

I saw the change in his expression when we heard the sound of footsteps upstairs. He looked up and there was a kind of utter focus in him that made me smile. *Boy, you have got it bad,* I thought, but I was kind enough not to point it out. Yet.

Claire practically floated down the stairs. Our fourth roommate—our booky little nerd, small and fragile enough that she always looked like you could break her in half with a harsh word—looked even more ethereal than usual.

She was dressed as a fairy—a long, pale pink dress in layers of sheer stuff, glitter on her face, her hair streaked with blue and pink and green. Soft pink fairy wings. It made her look both younger than she really was, which was still a year younger than me and Shane, and yet, also older.

But maybe that was just the look in her eyes that got more mature with every day she spent in Morganville, working shoulder-to-shoulder with the vampires.

Claire paused on the steps, looking at Shane. Her mouth

fell open, ruining her ethereal fairy look. "Seriously? *Leatherface?* Oh God."

"You were expecting something out of *Pride & Prejudice?*" Shane shrugged and held up the mask. "You don't know me very well."

Claire shook her head, and then caught sight of my own outfit. Her eyes widened. "Holy—"

I sighed. "Don't say it. Shane already did."

"That's really—wow. Tight."

"Catsuit," I said. "Kind of the textbook definition of tight."

"Well, you look ... wow. I'd never have the guts." Claire wafted over in her layers of pink to sit next to Shane, who gallantly moved his Leatherface mask to make room.

"You look fabulous," he told her, and kissed her. "Oh, crap, now I've got glitter, right? Leatherface does not *do* glitter. It's not manly." Claire and I both rolled our eyes, right on cue. "Right. Small price to pay for the privilege of kissing such a beautiful girl, what was I thinking? Sorry."

Shane was an idiot, but he was a good idiot, mostly. He'd never hurt Claire intentionally, I knew that. I wondered, though, if *she* knew that, from the look of concern that flickered across her expression. "Do you like the costume? Really?"

He stopped goofing and stared right into her eyes. "I love it," he said, and he wasn't talking about the costume. "You look beautiful."

That erased some of the worry from her eyes. "It's not too, you know, little girl or something?"

I realized that she was comparing herself to my Catwoman suit. "It's Halloween, not *Hello, Slut*," I said. "You look fantastic, CB. Hot, but not obvious. Classy." I, on the other hand, was starting to think I looked like a little *too* obvious, and not at all classy. "So. Are we going, or are we going to waste our amazing fabulousness on this B-movie fool?"

"Hey, Leatherface is an American classic!" Shane objected. Claire and I both smacked him, then she took the right arm, I took the left. "No fair double teaming! Don't make me hit you with my rubber cleaver!"

"Speaking of double teaming, until Michael catches up to us, you're *both* our dates," I said. "Congratulations. You can be Hefner tonight, if you go throw on a bathrobe and slippers."

He stared at me, blinked, and then tossed the Leatherface mask over his shoulder as he bounced to his feet. "Awesome. Back in a minute," he said, and dashed upstairs. Claire and I exchanged a look of perfect understanding.

"They're just so *easy*," I sighed.

• • •

It was the one-year anniversary of the Worst Halloween Ever, aka The Dead Girls' Dance party at Epsilon Epsilon Kappa's frat house on campus. And they were throwing it again, although this time it was a rave at one of the abandoned warehouses near the center of town. We'd gotten special invitations. I'd wanted to skip it at first, but Michael and Shane had both assured me that this time, things were under control. The vampires of Morganville were working security, which meant that the human frat boys wouldn't be slipping anything into anybody's drinks, and any would-be incoming trouble would be stopped cold, probably at the door.

Not that the EEK boys knew who (or what) they were hiring, of course. Students either didn't know, didn't want to know, or were in the know from the beginning, because they'd grown up in Morganville. I thought there were maybe six guys total in EEK who had insider knowledge, and none of them were stupid enough to talk.

Well, not too loudly. Unless the keg was open.

I parked my big, black sedan at the curb between a beaten-up pickup and a sun-faded Pontiac with so many bumper stickers on it I couldn't tell what their actual causes were. Guns, it looked like. And God. And maybe puppies.

"House rules," I said, and unlocked the doors. "Stay together. No wandering off. Shane, no fights."

"Aww," he said. "Not even one?"

"Are you kidding me? You've racked up enough medical frequent flyer miles to get a permanent bed in the emergency room. So no. Not even harsh words, unless somebody else throws the first punch."

He was happy about that last part. "No problem." Because somebody else *always* threw a punch in Shane's direction when trouble brewed. He had a rep, one that he'd worked hard to acquire, as a badass. He didn't look particularly badass tonight, wearing a moth-eaten old tapestry-patterned bathrobe fifty years out of date, old man slippers, silk pajamas that I *know* he must have found in a box in the attic, and a classic '50s pipe. Unlit, of course.

He made a surprisingly good Hefner, and as he offered us his elbows, I felt a rush of the giggles. Claire was blushing.

"I am *such* a stud," Shane said, and swept us into the rave.

As the resident dude, Shane was responsible for the acquisition of party favors, like glow-in-the-dark necklaces and drinks. Non-alcoholic drinks for Claire, however, because I am a stern house mother even if I suck as a role model. One thing I had to watch out for was the other kind of party favors being passed around, stranger to stranger—white pills, mostly, although there were the light-em-if-you-got-em kind, too. I let people pass things to me, then dumped them in the trash. It wasn't because I was Miss Self Restraint; it was more because I knew better than to trust most people in Morganville.

We'd had hard lessons about that last year. Especially Claire. This year, she was still polite, but fending off the weirdos with much more ease. Of course, having her own personal shaggy-haired Hefner at her side might have had something to do with that.

I started to worry about Michael. Usually, a side trip to the blood bank didn't take up more than thirty minutes, but by the time an hour had passed, he still wasn't in the house.

I went in search of a quiet corner to call him. My mistake was that I didn't tell Shane or Claire, who had their arms wrapped around each other and were dancing their hearts out.

No, I struck out on my own.

Hear that sound? It's Eve Rosser and her backup band, The Spectacular Lapse of Judgment.

The warehouse was loud, tinny, and crowded; dark spaces were already filled with the make-out brigade. I kept going, down a narrow little hallway, until the noise was only a thud, not a roar, and took out my phone from its hiding place (yes, in my costume, and I'm not telling you where). I started to dial Michael's phone.

Something touched my shoulder. It felt like an ice-cold electric shock.

"Hey!" I yelped, and whirled around. There was a vampire facing me.

Not Michael.

My heart rate went from sixty to five hundred in two seconds flat, because I knew this guy, and he wasn't exactly Mr. Congeniality. "Mr. Ransom," I said, and carefully nodded. I knew him because he was one of Oliver's crew, but I'd rarely seen him, even at Common Grounds, the coffee shop where the vampires felt free to mingle with the humans according to strict ground rules. He avoided humans as much as possible, in fact.

"Eve," Mr. Ransom said. He was a tall, thin guy with straw-brittle hair and a kind of vague look in his eyes. Tonight, he was dressed in a black jacket, black shirt, black pants, all straight out of the Goodwill box. Nothing quite fit him.

Mr. Ransom owned the funeral parlor, although he didn't work there. He was kind of a vampire hermit. He didn't get out much.

"Sorry, I'm on the phone," I said. I waved the phone for evidence, pressed DIAL, and listened. *Come on, come on...*

He didn't pick up.

"He will not answer," Mr. Ransom said. "Michael."

I quietly folded the phone and stared at him. "Why? What's happened?"

"He has been delayed."

"And you came all this way to tell me? Um, thanks. Message received." I decided to try to tough it out and walked right past him.

He grabbed me again. I spun, meaning to smack him good (a super-bad move on my part), and he caught my hand effortlessly in his. Now I was face to face with a vampire I hardly knew, with my hand restrained, and the noise from the rave had kicked up again to metal-melting levels, which meant screaming would get me nowhere but hoarse, and dead.

"Let me go," I said as calmly as I could. "Now, please."

He raised pale eyebrows, staring right into my eyes. His were dark, like puddles of oil, full of shine but nothing else. It looked like he was searching for something to say. What he came up with was, "Do you want to become a vampire?"

"Do I—what? No! Hell no!" I yanked, but I couldn't break his grip. "And even if I did, it wouldn't be *you* doing it, Mister Creepy!"

"Then do you wish Protection?" he asked, and reached into his jacket. He took out a bracelet, standard Morganville issue— a plain silver thing with a symbol engraved on the front of it.

Mr. Ransom's symbol, I guessed, which would mark me as his property. If I took the bracelet, I'd be free from casual fanging by all the other bloodsuckers, but not from him, if he took a notion.

I made a throwing-up sound. "No. *Let go,* you ice-cold moron freak!"

He did let go. It surprised me so much that I scrambled backward, tottering on my high heels, and bounced into the wall behind me. *Great,* I thought. *The one time I don't wear vampire-killing accessories.* Maybe I could use the shoes? No, wait, that would mean bending over in the catsuit. Really not possible. I settled for sliding against the wall, heading for the safety of the crowds.

Ransom slowly sank down to a crouch, his back to the wall, and put his head in his hands. It was so surprising that I stopped moving away and just stared at him. He looked... sad. And dejected.

"Ah—" I wet my lips. "Are you okay?" What a *stupid* question! And why did I even care? I didn't. I couldn't care less about his bruised feelings.

But I wasn't leaving, either.

"Yes," he said. His voice was soft and muffled. "I apologize. This is...difficult. Moving among humans in this way. I thought you wished to be turned."

"Why?"

He raised his head and mutely indicated his face, then mine, which was made up very pale under my Catwoman mask. "You seem to be playing at being one of us."

"Okay, first, I'm *goth,* not a vampire wannabe. Second, it's a fashion thing, okay? So, no. I don't. Ewwww." My pulse was slowing down some as I realized that maybe I'd read the situation all wrong after all. Mr. Ransom was a refreshing change from the vampires that tried to eat me first, talk later. "Why offer me Protection?" That was the equivalent of becoming part of a vampire's household. He would have to provide certain things, like food and shelter, and in return, the human paid part of their income to him, like a tax. Also, at the blood bank, their donations would be earmarked for him.

In short: ugh. Not for me.

"You don't have a bracelet," he said. "I thought perhaps your Protector had died in the late unpleasantness. I was being polite. In my day—"

"Well, it isn't your day," I snapped. "And I'm not shopping for a vamp daddy, so just…leave me alone. Okay?"

"Okay," he said. He still looked dejected, like some shabby street person whose bottle of booze had run out.

I thought of something less uncomfortable to ask. At least, I thought it was. "You said Michael had been delayed," I said. "Where? At the blood bank?"

"Near there," Ransom said. "He was taken away."

I forgot all about Ransom and his weirdness. "Taken away where? How? Who took him?" I advanced on the vampire, and all of a sudden the leather catsuit didn't seem ridiculous at all. I was practically channeling the soul of a supervillain. "Hey! Answer me!"

Ransom looked up. "Five young men," he said. "Wearing

the jackets with the snake."

Five guys wearing Morganville High letter jackets. Jocks, probably. "Did he *want* to go?" I asked. Michael had never been part of the jock crowd, even in high school. This was just odd.

"At first, they wanted me to go," Ransom said. "I didn't understand why. Michael told them he would go with them instead, and told me to tell you that he would be delayed." Ransom gave a heavy sigh. "That I have done." In about half a heartbeat, he went from a sad little man crouched against the wall to a tall, dangerous vampire standing up and facing me. Never underestimate a vampire's ability to change moods. "Now I will leave."

I worked it out a second too late to stop him from going. I guess five jocks had been hassling this sad, weird vampire, and he hadn't even realized what they were doing because, like he said, he wasn't out in the human world that much. He hadn't realized the danger he was in—he literally hadn't.

Michael definitely had. That was why he'd stepped in, sent Ransom to find me, and gone off without a fight.

Saving somebody, as usual. Although I wondered why he hadn't just flattened the creeps outright. He *could* have. Any vampire could.

"Wait, can you tell me where exactly—" But I was talking to the empty hall because Ransom had already beat it. Anyway, my words were just about lost in the thunder of a new tune spinning at the rave on the other side of the bricks.

I hurried out of the hallway, back to the rave, and found Shane and Claire still so into each other they might as well have been dancing at home. I dragged them out of the building, past impassive vampire bouncers, into the cool night air.

"Hey!" Shane protested, and settled his bathrobe more comfortably with a shake. "If you want to leave, all you have to do is say so! Respect the threads. Vintage."

"Michael may need help," I said, and I got their attention, immediately. "You want to come with?"

"I'm not exactly dressed for hand-to-hand," Shane said, "but what the hell. If I have to hit somebody, maybe they'll be too embarrassed to trade punches with Hugh Hefner—guy's got to be about a hundred years old or something."

I was more worried about Claire. Fairy wings and glitter weren't exactly going to intimidate anybody...but then again, Claire had other skills.

"You drive," I said to Shane, and tossed him the car keys. He fielded them with a blinding grin. "Don't get used to it, loser."

The grin faded just as quickly. "Where am I going?"

"Around the blood bank. Five Morganville High guys in letter jackets picked Michael up around there. I don't know why, or how, or why he went without a fight."

Shane's face went hard. "You think they lured him off?"

"I think Michael wants to help people. Just like his grandfather." Sam Glass had always put others ahead of his own safety, and I figured Michael was walking the same path. "It may be nothing, and hell, Michael can handle five drunk jocks, but—"

"But not if they've got a plan," Claire finished. "If they know how to disable him, they could hurt him."

Neither of them asked why a bunch of teens would want to hurt somebody they hardly knew; it was in teen DNA, and we all knew it, deep down. On Halloween, a bunch of drunk assholes might think it was fun and exciting to hurt a vampire. And then, as they sobered up, they might imagine that they'd be better off killing him than leaving him to identify them later. The Morganville powers-that-be didn't look favorably on vampire bashing.

"Maybe they needed his help," Claire said, but she didn't sound convinced.

We got into the huge black sedan without another word, and Shane peeled rubber.

• • •

"What do you think?" I asked aloud, as we started driving through the more unpleasant parts of Morganville. "Where should we start?"

"Depends on whether or not Michael's picking the place, or the jocks are," Shane said. His voice sounded low and harsh— Action Shane, not the one who arm-wrestled me for the remote control at home. "The jocks will go someplace they feel safe."

"Like?" Because I had no idea how jocks thought, in any sense.

Shane did. "Nobody at the football field this time of night. No games this evening." Because although Morganville paid lip service to other sports, like most Texas towns, football was where it was at. To know Michael was with five guys in letter jackets meant football was surely involved, if not at the center of things. "I'd say stadium. Maybe the press box or the field house."

I nodded. Shane took that as permission to hit warp speed. The engine roared as we shot down quiet streets, past derelict houses and empty businesses. Not a fantastic part of town these days. At the end of the street, he took a left, then a right, and we saw the columned expanse of Morganville High School at the crest of a very small hill. To the left and below was the stadium. It wasn't much, not compared to professional arenas, but it was a respectable size for a small Texas town. The lights were all off.

Shane piloted the car into the parking lot and killed the headlamps. There were a few cars parked here and there. Some had steamed-over windows—I knew what was going on in there. Kids. I wanted to run over, rap on the window and take a cell phone picture, but that would have been rude.

There was a cluster of vehicles, mostly battered pickups, at one end of the lot. The windows were clear. Claire pointed wordlessly over my shoulder at them, and we all nodded.

"What's the plan?" Shane asked me. I looked at Claire, but she didn't seem to be Plan Girl tonight. Maybe it was the fairy glitter.

"I'm the one with the stealthy outfit," I said. "I'm going to go take a look. I'll keep my phone on, you guys listen in and come running if I get into it, okay?"

Shane raised eyebrows. "That's stealthy? That outfit?"

"In terms of being black, yes. Shut up."

"Whatever, Miss Kitty," he said. "Call me."

I dialed his number, he answered it and put it on speaker. I slipped out of the car, wondering how anybody could scramble over rooftops dressed like this. Once I was in the shadows, I felt more at home. Nobody around that I could see, and as I did my best to creep along without being spotted, I felt more and more foolish. There was nobody here. I was skulking without any reason.

I heard voices. Male voices. They were coming from the field house, which contained the changing rooms for the teams, the gym, the showers, that kind of stuff. One of the windows was open to catch the cool night air. This was probably how they'd gotten into the building in the first place.

I sprinted—as much of a sprint as I could manage in the heels—across the open ground to the shadows on the side of the field house, and slid down the wall toward the window. "Shane," I whispered into the phone. "Shane, they're in the field house."

I heard a screech of tires in the parking lot and retreated to look around the corner. On either side of my big, black sedan, two pickup trucks had pulled in, parking so close that there was no way Shane or Claire could open the doors, much less get out. Another truck parked behind them.

They were trapped in the car.

"Shane?" I whispered into the phone. I could hear the drunk jocks high-fiving and booyahing each other in the trucks from here. A couple rolled out of the back and began to jump around on the hood of my car, rocking it on its springs.

"Well, the good news is you drive a damn tank," he said, but

I heard the tension in his voice.

"Can you get out of there?" I asked.

"Sure," he said, much more calmly than I would have. "But I think the longer we let them play on the bouncy castle, the fewer of these guys you've got to deal with on your end." He paused. "Bad news, I can't back you up in person if I do that."

I swallowed hard and went back to my original position on the side of the field house. "Stay put," I said. "I'll yell if I get in trouble. Rescue is more important than moral support."

If he answered, I didn't hear him, because just then a big, beefy guy rounded the corner of the field house carrying a case of beer. He dropped it with a noisy crash of glass at the sight of me.

Shane had been right. The costume was not stealthy.

. . .

"Look what I found prowling around," my jock captor announced, and shoved me into the doorway of the field house. My heels skidded on the tile floor, and I lost my balance and fell . . . into Michael's arms.

"Oh," I breathed, and for a second, even given the circumstances, being in his arms felt wonderful. He held me close, then pushed me away from him.

"What the hell are you doing here?" he asked.

"Saving you?"

"Awesome job so far."

"Fine, criticize . . . hey!" Beefy Jock Guy, who'd dumped the case of empty beer bottles outside, had plucked the phone from my hand, peered at the screen, and shut it off.

He looked tempted to do the macho phone-breaky thing, so I snapped, "Don't even *think* about hurting my phone, you jack-ass." He shrugged and pitched it into the far corner of the room.

"She's cute," the jock said to Michael. "Bet she likes to party, right?"

I ignored him, and looked around to see what I'd gotten myself into. Not good. Mr. Ransom's assessment had been right. Big guys, all wearing Morganville jock jackets. The smallest of them was twice the size of Michael, and my boyfriend wasn't exactly tiny.

I still couldn't figure out what Michael was doing here, though. He was just standing there, and he could have wiped the room with these guys, right? But he hadn't.

"What's going on?" I asked. Michael slowly shook his head. "Michael?"

"You need to go," he told me. "Please. This is something I need to do alone."

"What? Kick jock ass? Shane is going to be very disappointed." Looking into Michael's eyes, I saw the red starting to surface. I blinked. "Did you, ah, snack?"

"No," he said. "I was on my way in when they tried to take Ransom off with them."

"And you just *had* to get in the middle of that."

Michael's eyes were turning an unsettling color, almost a purple, as the red swirled around. It was pretty. From a distance.

"Yes," he said. "I kind of did. See, they wanted Ransom to come bite somebody."

My own eyes widened. "Who?"

For the answer, Michael turned, and I saw a frail young girl sitting on a bench at the back of the room, dressed in a cheap-looking Cleopatra costume. I recognized her after a long couple of seconds. "Miranda?" Miranda was sort of a friend, in that uncomfortable not-quite way. She was about ninety pounds of pure crazy, fragile as glass, and I knew from personal experience that sometimes she could see the future. Sometimes. Sometimes she was just plain nuts.

She'd been under Protection by a vampire named Charles, until recently. I didn't know for sure, but I strongly suspected that Charles had gotten more than just blood out of the kid. I was glad he was dead, and I hoped it had hurt. Miranda didn't need more screwed-up sprinkles on top of her utterly boned life.

"Mir?" I stepped back from Michael and walked over to her. She was very quiet, and unlike most other times I'd seen her, she wasn't bruised, or shaking, or otherwise in distress. "Hey. Remember me?"

She gave me an irritated look. "Of course. You're Eve." Wow. She sounded completely normal. That was new. "You're not supposed to be here." What, according to her visions?

"Well, I am here," I said. "What's going on?"

"They were supposed to find me a vampire," Miranda said, as if it was the most obvious thing in the world. I looked around at the jocks, an entire backfield of muscle, with blank curiosity.

"Why them?" And why, more importantly, would they be willing to do a favor for a kid like Miranda?

She knew what I was thinking, I saw it in the weird smile she flashed. "Because they owe me favors," she said. "I've been making them money."

Oh God, I could see it now. Morganville had a small, but thriving, betting underworld. What better to put your money on in a Texas town than football? The jocks had used Miranda's clairvoyant abilities to pick winners, they'd cleaned up, and now she was asking them to pay her price.

A vampire? That was her price? Even for Mir, that was just plain weird.

"Why Michael?" I asked, more slowly. Miranda frowned.

"I didn't ask for Michael," she said. "He just came. But it doesn't matter who it is. I just need to be turned."

I refused to repeat that because it would taste nasty in my mouth. "Mir. What are you talking about?"

"I need to be a vampire," she said, "and I want one of them to make it happen. Michael will do fine. I don't care who turns me. The important thing is that if I change, I'll be a princess."

I was wrong. She really *was* crazy.

For about fifty years in Morganville, none of the vampires had been able to create new ones—except Amelie, who'd turned Michael to save his life. Now...well. Things had changed, humans had more rights, and the rules weren't so clear anymore. Why did people want to be vampires? I didn't see the appeal.

Miranda obviously did. And she was going about it in a

typically sideways Miranda-ish way. *With my boyfriend.*

I wheeled on Michael. "Why didn't you just say no?"

He glanced over at the football guys. The defensive line was between us and the door, kicked back with a new case of beer but still looking like they'd love the chance to do a little vamp hand-to-hand.

Idiots. He'd absolutely destroy them.

"I was trying to," he said. "She isn't listening. I didn't want to hurt anybody, and I couldn't walk away and leave her like this. She needs to understand that what she's asking...isn't possible."

"I *know* what I'm asking," Miranda said. "Everybody thinks I'm stupid because I'm just a kid, but I'm not. I need to be a vampire. Charles promised me I'd be one." That last line came out like the petulant cry of a first grader who'd had her crayons taken away. I was willing to bet her vampire Protector (in name only—more like vampire Predator) had promised her a lot of things to get what he wanted. It made me feel even more sick.

"Mir, you're what, fifteen? There are rules about this kind of thing. Michael *can't* do it, even if he wanted to. No vamps under the age of eighteen. Town rules. You *know* that."

Miranda's chin set into a stubborn square. She would have done well in Claire's fairy costume. Fairies, as Claire had explained to me in the car, weren't kindly little sprites at all. Right now, Miranda looked like a fey come straight from the old scary stories.

"I don't care," she said. "Somebody's going to do it. I'm going to make sure they do. My *friends* will make sure."

"Miranda, they can't make me do anything," Michael said, and it sounded like an old argument already. "The only reason I haven't blown out of here already is because of you."

"Because I'm so screwed up?" Miranda's voice was dark and bitter. As she moved, I saw scars on her forearms, marching in railroad tracks up toward her elbow. She was a cutter. I wasn't surprised. "Because I'm so *pathetic*?"

"No, because you're a kid, and I'm not leaving you here. Not with them." Michael didn't even look at the jocks, but they got the point. I saw their beery good humor start to evaporate. Some set down bottles. "You think they're doing this because they like you, Mir? What do you think they want out of it?"

For a second, she looked honestly surprised, and then she slipped her armor back on. "They got what they wanted already," she said. "They got their money."

"Yeah, drunk, bored football types are always fair like that," I said. "So tell me guys, was this going to be a party night? You and her?"

They didn't answer me. They weren't drunk enough to be quite that cold about it. One finally said, "She told us she'd make it worth our while if we got her a vampire."

"Well, she's fifteen. Her definition of *worth your while* is probably a whole lot different from yours, you asshole." Man, I was angry. Angry at Miranda, for getting herself and us into this. Angry at the boys. Angry at Michael, for not already walking away. Okay, I understood now why he hadn't. He'd already known he'd be throwing her to the wolves (and the bats) if he did.

I was angry at the world.

"We're leaving," I declared. I grabbed Miranda by a skinny, scabbed wrist and pulled her to her feet. Her Cleopatra head-dress slipped sideways, and she slapped her other hand up to hold it in place even as she decided to pull back from me. I didn't let her. I had pounds and muscle on her, and I wasn't about to let her stay here and throw her own vamptastic pity party, complete with dangerous clowns.

Up to that point, Miranda had been all talk, but I saw the look that came across her face and settled in her eyes when I grabbed onto her. Blank, yet focused. I knew that expression. It meant she was Seeing—as in, seeing the future, or at least something the rest of us couldn't see.

The hair shivered on the nape of my neck under my Catwoman cowl.

"It's too late," she said, in a numbed, dead sort of voice. I drew in my breath and looked at the door. "Oh dear."

The door slammed open, bowling over a couple of football players along the way, and *three* vampires stood there. One of them was the vague Mr. Ransom.

Another was a particularly unpleasant bit of work named Mr. Vargas, who had the looks of one of those silent film stars and the temperament of a rabid weasel. He'd always been one of the dregs of vampire society. Oliver kept him around, I didn't know why, but Vargas was one of those you had to watch for, even if you were legally off the menu. He was known to bite first, pay the fine later.

The last one, though, was the one who really scared me. Mr. Pennywell. Pennywell had come to town with Amelie's father, the scary Mr. Bishop, and he'd stuck around. I knew he'd sworn all those promises to Amelie, but I didn't believe for a second he really meant them. He was old. *Really* old. And he looked like some androgynous mannequin, with no emotion to him at all.

Pennywell's cold eyes looked around, dismissed the jocks, and focused in on three things:

Miranda, Michael, and me.

"The boys are yours," he said to Ransom and Vargas.

Vargas's teeth flashed in a white grin. "I've got a better idea," he said, and stepped aside, out of the door. "Run, *mijos*. Run while you can."

The jocks weren't stupid. They knew the odds had shifted. They were severely in trouble. Not one of them was willing to stand up for Miranda, or for us, and that didn't shock me at all. What shocked me was that they didn't take their beer with them when they broke for the door and stampeded out into the night.

Vargas watched them go, and counted it off. "Twenty yard line. Thirty. Forty. Ah, they've reached mid-field. Time for the opposing team to enter the game, I think."

He moved in a blur, gone. I resisted the urge to yell a warning to the football guys. It wouldn't do any good.

Pennywell said, "You, girl. I hear you want to be turned." He was looking at Miranda.

"No, she doesn't," I said, before my friend could say something idiotic. "Mir, let's get you home, okay?"

Faced with the alien chill that was Pennywell, even Miranda's great romantic love of dying had a moment of clarity. She gulped, and instead of pulling free from my grip, she put her hand in mine. "Okay," she said faintly. I wondered exactly what her vision had shown her. Nothing that she wanted to pursue, clearly. "Home's good."

"Not quite yet, I think," Pennywell said, and shut the door to the field house. "First, I think there is a tax to be paid. For my inconvenience, yes?"

"You can't feed on her," I said. "She's underage."

"And undernourished from the look of her. Not only that, I can smell the witch on her from here." He sniffed, long nose wrinkling, and his eyes sparked red. He focused on me. "You, however . . . you're of age. And fresh."

That drew a growl out of Michael. "Not happening."

Pennywell barely glanced his way. "A barking puppy. How charming. Don't make me kick you, puppy. I might break your teeth."

Michael wasn't one to be baited into an attack, not like Shane. He just got calmly in Pennywell's way, blocking the other vampire's access to me and Miranda.

Pennywell looked him over carefully, head to toe. "I'm not bending any of your precious rules," he said. "I won't bite the child. I won't even swive her."

Leaving aside what *that* meant (although I had a nasty suspicion), he wasn't exempting *me* from the whole biting thing. Or, come to think of it, from the other thing, either. His eyes had taken on a really unpleasant red cast—worse than Michael's ever got. It was like looking into the surface of the sun.

Miranda's hand tightened on mine. "You really need to go," she whispered.

"No kidding."

"Back this way."

Miranda pulled me to the side of the room. There, behind a blind corner, was the open window through which I'd originally heard the boys partying.

Pennywell knew his chance was slipping away. He sidestepped and lunged, and Michael twisted and caught him in midair. They'd already turned over twice, ripping at each other, before they hit the ground and rolled. I looked back, breathless, terrified for Michael. He was young, and Pennywell was playing for keeps.

On our way to the window, Miranda ducked and picked up something in the shadows. *My cell phone.* I grabbed it and flipped it open, speed-dialing Shane's number.

"Yo," he said. I could hear the jocks pounding on the car. "I hope you're insured."

"Now would be a good time for rescue," I said, and yanked open the window.

"Well, I can either ask real nice if they'll move the cars, or jump the curb. Which do you want?"

"You're kidding. I've got about ten seconds to live."

He stopped playing. "Which way?"

"South side of the building. There's three of us. Shane—"

"Coming," Shane said, and hung up. I heard the sudden roar of an engine out in the parking lot, and the surprised drunken yells of the jocks as they tumbled off the hood of my car.

I began to shimmy out the window, but an iron grip closed around my left ankle, holding me in place. I looked back to see Mr. Ransom, eyes shining silver.

"I was trying to bring you help," he said. "Did I do wrong?"

"You know, now's not really the time—" He didn't take the hint. Of course. I heard the approaching growl of the car engine. Shane was driving over the grass, tires shredding it on the way. I could hear other engines starting up—the football jocks. I wondered if they had any clue that half their team was doing broken-field running against a vampire right now. I hoped they had a good second string ready to play the next game.

Mr. Ransom wanted an answer. I took a deep breath and forced myself to calm down. "Asking *Pennywell* probably wasn't your best idea ever," I said. "But hey, good effort, okay? Now *let go* so I'm not the main course!"

"If you'd accepted my offer of Protection, you wouldn't have to worry," he pointed out, and turned his gaze on poor Miranda. Before he could blurt out his sales pitch to her—and quite possibly succeed—I backed out of the window, hustled her up, and neatly guided her out just as my big, black sedan slid to a stop three feet away. The back door popped open, and Claire, fairy wings all a-flutter, pulled Miranda inside. It was like a military operation, only with one hundred percent less camouflage.

Mr. Ransom looked wounded at my initiative, but he

shrugged and let me go. "Michael!" I yelled. He was down, blood on his face. Pennywell had the upper hand, and as Mr. Ransom turned away, he lunged for me.

Michael grabbed the vampire's knees and held on like a bulldog as Pennywell tried to get to me.

"Stake me!" I yelled to Shane, who rolled down the window and tossed me an iron spike.

A silver-coated iron railroad spike, that is. Shane had electroplated it himself, using a fishtank, a car battery, and some chemicals. As weapons went, it was heavy duty and multi-purpose. As Mr. Pennywell ripped himself loose from Michael's grasp, he turned right into me. I smacked him upside the head with the blunt end of the silver spike.

Where the silver touched, he burned. Pennywell howled, rolled, and scrambled away from me as I reversed my hold on the spike so the sharper end faced him. I released the catch on my whip with my left hand and unrolled it with a snap of my wrist.

"Wanna try again?" I asked, and gave him a full-toothed smile. "Nobody touches up my boyfriend, you jerk. *Or* tries to bite me."

He did one of those scary open-mouthed snarls, the kind that made him look all teeth and eyes. But I'd seen that movie. I glared right back. "Michael?" I asked. He rolled to his feet, wiping blood from his forehead with the sleeve of his shirt. Like me, he didn't take his eyes off Pennywell. "All in one piece?"

"Sure," he said, and cast a very quick glance at me. "Damn, Eve. *Hot.*"

"What? The whip?"

"You."

I felt a bubble of joy burst inside. "Out the window, you silver-tongued devil," I told Michael. "Shane's wasting gas." He was. He was revving the engine, apparently trying to bring a sense of drama to the occasion.

Michael didn't *you first* me, mainly because I had a big silver stake and I obviously wasn't afraid to use it. He slipped past me, only getting a little handsy, and was out the window and dropping lightly on the grass in about two seconds flat.

Leaving me facing Pennywell. All of a sudden, the stake didn't seem all that intimidating.

Mr. Ransom wandered in between the two of us, as if he'd just forgotten we were there. "Leave," he told me. "Hurry."

I quickly tossed my whip through the window, grabbed the frame with my free hand, and swung out into the cool night air. Michael grabbed me by the waist and set me down, light as a feather, safe in the circle of his arms. I squeaked and made sure to keep the silver stake far away from him. It had hurt Pennywell, and it'd hurt Michael a whole lot worse.

"I'll take it," Shane said. He shoved the spike back under the driver's seat. "Well? Are you two just going to make out or what?"

Not that we weren't tempted, but Michael hustled me into the car, slammed the door, and Shane hit the gas. We fishtailed in the grass for a few seconds, spinning tires, and then he got traction and the big car zoomed forward in a long arc around the field house, heading back toward the parking lot. Oncoming jocks dodged out of the way.

Pennywell showed up in our headlights about five seconds later, and he didn't move.

"Don't stop!" Michael said, and Shane threw him a harassed look in the rearview.

"Yeah, not my first night in Morganville," he said. "No shit." He pressed the accelerator instead. Pennywell dodged aside at the last minute, a matador with a bull, and when I looked back he was standing in the parking lot, watching us leave. I didn't blink, and I watched until he turned his back on us and went after someone else.

I didn't want to watch, after that.

We'd only gone about halfway home when Michael said, raggedly, "Stop the car."

"Not happening," Shane said. We were still in a not-great part of town, all too frequently used by unsavory characters, including vamps.

Michael just opened the door and threatened to bail. *That* made Shane hit the breaks, and the car shuddered and skidded to a stop under a streetlight. Michael stumbled away and put his hands flat on the brick of a boarded-up building. I could see him shuddering.

"Michael, get in the car!" I called. "Come on, it's not far! You can make it!"

"Can't." He stepped back, and I realized his eyes were that same scary hell-red as Pennywell's. "Too hungry. I'm running out of time." And so were we, because Pennywell could easily catch up to us, if he knew we'd stopped.

"We really don't have time for this," Shane said. "Michael, I'll drop you at the blood bank. Get in."

He shook his head. "I'll walk."

Oh, the hell he would. Not like this.

I got out of the car and stepped up to him. "Can you stop?" I asked him. He blinked. "If I tell you to stop, will you stop?"

"Eve—"

"Don't even start with all the angst. You need it; I have it. I just need to know you can stop."

His fangs came out, flipping down like a snake's, and for a second, I was sure this was a really, really bad idea. Then he said, "Yes. I can stop."

"You'd better."

"I—" He didn't seem to know what to say. I was afraid he'd think of something, something good, and I'd chicken right out.

"Just do it," I whispered. "Before I change my mind, okay?"

Shane was saying something, and it sounded like he wasn't a fan of my solution, but we were all out of time, and anyway it was too late. Michael took my wrist, and with one slice of his fangs, opened the vein. It didn't hurt, well not much, but it felt very weird at first. Then his lips closed softly over my skin, and I got the shivers all over, and it didn't feel weird at all. Not even the buzzing in my ears, or the waves of dizziness.

"Stop," I said, after I'd counted to twenty. And he did. Instantly. Without any question.

Michael covered the wound with his thumb and pressed.

His eyes faded back to blue, normal and real and human. He licked his lips, making sure every spot of blood was gone, and then said, "It'll stop bleeding in about a minute." Then, in a totally different tone, "I can't believe you did that."

"Why?" I felt a little weak at the knees, and I wasn't at all sure it was due to a sudden drop in blood pressure. "Why wouldn't I? With you?"

He put his arms around me and kissed me. That was a whole different kind of hunger, one I understood way better. Michael backed me up against the car and kissed me like it was the last night on earth, like the sun and stars would burn down before he'd let me go.

The only thing that slowed us down was Shane saying, very clearly, "I am driving off and leaving you here, I swear to God. You're embarrassing me."

Michael pulled back just enough that our lips were touching, but not pressed together, and sighed. There was so much in that sound, all his longing and his fear and his need and his frustration. "Sorry," he said.

I smiled. "For what?"

He was still holding his thumb over the wound on my wrist. "This," he said, and pressed just a little harder before letting go. It didn't bleed.

I purred lightly, and nipped at his mouth. "I'm Catwoman," I reminded him. "And it's just a scratch."

Michael opened the car door for me, and handed me in like a lady.

Like *his* lady.

He got in, shut the door, and slapped the back of Shane's seat. "Home, driver."

Shane sent him a one-fingered salute. Next to him, Claire gave me a completely nonethereal grin and snuggled in close to him as he drove.

Miranda said, dreamily, "One of us is going to be a vampire."

"One of us already is," I pointed out. Michael put his arm around me.

"Oh," she said, and sighed. "Right."

Except that Miranda never got a thing like that wrong.

Hey," Michael said, and squeezed my shoulders lightly. "Tomorrow's tomorrow. Okay?"

I agreed. "And tonight's tonight." I put Miranda and her wild prophesies out of mind. "And that's good enough for me."

Wet Teeth

BY CECIL CASTELLUCCI

WET TEETH.

That was always the part of biting someone that Miles
didn't like. Sometimes, skin got on the teeth, too, and when he
rolled his tongue around his incisors, it felt like little pieces
of gravel. Some of his kind would say that the skin is a delicacy.

Not Miles.

Miles only fed on the homeless, people that society didn't
care about, which is why he liked the park. There was a water
fountain by the entrance. He headed for it so that he could rinse
the neck flesh, stringy veins, and clotted blood out of his mouth.

That's when he saw her for the first time. She was sitting on
a bench under a lamppost, wearing a raincoat and a scarf that
covered her head in an old-fashioned way that felt so familiar to
him. She had rhinestone-encrusted cat-eye glasses on and she
was looking up, maybe at the stars, maybe at the moon, maybe
at the shoes strung up over the telephone wires.

As he watched her, Miles put his lips to the water fountain
and began to swish water around in his mouth and then spit it
out. His mouth was still filled with leftover blood and skin. It
ran down the drain. He watched the water as it went from bright

red to pink. He kept swishing till it ran clear.

When he got up the girl was no longer looking up at the sky, but straight at him.

She waved.

Not knowing what to do, Miles waved back.

He headed out of the park and down the street and back toward his squat three towns over.

The girl had so unnerved him that even when he was long out of her sight and on an empty stretch of highway, he still hadn't been able to transform, which was a drag because it meant that he had to walk all the way back to his lair instead of fly.

Miles had a rule to never feed anywhere near his house, so it was a long walk. By the time he got home, the sky was just beginning lighten as dawn approached. He had been a little bit worried about having to find a place to wait the day out.

By the time he had unwound enough to lie down, it was well into the morning.

All day he lay in his bed thinking about the girl.

He wondered why she was sitting there alone in the middle of the night near a park that was notorious for muggings and killings. It was because of that reputation that it was such an excellent feeding ground for the vampires in the area.

It was best not to be seen in the same place too soon after a kill, and he didn't need to feed for another few days. But he was fixated on the girl.

Once the sun set, he wondered if he should go back.

Usually, he wouldn't. But there was something about the

girl that tugged at him. He hadn't felt compelled to act out of the ordinary since he'd been turned.

As soon as night fell, Miles transformed and flew to the park. He hung himself upside down on the lamppost next to the bench the girl had been sitting on and waited.

She arrived at 3 a.m.

With his sonar, he could see her approaching. He could sense her heart beating, her graceful walk, and the large object that she carried with her in her arms.

He was sure that she was human. There was nothing about her smell that suggested otherwise. She approached the bench and climbed onto it. Then she looked around. Seemingly satisfied that she was alone, she then pulled herself up onto the back of the bench and held herself steady by grabbing onto the lamppost.

She had to stretch as she took the object she had placed on the seat and began to attach it to the curly part of the lamppost. She was intensely concentrated. Miles could tell that she was happy and nervous at the same time by the way that her pulse quickened and then steadied, and by the smell that she excreted. It had the smell of hard work, not of fear.

The girl was so close, and yet, she was so fixed on her task that she did not notice him, in his bat form, hanging there. So he was comforted by the fact that he was not the reason why she lost her balance.

Miles could sense that her foot slipped before she did, and so he changed back to human form and grabbed her on her way down to prevent her from coming to any kind of injury.

They both fell to the ground gracefully. His arms were around her waist and they were crouched close together. His mouth was near her neck, and he could feel her rapid pulse. It was so close to him. So inviting.

He pulled away before he was tempted to do something that came naturally but that he consciously didn't want to do.

They both stood up at the same time.

"You're naked," she said.

Not, "where did you come from." Not a bloodcurdling scream because her neck, so close to him, had brought out his fangs. Not, "thank you."

Just, "You're naked."

That was the trouble with transformation. If you went from bat to human, you didn't have any clothes on. Miles got embarrassed, which surprised him.

He retracted his teeth.

"I'm sorry," he said.

The girl, now that he looked at her, really was a girl. No older than sixteen. She was staring at him hard, and then she put her hands to her face.

"Shit," she said. "My glasses."

They both looked around, and Miles saw them underneath the bench.

"There," he said pointing to them. He didn't want to make any movements that might change her state from strange calm to panic.

She scooted down and got them, and then held them up.

They were smashed. Not only were the lenses broken, but the very frame had cracked in two. Irreparable.

"My mom is going to kill me," she said. "These were my grandmother's glasses. Vintage."

"I'm sorry," he said again.

She took the cloth bag she carried, fingered a hole in it, and ripped out the bottom. She handed it to Miles.

"Here," she said. "You should cover yourself."

He stepped into the bag and covered himself with it. It was as though he were wearing a tiny, snug mini skirt that said WHOLE FOODS on it. He felt ridiculous.

He laughed.

"What's so funny?" she said.

"It's not too often that I feel ridiculous," Miles said. "Usually, I'm threatening."

"You don't look too threatening," she said.

He considered this. It was probably true if you didn't know what he was. Outwardly, he looked like an 18-year-old kid. He was tall and skinny, and looked a bit like the weakling in the back of the comic books that he had liked so much as a boy.

"What's your name?" the girl asked.

"Miles," he said.

"Miles," she said. "I'm Penny."

"Penny," Miles said. "I used to have a girlfriend named Penny. A long time ago. She wore glasses that looked a lot like yours."

He hadn't thought about her since 1956. The night he'd been turned was the night of the prom, and Penny was supposed to be his date. He'd never shown up.

"Can you climb?" Penny asked.

"What?"

"Are you a good climber?" Penny asked.

"Yes," he said. "Exceptional."

"Could you make sure my pig is secure?"

He stared at her, not really understanding the words that were coming out of her mouth. She pointed upward, toward the lamppost, and his eyes followed her finger. There, precariously attached to the post, was a ceramic pig with wings.

Miles scooted up the lamppost using his special skills; he investigated and secured the pig to the lamppost.

"It's all good," he said.

"Can you push it to the right a little bit? I want it to swing," Penny said.

He did as she asked. When the task was done, he came back down.

"I saw you here last night," Penny said. "Are you trolling the park for action?"

"What?" Miles said.

"You know, are you a hustler?" Penny said. "In the papers today it said that they found an old dead guy in the park who they think was killed by a hustler."

"No. I'm not a hustler," Miles said.

But standing under the light of a lamppost, under a swinging ceramic pig, wearing nothing but a cloth bag, he felt as though he wanted to tell Penny the truth. He had never in his life wanted so badly to tell someone the truth. So he did.

"I'm a vampire," he said.

Penny laughed.

"I used to be a vampire," she said. "In *seventh grade.*"

She laughed again.

"My mom was so mad because I would only eat everything *tartare*, or very rare."

"What are you now?" Miles asked.

"A street artist," she said. "It's way cooler."

Then they both had nothing to say to each other.

"Well," Penny said. "I would invite you to the 24-hour diner for a coffee, but no shirt, no shoes, no service."

"Right," Miles said. "I should get going, anyway."

"Rain check?" Penny asked.

"Sure," Miles said.

"How about Thursday?" Penny asked.

"Okay," Miles said. "I'll meet you there. What time?"

"Midnight?"

"Okay," Miles said and then turned to walk away from Penny. He would transform once he had walked far enough away from her. Maybe when he turned the corner at the end of the block.

He was excited that they had made a date. He hadn't had a date in fifty years.

Then he remembered that boys back in his day would always walk a girl home.

He stopped in his tracks, and turned around and called after Penny who was already halfway down the block.

"Penny," he called. And then he jumped in the air and landed next to her. "You shouldn't walk home alone at this time of night. There are dangerous people out."

He didn't say that he was one of the dangerous people to be afraid of, but she must have suspected something from the way he had jumped. After being so chatty, they now walked in silence.

Penny led the way, sometimes glancing at him while Miles looked straight ahead and tried not to feel chaffed by the cloth bag he was wearing. When they got to her house she spoke.

"I'm not going to invite you on to the property," she said. "You have to stay on the sidewalk."

"Fair enough," he said.

"And I don't want to ever see you again," she said.

"Okay," he said.

"If I do, I'll stake you in the heart," she said.

"That doesn't really work," he said. "But I get it."

"If you come near me again, I'll tell people what you really are."

He could smell the fear on her as she turned and ran up the pathway to her house. He could hear her struggling with her keys at the front door. Miles stood there for a minute, to be sure that she got into the house all right, and then he released himself from his body and flew home.

• • •

The next night, Miles went to feed at a town to the south of his lair. There was an alley in the skid-row part of town that had a lot of homeless people. They weren't tasty, but they kept him satiated. Once he got to town, he slowed down his extraordinary speed so as not to attract attention. He strolled down Main Street and over to Maple, down Independence and over to Metcalfe where all the shops were. He usually scanned the streets, checking the area for other vampires. He didn't get along with many of them, and he tried to steer clear. But that night, something caught his eye as he passed by the Goodwill. In the window, on display with the necklaces, pins and scarves, was a pair of cat-eye glasses, just like both Pennys had worn. He stopped and looked at them.

It made him wonder about this new Penny. It was Thursday, and Miles wondered if Penny would go to that diner and keep their date despite the fact that she had told him to go away. He wondered if that was where she usually hung out.

He ducked into the alley and fed.

He found that when he thought about Penny, he thought about his other life, before he was turned. The life where he went to sock hops and learned to drive his dad's car on Saturday afternoons. The life where he was team captain of the debate club and ran the projector at the cinema three times a week. The life where he had long make-out sessions with the other girl named Penny, the one who loved rock-and-roll as much as he did.

It made him lonely for the boy he used to be. It made him nostalgic for being alive. Now he was seventy-eight years old and a vampire. This new Penny made him feel human for the first time since he was turned.

He fed at the park again three weeks later. When he was done, he went to the water fountain and cleaned the bits of skin out of his teeth. While there, he noticed the ceramic pig.

It was swinging.

He decided that before he went home, he would go see if Penny was hanging out at the 24-hour diner. He would just go look.

She was there.

He stood in the shadows across the street. He watched her through the window of the place. She was reading a book. She looked happy, turning the pages and occasionally lifting the coffee cup to her mouth. He watched her for half an hour, feeling peaceful. He said her name.

"Penny."

He knew that she couldn't actually hear him, but it was at that moment that she happened to look out the window in his general direction. He stepped back, deeper into the shadows. He always wore dark clothing, so he blended in well, and he knew that she hadn't seen him. When he composed himself, he noticed that the glasses she wore now were round, ugly and ill-suited to her face. He was unsettled.

He released himself to bat form and flew away.

He thought he would go home. That was what he should have done. But instead he found himself standing naked in front of that Goodwill store, staring at the vintage cat-eye glasses.

He punched the window till it smashed and then turned into a bat, grabbed the pair of glasses with his mouth and flew away.

When he got home, he dropped the glasses on his night table, turned back to human form, and lay on the bed. He stared at the glasses. He knew what he would do. He would go to the diner, and he would give them to Penny.

For five nights, he staked-out the diner, waiting in the shadows until at last she showed up. She wore a tight-fitting rainbow skirt with a Victorian-looking white shirt. She had a big bag of books. And she was wearing those round, ugly glasses. She kept pushing them up the bridge of her nose.

"Penny," Miles stepped out of the shadows as she put her hand on the door of the diner.

She cocked her ear. He said her name again. This time she turned around.

They stood there looking at each other.

If he were alive, his heart would have been beating wildly. He did not know what to say. Words had escaped him. It was Penny who spoke first.

"I'm sorry I was an ass when I met you," she said. "I got scared."

It was not what he expected her to say. He expected a shove. Or a scream. Or something dramatic. Instead, she pulled the door open and motioned for him to come inside.

She *invited* him in.

Miles stepped into the diner. It had not changed much in sixty years. They slid into a corner booth and the waitress, as old as time in a brown uniform, handed them two menus. Her nametag said Stella. He watched her as she went back to the counter and leaned on it in a certain way. From the way she stood, he remembered that he had been in glee club with her. He looked at his menu for something he could eat.

"What are you going to get?" Penny asked.

"I don't know," Miles said. "I don't really eat this."

"Do you have money?" she asked.

"Yes," Miles said.

"Good. Then I'm getting the cheeseburger deluxe," Penny said. "You can pretend to eat my French fries."

She signaled Stella, the waitress, who brought over two glasses of water and took their order. Miles ordered a black coffee. He figured that he could make it look as though it were being drunk by using napkins and spilling some. Over the years, he had become a master of looking as though he were still human.

"So," Penny said. "What made you come find me?"

"I wanted to give you this," Miles said. He reached into his coat pocket and pulled out the glasses, placed them on the table and slid them across to her with his finger.

"Oh, wow," she said. "These are beautiful."

She put them on, and Miles thought that they suited her really well. She looked pretty. She took them off.

"Can't see with them. I'll have to get my lenses put in," she said. "Thank you."

She reached across to him and put her hand on his. Then she took her hand away.

"Wow, you really are cold," she said.

"I'm dead," Miles said.

"Right," she said. "I knew that."

She looked at him seriously. Miles poured a little of his coffee into the saucer.

"So, I actually was hoping you would come by," Penny said. "I thought maybe I'd put you off."

"I was taking a chance," Miles said. "You did say you'd rat me out."

"I know, I know," Penny said. "I was hoping that you'd know that I didn't mean it."

"I wasn't sure," Miles said.

"I didn't. And I'm glad you came, because I wanted to ask you something."

"You wanted to ask me something?"

Miles felt that it was the other way around. He wanted to ask *her* something. He wanted to ask her how it was that she could make him feel as though he had a pulse. How she could make him see the colors—that for him were beyond the spectrum already—seem even brighter. How she could make him remember tiny little details from when he was a living, breathing being.

"Yes," she said.

"What?" Miles asked.

"I want to paint you."

"Paint me?" Miles asked. "You want me to sit for a portrait?"

He had sat once for a portrait with his older brother when

he was seven years old. The portrait had hung in his Grand-mother's house.

"Not exactly sit," Penny said. "I want to follow you one night and do a lot of sketches as you do your vampire thing. Then I will make a bunch of art based on that."

"Out of the question," Miles said.

Stella arrived with the deluxe cheeseburger. She placed it on the table and gave Miles a sideways look, as though she were struggling to place him. He turned his face away from her.

"Anything else for you kids?" Stella asked.

Miles and Penny shook their heads, and Stella gave Miles one more hard stare before she walked back over to her station beside the counter.

"Why not?" Penny said. "You won't eat me, will you?"

"No," Miles said. "I won't."

He would never drink her blood. He couldn't. To him she was something more precious than food. She was *life*. His life. She was the thing that had made him feel something again. He would not do anything to put her in jeopardy.

"Hear me out," Penny pleaded. "My art piece will be three paintings side by side. Different stages of the hunt."

"No," he said. "Just no."

"What's the problem?" she asked.

"It's dangerous," he said.

"Why?"

"I can't tell you that," Miles said.

The truth was that he didn't want her to see him that way.

Fangs unfurled. Eyes wild. Running and hunting. Crouching over the victim and drinking. The ecstasy. He couldn't even bear other vampires to see him like that, which is why he hunted and lived alone. He was disgusted by how it made him feel. The power and blood lust were so overwhelming that he hated himself for the deliciousness of them.

"You are a stingy bastard," she said, shoving the cheeseburger in her mouth. She had ordered it rare, and there was blood that dripped off of the edge of the bun and onto her finger.

The sight of it made him catch his breath.

He wanted to take her finger and suck the juice off. If he wanted to be her friend, he would have to leave right away. It was either that, or he would attack her.

He slid out of the booth.

"Where are you going?" she said. "We're not finished here."

He was confused because she was smiling. She didn't look angry that he had said no. She was open and fresh. She smelled ready for anything. She put the burger down and noticed the burger juice on her finger and licked it off herself.

Miles almost howled. He could feel his teeth come out. He ran out of the diner. He headed for the park despite the fact that he had already fed here too recently for his liking. He could smell three other vampires in the area. It would be bad for all if there were too many deaths in one place, but Miles couldn't help himself. He was blinded by desire. He had to feed.

He went deeper into the park until he found himself under a bridge, hovering over a man. The man was passed out asleep on cardboard, wearing a large hoodie, and wrapped in a tattered brown sleeping bag. Miles leaned over him and exposed the man's neck. It was streaked with dirt. He smelled of urine, booze, and feces. This was not the blood that he wanted. He wanted the creamy neck of a fresh-smelling girl. He wanted the blood of someone who was healthy and not as sick as the homeless man. Miles yelled with frustration. He punched the brick wall of the bridge. He threw the man's possessions all around, ripping every item he could find to shreds. The man was so drunk he did not wake up.

"What are you doing?"

"Keep it down."

"You'll get us caught."

The three other vampires he'd smelled surrounded him under the bridge. Miles was so far into his rage that he thought he would kill them.

"He has the rage."

"He needs to feed."

"He wants sweeter blood than a derelict's."

They clucked at him. They felt sorry for him. They surrounded him and ordered him over and over again to feed on the homeless man. They wore him down.

Miles sank to his feet, plugged his nose up, and bit the drunk's neck.

As soon as the first blood hit his system, he relaxed. He drank his fill and then disengaged. Exhausted he sat next to his victim, leaning his head against the wall of the bridge.

He would not be able to feed here for a while. And he owed those three vampires a debt of thanks. Since Penny had invited him to the diner that evening, he now had a new place he could go to hunt. In his blood craze, he had fantasized about going back there and grabbing someone. Anyone. Maybe even Stella. Just to have blood that was not so tasteless.

It had been a curse to meet Penny.

After a time resting, Miles stood up and walked toward the water fountain to clean his teeth of the bits of skin.

"Hey there," one of the vampires called to him from behind a bush. "We saved you some girl."

Miles turned.

Spilled around in front of the bush, he saw the big bag full of books. There was a sketchbook near an arm that hung lazily out of the bushes. And not far from that was a purse whose contents one of the vampires was rifling through.

He threw the things carelessly out on ground. Keys. Lipstick. Wallet. *Cat-eye glasses.*

The vampire stood up and shoved the wallet in his coat pocket, and as he did he took a step back and stumbled onto the spilled contents of the purse.

The glasses snapped in two.

If Miles had had a heart, right then it would have stopped.

It was the last time he ever made a friend.

Other Boys

BY CASSANDRA CLARE

"THAT'S THE ONE." Bridget pointed with her fork. "That's the guy who says he's a vampire."

Jennifer, who had been picking distractedly at her tuna salad, looked up at her friend and frowned. "Who's a vampire?"

"The new kid. What's his name. No, don't *look*," hissed Bridget, who lived in mortal fear that one day a boy in the cafeteria would catch her or one of her friends *looking at him*, and the outcome would be—well, Jennifer wasn't sure what Bridget thought the outcome would be, other than some sort of unspecified disaster. "The one with the dark hair and the weirdo clothes."

Gabrielle, who was staring openly across the cafeteria, raised her eyebrows. "Oh yeah. I think his name is Colin."

"It is," Bridget said. "He said so in English class. He just got up and said: 'My name is Colin, and I just moved here. And oh yeah, I'm a vampire.'"

"He just said that? I'm a vampire?" Jennifer stared across the cafeteria, fascinated. The boy with the dark hair was sitting alone at a table, wearing a long black leather trenchcoat over a black shirt and black pants. He had black gloves on his hands,

283

too, the fingertips cut off. He had a lunch tray in front of him, but there was nothing on it. Under the black, black hair, he was pale as blank paper. "What did everyone else do?"

"Mostly laughed. Then Mr. Brandon made him sit down."

"He's a poser," Gabrielle said, and grinned. Gabby had a bright, white grin that had never needed braces. Jennifer often wondered how it was that the two of them were cousins who shared genetic material, and yet Gabby had gotten the perfect teeth and the blonde hair, and Jennifer had wound up with dishwater brown hair—something no one else in the family had—and four years of orthodontics.

"He never eats," Bridget said, ticking off her points on her fingers. "He wears sunglasses everywhere. He's super pale. And he never speaks to anyone. Maybe he *is* a vampire."

"Or maybe he's just a misanthrope," said Gabby. "Anyway, if he was a vampire, wouldn't he burn up in sunlight?"

"Oh, there's no such thing as vampires anyway," Jennifer said. "He's just some crazy goth kid."

"Oh yeah?" Bridget said. "Well, he's looking at you."

Startled, Jennifer glanced back in the boy's direction. He had something balanced against the edge of the table, a sort of book, open as if he were writing or drawing in it. He shook his head as she looked at him and even at this distance she could see the green of his eyes.

There was something else, too. A feeling that as he looked back at her, something zinged through their gazes, some kind of connection—

Jennifer turned around and looked back at the other two girls at the table: Gabby with her eyebrows up, Bridget chewing nervously on the end of her red braid. "You're blushing," Gabby said.

Jennifer shrugged. "He *is* cute."

Bridget grinned. "All vampires are."

. . .

On the bus ride home, Jennifer thought about vampires. She didn't know much about vampire legends: certainly less than the other girls in her school, who loved vampire romances and horror movies. She'd seen one vampire movie, once, when she was fourteen and over at Bridget's house. For the next week after that, she'd dreamed about beautiful people with pale faces who would swoop through her window and take her away from her boring parents and her boring life. She would live in Paris instead of Pennsylvania and drink blood out of wine glasses, except it wouldn't taste like blood—hard and metallic—but like something sweet and thin. Fruit punch, maybe, or black-cherry soda.

Not long after she'd been in a bookstore and asked her mother to buy her a copy of a teen vampire romance novel. *Blood Desire,* or something like that. She should have known better. Vampires and supernatural creatures and magic didn't fit with her parents' strict conservative worldview. Her mother had taken the book out of her hand and shoved it roughly back onto the shelf. Vampires, Jen was told, were not something girls her age should be thinking about; they were monsters made up by pagans and Satanists and had no place in a child's bedroom.

What her mother really meant, Jen realized later, was that vampires were sexy, and she wasn't supposed to think about sex, or boys. Unlike Gabby, Jen was never allowed to date—not even with a chaperone, not even a date to go to the mall in the middle of a Saturday with a million people around. She was forbidden to bring boys home, much less have them in her room. Sometimes Jen thought it was a wonder she was allowed to go to school at all, considering that there were *boys* there.

At home, Jen slipped in through the side door to find her mother in the kitchen, stir-frying onions in a pan. Jennifer slid onto one of the kitchen stools, twirling her backpack by one strap and watching her mother, thin and efficient-looking with her graying brown hair tied back in a braid and an apron cinched around her waist. None of the mothers of Jennifer's friends, even when they did cook, wore an apron—not Bridget's, whose mother only followed macrobiotic recipes she got off the Internet, or Gabby's, whose crazy artist mother didn't know how to make anything but Hamburger Helper. But Jennifer's mom stayed home all day—she disapproved of her sister, who worked—so Jennifer figured she had nothing *but* time to cook.

"Hey, Mom," Jennifer said. "I was just wondering..."

Jennifer's mom half-turned, brushing a lock of hair away from her face and smiling. "About what?"

"How come Gabby gets to date," Jennifer said. "You know. And I don't."

"Oh." Her mother stood for a moment, poking at the onions in the pan. "Look, you and Gabby—you're different."

Her mother had said this before, and it always annoyed Jennifer. "Different *how*?"

"Well—Gabby can handle herself better." Jennifer's mother had her lips pressed together. Jen knew how much her mother hated having this conversation, but she couldn't help it. It was like poking at a sore tooth. Of course, it was true that Gabby was more confident and self-reliant than she was, but how could anyone become confident or self-reliant when their parents kept them in a glass cage and never let them go anywhere or do anything?

"I can handle myself fine," Jennifer said. "I'd just like to be able to—maybe—go on a date." She held her breath.

She might not have bothered. "You know that's out of the question," Jen's mother said. "Don't be ridiculous." She gave a little shriek as a puff of smoke wafted up from the pan. "Oh! My onions!"

Jennifer sighed.

• • •

In the library the next day, trying to research a book on Norse mythology, Jen kept feeling her gaze drawn to other books—books that had nothing to do with the topic of her essay. Books with the word *vampire* in the title.

There were more of them than she would have thought: *The Encyclopedia of Vampires*, and *The Massive Book of Vampire*

Myths, and *Vampires through History.* Jennifer was just reaching for the last one when a voice spoke from behind her:

"You know, most of those aren't very accurate."

She whirled around. Colin was behind her, leaning against one of the low shelves of books. Up close, his looks were even more striking. He had one of those sharp, bony, delicate faces, like a British film star. His hair was pure black, his eyes a bright and feverish green like a cat's. There was a ring on one of his fingers. He couldn't be *married*, she thought. But no, it was on the wrong finger. She thought of what Bridget had said—that he wore weirdo clothes, but she thought they suited him.

Jennifer took a deep breath. "*What* aren't very accurate?"

"Those books." He stepped forward and took *The Massive Book of Vampire Myths* down from its shelf. "It's just going to tell you the same stuff. That vampires burn up in sunlight, don't reflect in mirrors, can't cross water or look at crucifixes ..."

"And you don't think that's true?" Jennifer's voice came out thin and high, almost a squeak. Standing this close, she could smell the scent that lingered on his hair and clothes. A faint charred smell, like a burnt match. Maybe he smoked.

"I think," he said, "that for vampires to have been around for such a long time, they must be pretty clever. Too clever to let their secrets get out like this. I think they'd be much better off spreading false rumors about how they can be killed—garlic, stake to the heart. Once people believe them, once they think they're safe ..."

Jennifer shuddered. "You're joking, right? Did you really tell

Mr. Brandon's English class that you were a vampire?"

He smiled. "Maybe I did. You have to admit it's more interesting than the usual introduction. Don't you think?"

"I don't know." Jennifer reached to put the book back on the shelf. "It all seems sort of ..." She turned back around, but there was no one there. Colin was gone.

"Morbid," she said, half in a whisper.

• • •

Jennifer stayed in the library for another half an hour, but Colin didn't return. When the last bell rang, she went to her locker to get her books and found Gabby leaning against it, holding a notebook across her chest. She popped her gum as Jennifer approached.

"Bridget said someone saw you in the library talking to Colin," she said.

Jennifer fiddled with her lock. "So what?"

"Did he say anything ..." Gabby paused. "About, you know. *Vampires.*"

"No," Jennifer said, partly just to be perverse and partly because she had felt a flash of resentment at Gabby's interest in Colin. Colin was hers. Except, of course, he wasn't. She jerked her locker door open—

And jumped back with a muffled exclamation as two books fell from the open locker and hit the floor at her feet. Gabby immediately bent and scooped them up. Both had lurid covers depicting a fanged male vampire looming over a prone girl in a long dress. "*Blood Desire*," she read aloud. "*The Vampire's Secret.* What is this crap?"

"Nothing. I was just looking for—" Jennifer broke off as something caught her eye. A piece of white paper fluttered, caught in the grille of her locker door. She reached to pluck it down.

I thought you might enjoy these, was scrawled on the paper in unfamiliar handwriting. There was no signature.

• • •

Gabby walked home with Jennifer, which was not unusual, especially for a Friday. Their houses were a few blocks from each other. Jennifer's mother hadn't wanted to move too far away from her sister even though they both lived in the same town. Gabby chattered about Colin the whole way home—about where he'd moved from, about the things he'd said in English class, and about whether or not he liked Jennifer. Jennifer barely paid attention. All she wanted to do was get home and read the books Colin had left in her locker.

She convinced Gabby not to come inside the house with her, claiming she had a headache. Locking the front door behind her, she raced upstairs to her room and flung herself on the bed, fumbling the books out of her bag. Their covers were even more lurid than she remembered—each one showed a powerfully muscled male vampire bent over the prone body of a woman, her back arched, her pale throat nakedly exposed. Unconsciously pressing her hand to her own throat, Jennifer opened *Blood Desire* and began to read.

• • •

She finished *The Vampire's Secret* after midnight, having read straight through for six hours, not even going downstairs for dinner. But she didn't feel tired. She felt alert and awake. Her mouth was dry, her heart pounding as if she'd been running. She was barely aware of what she had read—she'd taken in almost nothing of the stories—but images raced through her mind, as if they came swirling up out of dreams: pale bodies sinking back into darkness, dark hair blown on the wind, red fingernails scraping across the front of an old-fashioned white shirt, blood on an exposed throat, blue veins running under skin like a roadmap. Her own skin burned and itched. There was a pain in the side of her throat. Taking her hand away, she saw her fingertips stained red and realized she had dug her own nails into the skin of her throat until it bled. Her stomach twisted. *Colin*, she thought. *I want Colin*.

• • •

When Jennifer came downstairs that morning she found her father sitting at the breakfast table, half-hidden by a newspaper. Her mother was by the stove, flipping pancakes.

Her father lowered the paper with a smile that crinkled the corners of his eyes. "Good morning, sunshine."

Jennifer tugged self-consciously at the neck of her sweater. She'd worn it to cover the bruises she'd made on her throat with her own fingernails. "Morning, Dad."

He frowned. "You look a little peaked, kid. Is everything all right? You feeling okay?"

Her mother, coming over to the table with a plate of pancakes. "Do you need to stay home from school, Jenny?"

Staying home from school would mean not seeing Colin. Jennifer's stomach twisted, a feeling of nausea rising inside her. The sickly smell of maple syrup was overwhelming. "I'm fine. I just had a lot of homework to do last night."

Her mother and father glanced at each other across the table, their eyes meeting in secret parental communication. "We were thinking of going up to your grandmother's this weekend," her mother said. "It's been a long time since we've seen her. We thought you could take Friday off school."

Jennifer's grandmother lived hours outside the city in the middle of nowhere, a tiny house surrounded by trees, miles from the nearest town. And she was even more conservative than Jen's mother. She banned all books from her house, not just the ones with magic or supernatural creatures in them, and all music and movies, too. She was terrifying—cold and rigid and strict. Gabby said everyone was afraid of her, even her daughters. Gabby hated going there just as much as Jen did; they'd always used the place as a threat to each other when they were little.

If you do that, they'll send you to Grandma's house!

"Is this because I asked you about dating?" Jen demanded, whirling on her mom. "It's not like he even asked—"

She broke off, already knowing she'd said too much.

Her mother's eyes narrowed. "So there is a boy. A *specific* boy?"

"No!" Jennifer backed away from the table. "There isn't anyone."

"Jen," her father said. His voice was placating. "You know the rules."

But what if you met him? Jen wanted to ask, but it was pointless. She thought of her parents meeting Colin, with his rings and his strange black clothes and his claim that he was a vampire. She could only imagine how badly that would go.

And it wasn't as if he'd asked her out in the first place, anyway.

"I just don't want to go away this weekend," she said, her voice shaking slightly. "I have a lot of work. A big assignment—"

"Jen," her mother said. Her voice was soft; she didn't sound angry. "Whoever he is, just forget about him. Someday, when you're older, there will be other boys."

· · ·

But Jen didn't want other boys.

Colin was in his usual place in the lunchroom that afternoon, his feet up on the table, a black notebook spread out over his lap. As usual, there was no food on his lunch tray. Jennifer marched directly up to him, ignoring the stares of Gabby and Bridget from across the room.

"I read those books," she said. "The ones you put in my locker."

He lowered the notebook and looked up. His eyes seared into hers. "What books?"

Now he was playing with her. "You know what books." She

searched his face for any clue to what he was thinking, but it was unreadable. "Why are you so fascinated with vampires?"

Now he smiled. "Why not?" he said. "People have been fascinated with vampires for centuries."

"But *you*," she whispered. "Why do *you* care? Why do you know so much about them?"

"They're human, but more than human. They don't need to eat, to breathe—imagine being like that, so pure that you have only one need in the world, one desire."

"Blood," Jennifer said, and a shiver went up her spine as she said it. She was no longer aware of the cafeteria, the noise and bustle all around her, or even if people were staring. She was only aware of Colin, who was holding her gaze to his with eyes like green nails.

"Blood," he said. "So simple, but everything. Imagine looking around a room like this—" His eyes slid around the cafeteria, slow and contemptuous—"and knowing you're better than everyone in it. Better and different."

Jennifer shook her head. "I can't imagine that."

He leaned forward, his elbows on the table. His grin was florescent-bright. "You should. You *are* better. Different. Special. I knew it the minute I saw you in the library."

She swallowed hard. "I'm not, really. I'm ordinary."

He shook his head. "Come out with me this weekend," he said.

Startled, she could only stare. "Like—on a date?"

"Like on a date."

"My parents..." she began. "They don't let me go on dates."

"That's too bad," he said. He sounded like he meant it.

"And I won't be around this weekend," she said, and then, hardly believing her own daring, added: "But—my parents, they go to sleep early. Maybe I could sneak out..."

"Could you?" A smile played around the corners of his mouth. "I'll tell you what. You wait for me, tonight, in your room. I'll come to you."

Jennifer's throat was dry. It was all she could do to nod in response.

• • •

Leaving the cafeteria, Jen drifted through the halls like smoke, like a ghost. More than one person walked into her, but she only swerved to go around them, or stared through them until they moved on, muttering to themselves. *I'm seeing Colin tonight,* she thought, over and over. *Late tonight. He said he would come to me.* In one of the vampire stories she had read the night before, vampires had soulmates, humans who were bonded to them with a mutually interdependent bond—both vampire and human needing each other. The vampire would do anything to protect its bonded human. She thought of Colin being willing to do anything to protect her. She thought of his mouth on her throat, and a shudder went through her. She almost had to stop and lean against the wall to keep herself from falling over.

"Where are *you*?" Gabby's voice, bright as sunshine cutting through the fog in her mind. Jennifer looked up. Gabrielle was propped against the locker next to hers, a piece of her bright hair wound around a finger, her eyes inquisitive. "Earth to Jen."

Jennifer swung her locker door open, avoiding her cousin's eyes. "Sorry. I was thinking about something."

"You're always thinking about something." Gabby tugged on her hair. "You need to take your mind off stuff. Want to go out tonight? See a movie? Something dumb, with cute guys in it."

It was like Gabby was psychic. Jen bit her lip. "I can't. I have ...plans."

"Plans? Plans with who?"

"No one."

"Plans with Colin?"

Jennifer slammed her locker door shut. "Maybe."

"Oh my God, you *do* have plans with him!" A look of surprise—and something more than surprise—washed over Gabby's face. If Jennifer hadn't known it was ridiculous, she would have thought Gabby looked frightened. "You're not seriously going to go, are you?"

"Of course I'm going to go."

Gabby chewed her lip. "I don't think it's a good idea—"

Jennifer turned away, cutting her off. "I'm going home, Gabby. I'll see you later."

• • •

Of course, it wasn't as easy to get rid of her cousin as that. Gabby walked with her all the way home, talking excitedly all the way about Colin. Warning her that going out with him wasn't a good idea. He was weird, he was too silent, he was too pale, he was too strange, he acted like a serial killer, he never talked to anyone. He was probably full of himself and boring.

"So I'll be bored," Jen said, keeping her eyes straight ahead as she walked. It was easier to disagree with Gabby when you acted calm and didn't get mad. "So what?"

"So why subject yourself to that when you could spend the evening with me?" Gabby's voice was wheedling. "Where's the girl power?"

"Girl power doesn't mean never going out with boys ever, Gabs. You go out with boys all the time."

"I'm just looking out for you. Colin is—weird."

"So he's weird. *I'm* weird."

"Not like him." Gabby sounded unhappy. "I think he could be—dangerous."

That did it. Despite vowing to stay calm, Jen whirled on her cousin. "Is this about Bridget saying he was a vampire? Is that what this is about? I thought that was a joke."

"It was."

"So you don't think he's a vampire."

Gabby met her gaze, steadily. "No. I don't."

Surprise washed over Jennifer, and then something else— disappointment? It flared out quickly, and now she was angry again. "Then *stop* bugging me. I bet I can guess what's *really* bothering you."

"I bet you can't." Gabby's blue eyes sparked with matching annoyance.

"You're always the one who gets the dates. You've always got some cute guy panting after you. Now that I'm the one with the date, you're jealous. You noticed Colin first, and you're mad he likes *me*."

Once the words were out of Jen's mouth, she wished she could take them back. There was the strangest expression on Gabby's face. She'd never seen her cousin look like that before.

"Let me tell you, Jen," Gabby said, "whether you believe me or not, jealous is the *last* thing I am."

Jennifer opened her mouth to shoot back that she didn't believe her, then closed it again. Whatever else was going on— whatever was the real reason her cousin was acting so strange— it was obvious that Gabby was telling the truth.

• • •

Jennifer sat on her bed, looking at herself in the mirror that hung over her dresser. She had changed her clothes a dozen times, and finally settled on black jeans and a black sweater. Her hair was down, brushed out, with gel on the ends to stop it from frizzing. Between her dark hair and her dark sweater, her face seemed to hover in the mirror like an untethered white balloon floating in the darkness of the room.

He's not coming.

It was almost midnight. There were books spilled out across her bed. She had tried reading to take her mind off waiting, but that had only made things worse. She'd tried finishing the vampire novel she was halfway through, but it had only made her skin feel hot and unbearably itchy. She could hear the clock in the hallway ticking—hear the snap, snap, of each minute passing. The air in the room seemed close and suffocating, too, as if she couldn't quite breathe properly.

He's not coming.

She wished she hadn't told Gabby anything. It would be humiliating to have to go to school in the morning and admit that the date she'd fought so hard to defend hadn't even happened because she'd been stood up. Maybe Colin had just been mocking her with all his talk about blood and desire and—

It came then, a soft rap on her window. She whirled around to stare; the floating white balloon in the mirror veering as if caught by a gust of wind. She heard the sound again and stood up, going to the window and throwing it open, leaning out into the soft spring night.

He was in the garden below her window, a black shadow against the neatly trimmed grass of the front lawn, face and eyes printed white against the darkness. He beckoned to her with his hand. *Come down.*

• • •

She came down, and he was waiting by the front steps. He put his finger to her lips, shushing her before she could ask him any questions. When he took his hand away she could taste the salt from his skin on her mouth.

He took her hand. She let him, and he drew her toward the front gate and out onto the street. It was empty, the white lights painted down the center of the road gleaming in the moonlight, the parked cars still as sleeping animals. Colin pulled her into the shadows between two cars and kissed her, hard and hungrily, pushing her back against the trunk of a neighbor's Jeep, the handle of the trunk jamming into her back.

Colin's hands were alternately cold and hot on her skin, sliding up under the back of her sweater. His mouth tasted like salt. She was dizzy, floating, cut free from everything. Her fingers scrabbled against his shoulders, his neck. She could feel his pulse hammering. *His heart beats*, she thought. His mouth found her cheek, the side of her jaw, her throat. Desire and fear flared up inside her and she whimpered.

Colin pulled back. His lips looked bruised in the dim light, his eyes hot. He said, "You're right. We shouldn't do this here." He took her hand again. "Let's go."

"Where?" she whispered. It was all she had the breath to say.

He grinned, bright in the darkness. "You'll see."

...

The cemetery gate was unlocked. Colin pushed it open and slipped through, pulling Jen behind him. There was a gravel path running between the graves, lined with pale headstones. Some of the graves had flowers scattered across them, black in the shadows. Their feet crunched on the path.

Jen's heart was pounding. "What are we doing here?"

"Relax." Colin turned, holding both her hands in his, walking backward. He drew her after him, and she could have pulled away, but she didn't want to. "I want to show you one of my favorite places."

She let him lead her. "All right."

The path wound under the trees, where the shadows were thick and dark as paint, and came out by the side of a small lake. Hills rose around the lake, spiked with mausoleums and leaning gravestones. Colin let go of Jen's hand long enough to slide off his backpack. He pulled a blanket out of it, spreading it on the ground, and beckoned her to come and sit beside him.

For a moment, they sat in silence together, looking out over the lake. The wind had come up, and ruffled Jen's hair, lifting it away from her hot forehead, cooling her burning skin. The moon shone down on the lake, making it glow. Jen had the feeling of floating away from the rest of the world, being something holy and apart.

"Come here." Colin drew her down next to him, wrapping his arms around her, pressing their bodies together. She had never been so close to another human being; she wanted to lose herself in the moment, but kept marveling at how strange it all was—the feeling of the grommets on his jacket pressing into her skin, the cold air and the heat of his body, the slide of his lips across hers. He tangled his hands in her hair, raking his fingers down and through it. He drew up the back of her shirt in handfuls, and she felt the cold of his rings on her skin as he slid his hands under, fumbling with the clasp of her bra.

"No...don't," she whispered, but he just laughed, flicking the clasp open. He'd done this before, it seemed. His hands on her bare skin made her shudder.

"Relax," he said, again, but Jen didn't feel relaxed. She felt agitated—she didn't know why—every nerve in her body humming. Her skin *itched*. She felt awkward suddenly, not at home in her body. Even her teeth felt too big for her mouth.

"I want to stop," she said.

He pulled back just enough to look down at her, bewildered. His pulse was pounding. She could see it under the skin of his throat. "I thought you wanted this," he said. "You didn't want to go on a date. You said you just wanted me to come to your window."

"Not for this," she said.

He stared down at her. "Your *teeth*," he said. His pulse was hammering now. She couldn't look away from it, fluttering under his skin. Her stomach twisted, growling. She was—hungry. "Are those real?"

Jen blinked, bewildered. "What?"

"Baby, those are truly freaky." He was grinning again now. "I love how you're so into this stuff. I knew you would be the minute I saw you. So—you want to bite my neck?" He swept his hair back, leaving the pale side of his throat exposed. "Go ahead."

He leaned down, closer to her, until all she could see was the blue veins under his skin, the beat of his pulse, and she could—*smell the blood*. Her ears roared, the sound of the wind driven out by the audible sound of rushing blood. *Pale bodies sinking back into darkness, dark hair blown on the wind, red fingernails scrap-*

ing across the front of an old-fashioned white shirt, blood on an exposed throat, blue veins running under skin like a roadmap—

When her teeth met in his throat, he screamed. No one ever screamed in the books, but Colin screamed. He tried to push at her with frantic hands, but she had her legs wrapped around him, her arm across the back of his neck. She clung to him like a tick as he reared up and then collapsed, his scream turning to a gurgle.

And then there was just the blood. It exploded into her mouth, hot and salty, and she felt her eyes roll back, her hands digging into Colin's shoulders, kneading them the way a cat kneads its mother as it drinks milk. He was still struggling, kicking at her feebly, but it didn't last long. She didn't know it, but she'd opened his carotid artery with her teeth. He bled out in under a minute, going limp under her body, eyes open and staring glassily at the sky. She didn't notice that, either. She was still drinking.

The blood was gone too soon. Suddenly there was no more of it pumping into her mouth, there was only the dry sucking noise her mouth made against his skin. She jerked back, revolted.

She stared. Colin lay twisted on the ground, his neck bent at an unnatural angle. She reached to touch his arm, then snatched her hand back. His skin felt papery and limp, his body light as a husk. His skin was a dull putty color.

"Colin," Jen whispered. "*Colin?*"

The whites of his eyes were flecked with blood. She had made a mess of his neck. It looked like an animal had been chewing on him. No neat puncture wounds, just a ragged sort of hole. His clothes were drenched in blood. It was all over her, too. Her hair hung in sticky red tassels down her shoulders.

The worst part of it was that she was still hungry.

Jen wrapped her arm around herself and let out a wail, and then another one. They echoed through the silence of the cemetery like a fire alarm going off in an empty house. She was still wailing when someone stepped up behind her and put their arms around her from behind. She heard a voice in her ear, soft and soothing.

"Jen, Jen," Gabby said. "It's all right. Everything's all right. Let's get you home."

• • •

Jen's parents were waiting for them in the kitchen. All the lights were on: the room looked as bright and white as the inside of a marble tomb. Her father was leaning against the counter, her mother sitting at the table, turning a cold cup of coffee around and around in her hands. She looked up when Jen came in, Gabby leading her by the hand like a trusting child.

Seeing the blood all over her daughter, she paled. "*Jen*," she whispered.

"I'm all right," Jen said, automatically, but her mother was looking past her, at her cousin.

"What happened?" Jen's mother asked Gabby. "Did she kill him?"

"He's dead, all right," Gabby said. "Colin." She pointed toward a chair. "Sit down, Jen."

Jen sat. A great feeling of unreality had come over her, as if she were floating through a dream she knew was a dream. She was in her house, but it wasn't really her house. This was her kitchen, but not. These were her parents, but not. The words they said to her, to Gabby, had no meaning.

"Where's the body?" It was her father, still leaning against the counter. His face was set, almost expressionless. For the first time, Jen noticed that there was a duffel bag at his feet.

"The cemetery. Up by the lake," Gabby said.

"I'll take care of it." Jen's dad hoisted the duffel, affording Jen a brief glimpse of what was inside—a shovel, a knife, some lighter fluid. Tools. She stared as her father patted her mother on the shoulder and went out through the side door, shutting it carefully behind him.

"I don't understand," Jen said, softly, not to anyone in particular, and not expecting an answer, either.

"Of course you don't," Gabby said, an odd sharpness in her tone. "You don't know anything. You couldn't possibly understand."

"Gabrielle. *Please.*" Jennifer's mother stood up. Her back was very straight, and she looked at Gabby with a sort of tired disapproval. "Now is not the time."

Jennifer watched her mother with dazed eyes as she took a white dishtowel from the rack and dampened it under the sink. She came over to her daughter, and tenderly cleaned the blood from her face, even the crusted blood at the corners of her mouth, sponging the stains from her hands, turning the white towel pink. Jen sat silently, letting her mother minister to her as if she were a child and the sticky stuff all over her was spaghetti sauce or melted red Popsicle.

"He wasn't a vampire," Jen said finally, staring at the bloody towel. "Was he?"

"Of course not," Gabby snapped. "He was just a stupid kid who thought all that Goth stuff made him look cool. You're the one who—"

"Gabby." Jen's mother's tone warned.

"He said I was special," Jen whispered. "Different."

"You must have liked him very much," said her mother. "Humans have a way of sensing when a vampire desires them. It causes them to feel desire in return." Her voice was matter-of-fact. "It makes it easier to find prey that way."

"You *knew*," Jen whispered. "You knew what I was."

Her mother patted the side of her face gently. "I didn't know. I hoped the curse had passed by you like it passed by Gabby. Sometimes it skips a generation or two. Part of me hoped it had died out completely in the family. Seeing what my mother went through . . ." She sighed. "Hunting in the shadows, always fearing being caught. Your father's had to clean up after her in the past. That's why we moved here. To get away."

"That's why you wouldn't let me go out with boys," Jen realized. "Not because you were afraid for me, but because you were afraid for *them*."

"We knew that if you did have the curse, if you were . . . what you are, it would start showing itself when you were a teenager. When you got interested in boys. The desire to feed on blood, it's all tangled up with...with adult feelings. *Romantic* feelings."

She still can't bring herself to just say *sexual feelings*, Jen thought. Even though I just killed someone. Even though I'm sitting here covered in his blood, she thinks I'm a child.

Jen turned to look at Gabby, who was staring at her sadly. She looked so glum and miserable and ordinary. Jen almost felt sorry for her.

"You knew, too," she said to her cousin. "Didn't you?"

"My mom told me about the curse once she figured out I didn't have it," Gabby admitted. "Sorry I couldn't tell you. But honestly, I didn't think you had it, either. Not till Bridget started talking about Colin being a vampire and I saw how fascinated you were. It was weird, Jen."

"Gabby warned us what was going on," said Jen's mother. "It gave us a little time to be prepared. See, you can't control yourself right now, Jen. And that's why you have to go live with your grandmother for a while. Someone will have to teach you how to be what you are."

"I'm not doing that," Jen said, turning back to her mother. "I'm not leaving here."

Her mother looked startled. "We know what's best for you—"

"No, you don't," Jen said. "You should have told me all this stuff before. You said you were protecting me, but you set me up. I killed Colin because of you."

"And if you stay here, you'll wind up killing someone else."

"I guess you should have thought of that before," said Jen. Gabby gave a startled laugh as Jen stood up, pushing her mother's restraining hand away. "You called it a curse," Jen added.

"It is a curse," said her mother. "A family curse. Only the women in our family get it."

"Maybe I don't think it is one," Jen said.

Her mother's expression changed. Jen remembered what Gabby had always said about their grandmother—that everyone was afraid of her. Her daughters, too.

Her mother stood up, facing her. "You're upset," she said. "You should go to bed. We can talk about this in the morning."

"Sure," Jen said. "In the morning."

She turned and walked out of the kitchen, up the stairs toward her bedroom. She caught sight of herself in the mirror that hung on the landing. Her clothes were stiff with dried blood. Her face was luminous, her eyes glowing. She looked— different. Under the blood, her skin seemed to shine. She was almost beautiful.

She smiled, wide as she could, showing the sharp tips of her needle incisors, the ones Colin had thought were so funny and so fake. She thought of the way his skin had crunched under her teeth when she bit into it, like the skin of an apple.

Her mother had been right. There would be other boys.

Passing

BY NANCY HOLDER AND
DEBBIE VIGUIÉ

IT WAS ALMOST time—a few minutes before midnight on New Year's Eve. New Year, new vampire hunter. Would I be the one?

I sat down shakily in the ancient stone chapel of the former Universidad de Salamanca, the most ancient university in Spain. When the war broke out, most of the universities in Europe shut down. The Americans figured the vampires would never attack us on our native soil. We paid dearly for our arrogance.

For the last twelve years, Salamanca had been the home of the *Academia Sagrada Familia Contra los Vampiros*. It was the school for vampire hunters—my school. There were foreign students from all over the world, because the Academia was the best. Academia graduates took out the most vamps, and they had the highest survival rate. There were six living Academicians; Juan Maldonaldo had been a hunter for nine years. Unbelievable.

Not that the survival rate was very good—out of the original ninety-six of us in our class, we were down to eighteen. We shuffled into the chapel in our ceremonial black robes, our hoods concealing our faces. We were about to take our final exam. Only one of us would pass.

I had dreaded this moment for two long years—the moment my foot crossed the threshold of the Academy—and feared it for two months. Diego, our Master, had warned us that as the time grew near, we would experience high anxiety. About a dozen of my classmates woke screaming from nightmares. There was a lot of jogging in the middle of the night. Even though drugs and alcohol were forbidden, I knew that people were swigging wine and taking Xanax so they could get some rest.

None of them carried the extra burdens—or the accompanying terror and guilt—that I did.

I should say something, tell someone, I thought. But I would sooner cut out my own heart than tell them what I'd done. What I might do.

At the thought, my heart skipped beats, and I clung to the back of the carved mahogany pew.

In the last two months, I had broken a lot of rules. For some of the things I had done, they didn't even have rules. No one would have dreamed of crossing the line I had leaped across last Halloween.

Exactly two months ago, on October 31, everything had changed. The Vampire War had taken a brutal turn when the vamps had murdered the daughter of the president of the United States. The Cursed Ones didn't put it that way, of course. They claimed they had "liberated" her—changed her into one of them—and that *our* side had murdered her when we drove a stake through her heart and cut off her head.

Like everyone else, I demanded payback. I couldn't wait to

take revenge. Although we were pledged to run together, I wanted a vampire to die by my own hand. I ran with my *grupo* across the ancient medieval bridge as the dying sun turned the stone city a golden color. We scoured the hills for blood drinkers, Spaniards and Americans, Koreans and Swedes. In our body armor, we sang our song, which had always sounded so corny to me before. Translated into English, it went like this:

We are the vampire hunters.

Our cause is holy.

From Spain we come to save the world.

Race from us into the sunlight, demons of hell!

Better that you die in flames than by our hands!

That night, Antonio de la Cruz was by my side. Sometimes he held my gloved hand in his as we charged through the darkness. My crossbow smacked the bruises I had gotten in Advanced Streetfighting the day before.

Fog rose around us like smoke from a wildfire. I heard shouts and Antonio's hand left mine. I called for him; he answered, very far away. I saw a face floating in the fog before me, and I ran toward it. But it wasn't Antonio.

It was Jack.

Don't think about him, I ordered myself, my vision blurring as I focused on the stained glass windows of the saints. The Savior melted and blurred. *Think about your legacy, and the promises that you made. Think of your grandparents.*

Charles "Che" and Esther Leitner, my grandparents, were former revolutionaries, or at least that was their term for it.

Nowadays we called them terrorists. During the Vietnam War, they had bombed banks and military bases. I had a picture of Papa Che and Gram in a locket around my neck. In the picture, Gram was my age. Her super-curly hair—like mine—tumbled down to her waist. She wore a leather headband, round wire-rimmed glasses, an army jacket, and a pair of tattered jeans. My grandfather could have been her twin, except he was taller.

They were so proud of me for joining the Academia. My parents . . . not so much. Not at all, in fact. They were pacifists, and they said that it was time to stop the fighting and listen to the vampires, find a way to coexist. We fought about it, bitterly.

My grandparents said my parents were hopeless dreamers. When the war became more brutal, I sided with Gram and Papa Che. There was no way we could sit down and negotiate with the vampires. They were monsters, ravening beasts. We might as well walk up to them and show them our necks.

But now . . .

"Let us come to order," Diego said, as he swept into the chapel from the side door by the altar. We all had to learn Spanish. In the old days, before the vampires declared war on us, students came to Salamanca to learn Spanish, not hand-to-hand combat.

Diego stood in front of his ornate wooden chair, which was upholstered in black velvet. Black was our color, the symbol of darkness. The sun was not for us. More than once I had stopped to think how much more in common we hunters had with the vampires than with the rest of humanity.

So, it begins, I thought, trembling. The bell would toll at midnight, both a celebration of the new year and dirge for the seventeen of us who would not become vampire hunters. The vampires would hunt all of us for the rest of our lives. Our identities were known. Only one of us would receive the sacred elixir that would strengthen him or her for the ordeal ahead, and make them quick to heal. The rest of us would be vulnerable, easier to kill.

The elixir itself was magic. Rumor had it that it was made up of some incredibly rare herbs that could only be harvested on a single night of the year and lay in the heart of one of the vampire strongholds. Armand, one of the priests at the school, was the only one who could make the elixir, and there was never enough for more than one hunter.

I looked across the stone chapel at Antonio, who was busy crossing himself. He was dressed in a black robe, like me. Beneath the robe he wore body armor, like me. His profile was sharp. Tendrils of loose black hair brushed his cheeks. Like every other girl at the Academia, I had had an intense crush on Antonio. It took almost a year to understand that his heart had no room for romance or girls. Vampires had slaughtered his entire family. He was the only one left. *They took everything from me*, was what he said. He burned with a hatred that astounded me; it made him seem like a different kind of being.

In his presence I often felt foolish. No one had slaughtered my family members, or friends. I had come to study how to fight vampires because it sounded cool, glamorous, and because

I wanted to be more like my grandmother than my mother. I had been a stupid kid. As my thoughts drifted back to Jack, I realized that I still was.

On the night I met Jack—Halloween night—Antonio had told me that of all the girls in the class, he respected me the most. Would he still have respected me if he had known that I had fallen in love with a vampire? No, he probably would have killed me himself.

"You understand," Antonio had said, "why I cannot..." And then, and there, I knew that Antonio loved me. I don't know what kind of private battle he had fought, but he had lost it.

It was too late, but I never told him that. We never talked about it, and so I never had to tell him that I had been so careful not to let my feelings deepen for what I had assumed was a lost cause. Since he never told me that he loved me, I had no reason to tell him that old cliché—that while I loved him like a brother, it went no further than that.

As if to make my point, I sat alone, like almost everyone else. The only two who sat together were Jamie and Skye, both red-haired. The rest of us guarded ourselves; we had learned to harden our hearts. Jamie, a fierce streetfighter from Northern Ireland, was the hardest of all of us. Skye, a London goth, liked him, but it was obvious that he was oblivious. I was afraid that my own choices tonight might kill them.

Or Antonio, I thought, staring at the gut-wrenching carving of Christ Crucified hanging behind the altar. If you didn't enter the Academia a believer, you became one: crosses, holy water, and communion wafers really did work against vampires. *Most* vampires.

I knew one who was immune.

Or Jack, I added to my prayers. *Don't lay his death at my door.*

I could see my breath. My stomach clenched as Diego looked straight at me. *He doesn't know*, I reminded myself. *He can't know. I've been so careful.*

Beneath my black robe, my body armor was strapped on over a ratty old black sweater and a pair of faded, tattered jeans. It was what I'd had on the first time I met Jack. I wasn't exactly sure what I was trying to say by wearing the same clothes, but I felt better with them on. Safer, maybe.

It was dangerous to feel safe. Possibly even fatal.

My grandparents had never felt safe. They had been on the run all their lives. Warrants for their arrests were still active.

"And so, on your last night, we are assembled," Diego said.

I jerked upright. My thoughts were scattering. It was a nervous habit, a terrible one—"drifting," I called it. I had been drifting when I met Jack. He could have killed me.

After all this time, I still wasn't sure why he hadn't.

"First we will say Mass, and then I'll pair you up for your hunt this evening." Diego nodded to the back of the church. "The archbishop himself will give you communion. You will be as well armed as the archangels."

But only one of us would receive the elixir after tonight's exam. It seemed so horribly wrong, so unfair. To go through all the training, and make the vows, and then to be denied the best weapon our side had. They would try to protect us; some of us would make our way to other schools to try again. Or maybe to teach. But honestly? Most of us would die.

The archbishop and the altar celebrants arrived next, swaying down the center aisle as the altar boys and girls swung incense burners. One tall boy, a little younger than me, carried an enormous gold cross. The archbishop wore gold and white robes. He was old and solemn. Some people claimed that the church kept the war going because they wanted the vampires wiped out. There was even talk that the church had ordered the death of the president's daughter to make sure no one softened toward the Cursed Ones.

At last the archbishop arrived at the altar. He raised his hand high and blessed all of us. I swallowed hard. My throat was so tight I was afraid I would choke to death.

The Mass proceeded. I had imagined this night a hundred times, a thousand. The pageantry of the ancient Latin mass. The heavy symbolism. I had even dreamed about it—bats flying from the altar to be transformed into white doves. But whatever comfort the Mass might bestow on others was wasted on me.

I was shivering. It was so very cold. Then finally the archbishop gestured for us to sit in the pews.

Diego stood beside the archbishop. He raised his chin and began to read from a list held a distance away from him.

"Jamie and Skye," he began, announcing the first pair. Jamie glowered at Diego, earning a glare of disdain from the archbishop. Skye flushed to her roots.

"Eriko and Holgar," he continued. The two gestured to each other in the drafty room.

I looked at no one, and no one looked at me. Antonio stared straight ahead. Maybe he knew.

"Jenn and Antonio," said Diego, and there were actual sighs in the chapel, like steam. Some girls had not given up on Antonio. It seemed so ludicrous—and yet, I envied them. I hadn't let any of my strong emotions out . . . before Halloween.

Diego finished reading the list. Then the midnight bells tolled, waterfalls of music purifying us, baptizing us.

There were vampires in the hills. They had been sighted. They knew that tonight we would come after them, and they had probably already sown the forests and the hills with traps for us. Last year's vampire-hunter graduate had been slaughtered less than twenty-four hours after this very ceremony.

Then two by two, we took communion. I stood shoulder to shoulder with Antonio, as the short line progressed up the aisle, to accept the communion wafer and drink the ceremonial wine—the body of Our Savior, the blood of Our Savior. I was intensely aware of Antonio beside me. And then, as we knelt for our blessing, his hand brushed mine.

I had never understood why they sent us out two-by-two, as if we were animals on the ark, or Mormon missionaries—the Mormons kept each other company and guarded each other from sin, but they had a common goal: to convert others to their cause. We, however, were in direct competition with each other. Some of us believed that the Academia was lying to us; maybe we were put together because after the examination was over, we would work together.

Then it was over, and we were filing out of the chapel. Someone had put a candle in my hand. The golden glow played over Antonio's sharp features.

There had been talk of the savage vampire band in the woods. There were seven of them. Two of them were French, four Spanish, and one—the leader—was an American, named Jack. The Academia held Jack personally responsible for the deaths of thirty-six of my classmates.

This is insanity, I thought, as outside the church quivers of wooden stakes were slung across our chests like bows and arrows. We carried packs of crosses, holy water, and communion wafers. Modern weaponry was not allowed, nor did it work—another inexplicable fact, among so many, that made up what we had been taught about vampires and vampirism.

It wasn't true, for example, that being bitten by a vampire or drinking its blood changed you into one of them. Our side didn't know why some humans changed into vampires and some didn't.

I wondered if love had anything to do with it. I had a feeling I might find out for sure.

Tonight.

• • •

We fanned out, although there was nothing in the rules about having to separate. If we wanted, we could hunt in a group—*a grupo*—for the last time. As we stood on a rise and gazed down into the valley, Anita and Marica hugged me and wished me luck. Eriko and Holgar raced along the stream-bed, disappearing into darkness. Heavy clouds scudded across the cloudy moonlit sky, and fog rolled in like ocean waves—tall, relentless, wet, and powerful.

Can Jack command the elements? I wondered anxiously. My heart was trying to leap out of my chest, and then my throat. I was icy with fear. Diego had sworn to us that if we kept training and training, our reflexes would take over and we would fight without thinking. I hoped that was true.

The fog raced up over our ankles, then doubled back to sweep over our calves. We were hip-deep in it when Antonio turned to me and said, "I know."

Moonlight shone down on the crown of his hood like a halo. Fog swept behind his back and fanned out, giving the impression of wings. I couldn't see his face. His voice was hard and angry.

"You've snuck out three times to see him," he continued.

Oh, God. "Tonio," I said. My voice was hoarse. "They're not all the same. Just as we're not all the same."

"All of us here are dedicated to the cause," he said. "The holy war against *los vampiros.* Except you."

"I was," I told him. "And then . . . on Halloween . . ." I faltered as Antonio came out of the moonlight.

"You think you're some romantic heroine. Juliet. And he's Romeo. He's a murdering thug who takes pleasure in what he does. And you know that. *You know that.*"

I licked my lips. My tongue was as dry as the dust that coated the tombs of those buried in our chapel. Our revered dead. In some cases, there hadn't been anything to bury. In others— a hand, or a head.

"I know we have been *told* that," I finally managed.

Antonio's face contorted with rage. He raised a hand as if to strike me. "*Idiota*," he said through clenched teeth. "If you had these doubts and these beliefs, you should have spoken up. You should have left."

"I know," I said brokenly. I tried to look away. I didn't know what to say to him, but as it turned out that was the least of my worries. From somewhere close by, a girl screamed. The sound was high-pitched and terrible. Then it was cut off abruptly. Vampires were close, and one of my classmates was already dead.

Antonio grabbed my hand and pulled me in the opposite direction. "Shouldn't we be going after the vampire?" I asked, teeth clacking together as we stumbled over uneven ground.

"That's what they want us to do," he said.

"How do you know?"

"Because it's what I would do if I were them. Human senses can't match theirs in this darkness and fog. She only had time to scream because they wanted her to."

I pulled my hand free from his, fell to my knees, and began to wretch.

"What is wrong with you?" he hissed. "She is not the first you know to have been killed."

He was right, but how could I explain to him how I felt? For some twisted reason, that last two years hadn't seemed real to me. It was as though I was some contestant on a twisted game show. *Who will get the fabulous elixir? Tune in next week to find out!* I was changing. I wasn't a little girl anymore. I felt like a woman. And I owed that to Jack. I had felt so alive when he was holding me, kissing me. I had listened as he talked about his kind and how peace was all he really wanted. It had seemed the mature thing to do, to listen to him and try to understand. Now, I was wondering if he had been laughing at me the entire time.

I pushed myself to my feet. Maybe the girl who had screamed wasn't really dead? I knew it was crazy to believe that, though.

Antonio grabbed my arm to steady me. "Which side are you on? If it is not mine, then you should leave. Right now."

I stared deep into his solemn eyes. Why couldn't he have told me months ago how he felt instead of waiting so long? I should have been home, spending the night playing games with my family and laughing with friends. Instead I had chosen to leave, run away after a bad fight with my mom and dad. I had come to Spain because the Universidad took anyone who was at least sixteen. I was sixteen (barely) and I knew that my life was my own. My parents couldn't control me, not inside the halls of the Universidad.

I took a deep breath. Running had gotten me here. Running again would probably just make everything worse. "I'm with you," I pledged Antonio. But I knew I couldn't kill Jack. I still prayed he would survive. But the rest of his gang were fair game as far as I was concerned.

Antonio nodded but before we could move a vamp came out of the darkness behind him, its face a contorted death mask of fangs and lust. And Diego had been right; the training took over. I knocked Antonio to the side, reached for a stake, and plunged it into the monster's chest. It stopped it in its tracks.

It was a moment before either of us realized I had missed his heart.

Antonio regained his footing, just as I shoved a cross into the vampire's face. The creature lit up like a Christmas tree, flames licking at its eyes, making it look that much more demonic. The scream that came from it nearly paralyzed me. Antonio drew a short sword from beneath his robes and beheaded the creature in one move. The severed head rolled on the ground like some gruesome, flaming soccer ball. Before I could stop myself, I kicked it as far as I could. It sailed up into the sky, hanging for a moment as the flames danced upon the rolling fog.

And that was when I saw the rest of them. The vampires were in a loose half circle, facing us. They had Anita and Marica. As I watched, the vampires, with sick smiles, slowly sunk their teeth into the necks of the two girls.

"No!" I screamed, racing forward.

Antonio grabbed me around the waist and spun me. "Run!" he hissed in my ear.

The darkness pressed in, and I did as he said. We ran for ten minutes, twisting our way in and around trees, climbing steadily upward, away from the Universidad. At last Antonio pushed me into a cave and followed, lighting a single match to show the way. I had never been this far from the Universidad and I stared toward the back of the cave. I couldn't see a wall, just a bend in the path.

"What's going on?" I had so many questions but that was the one that crowded to the surface first.

"Things have gone wrong," Antonio said. "We were supposed to be hunting them, but instead they are hunting us."

"And at least three of us are already dead," I said.

"More," Antonio said darkly.

I desperately wanted to ask him how he knew, but I couldn't really stomach the answer. I thought of all my remaining classmates and wondered how many of us would survive the night.

"This cave is one of a network. We can move through them more safely than we can across the ground outside."

I looked doubtfully into the darkness which seemed deeper than the night. "I'm claustrophobic," I mumbled.

"Better terrified than dead," he said. "Speaking of which, take a moment to bandage your wound."

Puzzled, I looked down at myself and noticed that some underbrush had scratched me through one of the holes in my jeans. I tore a piece of cloth off the bottom of my robe, pulled a tube of antiseptic from my pocket and bandaged the wound. Once the war had begun, they had started putting extract of garlic in the antibiotic creams in order to neutralize the smell of fresh blood. I had never been more grateful for the innovation. The one thing vamps could do better than see in the dark was smell a drop of blood miles away.

"If we get out of this alive, I'm going to have to apologize to my mother," I said, making quick work of the bandaging. "And I'm going to have to thank her."

"For what?"

"For this," I pulled an unlit glowstick from my pocket. "She sent it in my last care package."

Antonio put away his pack of matches and cracked the glowstick alight. "I will thank her too."

"So, what's the game plan?" I asked, as ready to move into the confines of the cave as I would ever be.

Antonio led the way, and I followed him, forcing my eyes to stay on the glowstick in his hand. *I'm not descending into dark, terrifying caves and fighting for my life*, I told myself. *I'm ten and it's Halloween and I'm just trying to beat the bigger kids to the best candy.*

"We have to find a way to take the vampires out without exposing ourselves."

"And hope that they are tracking some of the others, right?"

"We won't be so lucky."

"Why?" I asked, scrambling to stay directly behind him and within eyesight of the light.

He hesitated. When he finally spoke his voice was tense. "There's something I probably should have told you before."

So, I wasn't the only one keeping secrets. The revelation gave me a sense of relief and something else to focus on besides the fact that the cave walls seemed to be getting closer.

"What is it?"

"I am known to the vampires, and I have made many enemies."

I waited for him to continue. Nothing he had said came as any real surprise to me. The silence stretched between us and finally he went on.

"I believe they will try to find us before they go after the others."

There was something he wasn't telling me. I thought about calling him on it, but I was still reeling under the weight of my own guilty secret. Where was Jack? Would we be bumping into him soon?

A sudden rustling sound ahead caused us both to freeze in our tracks. I had my hand on Antonio's arm, and I could feel the play of his muscles beneath the skin. He shifted slightly so he could press his back against the cave wall and I did the same, my heart beating uncontrollably. *I don't want to have to fight in here. I don't want to die in here. There's so little room, it might as well be a coffin. My coffin.*

I shook my head, trying to clear it. *Focus, focus, focus!*

I heard a soft whooshing sound and then a bat flew right by us, its wing brushing the tip of my nose. I jerked, slamming my head against the cave wall. All the stories I had ever heard about vampires when I was a kid flooded my mind.

"Vampire!" I gasped.

Antonio laughed, low and deep, and the sound cut through my terror. "You know vampires can't change into bats."

And he was right. I did know that. I had spent the last two years studying vampires, not the fictional kind, but the real, just-as-soon-kill-you-as-seduce-you kind.

We continued moving forward, slightly faster now, which was a relief because it required more attention on my part not to twist an ankle. We wove through several different tunnels, which branched off into smaller and smaller corridors until I knew I could never find my way back.

"You know I love you," Antonio said, breaking the silence that had once again fallen between us.

I didn't know how to respond. It was a statement, not a question, like there could be no doubt that I knew he loved me. I had managed to avoid the topic for two months. As I contemplated how to sidestep it now though, a couple of things occurred to me. First, I'd much rather talk about it than think about the caves we were walking through. Second, one or both of us would likely die before morning. Suddenly talking about it seemed like a really good idea.

"I'm not sure that I actually knew that," I said, grimacing. I was grateful he couldn't see my face. It was my intention to let him down easy. Still, there was a part of me that had actually wanted to hear him say the words.

"I don't know how I could have been more clear. I love you, Jenn."

All girls dream of having a guy say that to them. When I was younger, I spent countless hours imagining hearing those words, visualizing who would say them, where we would be, how I would feel. But in my wildest dreams, I couldn't have pictured a guy quite like Antonio. And although at least once or twice I had thought I might hear those words one New Year's Eve, I could never have anticipated hearing them in the middle of a cave while engaged in a battle with vampires. And I certainly had never anticipated having such a mixed reaction to the words themselves.

The moment he said them out loud I knew that I still had feelings for Antonio. I had so wanted to keep my heart shut up and stay detached, but maybe that was unrealistic. "I didn't let myself care for you in that way because it seemed pretty obvious to me that there was no chance," I admitted.

"It was . . . important . . . for me to stay focused on why we were here."

"I know that vampires killed your whole family. I thought that revenge was all you wanted."

He laughed, a hard, bitter laugh so different from the one before. "Yes, you're right, revenge *was* all I wanted."

"And now?"

"I've already told you I love you."

"I think . . . I'm in love with Jack," I admitted. There, I'd said it. I held my breath, afraid of what his response would be.

"No, you aren't," he said so softly I barely heard him.

That was one response I hadn't expected. "Why would you say that?"

"He's a vampire."

"That doesn't mean that I can't love him."

"I'm not saying you can't love a vampire, just that you don't love that one."

"I'm not following you," I said in frustration.

"He's mesmerized you."

I stopped dead in my tracks. Antonio took a few more steps before turning around. The light from the glowstick threw shadows around the cave in bizarre patterns, and they danced across his face. I wanted to tell him that he was wrong, that it was a lie. Somehow I asked instead, "How do you know?"

"I just do. Stop and search your soul. You know it, too."

Everything seemed to slow down, like in a nightmare. Where my obsession with Jack had flamed and burned, something icy and cold walked over my grave.

I gasped. I hadn't been myself. He had used me.

As awareness rushed in, I began to shake and cry. In two years, I hadn't shed a tear for the dead, or the pain. Now it all seemed determined to be released at once.

"What's happened to me?" I asked Antonio.

When he pulled me close and held me, he was shaking too. "I think Jack mesmerized you to get at me," he whispered. "I'm so, so sorry. Just remember that as long as you're aware of it, his mesmerism is broken."

I pulled away and wiped my eyes on my sleeve. But…but it had been so real. And now—just another vampire lie. They hadn't come in peace. Jack didn't come for love.

"Jenn," Antonio said. "I *am* sorry."

"We should keep moving," I said stonily. "We've got vampires to kill."

He nodded and took my hand. As our fingers interlaced, I

felt a peace I had not known for years. He turned and began to move through the caves at a half run. I kept up with him, grateful to be doing something at last.

Winding through the caves, I lost track of time. When we finally emerged from them, I was surprised to see the moon directly overhead. We scrambled up a rocky slope for about a hundred yards before emerging in a clearing.

The vampires were already there. The sick feeling in my gut told me that they had been waiting for us.

And there was Jack. He stretched out his hand toward me exactly as I had pictured him doing the last several, sleepless nights. His grin was wide, no longer as playful as I remembered it, but simply arrogant. His eyes were laughing and cruel. I could see everything that had been hidden to me before. He had mesmerized me. Damn him. He had tricked me.

But I was free now. And he didn't know it.

I gave Antonio's hand a squeeze, hoping he understood what I was going to do. I walked forward, a smile on my face, heart pounding out of control.

"Beloved," Jack said, when I was just a few steps away.

He had called me that before, but this time I blushed out of embarrassment instead of excitement. Out of the corners of my eyes, I could see the other vampires. They wanted me dead. I could feel the hatred coming off of them in waves. More than that, though, they wanted Antonio dead. I understood it all now. I had just been the bait.

If I could kill Jack before they could stop me, then Antonio would have a fighting chance. An owl hooted not that far off, and I did my best not to turn my head. None of the vampires seemed to notice, but I knew that it wasn't a real owl—it was our classmate, Jamie. It was a message: *You are not alone.*

And I smiled even more broadly. Jack had his *grupo* and I had mine. This then was the final lesson. We were not alone, not just single hunters against many vampires. We had friends who would fight and die with us, and for us. It was something not talked about in the Universidad because it was something that they couldn't teach. It was camaraderie built out of shared pain and adversity. I understood everything now.

"Did you miss me?" Jack purred. I came to stand before him. He reached out to me, wanting me to take his hand. I kept my face turned coyly to the ground. When I finally raised my eyes to his, he was still smiling, confident I was still under his spell. Bastard.

I ripped the stake free of its holder in a flash. "No, I didn't!" His eyes suddenly widened as I raised the stake and ruthlessly drove it straight through his black vampire heart.

His eyes flickered in surprise for a moment that suspended me somewhere humiliating and shameful. I would never let anyone use me again. Never believe in a vampire's lies again.

Then he was gone. I spun around to ward off the next, nearest vampire, but it threw me to the ground, knocking the wind out of me. Then it leapt in for the kill. Its fangs brushed my throat.

This is it. This is how I die.

Suddenly, something grabbed my tormentor from behind,

and he went flying thirty feet through the air. The only thing strong enough to do that was another vampire. And as I struggled up onto my elbows, that was exactly what I saw.

Antonio turned toward me. I knew it was no trick of the light. The fangs he was baring were real. I gasped and he smiled sadly at me. Then I understood exactly what he had meant that first day at the Universidad when he had said the vampires took everything from him. *His family, his friends, his life.* No wonder he hated them. And no wonder they hated him—one of their own kind who hunted them.

Jamie and Skye burst into the clearing. Antonio turned as another vamp came running toward us. Eriko and Holgar emerged into the battle, bloody and brutal. Vampires turned to ash around us. Our ferocity knew no bounds. This time we would take them all out! Jamie ran toward us, now covered in the blood of the vampires he had recently staked. He skidded to a halt when he got a good look at Antonio.

"Something new?" Jamie asked warily eyeing Antonio's fangs.

"No, something old," Antonio said.

"Bloody hell." Jamie lunged to stake him.

But I stepped in his way.

"No. He saved my life," I heard myself saying. I was trembling. "He's . . . one of us."

I want to say that then and there, we became a team. Five crazy humans and one vampire. But it took a long time, and we were tested over and over again as the nights unfolded.

But as we stood together on New Year's Eve, I turned and saw another half dozen vamps emerge from the trees. Their long teeth gleamed in the moonlight, and they were hissing in anticipation of the kill.

"I don't remember Jack having a group this big," I said.

"Looks like someone's been recruiting."

"Building his own little army," Antonio added.

I grabbed a stake in each fist. "Good thing we've got a vampire of our own.

"Let's get this party started!" Eriko shouted.

Antonio spared one look at me, and I felt a strange mix of horror and excitement. Antonio was a vampire. He'd said he loved me.

And I knew it was not a lie.

The knowledge propelled me into battle. I moved like whirlwind, fighting as I had never done before. I was almost crazy, I was so fierce. I felt my stake slam into vampire chests, taking vampire lives.

Miraculously, it was over in under five minutes. Even more miraculously, we were all bloodied but still standing.

"Everyone bandage up." I set to work on my own wounds. Antonio stood a safe distance away, and by his stance, I knew he was trying to regain control over his vampire self. I had so many questions, but they could wait. When I killed Jack, his power over me had vanished completely. At that moment, I remembered that before I met Jack I had loved Antonio. And not as a brother. Jack had twisted that emotion for his own ends. He had made me forget who I was for a moment. But that was all over now.

I had loved Antonio, and I loved him again. The idea was strange, and new, and yet it felt old. I thought of my parents and my grandparents, and felt a dizzying connection. Was I going somewhere in my heart that they had never been? Or were the hearts of humans and vampires more alike than different?

I had other questions. Some were for my classmates. Except for Jamie, they seemed fine with the idea of a vampire as comrade. I had fully expected them to turn on Antonio after we had dispatched the rest of the vampires.

I cleared my throat. "Are we going to have any problems?" I asked my new *grupo*.

"With Antonio?" Jamie frowned.

I nodded.

"He's okay with me," Holgar said. But Jamie said nothing.

I stared at them all in disbelief. After two years of training to kill vampires, of witnessing the horrors they were capable of, I didn't know how the rest of them could let this go so easily.

"Why? How?" I blurted.

Eriko smiled. "If Father Armand let a vampire study at the Universidad, then he must be one of us."

Us. Not one of us *humans*. One of us *hunters*. I hadn't thought about that. Father Armand personally screened every student for admission. He was a very kind, but intense, priest with a twisted sense of humor. Still, would he have even been able to tell Antonio was a vampire?

"You think Father Armand knew?" I asked.

"He knew I was a witch," Skye said calmly.

"And he knew I was a werewolf," Holgar added, as if it was common knowledge.

I stared at them all in shock. Finally I pivoted to face Jamie and Eriko. "Anything about the two of you I should know about?"

"No," a deep voice answered from the shadows behind us.

I spun around, my hand on a stake, and slumped in relief when I saw that it was Father Armand.

"Each pairing has one normal student, and one with special abilities," he explained. "It's safer for everyone that way."

"But—"

He raised his hand. "You think humans are the only ones who wish to fight evil? No. This war against the vampires has pulled in many people from many groups. A very few vampires retain enough of their original self that with meditation, study, and discipline they can control their bloodlust. Antonio is one of those. Skye is kin to some friends of mine and I recognized her talents when we met. Holgar, years ago, learned how to safeguard himself and others from his wolf aspect. This war touches us all and, I'm afraid, it does not stop here."

"Then we will continue to fight," I said. "Or at least, I will."

"And I," Holgar said.

"Me too," Skye put in.

The others echoed in the affirmative, Jamie last. Antonio appeared suddenly nearby, slipping his hand around mine. I fought the urge to lean against his shoulder. There would be time enough later for the two of us.

"I have only elixir for one," Armand reminded. "And it is for Eriko."

"Yes," I said. I wondered how I had managed to appoint myself spokesperson for the small group, and why no one else seemed to object.

The priest—our priest—smiled at me. "You understand, then. A witch may offer protection to her partner. A vampire may do the same. However, a werewolf has a wild talent. He could inflict unintentional damage on his partner and cannot change at will."

Eriko bowed her head. "I am not worthy," she murmured.

Armand put his hand on Eriko's shoulder and forced her to look up. "Then become so," he whispered.

We all will, I vowed.

"*Sí,*" Antonio whispered in my ear.

And so it began.

Ambition

BY LILI ST. CROW

"YOU I CAN change." He leaned forward, his lips brushing mine. His breath smelled like peppermints and desire, his hair was copper and chocolate. Then he rested his forehead against mine.

Sometimes I wonder what would have happened if I'd said no. But he leaned against me, his arm over my shoulders, our foreheads touching, and everything else was so far away. He was beautiful, and he was holding me as if I was his. It didn't matter that I was cold all over, that I was scared, or that my throat burned like gasoline. The only thing that mattered was that he'd chosen me.

Me.

So I said yes.

What girl wouldn't?

...

"God." Gwyneth lay on the bench, thick waves of golden hair touching the shade-dappled wood. Out here under the fig trees was one of the most desirable spots for lunchtime. "This won't ever end. I'll be trapped here for the rest of my *life*."

"We could skip fifth period." I hugged my bare knees, my bag a comforting slumped weight under them. It was a way to get around the indecency of wanting to pull yourself up in a ball while wearing a skirt. Double scabs from rollerblading were rough patches, I pushed my glasses up with the side of one knee in a quick sideways motion. "I've got the homework done. So we can get there at a reasonable time."

"But I'd have to change." Cornflower-blue eyes blinked. She held up one hand, inspected her French manicure. "I can't go in this."

"Schoolgirl is always in." *Besides, I don't have anything to change into.* I tried hard not to wheedle. But God, sometimes Gwyn even had to be talked into things she *wanted* to do.

"With perverts." She stretched again. "Let's skip fourth as well. You've got that homework done too, right?"

She meant, did I have something we could both turn in? I did. But there was a problem. "Quiz today." I hunched down, my shoulders sharp points. The shade felt good. Dry wind blew across the lacrosse field, full of the tang of sprinkler water and chemical fertilizer. Molly Fenwick and Trisha Brent and their whole crowd were at the benches in the sun, their jackets off and white Peter Pan-collared shirts unbuttoned enough to be daring. Mitzi Hollenweider was telling a story that involved a lot of handwaving and shrieks of *ohmiGOD!*, careless of whether any of the teachers could hear.

The embroidered badge on my jacket scratched as I rubbed my chin against the one unscabbed bit of my right knee. The hairpins hurt, holding my frizz tightly back. That was one of the things about St. Crispin's—every button buttoned and every stray hair slicked down. Gwyn's waves were placid and accept-able, laying tamely wherever she wanted them. But my mess of dark fritz was always working its way free of whatever was used to confine it. I would've taken home demerits for that, except I knew when to smooth the teachers over.

They liked me. Adults usually do.

"Dammit." She stretched again. "So we take the quiz and bail. Right?"

"Tricky." And it was—Brother Bob, as he liked to be called, pretended to be down with the kids. It was all a big act—he reported to the headmistress *and* to the bishop who made all the big decisions. The rumor was he was stuck in a girl's school because he liked the other flavor of young kid. Boy: The Other Catholic Meat.

You'd think we'd have some things in common to bitch about with Brother Bob if he liked boys so much. But he was a narc, no matter how much slang he tried to pick up.

"Well, then what do we *do*?" She was getting irritated now.

"We'll figure something out. We always do." The wind touched my hair, mouthed my knees. "Maybe we'll get lucky."

The bell rang. Second lunch over, freedom gone. A ripple ran through everyone. Mitzi finished up her story, glancing over at us. She always wanted to walk to fourth period with Gwyn. It was getting to the point where being Gwyn's best friend all the way from second grade was wearing a bit thin, and Mitzi was looking to get her into the popular crowd.

If she could get rid of me.

Gwyn hauled herself up with a groan, like she was forty instead of sixteen. Her knees were smooth, her hair settled into place with a few flicks, and she stood balanced on one leg, propping the other foot on the bench to flick imaginary dust off her shiny Mary Janes. Hers were always polished.

I stood up, and a dragging cramp went through my stomach. Gwyn snagged her brown paper lunchbag, wadded it up. There was half a sandwich still in there.

"We'll think of something," I repeated.

"*Gwyneth*!" Mitzi called. "Hey *Gwyneth*!"

"God," Gwyn said, *sotto voce*. "Her voice drills right through my head. Save my spot in fourth, okay?"

Like anyone else would sit next to me. But I nodded. "Sure. Have fun."

"Yeah, right. I'll see what the bitch wants." Gwyn gave me a weird, stretched-thin smile, and moved out into sunlight. Her hair caught it and glowed, and her legs moved long and lithe, dancing steps as she swung her bag back and forth. I sighed and almost fell off the bench while trying to get myself standing up. My skirt didn't flip up, though, thank God. Another cramp hit me sideways while I got my books all rearranged inside the regulation satchel.

St. Crispin's even decrees what bookbag you can buy. They're like that. Scholarship kids like me get a big break on the prices, though. Not enough of a break, but some.

Mitzi's voice kept hitting high ugly pitches. I sneaked a glance over while I shrugged back into my blazer. Go figure—

here we were in sunny Cali and they wanted us to wear wool.

The gaggle of girls in sunlight all giggled, the very same high-pitched nasal laughter. I was pretty sure Gwyn was laughing at them, though, not with them. I hitched my bag up on my shoulder and walked to fourth period. I only looked back once, and Gwyn was alight with the rest of them, standing in a flood of sunlight that picked out their glossy hair, their pampered skin, and the little glitters of gold jewelry—balls or small hoops, 24K of course—that St. Crispin's approved of.

My chest hurt. My stomach growled again, telling me I was hungry, but I ignored it. The school doors swallowed me. Smells of linoleum, oil, chalk dust, the janitor's harsh cleansers, and the funk of miserable kids in scratchy clothes, repeating drills when the whole world was outside waiting, all closed over my head. I trudged toward the classroom, and nobody yelled my name.

. . .

They were a couple minutes late to fourth period, but Brother Bob had been delayed with something or another. It was rare that he wasn't in the room on the dot, so I opened up my secondhand trig textbook.

Gwyneth slid into her seat next to me. Mitzi gave me a pitying look, tossing her blonde pigtails. I slumped down in my chair.

"There's a party tonight," Gwyn whispered. She'd gotten some gum from somewhere, and the perfume of Juicy Sweet touched my cheek. "Out in the Hills. Wanna go?"

"I thought we were—"

"Come on." She grinned while Brother Bob lumbered to the front of the room. He was sweating, and his round face was red. The collar always cut into the crinkled skin of his throat. Gwyn called the look "choked turkeyneck," and I agreed.

"I won't know anyone there." But it was a mumble, because the class had quieted. Bob's little, moist, dark eyes raked the rows of seats. Mitzi wriggled in her chair. Trisha shoved her bookbag under her seat and fiddled with her hair ribbon.

"Jesus, just say yes." Gwyneth's blue eyes narrowed as she stared at the front of the classroom. Brother Bob gulped and stood up straight. The chalkboard was freshly washed.

"Yes," I said.

"Quiet down, girls," Bob said.

Then the fire alarm went off. It was a drill, thank God. Gwyn and I glanced at each other, grabbed our bookbags, and got out of there. I guess we were meant to skip fourth period after all.

• • •

We stopped off at Gwyn's house. Her dad was at work and her mom was off somewhere, so there was only Marisa the house-keeper, who clucked at both of us as we tore in through the door, laughing.

"Did you *see* that?" Gwyn was laughing so hard she hic-cupped. It was a wonder she could drive. Her place was twelve minutes away from the St. Crispin's if the lights were right. Today they hadn't been, but we were lucky.

Driving with Gwyneth was like playing roulette. You just knew sooner or later you were going to lose. She got distracted and rolled through stop signs, forgot to check oncoming traffic, and didn't notice red lights sometimes until I pointed them out, usually by yelling *Jesus Christ!* and grabbing for the dash.

She was in hysterics from the fact that we'd rolled right past a cop at a stop sign, blithely disregarding the fact that it wasn't our turn to go. The cop hadn't even glanced or flicked his lights. He'd just been *sitting* there.

I was in hysterics because we'd come *this close* to getting pasted by a huge red Escalade. On *my* side, of course. Because nothing would ever happen to Miss Luckypants. But I just went along, laughing. At least hanging out with her was never boring, not since second grade when she fell out of the monkey bars onto me. And when I spent the night in her parents' glass-and-white-stucco mansion, sometimes I would close my eyes and imagine it was me who lived here and someone else who just visited all the time.

Gwyn dropped her bookbag on a stool at the breakfast bar and swiped her hand back through her hair. "Hi, Marisa." She tried to put on a serious face and failed miserably.

"*Ola*, Marisa." I waved, hitching my bag up on my shoulder.

She sniffed at both of us, but opened up the fridge door. In under a minute there was a plate of sugar cookies and two big glasses of milk. Like magic. Round-faced, round-shouldered, and round-eyed, she wore a black dress that seemed to be a uniform. A clean, starched white apron never had the slightest stain.

I took a sugar cookie. She gave me her usual tight smile, one that didn't reach her solemn dark eyes.

Our laughter drained away. Gwyneth dropped down on a stool, and Marisa pushed the plate a little closer to me. I took a gulp of milk, and my stomach eased up a bit.

"Rolled right past him," Gwyn giggled, and then we were off and running again.

It took a long time for the giggles to fade, especially with Marisa restocking the sugar cookies and pouring more milk. "So what did Mitzi want? Other than to invite you to the shindig of the week." I even managed to say it casually.

"Oh, just stuff. You know she doesn't exist unless everyone around her is adoring her. It's just sick the way they all stand around and valley each other."

Yeah. It is. "You sure you want to go to this party?" *With me* was what I meant, and Gwyn gave me a bright little sidelong glance. She looked so healthy, the roses in her cheeks blooming. I'd torn all the pins out of my hair and I felt greasy. The uniform didn't help.

"You can borrow my black silk shirt." She wasn't quite wheedling. But that black silk was her *baby*. She hardly ever wore it.

"Nah. You can just drop me off at my house. I don't want to go."

"You want to go to the Bleu again. The boring old Bleu."

That's where you wanted to go five minutes before Mitzi descended from on high to invite you. "No, I've got homework."

"Please. It only ever takes you five minutes to do your homework. I'm driving, you're coming with me. You have to. I can't go deal with those squealing idiots all on my own."

Why go, then? But I gave in. Oh, I played like I wasn't going for a while, until she got irritated and threw a cookie at me. Marisa sighed and whisked the plate away. I finished my milk and picked the cookie up. I didn't eat it though. I've got some pride.

But I did say, "Okay, *fine*. I'll go. Jesus."

Which made Gwyn all sunny again. She's always like that when she gets her way.

• • •

Some guy's house, up in the Hills. There was a keg, thumping music, and a lot of whooping going on. Someone's parents were away—I think the ratfaced guy in the corner taking shots with a bunch of pimpled jocks was the host, but I never found out for sure. It was a warm night, the winds just starting up. Full moon like a big wheel of boiled cheese coming up over the coast, rising above the broken pleats of the Hills. It was a nice view, through whole walls of glass. As soon as we got there Gwyn went for a beer and I was left all by myself near the front door, staring at groups of kids I didn't know.

I saw Mitzi in the corner, and she perked up when she saw me. When I say *perked up* I mean *swelled up like a frog preparing to spit poison*, and I suddenly got a very bad feeling about this.

The bad feeling lasted. I found Gwyn in the kitchen, her golden head together with Trisha Brent's. They were giggling over something, and I began to feel a little lightheaded. There had to be a hundred people in here. One kid started barfing in the pool just as I passed the wide-open French doors out to the patio. I peered out, the madrona trees down the hill moving gently as the wind poured past me.

It felt good. I wanted to step outside, but the kid horking into the pool kind of destroyed the mood. I stood there, hanging onto one edge of the open door, and someone got a little too close.

When I looked up, it was to see Scott Holder.

Half the girls at St. Crispin's were in love with him. Blue eyes. Blond floppy emo-boy haircut. Plays soccer and goes to Ignatius Academy, which is the closest thing to a sister school we've got. The end-of-the-year dances put Iggies and Crispies together, with the staff of both watching like hawks. Guess they don't want any of the Catholic escaping.

He was saying something, those chiseled lips moving. I stared at him. He was still in the prep outfit Ignatius makes the boys wear, though he'd ditched the jacket and unbuttoned the shirt. The necklace—a single canine tooth on a hemp cord, its top wrapped with gold wire—was definitely not regulation. He grinned at me, showing those white white teeth.

"What?" I had to yell through the music.

He said my name. "Right? You go to Crispy."

I nodded. *What the hell do you want?*

"Want to go outside?" He was too tan and perfect to be real. For a second I actually thought he was asking *me* to go outside with him, and a weird little double-track fantasy popped up inside my head. It was Scott Holder picking me up from St. Crispin's in his maroon Volvo, me throwing my bookbag in the back seat and getting in, and Mitzi and her pals watching enviously from the sidelines.

Then I woke up to reality, looked over his shoulder, and saw Mitzi and Gwyn, standing really close together. Mitzi looked like the cat that had swallowed the canary, and Gwyn's mouth was a round 0. They were staring right at me, and I recognized my only friend's expression.

It was the same way she looked on April Fool's Day. Gwyn doesn't have much in the way of subtlety. Mitzi whispered something to her, cupping her hand and rolling her pretty, avid, gumball-blue eyes. And Scott's smile was beginning to look like an inverted V because his eyebrows had gone up.

He looked really sure that I would follow him out the door onto the patio, where the kid throwing up had subsided into a gurgle and a bunch of laughter echoed around him.

Everything fell into place behind my eyes. It's the sort of thing that happens every day in schools across America. Someone makes a choice and hangs someone else out to dry.

I pushed past Scott, hitting him hard with my shoulder. He swayed aside. I plunged through the crowd and my stomach started revolving. I think I heard Gwyneth call my name once or twice, but I ignored it. The living room was a mass of kids all hopping around to some hip-hop anthem. I got jabbed with sweaty elbows and knocked around until I made it through to the foyer. Pot smoke hazed the air.

Normally Gwyn and I would've found a spot to sit and watch, sharing a beer or a joint and making snarky comments about every idiot in the room. But this time I slipped out through the front door and down the wide palatial steps.

The winds had arrived. They smelled dry and burning, but not as burning as the tears flooding my eyes. They splashed on black silk, and I made up my mind not to give the stupid shirt back.

The party had spilled out the front door. Groups of kids were standing around laughing. A line of shiny new cars stretched around the circular driveway and poured down the hill. I kept walking, my Mary Janes slapping the pavement. The roads up here were twisty but had shoulders and ditches, the madrona whispering and moving on either side. Stars of light were houses up and down the hill, none of the neighbors too close to make a fuss.

I had to walk for a while before I reached the little red Miata. Gwyn had left her door unlocked, so I could pop the trunk and get my bookbag and blazer. If I remembered rightly, down at the end of the hill was a crossroads and a higher-end Circle K, in case anyone ran out of booze or Twinkies up here in the rich section of town.

It was gonna be a long walk. The wind whispered and chortled.

Gwyneth yelled my name. It was faint and faraway, like she was standing on a train platform and I was pulling away.

I turned around, hitched my regulation bookbag up on my shoulder, and started walking.

• • •

There wasn't a cab, but there was a bus going downtown. I climbed on, swiped my pass, and sat right behind the driver. That's the safest place at night, especially if you're crying. I had to dig in my schoolbag for anything that might possibly be called tissues, found nothing, and ended up wiping at my face with my white school shirt. I had to do the laundry anyway.

It took a solid hour, though the bus only paused at one stop for no discernable reason. I could have been back at the party, necking with Scott Holder and making an idiot of myself. Or maybe they had something else planned. Who knew?

We dropped down into the valley, wound through one of the industrial districts, and ended up at the edge of downtown.

As a matter of fact, I pulled the stop cord before I thought about it, and climbed out in front of the Bleu. It was early yet in the night, only a few minutes after ten, and the all-ages club that was our sad excuse for party central was lit up like a Christmas tree. There was a gaggle of kids out front, some smoking, some just leaning against the wall and trying to look tough. Lots of eyeliner, lots of ratted-out hair, girls that weren't Crispies in tartan skirts and platform Mary Janes. The goths had taken over the club bigtime tonight.

I paid two dollars in dimes and nickels, got a fluorescent hand stamp. I plunged into the air-conditioned darkness flashing with strobe lights and thumping bass. My bookbag went to the check counter. I stuffed the tab in the little hidden pocket of my skirt and hit the dancefloor. They were playing some industrial trash, but it had a beat and the music shook me out of myself. Everyone was sweating despite the air-conditioning, and the hot salt water on my cheeks was touched with cool little puffs of evaporation.

When you're dancing, time disappears. Everything goes away. It's like being a drop of water in a body-temperature ocean, all the rough edges smoothed. When the crowd presses close and the sweat rises on the back of your neck, when you're jumping or waving your arms and there's the soft pressure of bodies against you, it's like not being lonely again ever.

I bumped against him four or five times before I realized he was dancing with me. A shock of dark curling hair, a white shirt, threadbare designer jeans and boots. He looked about seventeen, dark eyes and high cheekbones. The music welled up in crashing beats, he leaned in, and I smelled peppermints and the clean healthiness of a boy. It wasn't like Scott Holder's expensive cologne. It was something else. My pulse spiked and I whirled away, but the floor was packed too tightly. He was behind me, his arms sliding around me, and the tears came in a hot gush. I leaned back into the anonymous arms for at least two songs. We were a still point and the rest of the dancefloor whirled around us, a kaleidoscope of eyes and lips and kids dressed up and painted.

A chunk of the crowd broke, and I lunged for freedom. The arms fell away and I made it past the bar (only soda and overpriced water—all-ages means no fun) and through the stiles out onto the street where the wind was still blowing. Stopped, tipped my face up, my cheeks drying and my hair lifting. Kids came out behind me—it was about time for a smoke break, and they were all shouting and laughing. I swayed back and forth as they bumped me, and waited for the bouncer to yell at me not to block the door.

"Hey," someone said. Right in my ear.

I flinched. The bouncer, a thick pseudo-military guy who probably couldn't get a job at a real club, yelled. But not at me. I opened my eyes and looked up, and it was him.

If he'd been too pretty, I wouldn't have even paused. But he looked almost normal. Even the jeans could have been a thrift-store find. He was looking at me funny. A vertical line between his eyebrows, his mouth a little tense.

I swiped angrily at my cheeks. My feet hurt, and I'd wasted two bucks on this. Why? "Hey."

"Johnny." He stuck his hand out. "Hi."

I looked at his hand, up at him, and Scott Holder's blue-eyed smile, so full of itself, drifted through my head. But I shook his hand. "Hi." His skin was warm and a different texture, not sweaty like mine. I pulled away after one limp shake. My bare calves tingled under the wind pouring up the street and rubbing against the edges of buildings like a dry cat.

"Mystery lady." His eyes passed down me once, took in the silk and the skirt and the white socks and the Mary Janes. "I've seen you here before. With that blonde girl."

"She's not here tonight," I said immediately. He'd just struck out.

"Good. It's hard to talk to girls when they're with each other. You guys do it on purpose." He grinned slightly, the tips of his teeth peeking out. "You want a cigarette?"

I stared at him. My eyes were hot and grainy, and my entire face felt flushed and blotchy. "No thanks."

"Good. Let's dance some more, huh? It's early." He hunched his shoulders, sticking his hands in his pockets. His hair was like mine, only curls instead of frizz. He looked very sure. And there was something wrong.

It wasn't that he wasn't attractive, because he was. He just looked so *sure*. You never get a teenage boy who looks that certain about everything. If they do it's a front.

But he looked . . . it was weird. I couldn't figure it out and didn't want to stare at him. "I've got to go."

"You just got here."

How the hell do you know? I shrugged, rubbed one Mary Jane against the back of my sock, polishing it. My ankles hurt; I'd walked a long way down the hill to the bus stop. I was going to have blisters.

"Come on. Say yes." He didn't grin now. Instead, he looked serious. *Very* serious. His eyes had gone deep. "We have to stick together, you and me."

Say what? I don't even know you, kid. "Why's that?"

"Because otherwise they'll eat us alive. Let's dance." He offered his hand again, palm-up.

And I suppose it was true. And I'd paid my two bucks. And he didn't smile, just looked at me as if this was serious business and I was expected to know it. The wind just made its low rasping noise.

So I went with him. We went back past the bouncer, who glared at us but didn't say anything. Johnny kept my hand all the way to the dance floor, and we melded with the crowd. But we were in a private little space all our own.

• • •

When I opened my eyes Saturday morning, early sun striping my bed and my alarm clock wheezing instead of ringing, the first thing I realized was that my feet hurt like hell. The second thing I realized was that the trailer was empty.

Either that, or Dad was asleep.

I lay there for a few moments, feeling the sun. The trailer crackled the way it always did in the morning—like pork rinds in a mechanic's mouth. The backs of my ankles hurt, but I had clean socks. I'd done laundry the day before yesterday.

I got up. The hole in the bathroom floor watched me while I got ready. The water wasn't hot, but it wasn't cold either today. Which was all right. The spotted mirror over the sink was depressing, so I barely glanced at it enough to braid my hair.

When I got out into the kitchen, I found out why Dad was gone.

Job in Bakers today. Got report card. Strate a's. Good kid. Pay lectric bill! The letters scrawled across the back of a manila envelope from St. Crispin's, its official-looking coat of arms and Gothic typeface blotched from the coffee he'd spilled.

He had a job. Thank God. At least for a while. I opened up the card, saw the As in a neat row, breathed a sigh of relief. I'd really squeaked through in trig last semester, but Fate and Brother Bob had been kind.

So the scholarship money was safe. I was sure to get approved with grades like these. Who gave a shit what those rich bitches thought or how nasty they were? Who cared?

But Gwyneth. Sitting beside me on the dock at her family's summer cabin, swinging her legs and eating an ice cream cone. Watching out the window for her dad to get home while Marisa and I played checkers. Standing next to me in the choir, both of us bumping each other when one of the songs full of our little in-jokes came up.

There was cash in an envelope. I was supposed to go out and pay the electric bill. The cheap net curtains moved a little. He'd left the kitchen window open, probably to get the fug of cigarette smoke out. Three beer cans and a pan with scrambled eggs and a few traces of refried beans stuck to the bottom. I turned on the splattering faucet and put some dish soap in the sink.

My cheeks were wet. The wind moaned. From now on it would be a constant sound, the dry dust-laden whisper that wove around sharp edges every fall. If we hadn't gone to the party I'd be waking up in Gwyn's bedroom right now, smelling coffee and frying bacon, and hearing Marisa's faraway hum in the kitchen. Since it was a Saturday her parents might be there and she'd be itching to be gone before her pale, angular mother started up on the "are-you-going-to-church-tomorrow?" We would go to the mall and mock people, laughing behind our cupped hands while Gwyn shopped.

The phone rang. I looked at it and wished we had Caller ID. I'd like to know if it was Gwyneth I was ignoring as I scrubbed the dishes in the sink, rinsed them, dried them, put them away, and then cleaned out my bookbag. And really, who else would be calling over and over again? A bill collector, maybe.

When I left, closing the door behind me and locking it, the phone was still ringing. And I could still see the prints of Johnny's black Jetta in the dirt of the driveway, almost obliterated by the tracks of my dad's truck and the blowing wind.

• • •

Monday I didn't have class with Mitzi and her crew until fourth, which I was always grateful for. But Gwyn wasn't in second. I sat through a whole lecture on American history while her empty chair throbbed like a bad tooth next to me. The bell for third-period/ first-lunch rang, and it was like every other school day when Gwyn was sick or hungover and got Marisa to get her out of class. Nobody paid any attention to me, and I liked it that way.

Lunch I spent in the long, narrow library, staring at printed pages through the blurring in my eyes. My nose was stuffed up. I kept my head down when I heard voices at the door. Fourth period was what I was really gearing up for, and I wasn't disappointed. Brother Bob gave another quiz, the seat next to mine was empty, and Mitzi and her friends giggled all during class, glancing at me and whispering. I got out of there fast when the bell rang, but not fast enough.

"Where's Gwyneth?" Mitzi asked in a singsong as I passed her desk. I shrugged, hugging my books, and avoided her foot stuck out in the aisle. I got out the door before she could get in enough breath for her next sentence, and fifth period I only had Trisha Brent and Zoe McPherson to deal with. They were toothless without Mitzi there to goad them, and the final bell of the day was a relief.

The wind was up, full of dust and the smell of smoke, and the front steps of St. Crispin's thronged with girls. The buses crouched yellow off to one side, cars glittering as luckier kids piled in them and whizzed away. I was just about to break for the buses when a shiny black Jetta pulled up right in the fire lane and the horn honked once.

I would've ignored that, but Mitzi and her gang had beaten me out in front. I saw her heading for me, blonde ponytails bouncing, and let out an involuntary sigh.

The driver's door opened, and Johnny rose up out of the car. I stopped dead, hugging my trig and history books, my bag digging into my shoulder.

Holy shit.

In sunlight, his hair was full of red tints. He wore shades, and he turned around, rested his arms on the top of his car, and just looked at me. Like he'd expected me to be there.

Several girls stopped dead, staring. Mitzi was still heading for me, and I could tell she had mischief on her mind.

So I headed for the Jetta. No dust clung to its respectable paint job.

"Hey," he said, when I got close enough. "Want a ride?"

"Sure." I made it to the passenger door and saw Sister Agnetha, black habit flapping, heading down the steps in full sail. A *boy*. On school grounds.

Oh, Jesus.

"Anywhere in particular?" He grinned like he had a plan.

"Just get me out of here." I found out the door was unlocked. As soon as I dropped in and pulled it shut, the smell of a clean car closed around me. The heat and the wind was closed away, air-conditioning working overtime. He paused for the briefest of seconds, then settled in the driver's seat and glanced at me.

"You sure?"

"Hell yes." I didn't dare glance out the tinted window.

His door slammed, we both buckled up, and he cut across the three lanes in front of the roundabout. Someone honked, there was a screech of brakes and tires, and as we zoomed away I started to laugh.

It was just like driving with Gwyneth.

• • •

"So she just . . . huh." He sucked on the straw a little. His shades glittered. We sat on the hood of the Jetta, looking down at the valley. You could see the dust in the air, whirling in golden eddies like pollen. The trees whispered all around us. He was right—it was a nice place. He'd bought milkshakes and curly fries, and I was trying not to eat too quickly. I sat on my blazer, he perched there in his jeans, oblivious to the hot metal of the hood. It was nice in the shade, and you could see a big slice of smog-tinted downtown. The hills winked with sharp light through the veils of dust, glass-coated mansions sitting up above the scrabble. "You're sure?"

"She brought me to the party. I didn't want to go. And… well, you'd have to know her." I sighed. Took a middling gulp of strawberry shake. "And why would someone like him talk to me? He's one of *them*."

"And you're not?" But his tone said something else, like, *and I'm not?*

"I live in a *trailer park*," I reminded him. "And you seem like a nice guy."

"Huh." Johnny nodded slightly. His dark curls lifted on the hot breeze. "Let me ask you something. Can I?"

"You just did." I took another gulp of milkshake. "Shoot."

He acknowledged the joke with a flick of a smile. "Do you see a future for yourself?"

It was a cheesy question, but the way he said it made it sound completely normal. Reasonable, even. Like he was curious, and willing to listen. I studied him for a long few moments, sweeping my hair back and thinking about it.

"You mean like college?"

"I mean … beyond that. Beyond everything."

I set the milkshake down. "You really want to know what I think?"

"I do." He sounded like he did, too.

"I think the entire game's stacked. No matter how good you are, some people are chosen and some aren't. The golden people get everything, and the rest of us can work like hell to get just a little. So there's no future unless you're one of the golden people. But you can buy a little breathing room."

"And you're not one of the golden?" He was utterly still, except for the wind slipping loving fingers through his hair.

I laughed. It was kind of funny. "Oh, hell no."

"Do you want to be?"

"You can't just decide to be one. It's Fate." I dug in my book-bag for a piece of gum. "Can I ask *you* a question?"

"Shoot." He seemed to find that funny, or at least he laughed.

"Why did you pick me?" I tried not to feel like I was holding my breath, waiting for the answer. But dammit, I wanted to know. And his answer might tell me what kind of guy he was. Brain, jock, flash, plastic, gliefer, panda, goth—he didn't seem classifiable.

"What, you can't tell? Come on. Let's go somewhere."

"Where?"

"Wherever. Maybe just drive." He glanced at me sideways, and I wished I could see his eyes behind the shades. "I've got time."

"I should go home. I have homework."

"A good little Catholic girl. Okay. When can I see you again?"

I shouldn't have said anything. I should have just played it off with a joke or something. I've seen Gwyn shut guys down a million times. But I didn't want to shut him down. "Pick me up from school tomorrow." It was out of my mouth before I thought about it.

"Done. We'll go somewhere."

"Where?"

"Does it matter?"

The way he said it, it didn't.

. . .

I got him to let me out at the entrance to the trailer park. Dropping me off in the middle of the night was one thing, dropping me off where Dad could see? Something else entirely. The truck was in the driveway, and I was glad I'd been cautious.

Dad was home, and sober. He didn't give me the business at all. Instead, he just let out a sigh. "I've got a double-shift tonight, honey. They're payin' me on Friday."

"That's good." The wind moaned.

He didn't even notice my sweating palms or guilty face. "Your friend called. Gwyneth. It's that rich girl, right?"

I nodded woodenly. *That rich girl.* "Yeah."

"All right." He stood up. "She said to call her. I'm'a gonna go to work. You be careful now, huh?"

"I will." I swallowed hard. His eyes were bloodshot, but he didn't look angry. "Do you want dinner before you go?"

"No ma'am. Don't have time." He dug in his pocket and brought out his wallet. Two twenties, crisp and new, laid on the table. "See if'n you can get some groceries, honey. They pay me Friday, but we can have something before then. All right?"

Milk, at least. And potatoes and ground beef. Beans—we could eat chili for a couple nights. My stomach cramped at the thought, around its load of curly fries and milkshake. "All right."

He nodded. Big, heavy slump-shouldered man. "I got work shirts. You wash 'em."

"Yes, Daddy."

I waited until he was gone, his truck making the weird whining squeak of a belt too loose or too tight or something, before letting out the long breath I was holding.

"Jesus," I said to the empty kitchen, and picked up the two twenties. I might even be able to have lunch once or twice this week, if I skimped on the meat and got extra bread.

The phone rang again. I swallowed, hard, my throat clicking. It rang three times before I could get around the table and to the wall where it hung. I picked it up, but all I got was a dial tone and the sound of the wind.

I was already waiting to see Johnny again.

• • •

"It wasn't my idea," Gwyn whispered. I sank down further in my chair. Sister Laurel underlined the date of the Smoot-Hawley Tariff Act on the chalkboard. I made a note of it. "Really, it wasn't."

I didn't respond. She'd been at it since she walked into class late and settled down in her seat. A fading hickey on the side of her neck told me how the Friday party had turned out for her.

Probably with Scott Holder. She was lucky like that.

Gwyneth hissed my name, but I stared straight ahead.

Sister Laurel half-turned. Her profile was like a hawk's, with a hawk's beady stare. "Does someone have something to say?" she asked nobody in particular.

You could have heard a pin drop. The wind scraped at the windows. Sister Laurel went on about trade protectionism and the gold standard, and the causes of the Great Depression.

"Don't be like this," Gwyneth whispered.

I hunched my shoulders and didn't reply. We both eventually knew I'd forgive her, right? I always had before whenever she did something stupid or hurtful. That was my place in the cosmos—to be utterly forgiving. And in return, I got to lie awake in her bedroom and imagine I had her parents and her lucky golden life.

Do you see a future for yourself?

I kind of did. Getting through school on scholarship, making it through college, maybe getting an okay job. Working to afford a place of my own.

And then what?

Gwyneth would never have to search like that. Mommy and Daddy would send her to college and she'd catch a fellow rich boy, no problem. She'd make nice little golden babies and drink martinis in the afternoon. She'd never have to carry cash down to the utilities office and plead to be reconnected, or plead not to be disconnected. Dad sent me because I could talk my way around the employees. It was a fine art.

My cheeks were scarlet.

Gwyneth whispered my name again. Girls were shifting in their chairs, wondering what was going on between us.

Sister Laurel turned to face the class. Her gimlet gaze wandered over all of us, and I tried to look innocent and bored at once. I glanced down at my notes.

Did I see a future? Ink scratches on paper.

The Sister finally tapped her meterstick on her desk, a slight padded sound against piled papers. She called on Erica Angier, and I let out a silent sigh. Saved again by luck.

I made it out the door before Gwyneth could catch me. Let her go hang out with her popular friends. It wasn't like it mattered.

Not when I was going to see him again.

•••

Gwyn skipped Brother Bob's daily perdition. And the whole sucktastic day got better once I escaped sixth period and made it to the front of the school. Johnny was leaning against his Jetta, utterly disregarding the signs screaming NO PARKING! in the fire lane. He bought me a cheeseburger this time, more curly fries, and a Coke. He sucked on a strawberry milkshake, and said he wasn't hungry.

We sat on the hood of his car again, in the same spot overlooking the valley, and talked about nothing all afternoon. It was nice to talk to someone who actually *listened*.

The sun tended westward, and the wind's rasping moan settling drifts of hot dust over the valley wasn't nearly as creepy when there was someone's voice to shut it out. We lay back on the hood and looked up at the liquid movement of light through the branches, and when he kissed me he didn't take his shades off. But I didn't mind. I didn't even mind that I probably reeked of cheeseburger.

He even listened while he kissed. I can't describe it better than that. He braced himself on his elbow and his other hand didn't roam, just resting fingertips lightly along my jawline and occasionally dipping down to the curve of my throat where my pulse spiked frantically toward him. I bonked my cheekbone on his shades and laughed with a mouth full of him, and he laughed too. He tasted like strawberry milkshake, and he smelled like peppermints and desire and hot sun and clean clothes. He bit my bottom lip very gently, then kissed me harder.

It was so different from making out with the ugly friend of Gwyn's current conquest in the front seat while the golden people heavy-petted in the roomy back seat.

We separated, and I still couldn't see his eyes. "You wear those all the time?" I reached up, as if I was going to take his shades off, but he moved subtly back and I got the hint.

"Not all the time. Listen, I have some work that needs to be done. How about I take you out tonight? I'll wait at the end of your road."

My heart was pounding. I probably should have asked some questions, but I was tired of asking questions. I was tired of waiting. The air was bright and golden with pollen and dust, and I wanted to kiss the corner of his mouth again. His skin was smooth, a different texture. Like heavy silk, or something else matte and perfect.

He wasn't too perfect, though. He wasn't one of *them*.

"Okay." Getting out of the house wasn't going to be a problem, not with Dad working. I could be gone after dinner, and he'd never know. He'd probably think I was out with Gwyneth, unless she was calling again. "Where are we going?"

"Does it matter?" He laughed, and touched my cheek. The gentle flutter of fingertips spilled all the way through me, a tide of heat.

I should have cared. But I didn't. I let Johnny take me home, and I even kissed him goodbye. We didn't say we were together or anything. I didn't think we needed to.

. . .

If I'd known, I probably would have made something nicer for dinner. But I was in a hurry, so it was Hamburger Helper. Dad chowed down silently. I'd even ironed his workshirts, and he had one on. "Late tonight," he grunted as he stamped out the door.

"Yes, Daddy." *I'm going to be late tonight too*. We were probably just going to the Bleu, though.

The thought of being seen with Johnny, maybe by Gwyn and Mitzi if they didn't have another party to go to, made me laugh out loud while I cleaned up the kitchen. I even put on Gwyn's black silk shirt again. He probably wouldn't care what I wore. And dammit, she probably owed me the shirt. She could always buy another twenty of them.

The good mood lasted until I tried to shave my legs and cut a gash in my leg with the cheap-ass razor. I bled all over the bathtub while the sun went down, and all of a sudden I was sure he wouldn't show up. I'd wait out there in Gwyneth's shirt and my school skirt and feel like an idiot.

I stopped and put my sweating forehead on my knees. In summer, the tepid water that squeezed out of our ancient plumbing was pretty much a blessing. Right now I was thinking it would do me good. The wind licked the sides of our trailer, and I surprised myself by laughing again, a hard jagged sound.

If he didn't show up, I would know. And I'd call Gwyneth. And forgive her.

But if he did, I'd be ready.

• • •

It was a tinderbox night, the kind that usually starts with heat lightning and ends with a fire out in the hills and everyone jumpy. The Bleu was packed. It always was, even on school nights. I didn't mind, and Johnny didn't seem to either. We were glued to each other in the middle of the crowded dance floor. It was dripping hot, everyone breathing on everyone else, glow-sticks flashing and the lights smearing over blank young faces.

The music hit a thumping groove and stayed there for a long time. It was like swimming next to someone else's body. Johnny held me, and I got flashes of peppermint and clean heat whenever he leaned in.

Losing yourself in the middle of a mass of kids is easy. Losing yourself with someone else, that's hard. We made up a little private universe in the middle of the dance floor. When the lights went out, the only illumination was from the glowsticks and the sheen of sweat, and Johnny nuzzled along my neck. He had swept my hair aside and his chest was against my back. I tilted my chin up when his fingertips pressed gently, and his other arm turned hard across my waist.

His breath was hot on my skin, and I melted into him. I thought he was just giving me a hickey, but a weird thing happened.

Johnny tensed behind me. The music thundered, some singer wailing over the top about a missionary man, and a spot of heat began in my throat. It flushed down my entire body like lava running down a hillside, working inward from my skin and settling in the pit of my belly. Pounding bass drew it deeper and deeper, through my bones and down into the core of me, and the entire club went dark red. Like how you close your eyes against a searchlight and your eyelids turn everything into a crimson haze. The throbbing of my heart melted into the bass and slowed down, my hips jerked forward, and everything inside me exploded.

In the Bleu with the music going full-bore, nobody can hear you scream. Nobody can hear when everything inside you gets smashed. And nobody sees if you're dragged outside by a boy in a white shirt, darkness smeared on his lips and his shades on even in the middle of the night.

I huddled against the car door. He turned the engine off and sudden silence filled the interior. We sat there for a little while, the wind scouring at the respectable paint job.

"It's not like you've been told," he repeated. "Forget all that. Just think about it this way: I'm Fate. And I'm choosing you. *Inviting* you."

My throat hurt. I clutched the rough paper towel to the side of my neck. It was damp, but I couldn't tell if it was with sweat or... something else. I had to swallow twice before I could talk.

"Why me?" The words were husks of themselves.

"You said it yourself. You're not one of them. And we get lonely, those of us out in the cold." He measured off spaces on the steering wheel with his fingers. Measured them again, like he expected them to change. "You can *be*. With me."

I swallowed again. It felt like I had strep or something. My fingers were numb, even though the air pressed, crackling and electric-hot against my sweat-wet skin.

Then I asked the million-dollar question. "How?"

He smiled at me, and took his shades off. The red glow was vanishing, drawn back into the whites of his eyes in thin threads. His irises were dark now, like the first night I met him. "Are you sure you want to?"

I set my chin stubbornly. "First tell me how."

"All you have to do is give me a present, sweetheart. It's not so hard."

Jesus, I don't have anything. "I live in a *trailer park.* I don't have—"

"It's not money." He reached over and took my hand, and I didn't pull away. His skin was dry and warm, normal against mine.

Then he told me. I went cold all over. Ice crackled and settled over me, ground itself together in my heart.

"I do that, and then what?"

"Then you come with me. And there's a whole world out there for us. I won't be lonely, and you won't ever have to worry again."

He just said it, the way nobody had ever said anything to me before. He couldn't be lying. He sounded too matter-of-fact for it to be a lie.

And my throat gave another hot flare of pain. I was all frost except for the live coal on my neck, under my clutching fingers and the wilted paper towel.

"So, mystery lady? What's it going to be? You're going to spend your short little life playing by their rules, or are you going to take your chance?"

I thought about it, worrying my frozen lower lip between my teeth. Then I made up my mind.

• • •

"It wasn't my fault." Gwyneth was still on it. She hunched her shoulders, her golden hair playing over them. "I had no idea. Honest, I didn't."

"It's okay." I even sounded all right. I didn't have any Band-Aids, but the small twin punctures on my neck were white and worn-looking. You couldn't even tell they were there. "What are you doing tonight, anyway?"

"I thought you could come over." She slouched even further, the dappled fig-tree shade painting shadows on her arms and face. "We could watch a movie or something. Pajama party."

I couldn't agree right away. "What about Mitzi?" I glanced past Gwyn, to here the blonde bitch queen of Crispie cast a venomous little darting look our way.

"She's a bitch. You know she's dating Holder now?" Gwyn rolled her eyes. "It's amazing. The two of them are like two vacuum cleaners talking to each other. Let's skip fourth, too, and go shopping. Come on. What do you say?"

What else was there to say, except yes? And I already knew Johnny wasn't picking me up.

Not today.

· · ·

Her parents were out and Marisa was in bed. I lay very still until Gwyneth's breathing evened out, her old pajamas feeling like friends against my skin. I hadn't packed or even told Dad where I'd be. It was Friday, he'd gotten paid. He might have been at the bar even now. If he was at home, he was missing me.

It didn't matter. Nothing mattered now but the waiting.

She lay next to me the way she always did, elbows and knees poking. Even with a queen-size bed she took up all the space.

When she started the heaviest breathing of all, I slid carefully out of the bed. I got dressed quietly, my white shirt a ghost in the gloom. Tiptoed down her hall, avoided every squeak in the stairs with the ease of long practice. The kitchen was spotless and dark, the wind scrubbing the corners of the house and flinging dusty grit against the windows. Soon there would be a spark and the constant smell of smoke.

The glass diamonds on the kitchen door held nothing but the glow of a porch light. I stood there, my throat itching and my hand reaching for the knob and the mellow golden glow of the deadbolt lever. Each time the wind mounted another pitch, I would snatch my hand back.

He's not coming. Then I would think—*He is. I know he is.*

I don't know how long I stood there, feeling like an idiot in my rumpled school clothes, before a shadow appeared at the door. Just *appeared*. One moment, nothing. The next, a ghost of a white shirt and even through the distortion of the diamond panes, I could tell it was him.

I reached for the knob. Snatched my hand back again and stood there trembling as he waited. I didn't know how long he'd stay, and if I didn't open the door he would be gone in the morning. Just like that.

If I kept that door closed, I knew what would happen. I'd go to school. Go to college. Keep slogging away hoping the golden people would throw me a bone or two. And sooner or later Gwyneth wouldn't need my forgiveness. She'd go back to hanging out with her own kind and forget I ever existed, and there would be no more of this pale perfect seashell of a house that I could pretend was mine.

The deadbolt slid back. He didn't move.

I was cold all over and sweating again. The knob slipped in my fingers, and I heard a restless murmur. It was impossible to hear either Marisa or Gwyn muttering in their sleep, but I thought I did.

I twisted the knob and opened the door, and the wind came in full of dust and the smell of smoke. I guess the fires had started early.

• • •

Go wait in the car, he told me. So here I am in the Jetta. There's nothing in the glove compartment, and up at the top of the hill the house is completely dark. The porch light was on, but about ten seconds ago it flicked off. The wind rocks the car a little on its springs, mouths the paint job, and brushes velvet fingertips over the windshield. Something white flickers up on the hill.

I am shaking all over. My schoolbag sits obediently at my feet on the clean mat. The entire car smells new. I am cold even though it's ninety degrees and dry as the inside of my mouth out there.

I don't know what Johnny is. There's not a word for it. I don't even know if he's really coming back to this car. To me.

An orange wisp sparks up on the hill, behind one of the upper windows. Gwyneth's room, looking down over the semicircular driveway and the manicured lawn. The wisp unfolds. It isn't electric light. It's something older.

If he comes down the hill I'll see him silhouetted against the flames. My fingers are twisting together, slick with sweat. The puncture wounds on my throat feel hot and wet.

I am not sure if I want to see him coming down the hill. If he doesn't, what am I going to do?

What am I going to do if he *does*?

All Wounds

BY DINA JAMES

WITH A POWDERY crunch, the tip of the pencil lead snapped and slid uselessly out of the wood beneath her fingertips. It rolled across Becky's paper, leaving a gray smudge across the question she'd been attempting to answer.

She threw down her pencil in disgust.

"Now what?" her friend Robin asked in a hushed whisper, looking out from under her carefully styled-to-look-messy thick, blonde hair. Robin glanced around quickly, looking for Mr. Nairhoft.

"My pencil is being stupid again! Besides that, I really don't think writing an essay about the Spanish conquistadors is going to help Nana remember where her bedroom is, or not to turn on the stove," Becky sighed, glaring at the offending question on her assignment. "I need to get home!"

"Well at least make it look like you're working," Robin replied with another fast glance around for the detention room monitor. "Getting another detention isn't going to help your Nana either. It's a good thing she can't remember when you're supposed to be home anymore, or you'd really be in trouble!"

"Shh!"

"Is there a problem here, ladies?" Mr. Nairhoft said in a smooth, arrogant voice. "Rebecca?"

"Sorry, Mr. Nairhoft," Becky apologized with a sweet smile. She really, really hated it when people called her "Rebecca."

"This is the third time today my pencil's broken," she went on. "And I got frustrated with it. I'm sorry to have caused a disruption. May I go sharpen it again? That might help it, at least through the end of detention, anyway."

Becky gazed up at the tall, rail-thin Mr. Nairhoft, hoping her repentant smile would earn her his permission.

"Does anyone have an extra pencil Miss MacDonnell can borrow?" Mr. Nairhoft asked loudly, turning around to view the detention hall, which was really just the cafeteria with the tables moved around a little. He'd glanced around so fast that he couldn't have even bothered to see if anyone had an answer to his question. "No?"

Mr. Nairhoft turned back to Becky with that stupid fake smile he always had plastered on his face.

"Well—"

"Here, Mr. Nairhoft," said a voice from the far table in the corner.

Becky turned around to see who had spoken, as did Robin, and Mr. Nairhoft. Actually, everyone in detention swiveled their heads to see who was denying Mr. Nairhoft the occasion to be his usual unpleasant self.

A boy about her age, sitting at a table by himself, wearing a black leather jacket, faded jeans that were more gray than black, and a T-shirt in the same condition, waved a yellow pencil in the air.

"She can use this one."

He said it almost defiantly... like he was daring Mr. Nairhoft to come over and take it himself.

"Mr. Dugan, surely you haven't completed *all* of your *long overdue* assignments," Mr. Nairhoft said, folding his arms.

"I've completed all I'm going to," the boy replied, matching Mr. Nairhoft's tone exactly. The boy looked at Becky. "Want this?"

Becky nodded and stood up slowly, her frustration with her own pencil, assignment, Mr. Nairhoft and detention forgotten as all the attention shifted from her onto the boy.

"Becky, no," Robin hissed in a whisper.

The boy's eyes went back to Mr. Nairhoft's as he held the pencil out for Becky to take.

Ryan Dugan wasn't just a bad boy, he was *the* bad boy; everyone knew it. Always in trouble, always getting sent to the principal's office, always in detention. There was even a rumor that last summer he wasn't in summer school like he usually was, but in Mariposa Juvenile Detention Center three towns over.

And Ryan never, ever gave you anything without expecting something in return.

It felt good though, doing something Mr. Nairhoft couldn't really complain about, even though she was technically breaking the "don't leave your seat without permission" rule. Still, Mr. Nairhoft had asked if anyone had a pencil she could use, and

Ryan did, so she was going to take it no matter what everyone else thought. Really she just wanted to see the look on Mr. Nairhoft's face as she took the pencil from Ryan with a quiet "thank you."

"Don't worry about it," Ryan said with a big grin. He winked—actually *winked*—at Mr. Nairhoft as he held onto the pencil before letting Becky take it. "Wouldn't want you to get in any more trouble now, would we?"

Becky shook her head, stunned, and hurried back to her seat where she sat down quickly and bent her head over her assignment. She wondered if he knew what had landed her in detention. He *sounded* like he knew. Like he knew, and approved.

Becky's mouse-brown hair hid her blue eyes enough that it kept Mr. Nairhoft from seeing that she was secretly glancing at Ryan while she pretended to work. Her eyes went to the clock on the wall. Twenty minutes of detention left, then she could get home to Nana.

Ryan sat back, clasping his hands behind his head as he leaned against the wall. Mr. Nairhoft berated the boy until he was blue in the face, said something about "another week's worth of detention!" and stalked away to harass another student he didn't think looked busy enough.

Ryan just grinned and caught Becky looking at him. He winked at her.

Becky blushed and bent her head back over her paper, trying not to think about how much time she had left to sit there.

Or that Nana might be setting the house on fire.

• • •

Everyone else had someone to pick them up when detention was finally over—even Robin, whose dad looked unhappy as Robin got in the car, even though he smiled wanly at Becky.

Although Becky would have been perfectly happy taking the bus, Nana used to drive her to and from school, when Nana could still be trusted to drive. Nana hadn't driven in about three years. They'd taken away her license when Becky was eleven. Not that Nana was that old; there were plenty of drivers on the road older than Nana, but they could remember which house was theirs and which gear made the car reverse, and *where* they were going.

Nana couldn't.

The doctors called it "early onset senile dementia," but everyone knew that was just a polite way of saying that Nana was really too young to have Alzheimer's, even though it was obvious that she did.

The school busses only ran before detention, not after, so that meant someone had to pick you up, or you had to walk home. Becky offered Robin and Mr. Turnbull a little wave of apology—after all, Robin wouldn't have gotten into trouble if it hadn't been for her—and then shouldered her backpack and turned quickly away to begin the long walk home before Mr. Turnbull could offer her a ride. There was just no way she wanted to be in the car with that much tension, and she really needed to clear her head before getting to her house. Who knew what disaster would be awaiting her today.

The last thing Becky wanted was for Nana to catch on that she'd been in detention, and if she saw Mr. Turnbull dropping her off, Nana would probably notice how late Becky was getting home. That is, if Nana even noticed. If there was anything good about Nana losing it, it was that Becky could get away with a lot more than most of the kids in her grade.

Becky didn't see any smoke coming from the general vicinity of her—well, *Nana's*—house, or hear fire engines, so it seemed pretty safe to take a little time to breathe on the way home. She lost herself in thought as she walked, remembering all the little "funny" things she and her Nana used to laugh about, like Nana putting her keys in the fridge, or putting toilet paper on the paper towel rack. Then things had started to get scarier, like Nana leaving the gas stove on, or forgetting to turn off the water she was running in the stoppered sink for the dishes and flooding the kitchen.

I don't suppose I should complain too much to Robin about Nana, Becky thought as she pulled her jacket around her. *Because she could have given me up for adoption or something, after Mom and Dad died in the crash, and she didn't.* Becky sighed deeply. *She looked after me all these years, so it's only fair that I look after her now.*

Becky picked up her pace. October was cold, and it wasn't even Halloween yet. It was getting dark earlier and earlier these days, and when it got dark, it got colder, and she wanted to get home. It was getting close to dinnertime and Nana needed to eat, and if Nana got hungry when Becky wasn't there, she'd try to cook for herself. Becky really didn't want to spend another night in the emergency room explaining to the doctors how Nana burned herself again.

"First time, huh?"

Becky stopped in her tracks. She knew that voice. It was the same one she'd heard earlier, in detention.

Ryan Dugan stepped out from behind a tree that bordered the sidewalk she was on. He leaned against the trunk, brought a little box out of the pocket of his leather jacket, and flipped open a small, silver—

"Is that a lighter?" Becky asked, scowling.

"Yeah," Ryan said, bringing a cigarette to his lips. "You got a problem with smokers?"

"Way to add to the bad-boy stereotype there," Becky said, raising an eyebrow at his tone. "How did you get ahead of me anyway?"

"Back alley," Ryan said, lighting his cigarette. "You know ... the stereotypical bad-boy escape route."

He pointed back over her shoulder.

"If you cut through the gym and across the playground you can hop the fence and skip most of the block," he said, exhaling a cloud of smoke.

Becky fanned the cloud with her hand and wrinkled her nose.

"Where do you get the money for those anyway?" she asked.

"What is this, the Spanish Inquisition?" Ryan countered. He put a hand to his chest at her look of surprise that he'd mentioned precisely what had been on her assignment. "Wow, how about that? I actually *do* learn in school. Mr. Hair-off has a particular interest in the history of Spain, and he gives all the first-timers that assignment. So unless you want to learn more about the conquistadors and the Inquisition, I'd keep out of trouble if I were you."

Becky wanted to laugh at Ryan's use of the name everyone called the toupee-wearing Mr. Nairhoft behind his back, but thought it would only encourage him.

"What are you doing here, anyway?" Becky demanded, shifting her backpack nervously.

"You have my lucky pencil," Ryan reminded her, holding out his hand.

"Right." Becky rolled her eyes as she slung her pack off her shoulder. She pulled out the pencil in question and held it out to him. "Good to know you cut through the gym, across the playground, and jumped the fence just to rescue your pencil."

"Hey, this is my *lucky* pencil!" Ryan defended, though Becky knew he wasn't being serious. He reached for it and smiled a little as she held onto it for just a moment too long as he'd done to her when he'd first loaned it in detention. "For this I would even have rifled Hair-off's office ... which is where I got the cigs."

Becky looked horrified. "You didn't!"

Ryan grinned. "These things will kill you, you know. I did him a favor!"

He took a long drag off the cigarette, stabbed it out against the trunk of the tree, and put the remaining half back in the box. He tucked the box away in his pocket along with his silver lighter.

"Well, you looked like you were in a hurry, so . . . ," Ryan gestured down the block as if to excuse her. "Stay out of trouble, huh? You don't belong in detention with Hair-off and the rest of us delinquents."

"How do you know I'm not just starting out on delinquency?" Becky asked smartly. "I hear all the cool kids are doing it."

Ryan laughed.

"Yeah, and you're just being cool, aren't you? I've seen you around school, in class. You're about as cool as a jalapeño. See you around, Hot Stuff," he said, turning to go.

Becky blushed. Yeah. . . . one of the "cool kids," she wasn't. She was surprised Ryan even knew who she was.

"I'm really sorry that whole pencil thing cost you another week with Mr. Nair . . . I mean Hair-off," she blurted, shouldering her bag again.

Ryan waved a hand.

"Don't worry about it," he said, walking away. "He won't make it stick. Besides, some things are worth putting up with a little punishment."

Funny, Becky thought, *that sounds like what I was just thinking about Nana.*

Becky hesitated for a moment, watching him go, and then turned back toward home, hurrying even more now. She thought about Ryan, and what he'd said—he'd seen her around? Sure, they had a couple of classes together, but she wasn't the kind of girl anyone noticed. Just the opposite, really. The only reason anyone noticed her was because of Robin. Robin was the pretty one—the popular one.

Of course! That was probably how Ryan knew why she was in detention, Robin getting busted was the talk of the school, even though it had been Becky's fault. Robin had only been trying to help.

That might explain how Ryan had known about her, but how had he known which way she was headed home afterward? She could have gone in any direction ... unless he knew where she lived.

Becky shook her head, laughing at herself. He'd just guessed lucky or something. He didn't know where she lived.

Did he?

...

Becky forgot about Ryan, and Mr. Hair-off, and detention and Robin the moment she walked through the front door of her house. It looked like Nana was having one of her "good days." Becky was utterly relieved that everything was okay. Nana was sitting in her favorite chair, with Mishka on her lap. Mishka was a grouchy old cat—a big, white fluffy thing that needed lots of brushing. If Nana remembered nothing else, she remembered to brush Mishka.

Not that Mishka minded if she was brushed three or four times a day. That cat loved attention, and would happily sit all day in Nana's lap being brushed. But only Nana's lap. Mishka hated Becky, and the feeling was mutual. Mishka was Nana's cat.

Becky stowed her backpack in the foyer and made sure the doors were locked and the stove off and everything else was safe before greeting her grandmother.

"Hi, Nana!" Becky said as she entered the living room.

"Oh, Becky, you're home," Nana said, smiling even though Becky knew she was confused. "Did you have a good day at school?"

Becky nodded as she always did. Even though today had been a horrible day at school, she still told her Nana that everything was fine.

"Do you have a lot of homework?" Nana asked, earning a glare from Mishka as she stood up.

"No, I got most of it done at school," Becky answered honestly. You could get a lot done in three hours of detention after school. "And I'm really hungry. How about some dinner? It's my turn to cook tonight."

Nana's brow furrowed.

"I thought you cooked last night." She didn't sound at all sure.

Becky really didn't want to lie to her Nana, but Nana in the kitchen was dangerous. Becky cooked every night now, but let Nana think that she only cooked sometimes.

"I was really craving some spaghetti at school," Becky hedged, steering the conversation away from who was going to do the cooking. "I thought that would be good for dinner. It's easy to make—I know how."

Nana nodded absently and went back to brushing Mishka. The cat glowered at Becky as if to say "Well? Go on, then. You're not needed here." Becky stuck her tongue out at the evil cat and went into the kitchen to start supper.

. . .

Half the dishes on the draining board had been wiped and put away when she heard an insistent pounding at the front door, like someone kicking it. Hard.

Becky scowled as she looked at the clock. It was nearly nine o'clock, and they never had visitors. Well, not anymore. Nana's friends used to come by, when she could still remember who they were and what they'd been talking about. Becky never had friends over. Not that she had any besides Robin, but even if she did, she wouldn't have them over anyway. Other people just upset Nana now.

The noise came again, and Becky looked over her shoulder toward the bathroom door. Nana was in there getting ready for bed. Becky hoped she couldn't hear the racket.

Becky frowned and looked out the peep hole at the dark figure on the porch. She snapped on the porch light, and a blonde head cringed away from the brightness with a grimace, but remained still. He kicked at the door again, and Becky could see why. The bloody, unconscious body of the dark-haired boy who had just that afternoon come to get his "lucky pencil" from her filled his arms.

"Turn off that light! Do you want the entire neighborhood to see us?" the boy out on the porch growled sharply. "I don't know about you, but that's something I'd like to avoid!"

Becky had to agree with him and couldn't help but obey. She flicked the porch light off immediately before opening the door.

"That's better," the tall, skinny blonde boy said. He waited a moment, just standing there, looking at Becky and the interior of the house past her. When she just stared at him, he spoke again. "Well? Come on, Healer...I can't stand around here all night! I would have used the usual entrance, but it's sealed, so I had no choice but to come to the front door."

"What—," Becky shook her head, confused.

"If friend ye are and healing ye seek, enter this place and my blessing keep!"

Becky whirled around at the sound of her Nana's voice, stronger and clearer than it had been in years.

Nana was clad in her pink bathrobe and matching slippers. Her wet hair clung to her neck and shoulders. Becky suddenly thought that it was strange for Nana to have taken a shower at night. Maybe she'd gotten confused again as to why she was in the bathroom and had thought it was morning. Nana never took a shower at night.

The blonde boy expelled a deep sigh of obvious gratitude and shouldered his way past Becky. He strode into the living room with Ryan, muttering under his breath.

"My apologies, Lady Healer," the blonde boy said contritely as he reached Nana. "The entrance was sealed or I would have used it—"

Nana's hand cut him off, and she reached for a long-disused

candle lantern sitting on the mantelpiece above the hearth.

Why would she grab that thing? It's just decor, isn't it? Something of Grandfather's? Becky thought.

"Take him up," Nana ordered quietly, and followed the boy up the staircase, not faltering on the stairs as she usually did, leaving Becky standing dumbstruck in the open doorway.

Remembering herself, Becky quickly locked the front door. She ran up the stairs after her Nana.

She just caught a glimpse of the hem of Nana's pink robe disappearing through the door at the end of the upstairs hall. That was a linen closet. What ...?

Reaching the door, Becky found that the shelves of the linen closet weren't shelves at all. They were like those spooky fake bookcases in haunted houses and were now pushed aside to reveal a hidden passage.

Wow. She'd known this house was old and creepy—it had been in the family for generations—but a secret passageway? Really? That was just like something out of *Nancy Drew*! She hesitated only a moment before going through after her Nana.

"My apologies, Martha," Becky heard the blonde boy say, almost reverently. "I thought ... her mark ... she looked so surprised. Isn't she trained?"

Martha. The boy had called Nana "Martha." No one did that ... except Nana's old friends, and that boy didn't look like he was even old enough to be out of school. He didn't go to *her* school though. That was for certain. She'd remember a guy as good-looking as that.

"She's not of age," she heard Nana reply. "Set him down so I can have a look. Do something about the bed, would you? It's been a long time since I've been up here."

Was that her *Nana* talking like that? Like she'd suddenly... gotten better? Nana hadn't sounded that sure of herself in a long time, and certainly hadn't used that many words in that normal way for more than three years.

"She's here, listening to us," the blonde boy said softly. He lifted his voice. "Come out, little Healer. We know you're here, and you may as well see firsthand."

Becky stepped out from the secret passage and into the light of the candle lamp that had somehow become lit. Her Nana barely looked at her as she bent to examine Ryan, peering into his eyes and glancing at his clothed body.

"His clothes," Nana said firmly.

Ryan's clothes vanished instantly, except his underwear.

Nana glanced at the blonde boy, arching an eyebrow.

"Afford the boy *some* modesty, Martha," he said smoothly. "None of his injuries are around his middle."

"And you bit him as well!" Nana exclaimed with a gasp as she turned Ryan's head toward her and saw two small punctures on the boy's neck. "Sydney! Why would you... it *was* you... I can tell! Oh!"

Nana's eyes then lingered on the second bite on Ryan's bleeding thigh below the band of his underwear. Her fingers deftly touched the wound, and the unconscious Ryan cried out in protest.

"Becky, go into my room," Nana ordered, looking up at her sternly. "In the closet, on the top shelf, you'll see a leather suitcase. The one I always told you was full of old pictures? Bring that here, and fast. Go!"

Too stunned to do anything but follow orders, Becky nodded and ran back to the passageway and down the stairs, returning quickly with the case Nana wanted. The whole time questions ran through Becky's mind. What had the blonde boy—Sydney—meant when he said he would have used the entrance but it was sealed? How was Nana acting like her old self, *and* as though this kind of thing happened every day? Entering the hidden room again, Becky passed the case to her Nana.

"Thank you," Nana said in that same, calm voice. She reached for the case and opened it, pulling out various things as she spoke again to Becky.

"Go downstairs and bring me the two big pots, filled with water. The temperature doesn't matter. Sydney will help. Won't you, Syd? And Sydney? See to the boundary? That's a good boy."

Sydney looked like he'd been about to protest but nodded with a wry smile.

"As long as this doesn't take too long," Sydney said, standing up importantly. "After all, I left things in disarray. They'll need me back soon."

Nana waved her hand dismissively at Syd's words.

"This is more important than hand-holding your scared little clan. Now, tell me, what's this? Who broke the truce?"

"There really isn't time, Martha," Syd said gravely. He looked to Becky. "Shouldn't you be getting that water?"

"Look, I don't know who you are, but—" Becky was tired of being ordered around like a lapdog.

"Becky," Nana interrupted coolly. "Quickly now or this boy is going to die."

A glimpse of yellow caught Becky's eye. Ryan's lucky pencil was sticking out of the back pocket of the jeans that lay in a discarded heap at the foot of the bed. Becky felt dazed being in this strange hidden room with this strange, unfamiliar woman who was somehow working to save Ryan's life.

Why couldn't they have just gone to the hospital? Becky ran downstairs again, her brow furrowing. *Why did they come here? Why is Nana acting like her old self? Why is she acting like this is normal?*

The questions came faster than Becky could fathom as she filled a large stockpot with water. She was filling the other when suddenly Sydney was standing beside her.

"Holy crap!" Becky shouted, flinching away from the boy. She stared at him, wide-eyed. "How the heck did you do that?"

Sydney lifted the full pot into Becky's arms. She took it automatically, wrapping her arms around the bottom. Wow, it was heavy.

"The same as always," he said, confused by her question. "I just thought about where I wanted to be, and there I was. How hard is that? It's even easier with you worrying and fretting down here. I just had to focus on you, and I came to your side. You need help getting this stuff back upstairs, and your way takes forever."

He didn't wait for Becky to ask him anything else. Instead he put a hand on her shoulder and another on the second pot she'd just filled, and suddenly they were back in the dark room with Ryan and Nana.

Becky's stomach lurched and she set the pot of water next to Nana, just in time to be sick in the corner.

Sydney's eyebrows rose.

"First timer, huh? Don't worry, that happens to a lot of humans when they shift for the first time," he said.

"A lot of humans? What? I mean . . . Nana? What's going on?" Becky asked, her stomach tightening more at the disturbing suggestion in Syd's words.

"I don't have time to explain now, little dove," Nana said distractedly, soaking strips of cloth into water, which was suddenly steaming hot though it had been only lukewarm moments ago. "Give me a few minutes to see to this boy. What's his name, Syd? Names help, as you know."

"Ryan," Syd replied quietly. "Ryan Dugan."

"'Ryan," Nana repeated gently before turning back to Becky. "Give me a few minutes to see to Ryan, little dove. He's been bitten by a hellhound. *And* a vampire."

Nana muttered those last words under her breath in disapproval.

"Really, Syd. Did you have to bite him?" Nana asked.

"It was either turn him or watch him die. He's been good to us," Syd replied. "You know I didn't have a choice, Martha."

Nana nodded. "I know. It's just . . . well . . . he won't die of the

hellhound bite, that's for sure. If he survives the turning ... well
... we'll deal with that part when it comes. *If* it comes."

Sydney nodded and sat quietly on a chair beside the bed as
Becky watched Nana work.

Hellhound? Vampire bite? What?

It finally seemed quiet enough for Becky to ask a question,
but she didn't want to bother her Nana. Instead, she looked
to Syd.

"Because this is the place wounded Ethereals are supposed
to come," Sydney said before she could ask the question in her
mind. He glared at her pointedly, and Becky noticed his eyes
flashed in the light like Mishka's sometimes did. Funny—they'd
been a shade of dark blue in the kitchen. "This is neutral
ground, a haven, where the wounded can come for healing."

"Sydney, stop it," Nana said quietly. "She doesn't know any
of it. I ... I never trained her. I didn't want her involved."

Sydney looked at Martha, incredulous.

"You mean to say that she doesn't know you're a Healer?"
He sounded surprised and a little angry. "*The* Healer, if it were
told true? Lady Healer. Or that she's one of your line?"

"After losing my daughter, do you think for one moment I
would want Rebecca exposed to this?" Nana flared angrily,
pointing to Ryan's limp body. "We're mortal, and maybe you
don't know just how short a time that is, but to we humans, it's
too short! I'll not lose my granddaughter as I did my daughter!"

"Momma died in a car accident," Becky said suddenly. "You
said ... she and Daddy ... a drunk driver killed them."

Nana looked pained and guilty. She kept her eyes on Ryan's deep wound as she cleansed it with a concoction she'd made from the contents of a jar she'd taken from the suitcase.

Sydney stood up and reached for Becky's shoulders. She flinched slightly, but he held her firmly and guided her to a long mirror mounted on the wall of the room.

With a gesture of his hand, the unlit candles in the wall lanterns all blazed instantly, bringing much more light into the room, illuminating the mirror.

"Thank you," she heard Nana say absently.

Becky gasped as she looked into the mirror and saw only herself reflected back. She knew Syd was right there, behind her. She could feel him touching her. She looked to her shoulder and saw Syd's longish blonde hair mingling with her own, but there was no trace of it in the mirror. He smiled down at her slightly and nodded at the mirror again. Becky looked back, and though she couldn't see him do it, she saw her hair being moved aside and let him tilt her chin slightly so that she could see the small mark on her neck she hated so much. It was dark brown, like a freckle even though it was big like a birthmark, and was shaped like a funny asterisk. Robin always teased her for keeping it hidden with her hair. Robin thought it was cool—almost like a tattoo of an eight-pointed star. Becky realized, as Syd drew attention to the mark, that she could see the pulse that beat below the skin there.

"You see?" Syd whispered quietly in her ear. "You're a Healer...."

"If you're a vampire, shouldn't I be staking you through the heart or something?" Becky asked with a bravado she didn't feel. "I mean, you know . . . like in *Buffy*?"

Syd laughed gently and released her. She looked up at him with a scowl.

"Do you really think you could?" He smiled so that his fangs could be seen. Becky gasped and took a step back at the sight of them. "Tell me, little Healer—ever kill a spider?"

Becky nodded, wide-eyed. How did he know about—?

"It hurts, doesn't it, just a little bit?" Syd continued.

Becky nodded again, biting her bottom lip. She always tried to catch them instead, and take them outside. Because it *did* hurt. Physically. Not just like she felt sorry for them (which she did, as well, but that just made her feel dumb).

"Or when you want to hurt someone, like today in detention when you wanted to slap—"

"Did Ryan tell you about detention?" Becky looked sidelong at her Nana, hoping she hadn't heard. Fortunately, Nana seemed to be busy with Ryan and hadn't heard a thing; a great relief to Becky.

"Dude, shut up!" she hissed quietly at the boy. Well, he wasn't really a "boy," was he, if he was a . . . a . . .

Syd smiled again and laughed softly.

"'Vampire," he said dryly. "You can say it. I'm not as sensitive about the term as some."

"Sydney," Nana called suddenly. "I can't stop it. It's too late. He's turning."

Sydney instantly crossed to the bed where Ryan lay and

knelt. He took Ryan's hand as the bed shook. Ryan seemed to be having some kind of seizure, and looked all but dead to Becky.

"It's all right, buddy," Syd said quietly. "I've got you the best Healer here, and we're going to take care of you. Don't fight it. I know it's earlier than we planned, but take it in stride. Come on...."

Becky stood and watched as Sydney stroked a damp cloth over Ryan's forehead, which came away stained with pink and red. Becky realized that Ryan seemed to be literally sweating blood.

Nana stood and sighed, shaking her head. She noticed Becky and held her hand out. Becky came close and, like a child of five instead of a girl of nearly fifteen, took her grandmother's hand and clung to her side as she watched the wounded boy on the bed thrash.

"Come on, let's get some tea," Nana said quietly. "Syd will stay with him. There's nothing really to be done now but wait until it runs its course."

"This wouldn't have happened if the entrance hadn't been sealed!" Syd snapped, glaring at Nana. "Why was that done? You wasted my time, making me come ask for entry like a common human!"

Nana wasn't at all offended by Sydney's outburst or his accusations.

"Who broke the truce?" she countered with a question of her own. "That entry has been sealed for nearly fifteen years, which you well know, Sydney Alexander. After how the last battle ended, you know what precautions were taken."

"Precautions that included keeping your own granddaughter, the last of your line, ignorant of her own power!" Sydney growled darkly. "She doesn't even know...how could you not warn her, Martha Althea? If the flames of war have again been fanned, what makes you think her ignorance keeps her safe? She is a valuable asset to any side, and keeping her unaware can only lead her unknowingly astray!"

"Hey, I'm smart! I can handle things. I handle Nana well enough. That takes a lot more effort than you think it does!"

The words were out of Becky's mouth before she could stop them, but Nana hadn't seemed to hear them.

Neither, it seemed, had Syd. Nana and Syd continued to scowl at one another before Becky felt a tug at her hand.

"Come," Nana said quietly. "This isn't something you need to see."

Becky pulled her hand free.

"No, wait, Nana," she said, looking toward the now-still form of Ryan on the bed. "He...I know him. He goes to my school. He might...if he...He won't know where he is and he'll be scared when he wakes up."

"Sydney will stay with him, Becky," Nana said gently. "Let's wait down in the kitchen. It's not a good idea to be so close, even with the protections we have. A fledgling vampire is not easily controlled. It's fortunate we have a Master here with us to watch over him as Ryan turns."

"Turns?" Becky echoed, looking back to her Nana. "You mean..."

"Into a vampire, yes," Nana said softly. "And though turning a human is never easy or done lightly, Sydney had to do it to save Ryan's life. Ryan is fortunate that he was brought to me in time to wrest the dark magic from the bite of the hellhound. I'm sorry, Sydney. I wish I could do more."

"There is no cure for a vampire bite," Syd said quietly. He kept his eyes from Martha's as he wrung out the blood-soaked cloth with fresh water. "I know that."

Sydney brought the damp cloth back to Ryan's face and continued wiping it slowly.

"I couldn't let him die, Martha."

"I know, Syd." Nana smiled. "I know."

They left the two boys in the hidden room, and Nana led the way down to the kitchen. Becky put the kettle on and made a pot of tea. She felt very, very strange and needed to do something that made her feel somewhat normal again. Nana sat quietly in a kitchen chair, but without the usual, vacant look on her face that Becky was accustomed to seeing.

As Becky sat a mug of tea in front of her Nana—Martha—spoke.

"I never wanted you to know, but I see now I shall have to tell you, before Sydney leaves with Ryan," Nana said in pained resignation. "Once he leaves, he'll take his power with him, and I'll forget myself again. I'm sorry, Becky. I'm sorry for what's become of me, what you have to endure day after day."

"Nana—" Becky began to protest.

Nana held up a hand.

"Please. Let me talk and don't interrupt." She took a sip of tea and swallowed hard.

"Okay." Becky sat down, cradling her hands around her own mug in a futile effort to warm them. "I love you, Nana. Just so you know."

Nana smiled.

"I know, little dove. I still *know* everything. I just can't quite remember it all. It happens when Healers reach the age of sixty. I should have told you all these things long ago, but after Helene and Patrick died—" Nana closed her eyes for a moment.

She shook her head then smiled at Becky.

"While Syd's here I'm able to use his power to clear my mind, but he won't be here long enough for me to tell you all I need to," Nana said urgently. "I'm sorry for not telling you these things before. Syd's right. I've likely done more harm than good trying to protect you from your birthright with ignorance. I should have expected the war to start again. But the peace went on so long. I forget that mortal time means so little to Ethereals. Fifteen years is ages to us, but a heartbeat to them. Anyway, yes—you're a Healer. You were born with the gift to channel power to your own use, to share your life's force with those who are in need, and to heal those who are thought to be immortal. 'Immortal' does not mean 'invulnerable,' little dove. Your friend was bitten, very nearly lethally, by a hellhound who no doubt attacked Syd's clan. Vampires are a delicacy to hellhounds because they have no soul. It was only Syd's bite, the bite of a vampire, that saved Ryan. I don't agree with it, but it saved your friend's life."

Becky tried to process everything her Nana was saying. It was like talking to someone else, someone completely different to the grandmother she had grown up with. Nana was a vampire Healer?

"So," Becky said slowly. "We're a family of . . . vampire Healers?"

Nana laughed quietly and took a sip of her tea.

"More or less," Nana said after a moment. "Sometimes more, sometimes less. It's not just vampires. We help the hellhounds, too. Specters, shades, demons, werewolves—"

"Werewolves? Demons?" Becky interrupted, incredulous. "Nana, come on! All those things aren't real!"

"No?" Nana raised her eyebrows just like her old self. "Go upstairs. You'll find a couple of vampires up there."

Becky couldn't argue with that.

"We observe neutrality," Nana went on. "We don't take sides. We have the gift of healing those who cannot heal themselves—those who need power and the force of life that comes from a living soul like ours. Unfortunately, by using our life force in this way, it's depleted quickly. It gets used up by the time we reach sixty. *If* we reach sixty. A lot of us don't."

"You keep saying 'us,'" Becky pointed out. "Are there more of 'us' then? Or just you and me?"

"There are very, very few," Nana replied. "A great number were killed in the last war by the very beings we try to heal. Here, in a place of Healing, the ground is neutral—wars and battles stop here. Had the hellhound who bit Ryan tonight been in need himself, he would have been treated and sheltered just the same, right at the side of the one he harmed with no further hostility between them. Once they leave here, however...that's another matter. You are safe here, and your Healer's mark grants you certain clemencies both inside and outside the boundary, but you, like the Immortals, are not invulnerable."

"So...now what?" Becky shrugged. "You're not better, and you're not going to get better. The only reason you're okay right now is because that vampire guy is here. And there's someone from my school upstairs who's turning into a vampire himself. Are more of these guys going to show up? What did Syd mean when he said the 'entry was closed'?"

"The mirror up there serves ... *served* ... as an entryway," Nana said. "It was sealed after the last truce was declared. To put it in terms you can understand—I went out of business, so to speak. It seems now, however, I need to reopen. But I'm too old. Too slow. I can't remember much. Sydney is a powerful Master vampire, the leader of a vampire clan, and he's the only reason I'm able to manage at the moment. When he leaves...you'll be ...burdened with me again. An old woman who has lost her mind. I'm so sorry, Becky. You shouldn't be wasting your youth like this. Maybe you should look into a home for me."

"This *is* your home!" Becky protested. She went around the table to hug her Nana tightly. "You're not going anywhere! You're not a burden! You wouldn't let them put me into a foster home, and I'm not going to let them do it to you either! If anything, I'll chain Syd to the wall and he can just sit up there forever so you can be okay again!"

Nana gave Becky a squeeze.

"You know that can't happen. Syd has responsibilities just like we do, and if you really want to look after me, Becky ..."

"Yes, go on," Becky prompted when Nana fell silent.

"I never wanted you to know," Nana said again. "But I wouldn't let them take you away, so I guess that means you're going to be involved whether I want it or not. If you really want to look after me, Becky, you're going to have to look after those I once did. If the war has started up again, and it looks like it has, Sydney and Ryan are just the first of those who will need our ... *your* help."

Becky's eyes widened.

"*My* help?" she swallowed. "But ... I'm not trained, you said. And you said once Syd leaves ..."

"We'll ask him to stay a bit, both he and Ryan, but not too long," Nana said gently. "I drain too much energy now and can't focus on my work. I'm not going to be much help. I can teach you—train you—if Syd is willing to help, but you're going to have to learn mostly by yourself. It's easy once you get the hang of it. I have books with my notes and things. All my herbs and special equipment. It will be a lot of work, and you'll have to learn fast. But this is in your blood, and it is what you were born to do. I'm sorry I kept you from it for so long. I should have been teaching you since you were old enough to understand."

"Is this why I always wanted to be a doctor?" Becky grinned.

Nana smirked.

"Very probably so," she answered. "Now, let's go check on Ryan. He should be over the worst by now."

Becky nodded and rose to follow Nana upstairs.

The boy on the bed laid still and quiet. Syd still knelt by his side.

"He's shed his mortal coil," said Sydney.

Becky's heart broke at the grief and anguish in his voice.

"I'm sorry," she heard her Nana say softly. "Even if the entry had been unsealed—"

"I know," Syd interrupted. "And I offer my apologies. But he's like my brother, Martha. It wasn't supposed to be like this."

"But it is. Now we must both accept and endure, not lament what should have been," Martha replied in that same wise tone Becky had never heard her use before that night. "I need you to remove the seal. I don't know if you've realized, but I'm not fit for much anymore."

Sydney didn't acknowledge her comment, but gestured a hand at the mirror. It glinted seven times in the candlelight then returned to normal.

"He's going to need …," Sydney began, then trailed off, shaking his head. He looked helplessly up at Martha.

"I can't," Nana said quietly. "I'm not enough. I don't have enough to sustain us both."

Sydney nodded and looked back at the still form on the bed.

"But she does."

Both Becky and Syd looked up at Nana's words.

"I . . . do what?" Becky asked. She didn't like the way they were looking at her.

"Oh please, Martha. For this kind of healing, it has to be her choice. She's not even trained." Sydney curled his lip. "You know that."

"We can help her. If she's willing. Becky . . . remember what we talked about downstairs? Well, now's the time. If you want to help your friend and help me do what needs to be done, that is."

"What needs to be done?" asked Becky, warily.

"You'll have to feed Ryan"

"Oh, is that all?" Becky was relieved. "Okay. We have some leftover spaghetti . . ."

"Not *feed* him, you stupid girl," Sydney snapped. "*You* will have to feed him. As in 'be his food.' He needs life restored to him and the only life strong enough for that in his condition is yours. Get it?"

Becky blanched.

"Hey, I hardly even know him," she said, taking a step back and holding up her hands. "And Nana just said a bunch of Healer people were killed by what they tried to save, so thanks but—"

Sydney swore under his breath. Nana chastised him.

"Listen, young Healer," Sydney began calmly and with exaggerated patience. "He can't kill you here. He can't take too much from you either. That's why you're a rare and valuable commodity among Ethereals. You have mortal years of use, of life in you.

You more than others. He can't drain you. Of blood . . . possibly, but that's rare when a Healer is in her own enclave. That's right—Healers are always and only female. Healing comes from the life force created by a living soul, and it is the female who creates and bears life. Now, Ryan needs life restored to him. Will you, young, untutored Healer, restore my young fledgling?"

"Promise me I will not regret it." Becky didn't know where the words came from but she spoke them as though she'd known exactly what to say when asked such a question.

Sydney smiled and looked to Nana.

"Untrained she might be, but a Healer nonetheless," he said in approval. "She'll learn quickly, if such knowledge is that easy to tap."

He looked to Becky.

"Upon my honor, my lady," he went on formally, and offered her a slight bow. "I promise that you will not regret your actions." ·

Becky nodded unsurely but knew something had been done correctly. Then, without thinking about what she was doing, she rolled up her right sleeve and went to the bed.

Ryan's eyes opened and fluttered. He mumbled incoherently.

"Hey, Stereotype," Becky called with a smile. "I hear you didn't eat lunch. Did you get banned from the cafeteria, so that now I have to feed your sorry butt?"

Ryan didn't reply, but his eyes seemed to recognize something.

Becky closed her own eyes and pressed her wrist against Ryan's mouth. She looked away, over her shoulder and waited.

I can't believe I'm doing this.

Believe it, she heard Syd's voice in her mind.

Becky opened her eyes to stare at him. Syd couldn't help but grin back at her.

"You have much to learn, little Healer," said the blonde vampire.

"Ouch!" Becky gasped as Ryan's fangs pierced her wrist.

Then the pain faded, and she felt nothing. She really expected to feel *something*…but there wasn't anything at all. She didn't feel weak or dizzy, or like something was being taken away from her. On the contrary, she felt really, really good. Helpful and…and…

"Nurturing?" Sydney said out loud.

Becky blushed and nodded. "I guess that's as good a word for it as any."

Nana came to rest her hands on Becky's shoulders.

"You're strong," Nana said softly. "Stronger even than I was, I think. He won't take much, this first time, but he'll need more over the next couple of days."

"Days?" Becky echoed. "Doesn't this take—I don't know—just a few minutes?"

"This isn't Hollywood, little Healer," Sydney said with a roll of his dark blue eyes. "You don't get bitten by a vampire then change in moments to bite your friends."

"Well…no offense, but isn't that kind of what just happened?"

Becky countered. She pointed to the wrist Ryan had pressed to his mouth.

"Point taken," Sydney replied. "However, he won't remember himself for a couple of days."

Sydney glanced up at Nana.

"Though something tells me you're accustomed to people not remembering themselves."

Becky felt Nana's hands on her shoulders tighten slightly before Ryan dropped her wrist and began to tremble.

"That's enough," she heard Nana say. "Move away now."

Becky did as she was told, and Sydney reached for the damp cloth again as Ryan's trembling escalated into convulsions.

"Is it going to be like this…until he's…um…converted, or whatever?" Becky asked.

Nana nodded. "Mmmhmm. But don't worry. He's with us now, and safe. Comfortable. But it's also very late, and you have school tomorrow."

Becky looked horrified.

"Nana," she reasoned. "You can't possibly—"

Nana held up a hand, a familiar gesture that said she was through talking about a subject.

"I *can*," Nana said firmly. "Syd will stay and help me, won't you, Syd? That's a good boy. Becky, you can help in the evenings, *after* your chores and schoolwork are done, *not* before. It will be a lot of hard work, but you'll likely be trained enough in a year or so of hard study that we can let Syd go about his business as usual. That's not too long, is it, Syd?"

"A *year*?" Becky squeaked.

Syd voiced the same protest.

Nana looked stern.

"Sydney Alexander, you came seeking a Healer, and you've found one untrained. Rebecca Charlotte, you have a great deal to learn and a vast amount of power to harness. You'll be lucky if a year is all it takes. And that's just the bare minimum! Remember, you should have been studying intently these last ten years. Most Healers begin at age five. I'm sorry this is late, but if it's what you both want, it's all or nothing."

Syd looked mutinous.

Becky was just as unhappy, but asked, "Will you be more like your old self with him around?"

She jerked her head in Syd's direction.

Nana nodded. Syd rolled his eyes.

"Then that's worth a year of Blondie and hard work to me." Becky smiled a little.

The vampire groaned. "And I suppose, since I owe you my own existence more than once over, a year isn't so long a time, especially if it is given to train the granddaughter of Martha Althea in the art of Healing. Provided, that is, she works hard and doesn't waste my valuable time."

"Provided Blondie here doesn't go around provoking hellhounds into biting any more of my classmates!" Becky stuck out her tongue at Syd.

If vampires could blush, Sydney would have been crimson. Martha glared at him.

"*Provoking* hellhounds?" Nana said crisply.

"You didn't tell me she was a Seer as well," Sydney mumbled, embarrassed.

Martha looked at Becky, a bit surprised at her granddaughter's new talent. It was an uncommon gift among Healers, but not unheard of. It had been three generations since there had been a Seer in her own line. Becky's great-great grandmother, Agnes, had been one.

"You show up here, with a wounded boy—" Nana began sharply. It always made Becky cringe when Nana took that tone.

Sydney held up a hand.

"Can we please not talk about it?" he asked contritely. "I know this is my fault. The truce hasn't been broken. Some of us still . . . you know . . . get up to mischief . . . for old times' sake. Usually no one gets hurt. But still—what if the truce *had* been broken? What then? We'd have no Healer in this part of the world, and shifting through the planes is dangerous with those who are wounded. . . ."

Sydney caught Nana's look of disgust and trailed off, looking completely ashamed.

"Two years. For your serious lack of judgment," Nana said imperiously.

"Yes, Ma'am." Syd hung his head. "Two years indebted to your service. To train your replacement."

"Good," Nana said with a frustrated sigh. "At least one of us will have their wits about them for a while. Rebecca? Bedtime. It's well past midnight, and a school night."

Becky didn't have to be told twice as she hurried out of the hidden Healing "enclave," as Sydney had called it, and down to her own bedroom.

Two years. Two years of Nana being herself again. Wow. And Blondie *was* kind of cute. Okay...more than kind of. He was totally cute.

And she couldn't wait to tell Robin all about him.

Acknowledgments

"Falling to Ash" © by Karen Mahoney. First publication, original to this anthology. Printed by permission of the author.

"Shelter Island" © by Melissa de la Cruz. First published in *The Number of the Beast: 666*, September 2007.

"Sword Point" © by Maria V. Snyder. First publication, original to this anthology. Printed by permission of the author.

"The Coldest Girl in Coldtown" © by Holly Black. First publication, original to this anthology. Printed by permission of the author.

"Undead Is Very Hot Right Now" © by Sarah Rees Brennan. First publication, original to this anthology. Printed by permission of the author.

"Kat" © by KLA Fricke Inc. First publication, original to this anthology. Printed by permission of the author.

"The Thirteenth Step" © by Martha E. Bray. First publication, original to this anthology. Printed by permission of the author.

"All Hallows" © by Rachel Caine. First publication, original to this anthology. Printed by permission of the author.

"Wet Teeth" © by Cecil Castellucci. First publication, original to this anthology. Printed by permission of the author.

"Other Boys" © by Cassandra Clare. First publication, original to this anthology. Printed by permission of the author.

"Passing" © by Nancy Holder and Debbie Viguié. First publication, original to this anthology. Printed by permission of the authors.

"Ambition" © by Lili St. Crow. First publication, original to this anthology. Printed by permission of the author.

"All Wounds" © by Dina James. First publication, original to this anthology. Printed by permission of the author.

Author Biographies

KELLEY ARMSTRONG has been telling stories since before she could write. Her earliest written efforts were disastrous. If asked for a story about girls and dolls, hers would invariably feature undead girls and evil dolls, much to her teachers' dismay. All efforts to make her produce "normal" stories failed. Today, she continues to spin tales of ghosts and demons and werewolves, while safely locked away in her basement writing dungeon. She's the author of the *New York Times* bestselling *Women of the Otherworld* paranormal suspense series, and the *Darkest Powers* young adult urban fantasy trilogy, as well as the Nadia Stafford crime series.
www.kelleyarmstrong.com

HOLLY BLACK writes contemporary fantasy novels for teens and younger readers. Her books include the *Modern Faerie Tale* books, *The Spiderwick Chronicles*, and her graphic novel series, *The Good Neighbors*. She lives in Amherst, Massachusetts with her husband, Theo, in a Tudoresque house with a secret library.
www.blackholly.com

LIBBA BRAY is the author of the *New York Times* bestselling Gemma Doyle Trilogy, which includes the novels, *A Great and Terrible Beauty*, *Rebel Angels*, and *The Sweet Far Thing*. She has also written several short stories, some plays, one or two letters of complaint, and an occasional grocery list. She lives in New York City with her husband, son, and two bizarre cats. When she's not writing, Libba works on her Evil Author Overlord™ plan for world domination, which she will get to just as soon as she figures out the proper wardrobe.

www.libbabray.com

SARAH REES BRENNAN was born and raised in Ireland by the sea, where her teachers valiantly tried to make her fluent in Irish (she wants you to know it's not called Gaelic) but she chose to read books under her desk in class instead. After college she lived briefly in New York and somehow survived in spite of her habit of hitching lifts in fire engines. Since then she has returned to Ireland to write. Her Irish is still woeful, but she feels the books under the desk were worth it. *The Demon's Lexicon*, her first novel, was published in summer 2009.

www.sarahreesbrennan.com

RACHEL CAINE is the author of more than twenty-five novels, including the urban fantasy *Weather Warden* series, and the young adult urban fantasy *Morganville Vampires*. In 2009, she launches a new urban fantasy series called *Outcast Season*. She lives in Fort Worth, Texas with her husband—fantasy artist R. Cat Conrad—and a whole bunch of unusual pets.

www.rachelcaine.com

CECIL CASTELLUCCI has published three novels for young adults—*Boy Proof*, *The Queen of Cool* and *Beige*,all from Candlewick Press. She also wrote the graphic novels *The PLAIN Janes* and *Janes in Love*, illustrated by Jim Rugg, the latter of which was the launch title for DC Comics' Minx line of graphic novels for young adults. She has had short stories in Wizards of the Coast's *Magic in the Mirrorstone* anthology and Candlewick Press's *Cabinet of Curiosities*. She is the co-editor (with Holly Black) of the anthology *Geektastic*. Her new YA novel, *Rose Sees Red* will be published in 2010. Her books have been on ALA's BBYA, Quick Pick for Reluctant Readers, and Great Graphic Novels for Teens lists, as well as the NYPL Books for the Teen Age, and the Amelia Bloomer list. In addition to writing books, she writes plays, makes movies, and occasionally rocks out.
www.misscecil.com

CASSANDRA CLARE is the *New York Times* and *USA Today* bestselling author of *City of Bones*, *City of Ashes* and *City of Glass*. *City of Bones* was a 2007 Locus Award finalist for Best First Novel and an ALA Teens Top Ten 2008 winner. She is also the author of the upcoming YA fantasy trilogy, *The Infernal Devices*. She lives in Brooklyn, New York with her boyfriend and two cats.
www.cassandraclare.com

MELISSA DE LA CRUZ is the *New York Times* and *USA Today* best-selling author of many books for teens. To find out more about Dylan's story, read her *Blue Bloods* series, the fourth book, *The Van Alen Legacy* is due October 2009. Her latest works also include *The Strip*, the sequel to *Angels on Sunset Boulevard*, and the first book in a new series, *Girl Stays in the Picture*. Melissa divides her time between Los Angeles, Palm Springs and New York and has spent many summers (but so far only one winter weekend) on Shelter Island, where she has yet to meet a vampire. But she's always on the lookout for one in danger.

www.melissa-delacruz.com

NANCY HOLDER has sold approximately eighty novels and two hundred short stories, essays, and articles. She has received four Bram Stoker awards for her occult fiction, and serves on the Clarion Foundation Board. She and Debbie Viguié have written five novels in the *New York Times* bestselling *Wicked* saga together. This is their first published collaborative short story.

www.nancyholder.com

DINA JAMES After having three short stories published in vampire romance anthologies (*The Mammoth Book of Vampire Romance 1 & 2* and *The Mammoth Book of Paranormal Romance*), all set in the mysterious world of the Destrati, she decided to try her hand at writing something for a young adult audience. The result is the story in this collection, "All Wounds." Based on this story, a full-length novel soon emerged, introducing other vampires, hellhound puppies, and one very independent werewolf. The story featured in this book is, quite literally, just the beginning. www.dinajames.com

KAREN MAHONEY has been a Tarot reader, a college counsellor, a dating agency consultant, and a bookseller. Ever since she was six years old what she really wanted to be was Wonder Woman, but has instead settled for being a writer, which she thinks is the most fun you can have without bulletproof bracelets. She reads way too many books, hates bullies, and loves her two cats (even though they only have seven legs between them). She does nothing to hide the fact that she is a total geek. If she could be a character in *Buffy the Vampire Slayer*, she would have to be Buffy so she could kiss both Angel *and* Spike. She is British, but hopes that you do not hold this against her.

www.karenmahoney.net

MARIA V. SNYDER switched careers from meteorologist to novelist when she began writing the award-winning and best-selling *Study* series (*Poison Study*, *Magic Study*, and *Fire Study*) about a young woman forced to become a poison taster. Born and raised in Philadelphia, Pennsylvania, Maria dreamed of chasing tornados, but lacked the skills to forecast their location.

Writing, however, let Maria control the weather, which she happily does via a Stormdancer in her book *Storm Glass*. Maria enjoys hands-on researching for her stories. She had a blast learning how to fence and fight for this creepy vampire tale. www.mariavsnyder.com

LILI ST. CROW is the author of the Dante Valentine and Jill Kismet series, as well as the new YA series, *Strange Angels*. She lives in Vancouver, Washington, with three children, a husband, a variable number of cats, and other assorted strays. www.lilithsaintcrow.com

DEBBIE VIGUIÉ is the author of several books including *Midnight Pearls* and *Scarlet Moon*. She co-authored the *New York Times* bestselling *Wicked* series with Nancy Holder. Most of Debbie's books have a strong element of the supernatural to them. Debbie has been writing for most of her life and holds a B.A. in English and a Masters in Creative Writing. When Debbie is not busy writing she enjoys acting and traveling with her husband, Scott. They live in Hawaii. www.debbieviguie.com